Advance Prai

"Whenever the dull carapac   old, I
reach for Lucy Corin's books   elling.
Here is a writer light-years ahead of her time returning   ore the
recent past of our ongoing American crises. *The Swank Hotel* is pre-
monitory and grief-stricken and somehow gregarious in its lonesome-
ness, so generous in its weird humor and waterfalling surprises. In her
capacious vision, the 'rattlesnakes of madness' twine through a world
of starter homes and desktop screen savers, crushing debt and missing
sisters, a cruel, bewildering America where the runestones of love and
home can still, miraculously, make sense of us."   —**Karen Russell**

"In *The Swank Hotel*, Lucy Corin brilliantly fashions a world where
grief, familial love, ambulation, and detection are entwined as four dimensions of the same problem: time. Being in time. Accounting for
one's time. Accounting for time spent with others. Here we are offered
a place where people who have passed through can go on existing and
people who are present can be shattered so thoroughly that they end up
everywhere—where the dead go, where the living wander, where the
future holds. This is a devastating, enthralling, and mysteriously hopeful adventure."   —**Renee Gladman**

"Vivid, turbulent, intense, *The Swank Hotel* affirms, blow-by-blow,
our loneliness, madness, and longing for a place to settle down. Lucy
Corin's promiscuous gaze illuminates the impossibility of repairing the
breakdown by rebuilding the house from the outside in rather than
from the inside out."   —**Rikki Ducornet**

"With love, brilliance, humor, and weird wild energy, Lucy Corin has
written a perfect story of death and rebirth, of sisters, mothers, lovers,
of madness, of a broken, rocky modern world. No one writes like her.
No one could. Every page of *The Swank Hotel* is hilarious, heartbreak-
ing, strange. To follow Em and Ad, and the other radiant characters in
this novel, is to follow Jane Bowles straight into the future."
                                                         —**Deb Olin Unferth**

The Swank Hotel

The Swank Hotel

A Novel

Lucy Corin

Graywolf Press

"My Strange Addiction S03E08—Urine Drinker" © 2021 by Emily Hochman

This publication is made possible, in part, by the voters of Minnesota through a
Minnesota State Arts Board Operating Support grant, thanks to a legislative ap-
propriation from the arts and cultural heritage fund. Significant support has also
been provided by the National Endowment for the Arts, Target Foundation, the
McKnight Foundation, the Lannan Foundation, the Amazon Literary Partnership,
and other generous contributions from foundations, corporations, and individuals. To these organizations and individuals we offer our heartfelt thanks.

Published by Graywolf Press
250 Third Avenue North, Suite 600
Minneapolis, Minnesota 55401

www.graywolfpress.org

Published in the United States of America

ISBN 978-1-64445-066-6

2 4 6 8 9 7 5 3 1
First Graywolf Printing, 2021

Library of Congress Control Number: 2020951451

Cover design: Kimberly Glyder

Cover art: *Hotel Room*. © Emily Hochman 2021.

All troubles stem from the misconception that human brains are located in the head. They are not: human brains are blown in by the winds from somewhere around the Caspian Sea.

—Gogol, *Diary of a Madman*

Contents

I. Pulse

@ Message @

In the aftermath of 9/11, four or five apartments before the salary and the house, on a green princess extension with a light-up dial, Em got the first of many phone calls deep in the night about her sister being dropped at a psych ward across the country. This one from a pack of freaked-out friends. It was raining. Em's answering machine didn't know how to cut off if you picked up too late and she was always picking up too late. So at first, she was listening to her outgoing message overlapping with the voices of the friends. The problem with saying *first* is that it suggests a clean break between *before* and *after* when there isn't one, and nobody likes a cheat, nobody likes a liar. Not her literal thoughts—more the ethos of the time sliding into her.

Em sat up in bed and pressed the good, solid mouthpiece to her face. The cord bounced happily between the nightstand and the mattress. Sheets wound her in a nest. The air felt particulate, her whole body alert. She listened to Ad's friends through the rain and the machine, walls and states away, heard her own voice saying, "Please leave a message" because she'd never gone in for elaborate personalized greetings like your favorite song garbled, a dog getting scolded in the background, anxious insistence on screening calls, imagining hoodlums marking an empty house.

One friend spoke into the phone. Other friends talked in the background. They'd all gone to art school together, and now they'd piled into studio apartments in Los Angeles, trying to make something happen. Em's knee was illuminated by her bedside lamp. It might have been raining both out her window and on the friends, who seemed to be calling from a pay phone. They seemed to have been piled in a car and pulled over to call on their way home from dropping her. "I think you better come out here," the friend said. "I don't even want to say the shit she's saying. I don't even want to say what she thinks. Is there, I mean, like any *serious* abuse in her history? Like however bad you can imagine? God, never mind, you don't have to answer that. But I don't think your mom and dad should come." The friend gave the phone to another friend, who said, "She doesn't seem to think anything about you. She's still, *What do you mean? She's my sister.*"

"Couldn't it be art, though?" Em remembered asking the main friend on the phone, who it looked like was really going to make it as a real artist. Was already *getting big.*

"It's not art," the friend said. "I tried believing that. It seemed like that for a while but it's just not." One time Ad had been so missing that their mother hired a private eye.

Em had thought, wait a sec, that's a real job?

It's true. She must have assumed TV made up private eyes.

Sometimes Em wore contacts and sometimes she wore glasses. This was for myopia. Sometimes she'd walk around the house with her eyes naked just to feel free in the eyes for a while. She had dark brown hair, lightly freckled white-person skin, pretty good cheekbones.

Psychosis doesn't come from nowhere in the night, there's history, but so many people know so much history and still never see it coming, or when it comes it doesn't matter that they know it, they can hardly believe it, and even if they believe it, it's just different when it happens to you. Ad's madness was the contemporary kind with revolving institutional doors, impossible decisions, decisions that don't matter, *troubling* psychiatric practice, *troubling* pharma, Kendra's Law in the rubble of Ronald Reagan. What followed this first call was a variety of therapies and psych wards over the years that followed. A fuckload of failed drugs and diagnoses. For Em, a barrage of new information forming a new vast unknown sloshed like water in an ice tray, a lot spilling over. Over time, she'd come to put a single beautiful cube in her drink, and she'd function to the music of the clinks like a drunk, putting every effort into not losing track of her glass because the brain, keeping track of a glass, has a job within its capacities. Now we have our first black president, maybe some things would be more okay. Em did think that, in so many words, along with a lot of people. She had a good job that she went to, good like a step up from other jobs. Like steady. Wake up and it's still lying next to you.

But now Adeline was missing. She'd been missing before, but now she was missing again.

It sometimes occurred to Em when she thought about the night on the phone in the bed in the nest with the freaked-out friends in the rain, that Osama bin Laden remained missing. He was *on the loose*. It's important to remember that people aren't legally missing if they might want to be missing, and people are missing all the time but are not on the news. "Hey," you say on the phone, "I was just cleaning the kitchen, thought I'd call—" Then, once cell phones, multiplied: "Hey, I'm at the airport, in a car, at the store, on a mountain, up a tree, thought I'd call—" Everyone just taking and taking everyone's word for it because who really knows where anyone is. There was a bar near the house where Em and Ad grew up called *He's Not Here* that they wouldn't go to even in high school because it was sexist. Deep in the suddenly ubiquitous cell phones, beyond what any consumer knew, burbled nascent, inaccessible, morally ambiguous tracking functions. Someone called Dodd Frank was doing something with offshore accounts.

Em waited for news. She listened to the news on the radio. She let it be atmospheric, but sometimes voices or ideas would surface, take shape.

In her galley kitchen, combining her cereal with her milk, every day sort of a new day, Em listened in her distant way to the newspeople in the morning within the ordinary suspense of *where was her sister*. She took her cereal to the stoop and sat with the door open, eating the way she liked to, the news in earshot and a view of her driveway and the neighbor's garage. It was the standard broadcasting combo of cute things and atrocities, but then it was traffic and weather, and something was up. The anchor, with his warm, kind, familiar, authoritative voice, spoke from the station, and the reporter, with her firm yet getting-screechy-because-something-was-up voice, was struggling to be heard over the helicopter she was reporting from, live on the scene.

The scene was chaotic. It was *madness*, the woman in the helicopter said.

Birds came around the stoop for seeds or whatever had blown in from trees overnight, sometimes a worm that had dried up on a paver.

"What can you tell us?" the man said.

"It's difficult to describe—" the woman said above the beating blades. Em caught *fists raised*, she caught *willy-nilly*. She went back into the kitchen so she could hear better, and set her cereal down. She leaned on her elbows on the countertop, and put together that a man, apparently arguing with the wind, was disrupting traffic on the highway approaching the bridge.

He strode—"He's striding!"—across six rush hour lanes. The reporter narrated as he strode, tossing his head. She described his hair as wild in the wind. She said his hair was *stormy*. She narrated as the helicopter followed him to where he paused in an HOV diamond to lift his arms and *gaze into the billowing skies,* and then lean, waving, *dangerously and precariously* over the guardrail. She said he appeared to curse the sky, or to command it. She said he had climbed up someone's car, *scrambled* to its roof. She said, "He's cursing?" and the anchorman said, "Directing, perhaps?" She said, "Water *thrashing* beneath the bridge," and the anchorman said, "It really is quite a scene!" He seemed genuinely impressed.

Em listened, feeling the stillness of her kitchen as relative. She understood the man in traffic to be a madman. She knew there was a person within the effortful images the reporter deployed and that the anchorman rephrased, for impact and clarity, from his spot at some control panel she could picture with no difficulty at all. But she did not know how to imagine the man, the madman. He was obscured in part by the man and the woman anxiously pressing themselves into professional personalities, so intent on offering something both immediate and coherent. Not in so many words, but she felt it. She found it painful. She found it grotesque.

The anchor issued breathy chuckles. "He's really giving it to that traffic."

The reporter settled into a tone just a few shades from sportscasting. "Folks are starting to use their horns! He's disrupting them, but now—at least so far—refrains from mounting cars! It's difficult to maneuver! Everyone's confused!"

Em adjusted her relationship to the voices. She shut down. The radio became a small pet beside her. A helicopter hovered with speeding blades. Leaf shadows projected through panes onto composite surfaces. Helicopter, hair and weather, waves and airwaves. Versus soundproof wall tiles, giant window into another dull room. Versus checkerboard linoleum, silent kettle, grumbling, inefficient fridge.

She took her bowl of cereal in one hand, its spoon sticking out, to the back door again. Chewing, she stuck her hand, with the bowl, outside. It was as if she had already forgotten her own experience. It was as if she thought, based on the news, that she might be able to discern what was coming her way. The air was warmer than the bottom of the bowl, whatever that meant.

Anyhow, some people have to go to work. She pulled her hand back in, ate up, put on her bright blue rain slicker, and walked up the hill to her good job. The usual suspense returned: when would Adeline's condition and whereabouts become known, would efforts to locate her bear fruit, would messages left yield a reply, somebody finally thinking up something useful. Earnest memoirs on the subject of missing people—families on missions, the process of becoming your own detective—usually feature the giving-up-everything, never-giving-up mothers, the movies and documentaries based on them catching stumped fathers on furniture, red-eyed and wordless. Em's own father was actually kind of like that. Her mother, strident and prudish, would say, "I will never give up on my girls," but she'd also say, "No daughter of mine." Em's parents lived in the house where they'd raised Emilie and Adeline, a house in the woods with a river out back.

In these weeks with her sister missing, when Em returned home from work, she'd find herself expecting Ad to be there in the living room, as if they'd lived together in this house, which they had not, as if her own good citizenship had conjured her intact. She didn't expect it, exactly, she just made it home, felt spent, and was something like *let down* that instead of her sister there, all artsily tattooed with an even cooler haircut than last time, petting a cat in her lap, brownies in the oven, the house just sat there by itself, cutely, cutely. And then she sat down in it.

The sky was flat on the way up the hill. Em carried a compact umbrella in her fist like a mallet. Her (reluctantly finally adopted) cell phone slid around inside her briefcase, fish out of water. There had been a power outage overnight. Nothing happened that got through her sleep; she just turned on the radio when she woke and spent part of the morning visiting a sequence of machines—*Are you okay? Here let me reset you*—concluding with the microwave, pawing through drawers in the kitchen until she found the manual, eventually giving the clock a time, if not the right one, but on the way up the hill realizing she'd forgotten to turn off the terrible alarm noises it was going to make if she tried to heat anything with its default settings, and even as she walked up the hill to work she pictured, fast-forward, getting home, no news, sister not there, putting something in the white box to heat up, shutting the door, going to take her shoes off in the next room, and the terrible inanimate desperate screaming through walls and across the house: *I've heated something! Aaargh! Stop everything! Tend me!* And then, where had she put the manual after having thought of a better place for it, and the unfairness of needing a manual to stop your machine yelling at you.

She would avoid using the microwave.

She would consider throwing the microwave away in a fit of nostalgia.

She had seen someone use a phone booth in their home as a terrarium.

She would picture the microwave as a terrarium.

She would feel sad about someone dressing up a loss as something other than a loss.

By the top, she suspected she smelled bad. Her adorable starter home receded.

In her office, nothing to reset. Every office contained a desk, a chair, a bookcase, a wastepaper basket, a coatrack. A bunch of people had offices and a bunch of people worked in cubicle landscapes, one upstairs and one on this floor around some corners. Cubicle people had the same things as office people minus the bookcase and the coatrack, but could pin anything they wanted on their soft walls. Getting an office was supposed to relate to accomplishments in the hierarchy, but Em was pretty sure her office assignment was the result of least stuff to move at time of hire.

She hung her bright blue rain slicker on the coatrack. She stuck the umbrella into one of its pockets and it seemed to hold. She took off her blazer and hung it next to the rain slicker, but the two of them next to each other bothered her, so she hung the rain slicker over the blazer. She pulled the cuff of her shirt over the heel of her hand because anything metal in the offices might produce a shock regardless of the weather. She took a giant T-shirt out of the file drawer on the right side of her desk and put it on over her better shirt. The T-shirt didn't say anything on it. She made coffee in her personal coffeemaker because departmental coffee had been cut from the budget along with the watercooler. Em kept a gallon of water in the file drawer along with a gallon-size ziplock bag containing the T-shirt, tampons, and a pair of underwear. The smell of coffee filled the room. Somewhere—not here, because this place was crap, a middling firm behind the times—computer programmers were starting to work two per machine so that no element of their inventions would exist uncorroborated. Em understood from reading about her sister's illness that uncorroborated experience is symptomatic. A silent bell hovered near the crown of her head. It was golden, the size of a fist. She couldn't see it, just felt a presence. Where the hell was her sister?

Until eleven she worked at email. As she made replies, new messages arrived in the building, in the office, within the desktop, onto the floating square of one thing after another. The emails contained bodies of data, and her job was: look at a profile of the data, look at a statement from one of the *creatalitic team* explaining what the data should seem to demonstrate, and then turn it into a graph or a chart for a report, pamphlet, or advertisement. She learned exactly enough about software operation to accomplish these tasks. Beyond the walls of her office, people were drawing on their knowledge bases in administration, business intelligence, communication, data analytics, economic development, forensic accounting, greenwashing, human resource management, industrial organizational psychology, jockeying, keepage, leverage, merchandising, noodling, operations supply chain management, public relations, quality assurance through Q1, Q2, Q3, and Q4, reaching out, social entrepreneurship, transitioning, unbundling, visioning, workplace conflict management, xeroxing, yield management, and zerotasking. A little more than a year ago, after a series of phone interviews, she'd been offered the job by a person she never saw again who looked at her face and then at her résumé as if to see whether she ought to be allowed on an airplane. Em had her BA, ticket taking at a movie theater, temp office things, coming-of-age table waiting, one summer housekeeping at a motel near the ocean. "You'll pick it up quick," said the human resource manager she never saw again but whom, if she tried hard, she could re-member as a ruby mouth floating near a blue blouse with wide white polka dots. "I pick up quick," said Em, and dashed off to buy her house, thinking, *I'm on it!*

Because of a growing awareness of financing scams, she'd really impressed upon her father the safety of her mortgage. Her mother said if you can't live in a real city at least live in the country, and Em said, "But I can walk to work!" to no avail. The town was city enough to have people living on the streets in its business district, but most people shopped at the big box stores that sucked the life out of it.

Some months into the job, just back from sneaking a few sick days to see Adeline in a hospital in Dubuque—no one even tried to piece to-gether how she'd landed in Dubuque—an idea about the universe in-volving "three *you's*"—something—Em said yes to drinks after work, got drunk, ended up in a back corner booth with Magda (Design), who put on lipstick right there without looking, without even mess-ing up the story she was telling, put it on just by reaching into her bag and then putting it on, just timing the strokes for when Em made her contributions—*I know exactly what you mean—he is! he is just like that—that happened to me once—no, no, keep going*—it was so blatant, the way she put it on, and eventually Em told Magda about her last breakup, a breakup with a person who'd felt—you can't say felt like *the one* because that is stupid—but who'd felt, she said, "for *real*."

"Oh, honey, it's so hard," Magda said, and it's nice to be called *honey* by a peer. So Em told Magda that she hadn't actually been sick, she'd been visiting her sister in a psych ward in Dubuque. Did Magda freeze up? Not at all. Magda said, "Oh, honey, I know. It's just so fucked up when they won't take their meds." Magda also had a story about a friend with seasonal affective disorder. "I'll send you this article about fish oil," she said. "It really works. And there's a thing called a Happy Light," she said.

"Please don't send me stuff," Em said. "I won't read it." What she learned from this encounter was *don't*.

With the fluorescents off and the replica banker's lamp shining a rectangle on her desktop, by noon Em felt like she'd worked deep into the night. Nothing arrived for which she had no reasonable response, and the silent bell slid away from her head a little. People tapped and chatted in large and small grids above her, below her, all around, virtually, and beyond her senses.

In preparation for the meeting in the conference room Em removed the T-shirt. She had not dripped coffee on the T-shirt in months, but sniffed it to see if she should take it home to wash anyway. Then she put it back in the drawer. Later in the day, sister still missing, she tried to remember the smell. In the conference room, seven people sat around the ovoid table in front of a whiteboard. The custodial staff had requested they try not to use the board too much because they were no longer supplied with the special detergent to clean it.

Here were seven people with personalities like flags. Irene's eyes snuggled into the slim bridge of her nose, made her broad face broader. Her eyebrows were fierce. She'd be smart, then dopey, then smart, then dopey, slumping over her enormous breasts. Devin, redhead, elfin, trim and pointy facial hair, tiny bobblehead when speaking and always speaking or about to speak, white shirts under suit vests, never a jacket, shifting minutely in the seat, what am I about to say, what am I about to say *now*? The coherence of these people as entities mesmerized her. Tess under heavy glasses, short thick hair like a toupee, turned out not gay, just *uncomfortable*, and yet she arrived exactly like herself day after day. Katrina with earrings like drawer pulls, a little dip and rise with her chin to begin each vocalization; Billy fingering the ironed crease in his retro trousers; Reginald the full-on beard stroker, a man who lounged in doorways. There was Ben, who in typical Ben fashion tried to take the seat at an apex that was clearly designed to make sitting at the head impossible. He shrugged, a guy's gotta try.

From the doorway, Em thought, which one am I?

Em, in navy and gray, keeps her head down. Master of begging no questions. Never so reliable as to be known for it, always reliable enough.

Matchy-matchy Amber arrived late, pretending she was not always late, which it was just like her to do, wearing peach beads that brought out the peach in the peach and purple flowers on her blouse with its tan background, wearing a tan blazer over it just so.

With the onset of symptoms, personality slips. Back in her office, Em would feel her image of her sister vibrating in a way that frightened her. She'd peek out, witness people behaving in character, and get back to work.

About the whiteboard: a custodian had come up with his own solution for cleaning the whiteboard, which he kept in a spray bottle carabineered to his belt. Recently, after hours, Em had been waiting while he cleaned the ladies'. There were two doors between the hallway and the bathroom that defined a kind of decompression chamber, everything light green. At night, the custodial staff left both doors propped open for air. There weren't any fans or windows in the bathrooms, which didn't seem legal. She was just going to use the bathroom, finish packing up, walk down the hill, and stare at the telephone answering machine, pretending to shoot it with her finger for still giving no news. But he was in there, cleaning.

The top of his narrow head was visible above the stall door and his green coveralls, then tubes from shins to ankles, and his steel-toed boots, and the coveralls were too long, so that the hems were worn black and frayed from being stepped on. She knew he'd written *The Solution* in black marker on a spray bottle. How do you say nothing about Hitler in this situation? Em could hear him working away at the toilet with a brush. She said, "I've been meaning to ask you about *The Solution*," and he told her the issue with the whiteboards and his idea for this cleanser. He wondered if *The Solution* had to do with not being cut even though he was nonunion. He said some pretty virulent things about unions and cleaned steadily for the duration of their exchange.

Em said, "Wait a minute, does that mean we can use the whiteboard as much as we want?"

He said, "Best hold off on that for now." Who talks like that? He opened the stall door and moved on to the sinks. He was thin and craggy with rat eyes. She thought she learned his name and then she forgot it. He said he might take *The Solution* to market. She said something about the difference between your actual technology and the technology that technology keeps crowing about, and when she said "crowing about," she thought, who talks like that? He kept talking about his plans for *making it big* and she just took a deep breath and vacated the premises. She snuck down the hall and outside. Her sister was missing.

Outside was dark, practically no cars in the parking lot, just seven streetlights. As if there were no other bathrooms in the universe, she shoved herself between the building and a perfunctory hedge. One kind of humidity came from the bushes and another came from the wall.

She squatted and peed.

The meeting in the conference room concerned whether or not a crisis was impending. Afterward, Em followed two of her colleagues to a cafeteria-style eatery around the corner. The two colleagues kept their dishes on their trays while they ate but Em lifted her bowl of soup and side of mac and cheese from the tray and slid the tray under her chair. One colleague thought the meeting was sad and another thought it was funny. One departed saying, "Keep it real," and she couldn't gauge the irony. Em had only wanted something warm, and now tried to guess how long she'd have to wait until she'd stop feeling heavy. In her office, people came by toting diagrams to look at together. Between meetings, she'd produce email or yank the chain of the replica banker's lamp. She'd pull up a file with a graph she was working on, appreciating the stillness of pictures demonstrating basic math. She was no longer nervous in meetings when she had no idea what was going on, as she had been when she first arrived, gung ho, her sister *struggling* on an *upswing* across the country, new job, new meds—not yet missing again. Over the years Adeline had turned into a person who, by the time you found she hadn't just lost her phone again, wasn't actually living where you thought she'd been since the last hospital and no one had called you to say she'd left, and maybe when you talked to her she'd just not mentioned where she was or she lied about it or was confused but you didn't know she was confused and now nobody that anyone can think to call can find her, no one they reach has the same idea about where she went after they saw her, plus some of them are *shady*, and soon no one even knows what state to fly to and drive around staring into crowds. Meanwhile, Em was better all the time at keeping her head down, increasingly able to see things from other people's perspectives, buying into anything, who cares, asking the question other people were afraid would make them seem dumb. She worked independently, but popped in to say *hi* just because. She was fine saying, "I could get by with something basic," meaning cheaper, when it came to creating her charts and graphs out of data. Back from lunch, working independently, she encountered moments of elegance in her own visual rendition of a client company's subcontractor's findings. She knew that in terms of self-delusion she was a lot better off than people who thought their work was meaningful, and yet a feeling of being *interested* arrived occasionally. It came in a kind of *pulse*. An idea laid next to another idea would surprise her with its unintended applications. A shape could reach beyond its intended substance toward something new. She knew from her sister that a proliferation of the meaningful is symptomatic. She did not know the extent of the atrocities her sister had suffered physically or psychically or the relationship between what she suspected had been suffered, did not allow herself to imagine had been suffered, had been told by Ad or others had been suffered, and what had not been told by anyone to anyone—and who does? When Em looked up from her email, a wave of time would be passing over her and her heart would tilt with the possibility of a sweeping and profound *shift*. The bell that had been snoozing beyond the horizon would zoom in, clock her on the crown, and still not ring. Madmen are the ones who make and change history. Look around. We could use some Joan of Arc, is what Em thought.

Em's parents' house was located in the mid-Atlantic region, the central portion of a weather continuum that reached from the Bahamas to arctic Canada, in foothills known for not too hot, not too cold, but sometimes one or the other. Em could picture her sister only on the other side of the Mississippi from them, even when she knew she could be anywhere. Em knew *Mississippi* only as a song for spelling and a dividing line.

"I'm going to California!" people say when they're young.

"We're going to Florida," they say when they're old.

Their mother came from California. What were they doing, those sisters, toying with the past and the future? Em moved out there and came back. Ad moved out there and who knows what. Their father came from New York City. "They met in the Midwest?" guessed Em's ex calling long distance, back when they were getting to know each other from across the country, but diagonally, because the ex lived in the center of the lower desert known as the Southwest.

"Well, Chicago. Yes."

Currently, people Em cared about outside her family lived in secondary and tertiary cities, though she'd fallen out of touch with every one of them. Sometimes she'd try but fail to remember what had turned weird. In relation to her parents, Em lived the exact number of hours away that fly or drive was always an issue.

"If you will get my phone number tattooed on your ass," Em told her sister—this was before portable numbers—"I promise I'll never move."

When Em first stood in the doorway of her starter house with her responsible salary-backed fixed-rate mortgage, holding her first box from the truck she didn't have to pay for, thinking, I'll never have a landlord again!, there on the mantel of the humble fireplace was a 1940s 302-Type telephone, the first model with the bell in its base, one of the first made of plastic—but the kind of plastic before plastic meant oil and what we did to the earth, the oceans, its creatures. It's important to remember what's physical when you're talking about a machine that is supposed to connect people across distance when you're talking about people who mostly feel varieties of disconnection. Em could not remember if the phone had been there when she toured the house with the agent, but the house, also from the 1940s, seemed, in the moment, to have sprouted from it. Perhaps babies would sprout from it, now with the job and the house, as from the head of a god. Not *her* babies, just babies. She could not remember what happened, moving, apartment after apartment, to the princess extension she'd held that night with the friends who called in the rain, but it was gone by the time of this house. From her arrival with that first box, something in the act of purchase seemed to erase what was outside the house when she was in it—a kind of mutual occupation. First thing she did in this place that was hers, hers, hers was leave the box in the entryway, pick up the sculpted receiver, and hold it to her ear. Clearly no cord went to a wall, so why would she do that? She didn't wonder, she just did it. When she put the receiver down the bell moved in its housing. It's important to consider the cultural mechanisms of standards of communication when considering the rupture of madness. That dead rotary anvil of a phone: the first voices it carried all talked about war. Now the war was on terror, a feeling everyone knows you can't blow up.

End-of-the-day ritual, set briefcase on desk, slide eyes across objects, what to bring home, what to turn off, leave on, put to sleep. Her house was so adorable, the office so ugly and stupid, and still she prolonged her departure. This was not meant to be a job where you bring stuff home. A decade ago, many of her friends had finished school and gone to see the world on new credit cards. Em got one dumb job after another and finally this handsome briefcase, the most expensive thing she owned outright. She'd actually looked at things from the briefcase once—she'd never fall for that again—but the force of ritual, she could put anything in that briefcase—

Well, she brought it home. Home, home, home at the bottom of the hill the tiny red bulb could be blinking on her message machine. Or not. The whole short walk she imagined it blinking and then imagined it not blinking. What blinking could mean, news or no news, news meaning safe or not safe. What not blinking could mean. Opposite things. Or nothing. Those friends who traveled the world instead of getting jobs were probably still in debt. No they weren't. Family money. The hand-me-down Panasonic cordless with the full-sized tape that had finally replaced a Panasonic cordless with tiny answering machine tape that had lasted through the '90s could say, sweetly, increasingly obsoletely, *Someone is thinking of you even when you aren't around.* Or: *Found her. Got her. Girl on bridge disrupting traffic, girl in ditch—beaten—raped—girl on airplane to war-torn fill-in-the-blank looking for a revolution, girl shot self in the head.*

Then the machine was blinking. New day after new day and now this could be—was about to be—what was going to have happened.

She could see it on the kitchen counter from the doorway. It was still near the beginning of a long subtle rainless dusk. Since news of global warming, the relationship between the weather and human emotions had become more indeterminate. Em played it cool with the machine. She returned the blue rain slicker, dry, to the closet. She turned on lights, turned on the radio, left her clothes in a pile near the stairs. Standing in her underwear, she fixed a glass of scotch. She turned off the radio, pushed *message*, crossed the dining area to the machine's percussive throat clearing, sat in a soft chair, and put the glass on the side table, prepared to listen. Some atmospheric static, some plastic grinding of ten-year-old gears, clunk and clanking from a faraway life, human throat clearing, and then: "I'm just calling to see how you are."

It was her aunt on her mother's side, and that was the extent of the message.

Em got up from the chair, walked back to the machine, and pressed the *message* button again. This time, "I'm just calling to see how you are" *tilted*, making *how you are* a little funny. The machine rewound, flipped, and clunked forward again. Em returned to her chair, sat in it, and listened, lifting the glass as the message concluded.

This time, the aunt's *how you are* hovered existentially, not funny at all, the shape of the absence of Adeline.

She put the glass back on the side table and did it again—back to the countertop, smacked *message*, back to the chair—finally noticed what she was doing and did it again. The message ended this time with Em suspended between the dining table (hard) and the soft living room chair. She stood with the tips of her fingers resting on the side table. The living room window framed the cute tree in her yard. She looked at it because of the layout. It was spring and darkening in a diffuse way. She turned the radio back on, volume as low as possible, and got into the chair. She liked to doze with the news on so low that she could hear it only if she consciously tuned in as she had, long ago, that morning, now almost forgotten. She liked the distinct voices of the anchors to blend into what they had in common. She liked the carefully produced wrap-ups and in-depth investigations. She liked to tune out, because then all that was left was the rhythm of voices, like every good lullaby, skimming the surface of awful things in the world. There was still a nicely formed ice cube in her drink. White noise that's softer is pink noise.

In the morning, Em ate her cereal in her bathrobe in a band of sunlight on her back stoop. Her spoon was left over from childhood when her family ate with a mishmash of flatware acquired from yard sales. She'd always liked this one spoon, its basketweave decoration and the shape of the bowl in her mouth. People probably squint when they remember because that's what people do on television. At work she joined her boss in his office and got evaluated. He was thin, genial, anxious, the gray that comes after Nordic blond, and he liked to mention that he taught an evening class at the local university for the new PhD program in assessment. His office contained the same furniture the rest of them had but in wenge. In addition, a set of three department store African masks hung on a wall.

Data apparently showed that Em was give or take average for the company as a whole but lower than average for the department. It took a long time for him to get this across because he was trying so hard to be friendly about it. As he spoke, Em imagined herself smoking a cigarette—not lounging on a beach under an umbrella with a drink with an umbrella in it—but smoking a cigarette in a parking lot like back when she smoked. In the hallway after, she wondered how long she could hide an animal in her office. Someone's door opened as she passed and she didn't have to look to know everyone involved. Blocks of sound tumbled behind her back. People. She couldn't believe she had the energy to feel evaluated, but she did. She heard people deciding whether to go out and celebrate something tonight or wait for Friday. They were always celebrating. What she said to her sister once during an argument about reality: "But I know you, and you're not like this." Inside her office, Em compared celebration with evaluation. She contrasted her findings with images of a vast parking lot, a vast beach along a vast ocean, a cigarette, a sequence of umbrellas, a tree, a hiccup, a message.

False alarms, turns out, are followed by alarms.

At home were two messages, an automated one about calling your representative, and a hang-up with screeching feedback—or crying?—

sounds of birds in the background, parrots making their distinctive noises, and from trees or cages the rustling of leaves, of newspapers.

Em's breathing changed for sure, hearing the message of birds.

It was the time of day when you don't know whether or not turning lights on will help.

Inside her body, the liquids were contained in bizarre shapes.

Her eyes lit on one object after another around her house.

Then she called her parents and left a message. "I got a message, but it was just sounds. Call me back."

She turned the kitchen light on and then played the message again, the screeching, trying to parse the live from the mechanical, wings from the possibility of her sister's breath among them. She turned the light off in case that might focus her hearing, and played it again. Her parents should have called her back already, weren't they waiting by the phone? But what was the big news anyway? *Mom! Dad! I think she's with birds!* She listened past the birds, past the machine and the possible breathing, and thought she heard the vibration of measured speech—a faraway television, or a message from a sane person in the past that this message had recorded over.

She imagined playing this message of birds for someone. Her image of herself was standing just as she was standing now but with a winged or winglike shadow, and the two of them leaning together over the machine, she and the shadow pushing the button together, listening, ear after ear after ear after ear. Then she and the shadow methodically decoding what they'd heard.

People were out for drinks. Cocktail hour. She could turn the volume of the Panasonic down and pretend to be out with them like a person who thinks, life goes on. Let her parents sit waiting. One hour later she again called the house where her parents lived like neighbors, upstairs and downstairs from each other, and still no one answered.

Em left another message: "Even if the sounds are birds, I don't see what we can do with that information." She was crying in a way that wouldn't come out on the recording. Her image of herself was as an astronaut with its umbilical cord reaching outside the frame.

She had gone to LA as the friends on the phone in the rain requested. She put the flight on a new credit card with zero percent if you pay it back fast enough to cancel it fast enough. She stayed in Adeline's bedroom. A wriggly club kid named Rory gave her some blankets and a yoga mat to sleep on. He'd sold Ad's mattress for her share of electric. Could he be reimbursed for a bicycle? Ad was "amazing, like no one is like that girl, she's kind of a legend, I mean no one is like that girl and I'm worried as fuck about her—out of all of us, she's like genius level, paradigm-shift genius—" but he needed the money, he couldn't keep her stuff forever, he knew someone who could move in, also he had seen her car downtown sideswiped and a thousand tickets on it.

In a kitchen cupboard were a couple of mugs that she knew from way back. A Winchester Mystery House magnet on the fridge held a drawing in ballpoint on a square of DoubleTree stationery, clearly Ad's, the face of a monster, and the words *demon mother* infringing on its scaly neck. Em could not remember how she got from the bus to the psych ward. She could not remember entering the area where her sister was contained. It was her first psych ward outside of the normal amount of book and movie psych wards that a person growing up in this culture encounters. It was in the basement. There was definitely wire in the glass windows of doors. Em remembered a sameness to the rooms and halls that seemed both to encourage and emanate from being lost. She remembered her sister appearing in the common area, and the common area becoming vast and uninhabited around her. Adeline was wearing a dress she'd made by sewing to a silk slip clear plastic bags filled with clear plastic things like the caps of water bottles and the rings from six-pack cans. She was vibrant—actually vibrated. She was luminous—as in, the light that is technically emitted from a living thing came from her perceptibly. Em knew that if she ever tried to convey this to another person, she would not be able to protect it from the ridiculous. Even to herself she thought, but wouldn't Ad have been in some hospital-issue thing? No, she wasn't. She was in that thing she'd made, a gown. She was in the gown she came in.

In her memory, the LA psych ward was a vast concrete hall of tables dotted with mad people and their activities, but that was going on ten years ago, so Em's image of it could be that psych ward in composite with other psych wards where she'd been to see Ad, plus so many dreams of them.

She had not been able to get Ad to come home with her, and by the time Ad figured out how to fake sanity long enough to get released, Em was back on the other side of the country at the ticket-taking job watching movies repeatedly from twenty minutes in, which is when she was allowed to leave the booth where she was stationed to wait for latecomers. Someone must have signed a thing from the hospital saying Ad could live with them, or she could have just listed a shelter and gone directly to Venice Beach.

"It's not so strange to have visions," their mother had said to her girls, Emilie and Adeline, over a holiday spread in the house they'd all lived in together. Where the parents still lived. This was later, between diagnoses, but before the job and the house. Where was their father? In another room?

"I had visions," their mother said. "Don't worry, Ad. Having visions doesn't mean anything." She told a story about a hand that came up at her from the foot of the bed. Em saw Adeline look at her own hands quietly surrounding a bowl of gleaming sauce, then lift her eyes to meet Em's, who let her flatware rest and took the bowl. They were always checking with each other about what made sense. They were always reaching, quietly. Then Adeline's eyes moved toward their mother's. Their father must have had his head in the refrigerator, he must have been on the toilet. The sisters watched each other as they listened to their mother, and the mother's eyes must have roamed over their collusion.

"But the hand wasn't real?" said Em.

"Of course it was real," said their mother.

"Then why don't you *believe* me?" said Ad, and their mother said a bunch of things that Em forgot because no one was looking at her anymore and she felt left out. Some intensity was growing between her sister and her mother. In a way, she was relieved, as if they could take care of each other.

Em had tried to picture a culture where no one was necessarily freaked out by a person with visions behaving unpredictably. She knew they existed, but the best she could picture was a nice jungle family in history gathered at the base of its hollow tree. It's one thing to know the ideas you have are fucked up, and a whole other thing to access an alternative.

What would the imaginary jungle family think of these tense white Americans who had to explain visions to one another around a table? Some people need tea to get visions and some people don't, that family knew, eating from the same bowl, birds and animals one concentric circle away. Em pictured animals sleeping and blinking in the leaves just beyond the family fire versus sleeping and blinking just beyond the family brass plate chandelier—outside a house near a river in woods that would not be subdivided for at least another decade.

She managed to sleep some without hearing from her parents, and walked up the hill. At work, she brought her cell with her to the mail room, the copier, and the bathroom. How common is it, when a person is missing, for people to just *not check* their messages? She didn't call again because maybe they had their reasons, and she didn't call her landline from work to check her messages at home because she'd lost the manual before learning how to do that. Leaving for the day, she saw the custodian disappear around a corner with his cart, a yellow cord dragging a bouncing plug, then whipping it against the wall on its way out of sight. At home, people had called her back. Her parents, her aunt, other involved people. They'd been following leads. As she listened, the machine had the feathers of her memory of the message with birds, then was bare, then had feathers, and then was bare.

She called her mother. "Why didn't you *call* me?"

"We were following leads."

At night she had dreams that she remembered all the way up the hill in the morning but lost near the parking lot. At work someone came out of Frank's office next door and swooped down the hallway ahead of her. Frank was ex-management. She didn't know what he was officially, now. Steel doorknobs studded the space, luminous. A man in a pale flaring coat curved against the grid of the architecture.

In another house, a rental a couple of apartments before the adorable starter home, Em and her ex were still breaking up and they just wouldn't move out, neither of them could do it. Em would come home and pull the television up to her chair and plug huge puffy headphones into it, attach herself, put her feet up on either side of it and stare at it between her legs to get through time—and now, home from work, she brought her briefcase into bed with her and opened it on her lap. Inside lay the T-shirt, dripless. It smelled like something, but not coffee, and not her body. She had no memory of putting it in there. She left the briefcase open on the bed while she took the shirt downstairs to the laundry. When she came back to her room from the laundry, she curled up next to the open briefcase on the bed. Years ago her sister had called and whispered, "My cat is so smart. You would not believe the level of communication I have with this cat." Em didn't know if the cat spoke to her sister or if her sister could read the cat's mind. Both of these memories felt especially tragic with her ear on the bed near the briefcase that was open like a mouth noiselessly screaming or laughing.

It was spring. It was supposed to rain every afternoon like clockwork but this year it was not like clockwork, climate change or anomaly. Around the office, the impact of humans was up for debate. She'd carried the briefcase to work with only the umbrella in it. Weather, Em thought, is almost the opposite of a hall in an office building, if you think of it graphically. Her first sip of coffee, always the same level of hot, surprised her with its heat, and she dripped. She went to the bathroom, which was still propped open from the previous night, took her shirt off without thinking about the door. She lay the blue shirt over the bowl of the sink and located the mark. She squirted pink soap on it from the dispenser. Em never used that soap on her hands because it smelled terrible. She moved the fabric between her thumb and fingers. She hadn't thought of her sister's cat in ages, what might have happened to it along the messy way, but the day before—wait—two days before?—as her boss evaluated her, surrounded by appropriated masks, Em had thought, time to get a cat to come home to. The girls were raised to believe an animal is for life. Back when Ad and Em were living on the same coast, Em gave Ad a lost kitten and when Ad moved across the country, the cat went with her and that's where the cat had come from. Coast not necessarily near an ocean, but in relation to the rest of the country.

Your sister, Em thought, is always the other possible you.

My sister, she kept thinking, is missing.

Newspeople, office people, important people. Em held the shirt under the tap, trying to separate the wet spot from the rest of the shirt with her fist. She didn't realize until she was back in her opaque office that she had not looked in the mirror—not standing there in her bra, not when someone came in and shut the door without saying anything, not when she could feel the wet patch spread across her breast. She might still have been buttoning on her way down the hall and she didn't notice. A man in a pale cape-like coat had swerved ahead of her and around the corner. It's not like he had wings, but still.

Around lunch her father called. "So, bird sounds," he said. "What sort of bird sounds?"

"I don't know, Dad. Large birds, you know. Cage birds, exotic. Not little tweeting birds."

He made a cawing sound.

"No, Dad." She started to cry, the way she had on the machine. She felt as if he were making fun of her or her sister even though she knew he wasn't. She knew he had shut himself in his upstairs room to talk with her. It was not always clear to her what he was feeling versus what he was trying to assure her he was feeling.

He said, "It makes me think she's in paradise. Florida? Maybe illegal birds."

"Stop, Dad." Her computer showed a beautiful bar graph of yellow, orange, and green, and then went to sleep. "Don't say paradise."

He recounted recent efforts to pinpoint the path and current location of her sister. Em responded into her cell phone but caught herself looking at the speaker on the touch-tone on her desk as if his voice came from it. He recounted two telephone conversations with strangers, one with a cop and one with a bookstore owner, and then said, "So, how're you doing, how's work?"

"We're making over a hundred images this week," Em said. "About efficiency."

Her dad said, "What?"

Em said, "At my work. An air-conditioning company wants them," and then, feeling nauseated, she excused herself, woke her computer up, and made a plan to talk with him later.

"You're busy," he said.

Later, at home, her mother called. Em sat in her chair with a glass of wine and listened to her mother describe a series of conversations with people Ad had known or stayed with across many state lines. "Sal, the guy with the souvenir shop. What do you make of *this*: You can buy pashmina scarves and Mao alarm clocks right in Phoenix and another shop he has in Austin. You don't have to go anywhere. No one does! If Adeline comes by he has promised to call. I was very careful to build his trust. I believe he'll call. Marianne, remember? She called. She got a box in the mail. I made a list with the things in it. It's here. She sent an ashtray. With ashes, everything in the box covered in ashes. That was on the twenty-first. I kept trying to get Sal to tell me what he's near. He said he wasn't near anything. I thought he was giving me a hard time. But he's starting to trust me, I think. He told me something. The first step in alchemy is melancholy. What do you think of that, does that seem true? I think he'll call if she goes by. He said he put my number in the register. I called that woman Rebekah the baker. She doesn't call me back anymore."

Em felt her mother, through the phone, sink until the idea of her was one in a mass of people—breadlines or immigration in a movie, surrounding a bank gone bust in a movie, favelas in a movie, the followers of a cult leader in a movie, killing fields in a movie—tableaux that could make a wallpaper pattern if you back the camera up. She felt herself sipping on her glass of wine like a baby and made herself sip like an adult. Meanwhile her mother was getting wound up about danger to self and others. She'd found new chat rooms. When her mother entered a chat room she announced her situation immediately and began exchanging empathy. Her father just lurked. Her mother, Em learned, was reading just as many books as her father on what to do when your kid becomes a diagnosed crazy person, but the more they read the more they fought about, for example, freedom and containment. They fought about the meaning of love. Her mother, over time, had more to say and her father less. Her mother said, "That man is becoming useless. In this situation, I tell you, useless is dangerous."

Over Em's shoulder, in the next room, came the radio. Incidents of domestic mass shootings by lone white gunmen were increasingly common according to some sources, same amount as usual according to others. Along with the leaders of the Axis of Evil, shooters were *madmen*.

At night in the shower, drunk, Em considered danger. She considered use and uselessness. Her job was harmless, she liked to tell herself—like what if you worked where they made toxic toys, what if you worked for medical insurance, what if you worked for oil. By morning she'd forgotten she'd showered until she was in the shower again.

More than anywhere else in a building a bathroom exists outside time, so no wonder people like to fuck there. Later that day at the office someone was going to swerve down the hall in a billowing pale coat as if anticipating precipitation. Em's sister stood in the corner of Em's eye throughout the day with a cardboard suitcase and the world rushing past. In Adeline's suitcase could be anything— Windex, a change of shoes, a genie, a museum, a flak helmet, a pony. Soup could be in there. An industrious old lady came through the neighborhood on recycling day to collect bottles and cans to take to some site where you get something for them. She took them from people's bins, stuffed them into white plastic bags, and tossed them into the open window of the car Em was sure she lived in. She wore filmy yellow overpants that made her look official but certainly were not official. It's not often you get to see cans thrown *into* a car, and just the other morning Em was watching, with her cereal, from her back stoop. She could see, across the driveway and the street to the neighbor's yard, the old lady, with sharp direct movements, stuffing cans into bags. Then the neighbor came screaming out of his house, bathrobe flapping, waving and screaming about "being *robbed!*" He seemed staged from the nineteen fifties—striped bathrobe, hair combed and parted, pipe presumably resting in a breakfast nook behind closed doors trimmed with green curtains with lemons in phases from whole to slices. But the old lady was distinctly *now*, a contemporary gleaner, unaccountably agile. She hopped into her car through the window like a bag of cans and sped away. In the shower, Em tried to remember if she'd ever had *ambitions*, or if she'd just had *fantasies*. She liked the late-night joke segment "Difference Makers." She considered her body in the grid made by the tiles around her, her body parts, which are much the same as anyone's body parts. "She can't feel the weather," a friend of Adeline's had said into the phone some months ago. "It's forty degrees, it's *sleeting*, and she's out there in a T-shirt saying it's a beautiful day. She sounds like a *commercial*." Using language that is not your own is symptomatic— ventriloquizing—parroting. Em had felt through the phone the fizz of another person trying to make sense. "But that is *not true*. It's terrible outside. It's a *terrible* day." She put the stopper in the tub and slid down until she lay on her back so that the shower, water coming down in bits, transformed into a single entity that surrounded her, creating her outline. She remembered from linguistics people grown in isolated chambers of unique material—a world made all of wood, a world made all of plastic, a world made all of rainbows— exchanging, through a hub representing the space between us, marks scratched on paper. The lesson: receiving a message, even tattered and stuttering, is miraculous.

At work, the figure in the pale coat swooped down the hall and around the corner with the sound of a door breathing toward shut and then clanking in his wake, everything still by the time anyone looked. She remembered from a book or conversation that to dream of moving through a house is to dream of moving through yourself. She remembered from a book or conversation that architecture is the expression of a city's soul. She remembered finishing her cereal on the stoop of her house, a series of identical instances. People move around in architecture, painting it, eating on its stoops. Dreaming people, thinking people. She'd looked for herself in the concave part of her spoon, an old jingle singing in her ears. The house had been suddenly re-sided for curb appeal in preparation for sale, it turned out, to her—and she could feel multiple shadows of persuasion in the shapes that she'd agreed to inhabit. She chucked the spoon at the side of her neighbor's rotting garage, which was lined with bushes, the next-door neighbors who were never home.

There must have been a weekend. At work, Magda came by. Magda's fingers were always touching your desk when she talked to you. She was always wearing something like a secretary blouse or puffed-up hair, always picking up your little things and turning them over in her hands to test your boundaries. When she left with the stapler she'd come to borrow ("mine's jammed again—boy, they can put a man on the moon . . ."), she seemed for a second to leave an afterimage. At lunch Em sat with people, thinking *thieves*. On the way back to the office she saw a cat's black tail curled around the corner of the building and decided that if it was a stray, she'd take it home. She approached the cat, but the closer she got, looking at the dark tail shape in the shadow of the hedges not far from where she'd peed that time, the more she suspected it was something other than a cat. Someone called out, "Emilie!" and the tail disappeared.

The person who called out was Frank from the office next door. Spring, and he was wearing a black turtleneck with his suit. He waited for her at a different entrance. To get to it you had to go around a railed ramp that had been tacked onto the building for new accessibility compliance. Then to get from the ramp to an elevator once you were inside, you had to go around to the other side of the building. Not long before Em was hired, Frank had screwed up, working too obviously behind the scenes to *get it done*, circumventing protocol, going *around* people, pissing people off. Back to the ranks he went. It made sense that the next guy in charge was that weenie assessor with the masks. In her first meetings Em had felt Frank's lingering authority and looked to him at every juncture to see what the right thing to think might be. She hadn't registered his presence recently, though. She climbed the concrete stairs a step behind him, enjoying the way that climbing stairs makes masculine men look so funny. Clamminess created by the unventilated area fattened his outlines. Spiders in their webs clung in corners, as if none of the custodians were assigned responsibility for the space. It had been hard for Em to think of her sister and the madman in traffic as participants in the same condition. The Axis of Evil madmen weren't on the same continuum, because they were a lie. The madman in traffic had seemed lifted from books introducing God to children in the waiting room of a dentist's office. God is not a lie, God's a figure. But Adeline— was her sister. What linked Frank to the newsman, she realized, was they were both from the past, as her neighbor shaking his fists in his striped bathrobe was from the past. When Em reached the top

of the ramp, Frank gestured with his head for her to follow him inside. He had always seemed annoyed to see her near his office, as
if being placed in offices next to each other was supposed to make
them comparable.

He didn't say anything on the way up the stairs, so maybe he
was just being an ordinary kind of friendly. Friendly didn't seem
like him, though. They walked side by side down the hallway that
was exactly narrow enough to discourage people from walking side
by side. She kept going back and forth, guessing at his intentions,
and when they reached their offices, he waved her into his and shut
the door.

He was breathing dramatically through his nose. What a jowly
face he had, and below that, somehow both firm and expansive in the
trunk. The minute shiver of fluorescence filled the room. Crammed
binders filled the bookshelves. The coatrack held a hat, transforming
it into a hatrack. Frank laid himself out in his enormous green chair,
pushed back from his desk, and used his feet, flat on the ground, to
swivel rhythmically. Em stood against the wall near the door. There
was another chair, a small one, but she didn't take it. She wanted as
little as possible between being there and leaving. *He wants to nego-
tiate something,* she thought. She had no idea what that might be.

Frank said, "You may have noticed my recent absence."

She knew from somewhere that the power position in negotiation
is the other person talks. Preemptively outmaneuvering herself, she
said, "How long were you gone? I'm sure it wasn't a problem. I can't
imagine you missed anything—" and would have continued, except
that he interrupted her to say, "I'm *sure*?" as if she could be trying
to manipulate him in some way. *Was* it a negotiation? Why was she
afraid? Something left over from the evaluation, the way Frank took
that outrageous chair and left her floating in the room. In movies, the
boss says, "Have a seat," and that means, *this is going to be uncomfortable,* and the poor schlub about to get canned says, "No, I'll stand,"
because of the shred of dignity. *He can't can me,* she thought.

Frank said, "I'm not going to eat you."

"What?" she said.

"I'm not—I'm not trying to upset you."

"Eat?" In her mind, a man ate from a can with its lid wrenched open. He did it by the light of a trash can fire and an agile industrious old lady held a spoon out from the other side. She wanted to share.

"You're not in trouble. You didn't do anything wrong."

She was idiotic, obvious. She had no guile, tact, tactics. But the way he said it had no meanness in it, and that made her wonder in a new way about him. Like if he *got* her for a second, like maybe she'd been misreading the whole scenario. Some image of a break in the clouds. Relaxing for a second. Fading from your own view. Forgetting yourself. Fading as a person existing in relation to a missing sister.

He said, "Look. I don't know what of my history gets tossed around these offices but the past is the past. I may not be the man I was or was perceived to be." Whatever he was referencing specifically, what the office people *did* say about Frank was that he was *political*, by which they meant *connected*, by which they meant unfairly. And probably *deceitful*, but maybe, in the end, *necessarily* deceitful if you want to get anything done. And in that way maybe *courageous*? Also people were always thinking of ways his ideas sucked and then explaining to one another apologetically why they were going along with them anyway. They were not sure he would not return to power. They were not sure he didn't still have power in some way. All of which aligned with Em's initial response to him, except now he was talking and she was watching him talk from the supposed power position. "There are numerous asses in this building, but I don't believe you are one of them," he was saying.

"Gee, thanks," she said, low enough that he could ignore her if he heard her, which if he did, he did. He still swiveled in the chair, but now it came off as a tic more than an affectation.

"I apologize for the ruckus," he was saying. He put his elbow on his desk, kept trying to place his forehead in his hand and then taking it away. He took a box of tissues from the back corner of his desk and offered her one out of nowhere. She winced and waved it off.

She said, "Ruckus?"

He put the box close to his elbow. She thought, what on earth do I have on him?

"Look," he said, staring at his own fingers, braced tips against tips. It was an over-the-top sci-fi dictator position, but he was trying so hard—she was witnessing a man feeling *not himself*—or maybe a man feeling *finally* himself—most girls recognize this vibration as the fissure that precedes male violence—whereas if you are a boy you may know it as an opportunity to *move in*. If you have been close to the mad, multiply. So she was scared again.

"Look," he said, starting over. "That man you've seen coming and going is not a client." It was the man in the coat that Frank was referencing, but Em hadn't registered him, really, as a person. She'd experienced him as a figment, on the level of the memory of dreams that follow you during the day. Imagine how much of people's lives would be filled with figments if they weren't always shaking them off in order to function. She'd been trying hard to shake things off and do her work. So when Frank said *that man*, she didn't put it together.

"I don't work with clients," she said. "I'm internal."

"Internal, not stupid," said Frank, and she caught herself actually feeling flattered. The fear took a step back. He kept touching the tissue box, moving it with his index finger the tiniest hop away, then returning his fingers to their tip-to-tip position, then moving the box back where it had been. "Regardless, your discretion, noted and appreciated," he said. "I apologize if we were loud." His trousers were tasteful and pressed. His hair, too. His shoes were polished. She remembered walking down the hall to her office for the first time, her new job, her handsome briefcase, hoping that people would like her, and tried to picture herself as this man, all paunch and cashmere, walking down a hall. Meanwhile, his face was going through contortions like a baby's, one emotion after another. Finally, Frank's face went slack. He said, "It's love."

Em came from big valorized emotions on her mother's side. Her father's side put their stock in *keeping it together*, resulting in real or apparent dullness. It was clear to Em, when Frank said this, that he was high on feelings. She still didn't put it together about the coat, but *illicit* was clear, and *in his office* was clear. *Magda?* She wondered, mixing up her own space with his, Magda's fingers on his desk, on his stapler. "Oh, come *on*," she said. "I mean, *come on*. Aren't you *married*?"

"Well, you're some little priss, aren't you?"

"That's a word I haven't heard since grade school."

"I'm not married," he said.

I *am* a priss, she thought. "Oh! You mean that man in the coat!" she said. She almost said *cape*. How did that knowledge reach her? But it did, and as soon as she said it, the man in the pale coat swooping down the hallway was cousin to the shadow she'd imagined helping her listen for her sister on the answering machine, breath among feathers.

Just because she was right didn't mean she was sure of it.

He said, "I thought you knew," which was why he'd called out to her, and you could hear how foolish he felt, realizing he could have avoided this entire encounter. It was the most direct speech he'd uttered, but Em was distracted, the mechanisms of understanding new things clicking and clicking.

"You guys are *having sex* in here," she said.

"Well, he needs me," Frank said. He was recomposed now, full of himself. "You may not be equipped to appreciate . . . ," he said. Now she was sure of something, which was that the man in the pale coat was clinical, certifiable, a madman like her sister. She recognized what was coming off Frank, a quasi-cellular instability, because she suspected it came off of her, too.

Em said, "The man in the coat—do you know where he is now?"

Frank shook his head.

Em said, "Let me ask you this. Is he missing?"

"I expect to see him tonight. Sooner rather than later." She didn't believe him. Then he said, "He has a wife. His name is Jack."

"Maybe call that wife," Em said, suddenly furious, her face so tight likely nothing was making it to the surface. "She could be worried. Maybe give her a break. You know, talk to her. Or leave her a message on her machine."

Recently, a stranger called Em to say she knew where Adeline was. "I will talk with her, and I will call you." The woman was some kind of Russian. "I will call you four o'clock, no, I will call you six o'clock your time," she'd say, but then wouldn't call. Then she'd call another time, start all over, lead her on.

Em's mother would call: "Did she call? The Russian? Is Ad there?"

"She didn't call. I'll call you when she does."

The Russian called. She said she had a painting that Adeline had made and was keeping it safe. She said she had a steamer trunk filled with Ad's things, fantastic things, a fantastic camera, a marionette of a phoenix, bound notebooks illuminated with magic markers and nail polish. Clearly she was holding the things hostage. She said Ad was so special. "You, as her sister, know this, to be sure." She told a story of walking down the street in Los Angeles and meeting Ad, who was hanging out a third-story window with the sweetest smile you have ever seen "in your *life*!" arms open, calling, "Come on in! The water's fine!" and all kinds of people going up there and then coming back down with boxes heaped with stuff, walking down the street with lamps and plants. "In a parade," said the Russian. "In a parade that your beautiful sister had caused." She said she went up to the apartment and Adeline took her by the elbows, looked her in the eyes, and said, "Everything must go."

The Russian said, "I knew what she meant when she said 'everything.' Do you know what she meant? I don't think you truly do. A true sister knows." When someone came into the apartment and said, "How much is this?" Ad would say, "a dollar!" or "five hundred dollars" or "it's already yours" or "just fucking take it, will you?"

"I had to reach you," the Russian said, about three calls into the manipulation. "I have been feeling for your sister. I can feel all the love from you and I understand the sister feeling." But she wouldn't say where Adeline was.

"I would like to buy the painting from you," Em said. "How much would you like for it?"

"I am not for sale!" said the Russian, and hung up. When she called again, she said that Adeline was having wonderful dreams.

"Are you calling from Los Angeles right now?" asked Em.

The woman said, "Don't you be clever, I am her protector and no harm will come." This time she hung up and did not call again.

"Oh," their mother said, crying. "Grandmother's lamp. Your father's camera." Their father didn't have anything to say about the things.

Em pictured Ad in a house with the woman. She saw the woman feeding her and soothing her to sleep on a velvet sofa. In the image, Ad didn't even know people were looking for her, and when the Russian was talking about Ad's things they were code for Ad. It's not that Em mistook this for rational. It was just putting bits together into a narrative that had an answer, an enemy. It's not that Em thought Frank might be the Russian when it came to Jack. Jack was in his coat, disappearing around corners, no velvet sofa. But there was Frank, as real and corporeal as possible, between Em and a phone.

Em imagined Jack, a madman lover, mythic, chimeric, pure figure. He was down a dark hall dotted regularly with shine coming off doorknobs. Light from a moon snuck in impossibly. He knew something. He portended. She wanted to see him—or, not to see him so much as to *access* him—with such intensity that she thought this must be what people do who *conjure*. The feeling did not take place in the office. It was initiated there, but existed in a place so internal that it was located outside time. He lifted his arms in the coat but did not appear to have a body under there, like a bell with nothing inside it, nothing outside it, to make it ring.

Em kneeled in front of Frank's chair, a gesture you make of calm and support for creatures in crisis. A desk, a chair, an unappealing carpet, the faithful walls, burdened shelving, hazardous hatrack. She thought, I should tell him to call a hospital, call a NAMI hotline, call the police. But she knew what happened when you did, because that's what her family did. What happened was nothing, or nothing good, or it was going to be good and then wasn't good and was sometimes ruinous. They both looked at the telephone on his desk. Square light-up buttons, speaker, woodgrain veneer detail.

"Get up, would you?" he said, as if to the phone. In negotiation, that is a way to say, "No. You're being pathetic." They both stood. Frank was enormous in his black turtleneck, a jacket over it, in the air-conditioning, in the spring. He opened the door so that she would leave and then he followed her to her office to make sure she went. When she opened her door, he leaned close to her ear. He said, "If it is easier for you to believe in *humping* than it is for you to believe in *love*, that is your business. Discretion, Emilie." He wagged his finger. "That's all I ask. Imagine humping if beauty is so unbelievable to you. Me and Jack. Gettin' it on." He made the hips-and-fists gesture of humping, right there in the hallway among the shut doors. The tails of his jacket flapped. He turned to go. "The world is a better place than you think," he called, and she watched after him. "Imagine that with your pea of a mind!" Then he disappeared into his office. She scooted into hers. Shamed, fearful, obstinate—still she wanted to shake him—*we're the same*. She tugged the banker's lamp on, off, on.

At home it seemed preposterous that big-whoop Frank was in love with a man off his rocker. For one thing, he was *straight*. For another, he was *right next door*. She understood that *over* a certain level of serendipity was symptomatic, but she did not know what level of serendipity this business with Frank had reached. Even in her living room where she sat with the scotch on ice that she'd been counting down to for hours, she felt a rent in the room, shards coming through from him, as if he were sitting in the chair she never sat in even though it was exactly like the one she was sitting in, just another angle, and at the same time as if he were still splayed in his office chair using that swivel, a little left, a little right, to gauge her psychically. Methodical radio newspeople explained that many terrible things were happening around the world near and far, *but not to you, not to you.*

Soon after Adeline's diagnosis came to include delusion and hallucination on top of the mood disorder, their mother told a story at the dinner table, girls returned from school for a holiday, father late to join them as usual, head in the refrigerator, finishing up on the toilet, watching a spider build a web in a window.

"When I was a child and we were Catholic," their mother told the girls, "I had a guardian angel who walked with me all through the day as I went to school and played in the forest, and he stood at my bedside at night to protect me from my parents and also visions that might scare me. The angel stood there to keep it at bay. In college I read philosophy, and now that I don't believe, I don't have an angel."

"So what do you think it was?" asked Em.

"Weren't you listening? It was an angel," their mother said.

"Oh," said Em. "Did the hand come? Did it come without the angel? Does the hand come now?"

Their father arrived at the table and reminded them that relativity theory, in its efforts to understand which events in space-time may be causally related and which may not, *quantifies* the time separation between causally related events according to *how* given observers are moving, *relative* to the events. Now (he said), these observers will not necessarily agree on the time between cause and effect, but they will agree on their *order*; so that while cause must precede effect, if two events are causally related according to one inertial observer, then they will be causally related according to *all inertial observers.* It's important (he concluded) to remember that two events are causally related if an observer exists whose timeline contains both events, because in that way, relativity informs *even* metaphysics.

Their mother turned to Ad. She said, "You still have to take your medication."

Back at the ranch, on the radio in her living room, one familiar voice after another led Em from place to place, no one sitting in for anybody. She changed her position in her chair. She handed her glass from her right hand to her left hand, took a sip from there, handed it back. Back in LA at the psych ward, that first psych ward, she'd left her sister in the vast concrete hall of tables dotted with mad people and their activities and returned to the waiting area. Sitting among the sane people, each in association with an insane person on the other side, everyone waiting to see doctors, everyone waiting to see *loved ones*, what Em felt was collective layered motionlessness. Circles under everyone's eyes came to points as if lead beads pulled them down. Whatever else they were under there and beyond the psych ward waiting area was rubbed out, lopped off, half-buried, passed out, sleeping, missing. The doctor, when she met him in his office, which she couldn't remember but seemed, in retrospect, aesthetically aligned with the office of her assessor, was not that much older than she was, but he probably thought he was *much* older. Or maybe it wasn't that he thought he was older, or that what she was wearing was—well, she couldn't remember what she was wearing but it was definitely not *work clothes*, and she was definitely not *put together*, but wherever it came from, he was just so full of himself or who knows maybe just so burned-out—whatever, she did not want to think about that man and what made him whatever he was—but this is what he said when Em asked, *What should I prepare for? What can I expect from here?* He said that she—meaning Adeline—would likely be on the streets increasingly, would likely be raped and probably had been already, so raped *more* was maybe more accurate, more "accurately precise" he said—and he said she'd have serious drug problems if hers weren't serious already, he didn't know her particular case, he mentioned data supported by dead celebrities she—meaning Em—may have heard of about a lot of suicides around the age of twenty-seven, which seemed to be around her—meaning Adeline—ah, right, well, she had a ways to go—but if she made it to thirty, a lot of people could settle down after that, some of them were able to have jobs. For a second, she thought she recognized this doctor from school, like from some giant required lecture and you'll never be in class with any of these people again.

At some point Em said, absurdly, "But isn't there a pamphlet?" At some point she said, absurdly, "But I'm her sister, and she has me."

Next day at the top of the hill on her way into the building Em saw that someone had abandoned a section of the paper on the steps. It was stiff and warped from rain that had come but she'd missed, and right below the fold was an account of the man from the traffic on the radio. He was an African American male, mid to late thirties, name as of yet unreleased, and while she was afraid to read the article, she did *glance* at it by allowing her eyes to drift toward the text with a desire to know without having to go through the process of *coming* to know, which she knew would hurt. Clearly it had been difficult to contain him. Euphemisms and erasures were in play. He had been on the loose. But he did not appear to have been killed via apprehension, so there was that. A photo showed him being pushed against a car by officers. You couldn't tell anything about him. You couldn't even tell what he was wearing to get some sense of who he was from that. Em squinted at the photo for a bit before she went inside. A couple of the officers had their sticks drawn. Despite all evidence, she thought, but what if that man *did* command the weather?

On the stairs, she discovered a tissue in her pocket and used it to ruin a spider's web that was in a bottom corner of a landing where she could reach it. She did not habitually keep anything in her pockets, was not an allergic or sniffly person, did not know why she even thought there might be a tissue in her pocket but there it was, and she carried it in her fist worried that she might have also got the spider with it, what if it's in there dead, what if it's in there alive, all the way to her office because there were no communal trash bins along the way. In her office, she listened through the wall and it was the sound of big men surreptitiously fucking, or it was the sound of office supplies at work amplified by an agitated imagination, or what Frank had said about fucking haunted her. Could be that chair rocking against a wall. Could be a man alone, crying. Eventually she heard Frank's door slam and could see the curve of the man in the coat, not missing, move like a sail in wind down the hall, defying its structure. She made herself not look out of her office to confirm or deny. She turned the light off in the silence of his wake and listened. Animals who live together often end up symmetrical in rooms or fields at intervals through the day because they know each other in their bodies. She listened for Frank, a person like her in this way that mattered now, shoving other characteristics to the side. A person in proximity to madness. Loving a person who is inaccessible because of it and becoming unformed by the ripples of its force. *Deepwater Horizon*, an adjectival phrase, came from the radio. Amber and Reginald, Devin and Tess, at their desks in the grid, appeared in her imagination as prisoners of the thudding stark outlines that contained who they were and could be.

She took her extra underwear out of its ziplock, wet it with water from the jug in the file drawer, pulled her stockings down and wiped her vagina, then threw the underwear into the trash container. There were rumors that the custodial staff watched porn on the office computers at night. She had sometimes pictured it, custodians, in her office, at her computer, jacking off. She wondered if it would matter to custodial staff in whose office they were jacking off, would custodians pick someone they thought was attractive or someone they thought was an asshole or what might their rationale be. Or the location of the office, if that would matter in relation to feeling safe from getting caught or what level of danger the custodial staff might be going for. She tried to think, if she were custodial staff, and if she were going to jack off in someone's office, whose would it be? The custodial staff doesn't care who you are, she thought. The custodial staff just wants the internet, like everyone else. They want a nice place to jack off, like everyone else. She thought of that custodian with *The Solution*, his narcotic eyes and old skin. Symptomatically, cycling, Adeline would say things that sounded like sentences, had the rhythm of sentences, but were not really sentences. *Not really sentences!* Like the punch line of a campfire story no one actually thinks is scary—*but she didn't have a head!* Soon Em was weeping and masturbating in her office by desklight as if she could find her soul in the act. Jim, John, Jake, what's his name, the figure in the pale coat, was in a constant state of disappearing around the corner. An angel is a messenger. A ghost wants life as it knew it. A chimera is many animals that escape us. Jacking off is the effort to leave your literal circumstances. Jacking off is a body without language. Em did not think that in so many words, it was just *in there*. What would a message say when it finally came and said something real and complete—a real message for Em from Adeline? Here I am at the following coordinates where you can come to pick me up hoping that I am a-okay superfine sugar (and might be magic), but arrive to discover that I am not fine (and might be magic), and there's nothing to be done so we'll all just have to take me out back like a sack of cats and shoot me.

& Following &

If animals separated by walls are sometimes symmetrical—

If a stranger can cause a—what would you call it?—association—vibration—resonance—a stranger who walks in—comes over—calls out—

What then, what then—

Is what you ask, then—

I mean what I ask, then—because trails are warn—

I mean worn—in the brain, I mean how a sentence goes—I mean—

Okay. Okay, so. So when—

When Em joined the company and was introduced at a meeting—"Emilie what's-her-name comes to us from a shit job with shit qualifications . . ."—Frank thought, there is a person trying very hard to look like nothing, and hardly noticed her again.

Okay. Frank.

That morning, the morning it rained—no, it rained *before*—so the morning Em read the rained-upon paper on the steps on the way into the building—Frank, from his office—animals side by side—had heard sounds that he hoped were Jack approaching—

walking-in-clothing sounds, picking-up-and-putting-something-down sounds—but realized were just Em in her office. All morning he was plagued with the sense of her working away at her desk behind her perfunctory haircut *pretending* not to know that Jack was in there with her. He could not shake it, no matter how dumb it was. He felt a level of jealousy that was as close to murderous as he'd known since he was a boy watching his father stare into a magazine and scared himself by too vividly imagining impaling him with the fireplace stoker.

No one at work knew about Jack. Frank had practiced—in marriage, through marriages, making his way in the world—covertly moving Jack in and out of existence. Whatever they thought of Frank it was not this. Now he'd missed work for a week and no one seemed to notice. He'd been back for a week and no one seemed to notice that, either. He found it disturbing not to be missed, because he'd always been, at least relatively, *important*, but also because *really*, were people *blind*? Were they *deaf*?

For lunch he tried to find something dignified to eat in the cafeteria-style eatery down the street where everyone went. He settled on a Sodexo mixed-greens salad with tiny cold shrimp from the soup and salad bar. He'd feel a flicker of Jack and look around to try to see where it came from. Returning from the cafeteria, he saw Em.

"Emilie!" he called out to her.

She changed her angle of approach to the building and made her way toward him up the wheelchair ramp. He tried to see, as she approached, whether there might be anything appealing about her. Nothing in any of her features prevented it.

She'd followed him up to their offices. He'd sussed her out. His performance had been terrible—fidgeting with those tissues, calling her *priss*—truly infantile—but some of his anxiety had been warranted, he decided, once she was back next door. He hadn't brought it all on himself. He didn't feel outed so much as misunderstood. What sort of woman doesn't care about love? Debra, he thought (his first wife). Miriam, he thought (his second). But he knew that was untrue and

unfair. Jack was in such an unpredictable state—it had been accumulating for weeks—that Frank spent the afternoon thinking of all the
places a person can get to in an hour, in two hours, three, proliferating
internal maps, mapping via ethernet in his office. Jack did not come.

He left the office for home like everyone else. Got into his robe
and ate something from the freezer that his sister had made. Couldn't
stand it anymore, got in the car, and drove around the cluster of
motels near the highway, then drove around downtown as if he'd
catch Jack coming or going from a building. Still in his robe. On
the wraparound porch of the house his second wife left him in, he
slept on a wicker sofa so he wouldn't miss anyone approaching. He
remembered her always in shoes that clopped. First wife remained
suspended in the middle of the country, alimony on autopay, kid
he'd met twice, now, somewhere, adult. He had a photo of the boy
in braces grasping the rigging of a small docked boat. He'd taken the
boy on a weekend of father-son lessons and had not been able to age
him in his mind after that.

But the next day at the office Jack did show up.

"Hi."

"Hi."

"Come on."

"Come on."

"Asshole."

"Asshole."

Grab, kiss, something falling off something.

"Where are you staying?"

"Shhhh."

Fuck, fucking, fuck.

"Don't go."

Clothes righted, locate wallet.

"When are you coming back?"

He was out the door. He was down the hall.

Frank felt left. Then he thought, no, I'll see him later. I'll see him
later tonight.

When it was time to head home, Em knocked on Frank's office door. She felt tiny at the door and tiny when he opened it. It had been a day of no news, no sister.

Frank slumped visibly when he saw it was her.

"Any news?" she asked.

Her tone was off. She said *news* as if they had a secret together, sounded accusatory when she was going for *neutral*. She'd also addressed the suit jacket on the back of his chair in the depths of the office because she had been too anxious to look at him. "Did you call someone? Did you call a hospital? I know, they can't do anything. Did you call the police? Just to keep an eye out. I mean in case they find him maybe they won't beat him up. They have awareness training."

"You're doing all you can to avoid saying 'crazy' now, aren't you?" Frank said.

"Yes," said Em. It was true. "Some people find it offensive."

"I find it not your business."

"Hey, you came to me."

"Not exactly."

"You called my name!"

"*Honestly.*" He shut the door, nearly clipping her nose.

Em got back behind her own door and prepared to go. Papers, drawers, outerwear, yanked off her banker's light, then stood there like a hole in a hole. She felt her briefcase in her right hand and the sweater she brought for air-conditioning hanging over her left elbow. She tried to run her mind along the outskirts of her body, but lost track. The ache for her sister pulsed. The coat covering the madman lover phased in and out of being the rags of an ancient wanderer and the wings of a pale bird. She heard a phone ringing, and it wasn't hers—she was sure it was Frank's. She pictured him picking it up—it seemed he had picked it up—and hearing the anchorman from the radio on the other end. With a real news update. Two men cut from the same cloth is what she pictured, passing knowledge under the table. Maybe a few years ago they each looked up from an enormous desk to find no one listening, but they still trafficked in some ether of knowledge she was still outside of, some cultural current of access. Anyhow a phone rang, stopped ringing, and something made Frank leave swiftly. She heard his door and when she was able to open hers and step out, his brown shoe was just disappearing around the corner like a rat. She thought two possibly incompatible things: that Frank was enabling a man in a medical crisis, and that Frank knew how to love a person who was in touch with the divine, and she did not.

Em's most recent bright bulb about Adeline was, "Come on, Ad, just come stay with me, stay in my house." It was the last phone call before Ad went missing. It was the first time since the LA psych ward that she'd dared to try to get Ad to come live with her. She didn't know if she meant it anymore. Ad was intensely agitated. Part of Em knew she was hearing voices, and part of her steadfastly insisted on something like *giving her the benefit of doubt*. Em said, "I have this completely adequate job, I have so much room here, you can have the whole dining area for your weird art, the house is so cute, you can just be there doing whatever, I'll go to work, they're trying to do something with downtown, there could be people for you."

Adeline said, "My jam is not your jam, your jam is not my jam."

Em said, "Jam? God, you're so funny," her heart cracking with shame and relief. It's terrible to think you know what's going on when what's going on is someone losing her mind. In retrospect she knew she was pretending her sister was joking when she wasn't. She was trying to give her sister a chance to *turn back now*—when she didn't have the courage or knowledge or imagination for anything else—as if Adeline had a choice in the matter.

But in the office, she thought, I bet that asshole is onto something. For one thing, he believed in what he was doing. So she stopped thinking and followed him.

Frank took the back stairs, a damp and spotted echoing cinderblocked air trap, no way he didn't hear her coming down a flight behind him.

He established a solid pace across the vast parking lot, weaving between cars, seeming to set one off as he passed and it pulled away. He stopped somewhere in the middle of the lot to take his suit jacket off and put it in his briefcase, and Em, a few rows over, took off her sweater and put it in hers. From above, the parking lot looked like a cheerful sheet of wrapping paper, the candy-colored cars with their slant-light shine, or a computer, mid-defrag. Day was cooling into evening, but they walked along with the cars leaving the lot, and then along with rush hour traffic, their bodies heating up. They passed the turn into Em's neighborhood and she didn't blink. Frank stopped at a light and took his turtleneck off and tied it around his waist. He squinted around in his sleeveless undershirt, then scrambled up an embankment to an overpass. Em stopped at the railing to take her stockings off, stuffing her feet back into her pumps barefoot. The string between the two of them expanded and contracted.

She followed Frank through downtown, past its banks of several stories, its waning department store, its retro diner, its internet café and karaoke, gutterpunk runaways on the sidewalk with wild dogs, veteran or man dressed as a veteran on the corner with incense in his hair floating with the smell of live body rotting. Frank stopped every so often to gaze into the eyes of taller buildings, and that gave Em a chance to rest her feet. Every so often he whirled around to flip her the finger, but now she thought his mood was shifting from being angry at her to being amused by her. He turned a few corners on the compact blocks of revitalized downtown.

After passing a busker at rest, he came upon a large cardboard box that had a flap cut into it and a person inside. Written in red marker in a sentimental arch over the box flap was: "Home Sweet Home." Just outside the box, a can sat on a mechanical platform like a pet. As pedestrians walked by, the person inside, a madman-in-a-box, pulled something that made the platform move, which bounced the can so that the coins in it clanked violently. Em saw a lady walk by the box without seeming to notice it and cry out when the machine jerked and clanked at her from behind. The lady hurried down the block holding her blouse at the neck as if she'd been caught in a sudden storm, the machine jerking and clanking as she fled.

Apparently Frank, too, had been watching, because he approached the madman-in-a-box. When the machine made the can jump, he stopped and took coins from his pocket and dropped them in the can. A hand popped out of the box flap and gave a thumbs-up. Frank crouched down near the flap. He said something and the hand retreated. The flap fell into place. Then it popped back out and gave a thumbs-up again. Frank put a bill into the jar. Then he patted the top of the box and continued along at his previous pace.

Em mocked him silently. What, now he's in with the downtrodden? Got 'em on the lookout for his man? Here's some crumbs, now you work for me? She watched a woman approach the box. This lady had also seen the can jump, so when it jumped at her she was ready. She gave just a little start and a little laugh, and she put some coins in the can. The can bounced again and she said, "Well, you're welcome!" This made Em angry, too. Then she saw Frank was making a right at the end of the block, and she sprinted to catch up with him.

They passed single-family rentals, a complex of apartments, long vacant lots overflowing with budding thistles. Frank began to whistle a song that she knew she knew, but took some blocks to identify. It was one of the most annoying songs in history, one she had been fascinated by in childhood but hadn't thought about since—a ballad, sometimes sung in a cowboy style, about a stray cat that a man takes in, and the inventive ways that the cat torments him until he regrets taking it in, how he throws the cat out of the house but it comes back, and he throws it out again but it comes back in a new way, and he throws it out and it comes back, each round escalating in violence and strangeness until he kills the cat and it comes back as a ghost, purring and meowing for food as if nothing bad has happened at all. She called out, "I get it, I get it!" but Frank didn't stop whistling until they reached the train station. He picked up his pace to blend into the rush of commuters. When they emerged on the other side of the station he was silent.

He led her past corrugated warehouses along a gravelly path to a ridge that wound upward, telephone wires scalloping the edges of the town below the increasingly glowing sky. They crossed a single-lane, single-cantilever bridge over a stories-high gully with a river moving in it, and back up on the ridge, made silhouettes in the dusk, Em narrow against the color blue her rain slicker had been going for, currently a sliver in the closet in the hall in her house, Frank bulging against the sky but retaining dignity, a sense of Em behind him, a sense of Jack ahead. Stars and satellites wobbled out like little kids in tutus. Em saw a cell phone tower in the distance and in sudden terror went into her briefcase to check her phone, but she'd lost reception. She stood, poised to run like a rabbit in the road, back into range, but then she just didn't. Frank was far enough ahead that it was hard to see him, and she just kept following him into the hills on the edge of town that accumulated mountainous qualities until finally it was just mountains.

In the last sustained minutes of dusk, they reached a postindustrial ruin. When Em came upon it, Frank was standing in a squarish depression in the earth, leaning against a mossed-over pylon next to a satellite dish, waiting for her—behind him, cables like diagrams of funnel clouds, buoyant over his head, and behind that, five smokestacks like their own city skyline. Frank had been near here with Jack, before. This exact spot was new to him, but these ruins in this weather in this light felt like a stage set for contact.

When she caught up, Em said, "Frank, I'm serious, it's important, are you getting reception?"

"I'm a dinosaur," he said. "I forgot my phone." In fact, his phone was in the pocket of the jacket he'd stuffed inside his briefcase. He did not want to be interrupted in this place. And he was very tired.

It was almost dark. Em took her sweater out of her briefcase and put it on, relatched the briefcase, and let it lean against her calf when it wouldn't stand on the rubbly ground. She smelled terrible and started to cry.

She said, "What are we going to do? Are we going to go back?"

"What are you, a child?" Frank said. "Do as you like." Colors were draining from their surroundings.

She said, "Are you meeting Jack here?"

He flipped her off again, but mildly. He took his suit jacket out and draped it over his head. It was a little buggy out. He sat on the concrete slab chunked into the earth. "You know what, Em, what's it to you anyway?"

She walked closer, stood over him. "It's not just love, it's sex, right?"

"Yes of course there's sex. Are you deaf?"

"I just wanted to make sure. I think things, but I'm not always sure."

"Things aren't always what they seem," Frank said in a sarcastically spooky voice. "'*Just love*,'" he said. "Outrageous." Em didn't care.

"Jack's wife, does she know what's going on?"

He looked hurt. A lapel cast a shadow across his brow. "The thing is," he said. "The thing is, the thing is."

"Come on," she said.

"He's from my personal history," Frank said. "He's no one's business. I just don't know where he is and I want to find him."

"Here? Why here?"

He took a package of saltines from his briefcase. "Want one?" She shook her head. He stripped the plastic off and ate them. "He mentioned something one time," he said. "I admit it's rash, coming out here." She let it go. They poked around the ruins and found a ragged blue tarp blown into the corner of the exposed foundation like a magic puddle. They spread it on softer ground and lay on it.

"Are you worried he's not okay?" asked Em. "Are you scared of where he is?" But he didn't answer.

Frank's mother died when he was midway through high school. He and his father had never, as his mother put it, *gotten on well*, but after her death they fought in a newly direct way. In the midst of one fight, Frank left out the back of the house and into the field beyond their lawn. His sister, who had crept halfway down the staircase from her room to listen, came out to the porch and watched him go.

As he walked, he slashed at the air with a stick, which he'd done as a child, clearing the way and cutting down enemies. Late-summer grass hung with seeds. A stranger was out there. This was Jack, eating a sandwich, looking up at a row of conifers that sketched the property line.

The trees had been topped. The neighbor must have done it himself because Frank's father would have hired an arborist to trim them properly. Jack was a couple of years younger than Frank, but he did not seem younger, and he did not go to school. He'd come from a town away and was working at a gas station, but his hair was as light as the grass and to Frank, in grief, he seemed to have come from the field itself.

"Hey."

"Hey."

Soon they had each climbed a tree in a contest that Jack won easily but didn't make Frank feel bad about, and were sitting on the tops of the lopped-off trunks. In a new contest, they were soon each standing. Jack removed a half-eaten sandwich from his shirt pocket, and finished it standing on the top of the tree, which made Frank laugh so hard he had to sit down to keep from falling.

It took a while for Frank to realize that Jack was a real live runaway, even if he had a job, even if no one was looking for him.

This time, a week—two weeks?—ago, Jack had appeared in Frank's driveway, in cropped hair and beat-up khakis, with an impractical decades-old orange Samsonite suitcase. They hadn't seen each other in over a year. Two years, maybe. Jack had been busily married. Frank had been getting divorced. Frank was reading the paper on the wicker sofa on the porch with a brandy. He always skipped local coverage to focus on world affairs, so he missed the article about the man who'd cursed the skies and held up traffic, but it was there, in the section folded on the side table, being a coaster. When Frank looked up, a taxi was just disappearing into a patch of fog down the block, but it had not brought Jack, because Jack was standing with the suitcase next to a junk heap of a car.

"Come on, old man," Jack said. "Let's go." He was clearly in a mood. Frank followed him into his house and up the stairs holding his glass of brandy like a lantern. He said, "Jack, it's great to see you— amazing, actually." He said, "Jack, what on earth—" But Jack was being evasive. He split the suitcase open on the bed and moved to the bureau. He opened each drawer and tossed something from it into the suitcase. He scanned the room, fixed on a small framed painting of a tree near the nightstand, tossed it in with the clothes, snapped the case shut, and turned it upright. Frank set his drink on the bureau.

It was Thursday. He had a date Friday with a woman his sister liked for him on the internet. They fucked and slept, or Frank slept. He woke to Jack shaking him by the shoulder.

He pulled on the trousers he'd let fall at the foot of the bed and followed Jack down the stairs and down the driveway. The thin coat lifted, making him seem even lighter. Everything felt bygone. Remnants of stickers on the suitcase suggested that it had been on the earliest commercial flights and the last transoceanic steamships. In this context, Frank completed the ordinary actions of getting into an unpleasant-smelling car and being driven in it. He thought something glowed in the car with them on the bench seat, at the level where a third rider's head might float. Foam bulged through cracked vinyl, ceiling fabric sagging. The broad curved windshield had a notch from a rock with a single crack reaching out.

They left the car at the train station. Jack liked to say he'd been born in the wrong time. He pulled the suitcase from the back seat, then put his hands in his pockets, both sides, jangling, probably, coins. Frank followed him into the station lugging a suitcase only a quirky thrift shop girl would still use. It was embarrassing to cross the parking lot in that manner but he did it. It was already hot and bright out. Jack walked ahead just jangling, and Frank lumbered along after. A porter is what someone doing that is called.

Then: train moving through stations. Jack handling the tickets, handing the tickets over. Moving through train cars. Playing along. "Fun, Jack. Okay, Jack." Days ("Really, Jack? Okay, Jack"). People filling aisles like old-timey soda bottles elbowing down a conveyor belt for capping. In crowds, he jostled cellularly, feeling himself as part of a unity with Jack. "Come on, Jack, where are we going? Where are we going, really?" In crowds, people were parts of themselves, a flat shoulder, a lurch, a foot maneuver, whatever luggage. They seemed already in the past. Focus on one body and it will keep disappearing. Touch an arm and beneath the fabric you'll be shocked there's bone. Jack rubbed his hands together. He said, "I'll give you a hint, motherfucker. A big apple. Wait till we get there," and then bought tickets going another direction.

Back when Frank was married they'd once met up in a tropical paradise and spent no time at all on the beach. Before that, a place Winston Churchill had stayed in Morocco. Before that, following Jack to an array of nightclubs. One sex club where Jack explained, "You're a ghost and when you're a ghost you don't have to worry about anything." Scenes. People in costumes. "The costumes are not disguises," Jack said. "They're expressions." Jack liked sex clubs. He also liked to walk where everyone was poor and talk to people. He'd trade a camera for supper in a family's shack. Frank, shoving embarrassment down, eating someone's dark stew, thinking, I'm a ghost and I don't have to worry about anything. Sometimes with Jack he felt like his real life was finally happening, and sometimes he felt like his own lesser twin. Kids half a generation younger than them selling their stuff on the ground leading out to some warehouse in a field and he'd wonder what was between him and Jack and those kids, because we're not like them, we would never be them. And he'd wonder, is Jack thinking the same thing?

"We're going to New York City?"

"No, an apple." Frank couldn't tell if this was sarcastic or not. "We're going to something in it," Jack said. "I said, *hint*."

Frank obliged, thought about seeds, worms, seeds of the past, his past, worms of an apple. It's not that it made sense. Someone says, *trust me*. You are and are not quite yourself, and if you're Frank, you believe yourself to be a good judge of character, a man with a nose for bullshit. You take pride in your taste for grandeur. You believe yourself to be, in your daily life, not fully recognized.

Train covering ground and the memory of trains covering ground, the view out the back making tracks. Having lugged the suitcase, stashing it in the footwell of an empty row across. Light geometric, light slipping, light in spasms, leaping back into place, slipping, the rows of windows, grid of seats, the printed upholsteries, the shadowy rubber-ridged aisle, Jack's arms spilling over with cans of sodas from a vending machine last stop. Spilling over. Someone says, *how about a little faith*. You are not the boss, not anymore. You would like a little faith.

Time, and then, "No, come on, where are we going? A man has obligations." Jack unfolding the hinged table. Going through a lot of newspapers. It was not clear that Jack's eyes took in words as they moved across the pages and turned them. Some play between men acting like boys, sitting at the train table, some touching as if they weren't touching. Swapping sections. Ha, look at this. Some small rejections. Flick the paper held up like a screen. Don't flick my paper, dick. Flicky-dick. Upon the table, unfolding a map of the coast. Upon the map silver cans from the café car sweating on the states. Light fooling around on the map. Frank pulled the curtains. Jack pushed them back. He said something about the skin's receptors, something like, *Cells are pixels under microscopes*, he said. "Fuel cells, chromatophores, Argos, millions." He said, "This very window." Something like, *Towers in Japan made of pills called capsules*. The train picked up after a stop and Jack said, "Slow film flapping." When Frank didn't respond he said, "Right?" He looked out the window and then moved a can on the map.

If he just gave it a minute, Frank thought, what Jack meant would come together.

He picked up a section of the newspaper. Jack had been studying it, glancing dramatically at Frank to warn him off peeking. It was the *New York Times*, declining paper of record. Frank was not sure if the warning was ironic. He read parts of a few articles (Jack didn't seem to notice), settled into one about a new high-end condo, a golden tower of glass cubes that provided a choice example of *the hubris that led to the financial crisis*.

In the paper, construction had halted. The floor intended for a swimming pool, a spa, and a wine bar remained a cavernous shell, Frank learned, its role in the skyline, the glinting reflections and labyrinthine scaffolding, *jolting the neighborhood into the present*. Maybe they were going to ground zero, he thought. That would be significant. The photo of the vacant, gleaming skyscraper in the sun did make him think of a black hole.

The article applauded the caliber of the architecture, a stack of multistory glass cubes plugged into one side of a bronze-colored shaft. People could take a measure of solace in the quality, the article said. Celebrities had meant to live there. Light rippled through the glass as if a lake could be floating in the sky for the sole purpose of being reflected. Jack kept working on his map, moving the cans, marking with a pen. Frank said, "You're leaving rings." He thought he could see a pattern. He tried to make a joke about the Olympics, as if he could suddenly become a funny person, or make Olympics funny.

"Rings?"

Jack looked at Frank as if he were crazy, which means he looked at him with disgust.

It's a matter of fidelity. You love someone. He is going through something you don't understand and your attempts keep failing. You believe him. With his wives, what Frank felt was *accomplish-*

ment, he now thought, not love. Interaction by interaction, he took his own ideas and just shoved them over to make room for Jack's. What Jack thought, he told himself, could just as easily be true as what he thought. Sometimes his body felt extra heavy when he made this mental move, but sometimes it felt thrillingly, almost chemically, light.

Watching, out the static window together, the land in motion. Uncountable items upon it. He tried to guess which ones were the right ones to strike him. Out the window an airplane flew low alongside the train under a storm that never hit them. Migrants had built homes against a stone wall in a field. On the other side, an industrial lot for boats in a bay. Jack said, "Well, *that* means something." He said something about weather in the Dust Bowl, dozens drowning in a plaza in China with sixteenth-century pipes. "Natural disaster that is not a natural disaster," he said. "Mark my words, my man."

"I thought we were going to New York," Frank said, trying to sound jocular to cover *whining* or *frightened*.

Jack rolling his eyes.

Jack took a Walkman out of the obsolete suitcase. He drew cheap earbuds from one khaki pocket and a bottle of Wite-Out from another. He put the earbuds in. Jack sticking things in ears like that. Something fetal about an earbud. In the car, bulging, splitting. In the train, endlessly forward even as they must be drawing scribbles. When a dynamic shifts and everything gets stupid and you can't say anything that's not stupid. When everything he says back to you can't possibly be real. When people don't really act like this.

What's going on with you? What did I do?

What's going on with you, man?

What's all this *man*, since when do you say *man*?

Frank thought, but he comes to town for me, over all people. Remembering a time on some beach when he asked Jack about a woman he'd claimed to love, and Jack said, "She is no longer in the picture." Why he didn't push it. When you don't want to know because it would be disruptive. Someone comes to town and wants you so much it allows you to defy your life.

In the café car some commuters were getting drunk. They'd lined up their tiny empty wine bottles along the chrome edge of the table. As Frank passed them, a man in a bow tie flicked one off the table. It made Frank turn and go back the other way. He passed Jack again and caught half words coming from his moving lips, maybe singing? He saw Jack's attention moving between the reflective surface of the window and he was still bent over his map, adding, erasing, moving his lips. In another car, Frank rested his hand on the back of a seat and watched a teenaged boy sleeping, his face not far from the hand that had landed near it. The boy appeared to be traveling alone. He had a silver bone through his ear and splotches of receding acne. Eyebrows unruly for perhaps the first time. He rested his face on his crumpled hand. Frank had watched his sister watching her children sleep the way people do because you can't fuck a kid up if he's sleeping. He took a seat in the empty row across from the teenager and reclined. He had sex dreams that were partly sex memories. Later, he remembered only the part of the dream during which he was simultaneously fucking Jack and unable to touch him. In the night, a batch of people getting it together and disembarking in the night intersected with people entering and settling in for the ride. He did not know where on the train he was, or where in relation to the suitcase, map, Jack, or where the train was in the country. He woke with his feet lying like dolls pressed under the seat in front of him and thought he saw, out the window, a row of trees smoking. His body reacted, but it was a cloud. It was morning. His vision crackled with white branches, some somatic optical thing. He straightened up. Jack was there in the aisle, and the teenager was there, too, up and animate, Jack's face working like a rubber mask.

The boy yelled, "Are you off your fucking meds?"

People had half risen in their seats, craning around, heads over seat backs, just up to the eyes, or just up to the nose. They didn't want to have to do anything. *Please don't make me be supposed to do something.*

The train was decelerating into a station.

"You need help, asshole. Help." The boy was zipping a backpack, pushing toward an exit. His hair blocked most of his face. Jack scrambled after him. He must have been saying something, making noise. They pushed each other off the train. Some other people got off, too, and skittered away. On the platform, that schoolyard thing. Push, push back, wanna make something of it? The boy threw his backpack to the ground. Jack bounced like a boxer, possibly making fun of boxers, in his long coat. Frank could see all this from the window. He touched the glass and then pulled his hand back. He was grateful for the window. It's not like the stop came and went too quickly for him to make it off the train after them.

He made a decision not to move.

Frank stayed in the seat until the next station was announced and he remembered the suitcase. He was trying to retain what Jack's face was like fighting with the boy. He moved down the train aisle using the seat backs, hand by hand. When he saw the table open with the mess of map on it, he felt his stomach contract. The suitcase was there, wedged between sets of seats, rocking, two generations of vinyl making a sound that disgusted him. He took the suitcase to make it stop rocking. The train stopped. He got off the train. In the station, he stood in front of the electric monitor for departures. There in white glowing letters and a number next to it was the code for a city near his city. He took that train, then he took another train, and still humming from it, he set the suitcase down in the kitchen of his house that his wife left him in. He dropped his clothes by his bed, the sheets still in whorls from when he'd followed Jack out. He bathed in the darkness of very early morning. He stood in his bedroom and then his living room with a towel around his waist. Back in the kitchen, he stood next to the suitcase, one hand on a knot of damp terry cloth, the other resting on the tiny lock. He thought of making toast but was unable to do it. Choosing a jam, choosing a tea. Upstairs, his sister had left clothes from the dry cleaner hanging on the door to his closet so he'd see them. Every few days since his wife left, his sister came over to clean. He'd lie on the sofa and follow her with his eyes—not turning—just the eyes—her smooth body of uncooked heaps, her skin always pink with feeling. Sheila followed the vacuum, or followed her own hand outstretched with a rag like a sick bird that groped through the house after the furniture. He put the dry-cleaned clothes on and left the house again. His wives had not known about Jack, he was certain. He always felt more truthful, more faithful, knowing that they left him without Jack as a reason. The wives knew about a friend from his youth who made him happy. They had not left because of Jack. They left because of him.

Then he went to work.

In his office, in clothes his sister had dry-cleaned for him, tasteful but unseasonal, Frank bent over his work, worried about Jack, missed Jack, felt like an asshole, felt upstanding, and his mind returned to the vacant skyscraper so regularly that he began to imagine Jack had wanted him to read that very article and for it to explain their journey. The *Times* suggested that our economic woes were in fact due to aesthetic stagnation. As captivating as the wandering tenants, Frank remembered from the paper, if not in so many words, were the ghosts that the design conjured, radical experiments in mass production for an increasingly dense and urban postwar society, a latter-day version of the modular approach used to envelop the rich in an aura of luxury while insulating them from the masses. The author approached the building at one angle after another in order to decide which angle was most handsome and, once inside, found it was all about views, views, views. I miss you, Frank thought as hard as he could, gazing from his own interior, imagining the glass cubes scraping the sky. He had learned to read late, and remembered palpably what the idea of reading felt like as a child before he could do it, and then the liberation of finally, and suddenly, being able to do it.

Longing broke over him and the luxury structure rose from the pit of the Twin Towers.

Cities were once considered a cause of madness. Kids from the farm stepping from trains with their single suitcases would find their circuits overloaded, whatever brain gears whacking out, coils sproinging, whatever you'd call it back then, when people were like clockwork instead of like time. As the *Times* noted, even those who will never enjoy the luxuries of such a construction can still appreciate the building as a valuable addition to a prominent historic site, and as part of an incremental improvement in aesthetic standards, it at least feeds the fantasy that someday high-quality architecture will trickle down to the shrinking middle classes. The reverse, the *Times* lamented, is too depressing to contemplate.

Then Jack in the office, arriving and leaving like light. Too many hours and Frank would start phoning. Too many hours and Frank would start to wonder if anyone else saw Jack. Jack's hand over his mouth. Something falling off something and landing like a backpack. Jack would not say where he was staying. He said he was assessing the situation. Frank thought if he left his office and stepped into the hall there was some chance he would find himself in a golden glass high-rise.

Then the thing with her in his office, then the thing with her in her office jacking off. Symptomatic is when you are making choices your usual self would never make. Two children fighting over the true shapes of clouds.

On the tarp, Frank and Em looked at each other in the coming dark and then the dark. The air, the darkness, and no dinner made them a little drunk. Stars and airplanes went blinking and made them a little happy. They each made a wish for the spectacular, but silently and in separate ways. Em's sister floated in a cool halo that had slipped out of sight behind her head like rings of sound or ripples from a stone in water. Em's idea of Jack could easily be hunching behind any mound of earth or concrete chunk.

She tried again to get Frank to tell her something that would make him real for her. He tried a little. "Jack is filled with wisdom," he said. "Jack has a way about him, he brings something that you don't normally—" shrug "—it's useless, someone else's emotions . . ." Em could only see a figure disappearing around a curve on a mountain trail. "He mentioned something one time," he said again. He said, "Jack wrote me letters from Iceland and Alaska. He was gone for a year in a rain forest once, living with people." He said he knew, too, that Jack sometimes lied, or lied and then said, *But you must have known that couldn't be true.*

"He's perpetually on a quest," Frank said. "It's compelling to be part of a quest."

Rocks jutted from the mountain that rose from the edge of the ruin. Frank's eyes flicked up at them, and Em imagined that he expected Jack to jump down, coat flaring, skin flashing. But Frank was not much of a nature guy. He'd never spent the night outside. He was wondering about animals. A quest is symptomatic. The collapsed architecture was both beautiful and pollution. Em knew there were supposed to be a lot more stars and still felt deliciously lost in them.

Frank said, "I don't understand why it didn't rain today." He reclined with his suit jacket draped over his shoulder, propped on one elbow, one hand flat on the tarp, shining. He wore a strange ring on it instead of a wedding ring—a thick one with a large black stone in it that didn't shine.

He shifted onto his back, lacing his fingers across his chest. "Jack makes me feel things I mock in others." Then he said, "Why are you following me?"

Em said, "My sister's missing." She focused on whatever was poking from the ground into the flesh near her hip and its relation to her hip pushing into the ground. "The person I love the most. Don't you think that's meaningful? Don't you think it's—I don't know—*remarkable* that you're in the office right next to me?" And she didn't say, because otherwise we have nothing to say to each other and may even be mortal enemies. Em did think the coincidence was remarkable. She also still thought he might know something she didn't, something about *honoring* a person even when you didn't understand them. But it also pleased her to see him so wrecked. A man used to being boss. A guy like that. A memory from a party, back when Em lived somewhere with parties she wanted to go to: entering a stairwell, a guy a few steps ahead of her, someone's impressive boyfriend. "I'm not following you," she'd said, and the boy laughed. Then back in the party fray, Em had sidled up to his girlfriend. "I had a little chat with your guy," she'd said, and the girl gave her a look. "What?" Em said. "Nothing happened." But something *had* happened. There'd been a—what would you call it—resonance, vibration—a *charge* with that boy and she'd used it to create a charge with that girl. There was a charge with Frank. It must have been there even as she followed him up the clammy spiderwebby stairs after he'd called her name. She'd felt the bulge of his proximity, the molecules that buzz around a person because they're alive that you never notice unless there's a charge. What was the charge made of? Potential. Everyone is looking for their people. Newspeople, office people, street people, important people, mad people, people near mad people.

Frank looked at her. What a plain, plain girl. Inside, he was drenched in one meaningful memory of Jack after another. He tried to attach some words to the memories, but every word he thought of was definitely wrong. Everything, he concluded, is an inside joke. You'd just have to know him the way I know him, you'd have to be there down to the molecule. He kept trying to remember a line from a letter Jack had written to him about landscape, and what he'd once said about a trail that went up this way, which their trail might or might not have ended up being, but which he thought he'd been following from the back of the train yard. In his office that afternoon, he'd looked up pictures of the progress of the 9/11 memorial. The footprint of the building had been lined with steel, turning the ragged hole into a clean square. Beyond the construction cranes in one of the photos he found, a sign on a building read in giant letters, "Shhh! New York's Best Kept Secret!"

Em and Frank lay on the ground in the dark, physics everywhere.

"Well, I feel a kinship," she said. "I think it's remarkable," she said, "that we both turn out to love such similar types of people."

"Blonds, you mean, I'm sure," he said. His tone had softened.

What shifted him was that he realized he'd inadvertently been doing to Em what Jack had done to him, teasing with the idea of an apple.

"Okay," Frank said. "I have something for you. There was a girl in my class, the best-looking girl of all of them, breasts before any other girl." He meant deep in his past, he meant childhood. "She had a black father and a white mother, which was very interesting to me at the time and made her even more beautiful. But for some reason she said to me in my ear one day—I was drinking from the fountain— she leaned toward my ear from behind me in line: *Why don't you come into my window at night?* It was like a song." He was telling the story from a parallel space, with leftover authority, through an assortment of damage.

"I froze there at the fountain letting water pump up into my lips until she leaned in again and said, *Hurry up.* I'd been tantalized by her every day since she'd arrived at the beginning of the year, a new kid in my class, and down my block, and at my bus stop, so I saw her in every weather, and was under constant threat of seeing her in a million circumstances I could not control. She'd suddenly be there on the corner when I came off a curb like an oaf on my bike or suddenly when I was doing some horrible chore for my father, or my mother called for me in a horrible voice I was sure betrayed all the pain in our home that embarrassed me. I went, though. I knew from the movies that I was to throw pebbles at her high window, so I collected a pocketful from our driveway. I knew she was forbidden because of her girlness and her blackness. I was afraid to go alone so I brought Sam, a boy that I, along with other aggressive boys, terrorized at school, but who lived next door to me and was my closest friend."

"Is Sam Jack?" Em asked.

"No," he said. "He's Sam. This is well before Jack."

"Is the girl—what's the girl?"

"Sam and I wore dark clothing and snuck along the base of the hedges looking at the lit windows for clues. Their house didn't even have two stories and her window was low. All I had to do was tap. I didn't know what to do but I managed to roll around in her bed with her with my nose in her hair and pebbles pressing into me. A voice came at her door—it was her father—terrifying to me because of his blackness, terrifying because of his—fatherness. I knew what to do. I slid off the bed and under it. There was Sam under there. I hadn't even thought of him since we entered her room. We looked right at each other the whole time, huddled together."

"Sam was under the bed?"

"Oh, that girl. She was valiant and believable."

"Did you say the girl's name? I forgot, if you did."

"Her father pushed his head in the room and said, *Honey?* She mumbled from her covers, *What, Daddy?* as if from sleep, as if with pebbles in her mouth. He said, *Okay, honey, I thought I heard something.* She said, *No, Daddy.* He said, *Sleep tight, honey.* I didn't know that Sam was a homosexual until many years later when he killed himself. Those were the times. They still are, I know, but they really were. That night, I went home. I brought Sam with me. We went into the kitchen and I took down a jar of honey, and we ate it with a spoon."

Em pictured little Frank in the bed with the girl and Sam below them. She saw Sam lined up with the girl on another plane. Frank had not answered any of her pressing questions, and he had not told her anything about Jack that she understood. He had not asked her anything about herself or what she had revealed to him, or what was beyond what she'd revealed. The girl in his story remained alone and safe in her bed. Next to Em, Frank was in his own world, self-absorbed. Still, one part of her brain told another part of her brain, *you were right!* Because of the story, Em felt calm with her secrets and shame. She'd been in the presence of a person taking quiet indulgent pleasure in speech, expecting nothing, leaving a story there for her—a little familiar, a little out of reach—just in case—and she slept like that. The air was softly particulate, night birds swooping and not colliding over and over again, not extinct yet, the almost entirely unpeopled landscape suggesting the curve of celestial organization.

"What's it to you?" he asked, one more time, half-asleep, and she was so close to him she sensed his gratitude when she didn't respond.

After a while, she heard him say, "I wanted to champion excellence . . ."

After a while, "He brought a sunny field beyond the house."

When they were asleep in the ruins—when the place was a little magic with the sense of what can pass from one person to another—

When meaning hums nearby but won't resolve—

Something poking from earth, shifting sleep—

A cat around a corner—

Or other animal—

Briefcases and grocery sacks brushing I beams, catching on orange netting that cordons off safe zones—

When *you are off your meds* comes like a song down the street—

When something nudges a brain such as the weather, the world—

When shoppers among panhandlers—how about this one?—this one looks so—a dollar for that—

A whistle—

When *what happened?*

Nothing! Nothing happened.

When a chase in a small dark room, in a mental state—

An erotics of inside and outside at once—

Jolting.

When you are off your meds—

When you get the message—

"Off!"—what you say to a dog on the couch—

Come on, let's go.

Your tiny bottle bouncing in a footwell—
Your soft chair with a glass that clinked—
When a box of tissues, when home sweet home—
A code for a city near your city to a place you remember—
When *take your mask off,* to a man in a box—
When I'll show you mine when you show me yours—
What do they call it, a black box theater—
It's not my box, it's my face—
When the cat came back—
Up a hill, so close to your feet as they follow—
It's August, Ad's walking Venice Beach in a parka with fur lining—*fur*!
She can hear what every person in the crowd is saying—"like Septimus, and that book is a *masterpiece*"—
When she's running barefoot along a hillside strewn with cacti—
Her feet hooves—
She can feel vibrations, boulders up her bones, legs shredding—
When *how are you doing?* I'm doing *fantastic!*
When *mark my words*—
When animals and the dead speak to her, the future visible in a saltshaker—
When a butterfly flapped because she thought it did.
When *finally everything makes sense.*
When you are assessing the situation—
When you are following leads—
Handbooks with sample dialogues in bubbles for defusing—when compliance—
When you use your knowledge of a person's private universe, lie to a judge so a person has to—
When self and others—
And you have to trick a person into a hospital—do you have to—you trick a person—
A parade of doctors and snotty asshat students putting you on a scale of 1–10—

When you are evaluated—evaluating—

So you're a little weird—

So *inconvenient—so disruptive*—

So you're *expensive*—

When you're not listening—

No, *you're* not listening!

Count backward by sevens, who can do that?

When remember these words: car, book, umbrella, who's the president, what day is it, what does this mean a stitch in time, what if there's a stamped addressed envelope lying on the sidewalk, what would you do? What would you do if you saw a fire? I'd put it in a mailbox, right?

You know what I'm doing? I'm drinking urine down the pike. *My urine.* You find that upsetting? You find it vulgar. I'm doing it right now.

People do it all the time in history.

My brain is a *gift*—my brain is a *gift from*—

My ass is a six, my soul is a two, my heart is hovering at eight point five—

Put that in your pipe—

Locking up my people—*my people*—who are *visionaries*—shamans—Huna—

What's a Huna?

If you really mean something to each other a sticky thread comes into existence and connects you forever.

But Adeline—

You know what matters to hospitals is liability, don't you, Em? You know you can be a little pompous, don't you, Em—

But Adeline—

What? What? What?

If we get the meds right—

Protect you—erase you—(a curse?—a spell?—)

You? You who? (a joke?—yoo-hoo anybody?—)

Great, so I can what, get a job? Push a mop?

Not a mop. There's nothing wrong with a mop.

You want me to *push a mop*?

When Em and Ad each recall their mother, stories of her visions from her childhood transformed magically into memories of stories from theirs, the domestic creatures that filled the house they grew up in with fur, with animal sounds, and the woods with the river outside it that in the past must have brimmed with birds and beavers, fishes and foxes.

And when Frank recalls his mother—

And really, what do I know—who am I—who am I to say—

When Jack turned to look back at her, Em didn't want to look, even in her dreams or remembering imagination. His face was shadowed in a way that suggested, for a moment, the distant profile of a seahorse, a Chinese dragon, and, for a different moment, a sort of waxy proto-person with white smoothed-over features like an out-of-focus elongated infant. Or he turned to look back at her and his face appeared hyperreal, a projection of a mannequin. Or he turned looking like a stylized mash-up etching of an android: a figure by a lake that spread at the foot of a castle over which hovered a flying saucer with beams where a heavenly object would be. She knew he judged her for the inadequacy of the images.

In the morning Frank was covered with dapples. Grasses with dew like fiber optics fanned around the tarp and among the ruins and collapsed pillars, interior cables exposed and tumbled with mouthy morning glories, naturalized hostas, and irises, white and purple, from old landscaping. Now Em could see a pond, too, across the foundation. She left him and walked over to the pond. The black bodies of fish moved in and out of patches of clear water, milky-green water, and underwater forests. Romance, romance: everything populated by the spirits of poems and poets loathed in high schools across the nation. She listened to the honking of frogs, and then some bird imitating a car alarm, that whole repeating sequence of patterns they might not even put in car alarms anymore. Before these fish were native they were invasive, and now they were genotoxic. A feather floated on the surface and one after another—perhaps the same fish, never learning—surfaced to peck at it. Several tubular smokestacks, once six, ten stories high, had toppled over each other and partway into the far end of the pond. She thought this might be what it was like in her sister's brain when her sister was sleeping dreamlessly. Something mewled. A leaf of ash floated by on a breeze.

When Frank woke, they just walked back along the ridge, across the bridge, and descended toward town. They looked like rags. At one point Em noticed that Frank had his briefcase, but she'd forgotten hers, though her cell phone was in the pocket of her poor skirt. Then their reception came back, and they both had messages. "Dinosaur my ass," said Em, under her breath. But she wasn't angry.

Frank's message was from his sister, Sheila, about the woman he'd stood up so long ago. Sheila had gotten emails from the woman twice already, and now a third saying, "Well I guess nothing's gonna happen," so what should she tell the woman, now? Em's message was from Benny, who lived in the house with her mother and father. It said her sister was dead, that her parents were with the body at a hospital in one of those states in the middle of the country, he'd get an address. She told Frank. Frank called a cab. Birds that had been on a machine in the background came to nothing. They took the cab to Frank's house. He had it wait in the driveway with her in it while he went inside and came back with some drugs. Then they took the cab to her house and he put her in the bed and gave her some of the pills. He left messages on her behalf on the machines of some people who didn't know him while he sat in a saggy plaid chair near the edge of her pillow, waiting for the pills to kick in. She said she wanted the radio on, so he brought the little transistor in from the kitchen and it played, low, from her nightstand. News of the world. Then while she was crying and sleeping, he talked to Benny and booked her a flight. The message had been from Thursday, it was Friday, and he bought the ticket for Sunday morning. The girl was dead; Em should sleep. In the chair, when he dozed, Frank was wearing a golden condo like a suit of armor, striding among the mood-enhancing plasma screens of its lobby. In the evening he called his sister and she came bustling with some food, to sit with Em while he went home to change clothes and look for Jack. The orange suitcase was still in the kitchen and, as he set his briefcase down next to it and left it, again, in the house on the ancient linoleum, he remembered the small framed picture Jack had taken from his bedroom and put in there, and then nothing had come of it. It was just a picture of a tree in spring. Across town, his sister took a suitcase from Em's closet and they talked about what to put in it. On Saturday afternoon, Em talked to her father, who said Ad was brain-dead but, as an organ donor, remained on life support. Sunday morning, as Frank's sister was driving her to the airport, Em's father called and said Adeline had moved her hand.

Experts

In line at the airport Em focused on the stillness of her body in relation to the airport rattling with everyone's luggage, name tags swinging, children lurching alongside their parents, attached at the hand or waddling away dizzily or with shrieks of resistance, the constant and too-loud music meant to drown out the people in fucked-up-flight trauma, to trick people from recognizing their own infuriated boredom. To protect herself, she tried to understand her body as a separate entity, but the more she focused on it, the more she could feel the ways it, too, would not be still, and it would not be still because it was not dead. First there was life then death, and now there was life then death then something. *Something* like the chasm of an open mouth. She closed her eyes and tried to feel people as good as gone, and then she tried to put herself back on the tarp with Frank. She reoriented in space, vertical from horizontal, *adobe acrobat rotate clockwise*, but the universe turned in relation to her and remained askew. She tried to put herself into the story with the girl in her bed and the boy Sam under it, to give herself a quiet place in the layers of the real and imagined. She'd slip, and then put herself back.

After security, she took a pill for the plane.

After the plane, she took a long taxi ride from the airport. Her father and mother had come on separate flights (one day ago and two days ago) and dropped their stuff in separate rentals. The aunt arrived, the one who'd wanted to know "how you are." Friends of Ad's had been emailed (dead!), then re-emailed (not dead!). Now some were en route. The hospital was in Kansas City. No one in the family had ever been there. Maybe driven through. Em started off nights, solo, in Adeline's blue hospital room. There were now only three other places in the world: a motel with a pool, a sunny patio outside the ward where people smoked or made phone calls, and wherever cable programs came from. The brain is a blueprint of an imaginary building that defies physics every day. In computer simulations, something removes the skull, into which the brain has been stuffed like a rag, and uncrumples the coils into a flat sheet of cells. Someone had placed a small painted wooden plaque depicting the patron saint of the mentally ill and their caretakers on the bedside table like a radio. It must have been the aunt, here from the desert. Sometimes a nurse from another floor came into the room, looked at Ad rising in and out of hallucinogenic consciousness, and said, *miracle*. There was no *before* and *after* madness, but there was before and after this happened to Ad—I mean Ad did this.

The story of the girl on the plaque was that she loved her father, the petty king of Oriel. Her father loved his queen, and the girl had a priest who loved her in a fatherly way. To the king, the queen was perfect, but the queen died and her death made him mad with grief.

The people called for a new queen. Her father wanted only his wife, but his wife was dead, dead, unambiguously dead. He said, "Find a woman to match her," and like leaves bursting from a tree, his subjects traveled the roundness and flatness of the earth—never to return, or returning spent and empty-handed, or returning with specimens of women the king rejected. Soon the girl's priest saw the father's eyes, sexed-out, shift to the girl. She was thirteen, shade of her mother, and not dead. The priest arranged escape on a ship to whatever Antwerp was in the seventh century, and friendly villagers in the hills there sheltered them, a girl and her priest. Well, the priest had used the girl's royal coins for their passage and then the girl used her coins to set up a caretaking system for the mentally ill of the friendly town, so follow the money.

The king and his search party tracked them down. "Bang, bang," on the door of the hut from which they administered their facility, which matched the mad with families to house them. "Let us in!" The priest took the girl by the hand and off they ran, out the back and into the woods, horses and dogs after them, into the mountains, until the two were surrounded in a clearing. The king dismounted and stepped into the grassy circle. The sun spotlit them greenish through the trees. The king's subjects with their horses encircled the king, the priest, and the girl. Villagers arrived limping and panting, and joined the audience. Mountains like hats surrounded them all, and this may have been the very moment they all transformed from people into figures.

"Return!" the father moaned, as if calling the dead. "Return to me!"

He spat a monologue of pagan shreds: hands of silver, secret pigskins and horse ears, stones crying out, apples falling from cooking spits like dung, a butterfly blown into a brimming cup, a woman scratching the plans for a fortress into his heart with a brooch. Grief was under that churning surface of words like a great and implacable fish, and the fish meant fecundity, reincarnation, and took the symbolic form of an arc, fish were a secret knock among the oppressed Christians, and don't little American children get goldfish in baggies to learn about life and death, and don't the parents of little American children like to replace one dead carp with another as if a fish is a fish is a fish, they do it with the trickery of coins and behold—death, what death?—and so, and so—and so the priest said, "You are *off your meds!*" and the king commanded his people to kill him, which, from their steeds and with their swords, they did: dead, dead, unambiguously dead. Now the girl kneeled before her father, her love so large it enveloped madness, like a big fish eating a little one because a love so great, because a love divine.

The king struck her dead himself. She was sainted. The villagers made relics of bits of her body. Someone in a desert produced a plaque. Ad began rising in fidgets after three days so dead that no one closed her eyes until her father saw his daughter dead with her eyes left open, and shut them. Benny had said nothing untrue on the machine. When he called she was dead. There are a lot of books, movies, and stories about people condemned by doctors to die and then not dying that people will begin to point out to you when you are suddenly in that situation. Ways the past might contain or predict the future. How to hedge your bets.

Benny had lived in the house with Em's mother and father since he got out of prison rehab, was the story. He was a small man who often wore a straw hat called a trilby. They all went way back. A superb carpenter, he worked on the house under the mother's direction and played chess with the father.

A boy from Chiapas named Tasio, age seventeen, worked under Benny and lived in the garden in a shed where Ad once ripped out rotting floorboards looking for dead celebrities. Em didn't know him, but she pictured him from stories told over the phone. Madness ran in his family. His mother (likely) named him Anastasio because of it, saw doom and yet hoped, and Em's mother (likely) hired him because she knew the name meant *resurrected*. Em cared about him because of these stories.

Ad had not yet died. She was between episodes when Tasio took the job at the house in the woods, and they came to know each other there. But by the time Ad died, no one had heard from him in a while. Months. When did the king die, or in his madness did he go on and on? Death is a swinging door, a witch at night who sees the world through an unlit mind, among leaves, between thighs, in magicians' sleeves, pulling up sheets against time. That's a song. Em had sometimes called the aunt to ask about the deep past of the family that only the mother and the aunt knew. She'd ask about her mother's stories and then get the answers mixed up. Is this story true? Is this?

On the hospital patio, a small woman in spectacles and a large man with a new liver were enumerating the details of a sex-murder case they'd both been following in the papers. They were coming up with scenarios and then poking holes in them. People landed on the patio in a mysterious pattern over time, returning and being replaced like starlings. Em used them, when she was in the sun, to pull at her mind. She'd arrive in the deep-blue room after waking in the afternoon in the motel, presumably eating something, walking down the dirt path along the highway, then through a parking lot, into the hospital, through corridors and units, along the green path to the ICU. Monitors blinking, making low groans and faraway rhythmic beeps in watery electronic darkness. Not recording normally is how she felt in its vicinity. The blue room. Going in as her mother and aunt were coming out, registering peripherally that her mother was unable to look at her, or uninterested in looking at her. Adeline's eyes closed. The parents, the room where they put her, the daughter, sister. The machine light, glowing tubes of liquid. Monochrome. Unisonic. Night shift, then motel. The pool in the dark. The parents and nurses. Hours into night. Patio sun in the day. People smoking and sucking Cokes on wire chairs. Heads in the water, Ad's friends on telephones. What fish are for. Television psychics and naked interviews of strippers. Ambien, and Em's ex, feeling guilty, a voice on the other end of a stiff pillow, who kept a gun in her nightstand. Her mother's sister from the desert with a lot to say. The drapes in the motel room, the thickness, the invisible embossed patterns, their several layers. One layer shining like the white border of a photo of a certain amount of black. A pink thing you call a noodle in the pool. Blue strands of fluid through the room, with moving numbers. The father with travel chess on a tray. The sun like ringing and wounds on Em's feet from the past in pumps. She stood on the path to the pool in the dark, looked up and moved her neck in ticks, causing the stars to blur geometrically. We are surrounded by math. The blue room pulsed with rhythms and chemicals, numbers on machines running. It was outside the structures that it was inside. The numbers represented something about the body for the sisters. Em would watch a set of numbers and tell nurses if certain levels went beyond something. *I forgot the numbers.* She went out and asked. *What were those numbers again I'm watching for?* Went out and asked again. She kept letting information go like balloons. She kept looking at Ad's hands. Her father had said her hand had moved. Which hand? That one? She'd look at one and wait for it to move. Sometimes the room resembled nightclubs she remembered. She stayed through dawn, when her father arrived with the tiny chess and a paperback book of games to play through as lessons, which he'd play until lunch, when her mother and aunt arrived with takeout and stayed through the afternoon until Em returned from the motel at dusk.

In this way they followed one another while the body rose and fell according to science.

Look, a rubber monster thing for my finger, maybe she'll like it?

That's funny, Dad. She will.

She really likes presents.

And monsters—

Over the weeks, the flux of coma. Ad's consciousness moved in waves. Bizarrely shaped and otherworldly blisters on her knuckles silently deflated. Arrivals shifted, everyone coming a little later, a little later, a little earlier, moving in relation to each other around the clock around the body. Something about time—about a clock—about a clock that can feel. It was from a poem. The clock feels time, but can't know what time means. Ad's mind rose and fell. She'd move her lips. Her face would move. Em rolled closer in her rolling chair, whispered to Ad, her complicated face, rolled back. Once she was looking out the window of the blue room at a certain amount of darkness and some stars. When she looked back, a teenaged boy in jeans and a plaid shirt cut off at the biceps, black hair to his shoulders, was standing at the foot of the bed, watching Ad breathe among fluids and numbers. Em thought she might be having one of her mother's visions from childhood. She thought of Frank in her plaid chair. He was as if through a telescope. She remembered looking at the keyless lock on her suit-case by her side in the back of a taxi and thinking of the very small number of ways locking a suitcase could possibly help. If you have another person's vision it must be true. When the boy saw her look-ing at him, he said, "Sorry," and left. From under the slippery cover-let in the motel, she watched the prettiest, cleverest little stripper in the world sit nude on a stool on an empty stage at the foot of the bed answering every nuanced question posed by a voice from the theater. On the patio, the woman in spectacles asked the man with the new liver, "What do you mean 'crazy'?" while she smoked her cigarette slyly. Em almost bolted, but the sun in her eyes or the tippy chair—

He said, "I'm an expert on crazy. I mean *literally* crazy, like I would think, 'I just can't be here, I have to go to Berlin.'"

"That's not crazy, that's instinct," said the woman, smoking.

"No, I mean when Regina finished the marathon I went up to her with a cup of water and a power bar and said, 'I can't be with you,' and left after fifteen years together."

"Revelation," she said. "Choice."

"No, no, listen," the man said. Em thought, this is too much. I could go. But she didn't go. "I met a woman in a dining room at the resort, she was wearing a thing on her neck, a neck brace—" he looked around the patio, there were a dozen people out there and he spotted one "—neck brace, like that," he said, pointing. They both swiveled their heads to look at it and then swiveled back to each other, but Em didn't look where they looked. She kept her eyes on them. It had become, just that quickly, a responsibility. "Lady keeps pointing like this at her neck saying, 'What's this?' and I keep say-ing, 'Neck brace,' and she says, 'No, what's this?'—she's German, we're in Geneva. I kept saying 'neck brace!' when what she wanted to know was the name of my cologne. It turned out she's a shrink, so I start seeing her because I'm going crazy. One day I was wound very tight, I'd been at a dinner and felt foolish, I was always having my pride wounded, and she said, 'You need to throw that feeling up,' so I went into her bathroom and put my fingers down my throat—like this—and threw up. I was hearing commands. She was right, I felt much better. I started doing that, I'd have a feeling and if it got too much I'd just throw it up. I'd be walking down the street with people and have to excuse myself to some bushes." He made the gesture of wiping himself on his sleeve with a flourish that concluded with his head sweeping back on its agile neck and pausing there for effect. "And look at me now!" In the motel, when Em thought of the man with the liver making that gesture, she thought of a figure in a crowd watching a resurrection, and how she'd once walked down a hall in a museum dedicated to painting after painting of crowds watching one resurrection after another.

In the motel, on the computer in the lobby, Em looked up the hotel where Ad was found dead and recognized it. They'd driven past it to get to the crappy place where they stayed one night, sisters passing through in a rental that had replaced the car that died near Cincinnati, cross-country from Baltimore to LA. Ad had said, "Now that's *swank*." Why did Em remember that? But she did. She left the motel lobby and walked under stars along the corridor of rooms on one side, pool on the other. Dark wet heads of three people floated there, backlit from light coming up through the water, the pool's blueness cracked with curves of white where light bulged from the edges of ripples. A pink noodle floated with no one touching it. Guests. She stood holding the black iron bars of the fence that surrounded it. Her image of herself was a bucket of warm water on a hill in a storm.

The next day, as Em was moving in and out of Ambien sleep behind the drapery, she saw that the boy who'd been at the foot of the bed in the hospital was Tasio. Tasio was always coming up in conversations on the phone—mother, father, sister over landlines, pre-VOIP jerking you around, chopping everything up. Her image of him was solid, 3D. He was part of the way the house must have changed so much since she'd been there, Tasio was *this* with the house, Tasio said *that* while he was *this* with the house, I was *this* and then Tasio *that*, did you know Tasio *that*, that he *this* back when he—? At the

foot of her sister's bed, the feeling of the center of the blue room—
the distinct transition from architecture and ambience to the flesh
that was Adeline—extended to reach him. A phone rang from the
bedside table while she was dreaming. She thought, it'll be Benny
to say Ad's dead again, and picked it up, but it was the motel phone
with a dial tone, so she hung up because what had rung was her tiny
cell phone next to it, but when she picked it up there was her ex: "Oh
Em, I feel so bad, tell me everything, I'm going crazy here." For a second Em thought the ex was trying to say, "I love you! Come back!"
because as soon as she heard the voice, love and longing flooded her
despite everything, but the ex said Ad had shown up at her place
and stayed for a few days maybe a month ago. They got high a lot,
they talked a lot about no one getting it about magic, sadness, and
hell. *You've seen hell?* they said to each other, *I've seen hell, too!* In the
motel, Em said, "But she was missing. But I was looking for her. I
can't talk. I took drugs. I'm asleep." She thought for a second that
a gun was under the pillow, but it was just the shape of the phone
with her ear to it, and the pillow on the other side. The noodle in
the pool when she remembered it was synaptic, someone's hands not
quite touching it. In the blue room in the hospital Ad made word-
like sounds in sentence-like rhythms, slipped from dream to hallucination and back so quickly Em could only sense that something was
out there, like real math. She slipped from talking to Em, to talking
to someone she thought Em was, to talking to invisible people like
cars going by, something about Tolstoy. "Is someone near my feet?"
Ad asked. "Is that a real mouse?"

Do you hear what she said? It was so funny.

What did she say, Dad?

Her hands were in the distance—she said, "What is that, is it carrots?"

She couldn't take in that she had a catheter: everyone explained,
she understood, and then couldn't believe it again several times an
hour. "Don't you know it's a form of *torture* to make a person piss
herself?" The television stripper was sitting on the tall stool gleaming against the dark stage, just one set of toes on the ground, her

other heel on the footrest, her ass minutely tipped, and Em could tell it was only the base of her pelvis touching the seat of the stool, the vaginal opening balancing there. Some days after she wasn't dead anymore Adeline had to shit the charcoal they filled her with to soak up toxic material, she had to shit while in the bed because she couldn't be moved, and she had to shit while ambiguously conscious. Brenda the nurse and Em had to convince her to shit in the bed as they lifted her over the pan. Em stood at her sister's shoulder and put her arm around her back so she could place her arms under her sister's arms as a layer. Being crazy, Ad said, is like having the skin ripped off your consciousness. It's *that* naked, is what she said. Through her arms Em felt the unaccountable strength of her sister's arms gripping at the arms of her bed to lift herself, and another set of arms, Brenda's, under her back, and another set of arms—some other nurse for under her legs—also the further strength to make herself do this thing that whatever is left at the base of consciousness does not want to let you do. Woman shitting black in a wombish electric room, six arms tangled around an act of expulsion. Em kept looking to Brenda like, *should I be here?* And when Brenda looked at her to say yes, it was like a pact had been made in the room to keep something safe, something sacred.

At the bottom of the bed—the motel bed—least intimate object ever—when the stripper wasn't on, a narrow man with hair like a giant spider glowered magicishly and punched nails through his nose against a backdrop of the cosmos. Em could sense, behind the production, a clump of producer-like people asking her to find it arousing, to get sexy about a spooky man in a motel at some time of day with the blackout shades drawn between her room and a pool, feeling the outskirts of her body, just claustrophobic enough between the mattress and crappy coverlet, disgusting *bedspread*, to confuse the edge of panic with sex. This guy put pins in his eyelids, arrow after arrow into his face, his head under that spider of hair (and is there a difference when you watch a cheesy TV guy do that versus "In the Penal

Colony" versus who was that art guy who shot himself as art—like besides authorship, besides venue—of course it's different, because the feeling's different), and right next door on the dial, or what do you say—one click over, up, what was it called before computers, was it *clicking* with a dial? But next channel, brain-sucking aliens, and Em lay with her hand between the pillow and her face, fingers to her own hairline like arrows, thinking about her sister's brain, comorbid difficulties distinguishing between agitation, psychomotor acceleration, and goal directedness free-floating anxiety, epiphenomenon of mood symptoms iatrogenic from pharmacology and the long-term of particular lithium neurogenerative stabilization as addressing neuroprotective, neurotoxic, neuropathic structural brain changes in cognitive potential decline delays such as anticonvulsants, robust or minimized not as a class of psychotropic property effects confined to divalproex, carbamazepine, and lamotrigine, but cyclicity topiramate gabapentin as add-on treatment or monotherapy *off label* in a regimen as a possible benzodiazepine polarity change, impulsivity, chronobiologic disruption for consequent behavioral or interpersonal methodology. "I'll tell you about some prominent fuckin' families," someone said on the patio, right as Em registered that she'd been staring at the plaque on a bench nearby, *a gift from*. The girl saint's name—Dymphna (such an ugly word)—meant *poet*. "It's too much," someone said, or "You are too much." Being *too much* is symptomatic. The slip of paper glued to the back of the small painted picture from a souvenir shop in an airport in the desert on Ad's bedside table in the blue room concluded with the saint's love. The mad are in conversation with invisible interlocutors, raveling, unraveling. The saint's father had aspired to transform her into her mother, which would eradicate her, mythically, but he managed only to eradicate her in the mundane, disappointing, and medical way of violence. Did that father sink to his knees over the body as they cuffed him? Did he throw his bloody hands in the air and run into the mountains, never to be seen again? The villagers had babies, and those babies had babies, passing stories along until whatever descendants sainted her, authoring, making ends.

In the blue room Em watched emotions pass through her sister's face, below consciousness, still yet moving, what amount dream and what amount madness persisting. What intricate musculature in the face adjusts its shape so minutely in conformation with what's beneath.

Seventeen, six months in the US, Tasio held a slip of paper torn from the fringe of a flyer on the door of the 7-Eleven: cash job plus room. He had no phone and did not want to speak in English, did not like to sound slow. Days, he looked around for work. Nights, he hung out with his uncle and his uncle's friends. Where was Ad? Missing and no one knew it. In an apartment, everyone assumed, across the country with other tattooed artsy kids. Between episodes, with the retail job of a girl like her, in an occult bookshop on a trendy street, what did they know? Probably already she was keeping her own hours, lost in the stacks with her own agenda. This is when Tasio's uncle drove him out a secondary highway and onto a dirt road that split a bare field toward a stand of trees that became woods.

Something shiny blinked from a house that was partially visible behind a stand of trees. The boy might have been a little nearsighted. His uncle parked where the trees started, firs with clean trunks and tips that made a frill against the sky. Driveway stones pressed under a crust of dirt that blurred into lawn that blurred into woods. Tasio got out of the car and his uncle leaned the seat back and turned up the radio. A dirt path lined with monkey grass led to a red door visible behind pale scaffolding. Translucent plastic tarps moved in competing rhythms, though he felt no wind where he stood. The red door opened and out came a woman, parting the plastic with an elbow, her hands behind her head, something in her teeth. It glinted and then she stuck it in her hair. A clip. Just an ordinary hair clip you could pick up at the drugstore. The ends of her hair splayed at the crown of her head. Some gray streaks slid through it. When her hands were empty, Tasio held out the bit of paper with her information on it and she took it. Four sleek dark dogs arrived and bounded around her. A fifth arrived at high speed from the forest and sped past. He didn't notice when she started talking. Later, it was as if she arrived in his life talking and had just paused for that moment with the clip in her teeth to put her hair up. Her hand that wasn't holding the bit of paper started pinching dead leaves off a bush as she talked. She told a story he came to realize was about the life of a man from the phone company. "You might have noticed a yellow truck," she said, and nodded in the direction of the access road. She described the complexities of getting service and some recent electrical storms. *In any event*, she said. *Oddly enough.* Then she went over to the car where his uncle was smoking and asked him not to smoke. She said she used to smoke, everyone needs a vice, it was fine to smoke just don't ash out the window. Then she came back to Tasio and said, "Fires." A dog came by, pushed past the bush, and sat leaning against her leg. She pulled shedding hair at the back of the dog's neck. The door had not caught in its latch so she pushed it open with her hip. "Come in," she said. "I'll show you what I've been doing."

Tasio touched the large egg-shaped knob of the door as they stepped through plastic sheeting onto a concrete composite floor, recently sealed. They were surrounded by plastic, gray space, blurred distance. She talked about the history of cement as distinguished from concrete. "This," she said, pointing to a dog's footprint, sealed in, "has *substance*." The shape of a dog trotted in the pastel depths beyond the plastic, and plastic made it stretch, the nose leading, body rippling to catch up. She located a slit in the tarp and they stepped through. It was like stepping into a photograph of a flock of birds.

It was a kitchen. The woman pointed around, talking about a lot of animals who had lived here in the past, and a few people. As she spoke and Tasio's eyes adjusted to the clutter, he began to sense an order to the layers of stuff on every surface. A relative balance among the piles on the table. A cityscape of canisters and dishware on the counters. Pots and baskets hanging from the ceiling beam not unrelated to the lamp that hung over the table. A dirty computer on a desk in a corner with its keyboard balanced on a tray stacked with mail. A dog trotted by. Another arrived to lean against her leg again and slid the flat of his head under her hand. The woman kept talking, and he let go of the need to keep up. He learned that this was one of three rooms that had been part of the original structure, that the original house was a replica of the childhood home of the original owner, that the dishwasher no longer worked but stored dishes, that he would have a shelf in the refrigerator and a shelf in a cabinet. The woman shoved a couple of things on a shelf in the fridge into the door of the fridge, and took a couple of things out of a cabinet, couldn't find a place for them, and left them on the counter.

"There should be a window here," she said. "What kind of idiot builds a house on a river and you can't see the river? See these beams? Not structural. So stupid." The wallpaper—itself a replica of something Arts and Crafts, was inappropriate for the architecture, which was also inappropriate for the region (she explained)—was almost entirely obscured by the things tacked, taped, and nailed to it—painted plates with gold rims, a calendar covered with circles and arrows, framed photographs of the landscape he'd just ridden through, the art of children fading from brittle paper, greeting cards flapping open, a stack of receipts impaled near the telephone, numbers written in many colors of ink in the ivory spaces between dark leaves and curling petals, dense near the phone and thinning into the leaves and flowers around it. He tried to pick out information about the job. The table contained stacks of multicolored file folders with yellow and white paper jabbing out of them; a can opener; a bowl that appeared to be made of woven wood—he touched it and it was plastic—and held a calculator; a large black feather; a pad of thin sticky notes and a pad of fat sticky notes; a cookie tin containing dry speckled beans. Vases and empty plastic jars from bulk purchases lined the counters stuffed with wooden spoons and paintbrushes—in fact, all the surfaces he could see as they shifted from kitchen to living area were cluttered with vessels—things that were made to be vessels and things that were repurposed as vessels—blown glass, chipped pottery, lidless cardboard packaging for fancy tea with inky landscapes. Dusty dried flowers stuck out of some, along with old wooden folding yardsticks and metal protractors, chopsticks, a riding crop, perhaps hundreds of pens—fountain, ballpoint, rollerball—and pencils—mechanical, wax, lead, charcoal— and magic markers, if Tasio registered these objects. There were a lot of bookcases containing a lot of books, cheap taped-back-together ones and expensive showpiece ones, and vessels on the shelves in front of the books. In a corner, shoved between record albums, was a television, and in front of the television was a stuffed chair with its footrest leaping into space on metal hinges toward a coffee table also covered with stuff, including a gun on a stack of magazines, a stethoscope, a cereal bowl with a spoon still in it, and on the other side of the coffee table was a sofa with its back to them.

The woman pointed to a plank door beyond the sofa: "My room." She pointed to the ceiling: "Husband's study." She opened a door near the telephone that might once have led to another room or a garage and now hung over the foundation.

"Out," she said to the dogs, and they leaped, one after another, off the cliff. "Out, out, out," she said, and smacked the last on the haunch as he leaped. She closed the door behind them.

Then the woman led Tasio through another sheet of plastic into a region of plywood subfloor. She clicked on a couple of caged bulbs hooked to nails. Now she stood a step behind him taking in the space for herself. He felt her there. Pale studs echoed trees in the yard. Extension cords squiggled like skywriting. He thought he could hear the dogs in the distance, onto something. Here, the woman explained, summer heat would rise into the dome-y space beneath the high ceilings and out these clever vents, and here—she patted a stud—thick walls for warmth in the winter. Many innovative insulations, many not very toxic at all. A place for a tub held by stones from the field *for my back issues*, and then the history with her back and here in her pockets were some capsules she took for it, which he might want to start taking himself if he planned to continue with manual labor. Windows, expensive, anything decent, she said, but how can you have a river and never frame it? There was, in fact, something *immoral* about disregarding a river, she said. This one for example, leaning in this stack. Pretty enough, very expensive. She found it on discount. But improper seal. "We're in court for it," she said. Now, here are some things you might want to know about windows. Here are some things you might want to know about rivers in general, now some things about this river particularly. Here is some information about trees, and these trees beyond the river, and here are some things about building we could learn from ancient cultures, "including your people the brilliant Aztecs," and here are examples of innovations coming down the pipe. So many material options nowadays, such sophisticated chemistry to make things out of stuff that's not oil, so much promise, her body sharp against the multiple pastels and transparencies. The cheap clip in her hair began to slide. An aluminum ladder reached through a hole in plastic that glowed. For a moment, it was as if he had not seen the outside of the house at all. Like up that ladder, if the glow didn't come directly from the sky, the house could just keep going up endlessly.

She led him through another sheet of plastic into the living room and from this angle he could see that a man was asleep on the sofa with a trilby on his thigh. He would not have known the word for that straw fedora-looking thing—*trilby*. Who knows, maybe he would. It's hard to say what words he'd have picked up. Dogs had returned, streaming and bobbing beneath her hands. He didn't care about dogs, he didn't care about Aztecs, his people weren't *Aztecs*, but he thought the woman might be helpful to him. And he might like her.

"Benny, I'm glad you're awake," the woman said to the man on the sofa. "Benny is a master carpenter," she said to Tasio. "A real artist. He can make anything."

Benny said from the sofa, "I'm not awake." Then he said, "Ever hear of a passive house?"

The woman said, "You can heat it with a single bulb." She made a light bulb flash with her hand and a dog leaped at it. "Up," she said to Benny. "Up, up."

"She take you on the tour?" Benny asked.

"Tour?" said Tasio.

"If he's going to work here," said the woman, "he needs to know the whole elephant."

They were performing something for him, but he wasn't sure what.

On the coffee table, along with the cereal bowl, the magazines, and the gun, a game of full-sized chess rested in progress next to a beat-up paperback splayed out. Its cover showed a man playing chess, making a move across from you. Dogs jostled the table, the board jiggled in one direction, pieces jiggled in the other, nothing fell. On the way outside, Tasio tapped the dog's footprint in the concrete with the toe of his boot and as they walked the woman pointed at one, two, three heaps of debris: stuff pulled out of the house that might get repurposed; stuff she'd found cheap and had plans for; and compost with an opportunistic garden growing out of it. Beyond was the road parting the dirt field, woods either side, and the black country highway curving along the horizon. The other way, down a slope, a little winding river and more woods. She led him to a creosoted shed and opened the door. Across from the door, a window looked over the river. It had a shutter, but no glass. "When it floods you get lakefront," she said. "Benny taught himself marquetry on this floor. Instead of just fix it, make something beautiful. That's an artist. Do you know the word *autodidact*?" The pattern was a sun—a circle of white wood with multicolored pieces beaming from it and an intricate frame border of patterned waving triangles, some number of sizes not immediately countable, some number of colors of wood that switched beats around each corner. The walls of the shed were raw cedar tacked to pine two-by-fours, but the floor, the woman explained, was birch, oak, maple, mahogany.

Tasio hung his knapsack on a hook and looked out the window at the river disregarding its banks. "No, not from the woods," she said, because he was looking out the window. "Benny collected endpieces from other floor jobs. Rich people's floors. Where's your ride?" said the woman. His uncle was no longer in the driveway. "Do you want the job?" Two dogs came in and then left. He took the job. The job was living there and helping Benny build the house.

In the following weeks and months, Tasio learned, learned, learned many basic and technical things about construction and also about the people in the house including: that Benny played chess with the husband, but the husband did not come down from his room very much; that Benny had lived with the family on and off for a long time; that some units of measurement came from one king's body parts, and some units of measurement came from another king's body parts; that Benny was devoted to talk radio; that for some years chess games had been conducted through the mail while Benny was in prison; that the husband was *melancholic*, that the husband had been, for many years, a lowly professor of mathematics at a state school but was no longer; that the sounds of the house shifted with any gentle change in weather and he could feel the changes even under the racket of hammers and scrapers; that the house was meant to turn as they rebuilt it in order to align with the sun, which entailed—hypothetically—essentially raising a new house around the original at an angle and then extracting the original house from within it; that the woman bought materials in batches as money came in, that money came in by going to court for chunks of principal left in trust by her grandmother, the rags-to-riches fruit farmer from California ("migrants, like your people"); that the plastic sheeting was known as *wrap*; that the woman was *a pussycat*; that if she was really truly angry with a person, she would take something that belonged to that person, break it in front of them, and declare, "I've *had* it!"; that the birth of her second child had torn her open *down there* and when the doctor sewed her up, he sewed crooked, which she knew was on purpose, so that's what was going on when she said, "Things would be different if I'd sued that prick"; that for a time in her youth she had been on welfare; that in winter, she wore a white fur coat from the steamer trunk; that the steamer trunk came from the rags-to-riches grandmother and she wore the coat inside and outside, whether she was hauling stuff around for the house or appearing in court, and the coat had turned pink from the earth—"A man should take a woman out in that coat," Benny said, "and now it's ruined. *She* says she wears the coat because it's warm. I know why she fuckin' wears it." He said the thing with the light bulb only works if a house is simple. He said of the three heaps of debris: "I put stuff in, she takes stuff out. I take stuff out, she puts stuff in." He said, "Obsolescence overtaking vision."

Tasio said, "It's not possible to build this house?"

Benny said, "It's not possible to build this house," and that is how Tasio learned that Benny had loved the woman for longer than he'd been playing chess with her husband.

Evenings Tasio used the shower and drank beer at the kitchen table with the woman until dark and his uncle picked him up and drove him even farther into the countryside where they met up with his uncle's friends, usually at a bonfire. He touched the paw of the dog with his boot on the way out, and touched it again in the morning on the way in. If he went from the shed to the car and had not touched the dog's paw, he'd tell his uncle he forgot something in the house. When his uncle dropped him off—two, three in the morning—he could see a light on in the husband's study. Deep in the countryside, one of his uncle's friends was slow, or maybe not slow, but something was wrong with him. Other people enjoyed the guy, but Tasio had no patience for him. The guy told stories with his eyes and his hands, just noises coming out of his mouth. People stood around and listened, clapped him on the back. The guy made faces, raised his arms at the climax. People would just go with it: *Great story, man.* They're all lying to the guy, is what Tasio thought, pretending they think he's so great. Evenings at the kitchen table, drinking beer with the mother among vessels undergoing repair, she used toothpicks to spread glue and propped them to dry, she touched up chips with oil paint. She used a squirrel-hair brush: *It's called a squirrel-hair brush because historically it was squirrel hair.*

Deep in the countryside, at a bonfire with his uncle's friends, the slow guy started telling a story with his eyes and hands. Tasio stayed focused talking with the normal guy he'd been talking with, leaning on someone's car. But then the slow guy really started getting into it. He stood up from where he'd been sitting and continued his story before the flames. People let their conversations drop and turned to watch him. His hands were huge and glowing. Tasio did not want to pay attention. The guy was exaggerating his eyes and mouth. Tasio thought, I hate him. But he was losing the attention of the guy he'd been having a beer with, so in order not to be an asshole, he turned, too.

All these drunk men, Tasio thought. Look what they're latching on to, a mute. He thought it in Spanish, which every American should know by now, and I do not. But not even Spanish exactly. Gist of thought. "What's with that guy?" he said to his uncle in Spanish on the ride home. "Why's everyone listen to him like that?"

His uncle shrugged. "It's impressive."

"Guy thinks he's a poet," Tasio said. "He's a moron." His uncle laughed.

At night, Tasio usually pissed on a tree near the shed, but sometimes he'd come in to use the bathroom and see the woman's husband hunched in the refrigerator light pulling food onto a plate, or watching TV in the living room in the stuffed rocking chair next to the sofa, not rocking, next to the sofa where Benny slept under a heap of blankets, anything with a laugh track, insomniac. In the shed, Tasio slept in a brown down bag on a blue carpet remnant on the wooden sun. Over beer at the kitchen table he and the woman laughed together—they thought so many of the same things were funny. A dog dropping a bicycle chain at Tasio's feet, so funny. "What's so funny?" called Benny from the sofa a wall away. Over beer in the kitchen, she explained her beliefs and recommendations such as never to confuse the beautiful and the expensive; such as cities are good, the countryside is good, suburbs are evil, Florida dumb but California evil. A dog came through and hopped his paws up on the table. The best way to punish a dog, she explained, is to refuse to look at him. In a relationship you abide by your contract, she said. People act like they invented sex, she said, but a body, look, it's just a body, it goes dust to dust (reaches across table to touch his biceps, receipts slide off the surface and in all directions across the floor), we've all got bodies, and so what? (pulls a hair from the glue she's using on a child's broken clay pot). People flying all over the world, people jumping out of planes to prove something, then the money's gone, what do you have to show for it? (Tasio by this time, months in, catching almost everything, saying next to nothing, hearing words he thinks he could say if they could make it out of his head.) People have no imagination, the woman explained. (It didn't matter how well he knew her, she stayed for him always at a certain distance—even in his thoughts she wasn't *quite* her name.) People are lazy. People need a place, and not everywhere you go is a place. Just because it's there, doesn't mean it's a *place*. She used an awl to poke a hole in the mouth of a clogged tube of paint. Looked around the room. I love it here, she said. Doing something to the room with her eyes. I used to think that was pretty, for wallpaper. She explained the difference between good patterns and bad ones. Gist of speech.

Mornings she came out of the bedroom in a bulky flannel nightgown surrounded by dogs and fed them in silver bowls she slid across the floor, Benny on the sofa, husband somewhere above in the unfinished reaches of the house, no staircase so far, just up a ladder. Nights the husband hunched at the edge of the rocking chair studying the chessboard by the light of the television, holding his plate of food where during the day any dog might snatch it. Tasio came out of the bathroom one time and the husband had not moved since he'd gone in, the plate still in the middle of nowhere, a fork pointing out of it. He stood in a slit in the plastic sheeting. The husband felt him there. He said, "I love to beat that guy. Doesn't matter how many times I beat him, always feels great." Oh, Tasio thought. Benny loved the woman, the woman refused to notice, and even if she did not love the husband anymore, the husband took a warped comfort in the complexities of the rejection. Not in those words, but the dynamic—when the husband said this—rose and revealed its shape to him. He also thought so many things that had nothing to do with the family at all, like about just the other night, when he'd been trying to explain some things to his uncle that he was going through—not about this job but about his heart, and his life—and his uncle just kept watching the road and told him he was starting to sound like his father, and Tasio thought, I'm trying to tell you about my heart and you're threatening me with my father? and his uncle said (in Spanish), as if he could hear him thinking, "The problem is sometimes you don't make any sense."

"I'll tell you how the house came to me," the woman said one day. "I lost my family at a young age. I will not," she said, leaning close, "I *will not* lose another." She said, "A family needs a place to come home to."

She said that some cultures seemed to know this but not this culture, this culture was losing its mind. She said you could tell from the sprawl. She said when her girls were little they were like Snow White and Rose Red. Now Rose Red had a house, she said, and a house is an investment in the future he should keep in mind. Being boundaryless and uncontained is symptomatic. She said it must be terrible to have your family scattered across continents. She said, "Who do you have back there in your country?"

"My mother," said Tasio.

She asked if he was planning to return home, but he didn't know how to explain in English, so he said he didn't know. He asked himself if he wanted to tell the woman about himself. But then he thought, if she's meant to know, she'll feel it from me like a poem. She asked if he was planning to bring his mother here.

He said, "To the shed?"

She said, "Well, I was thinking the country."

He said, "I don't know."

The woman called the men from wherever in the house to the kitchen. The husband was with her, sitting at the table with a spot cleared off for a glass of water. She said they'd need a staircase, forget the drawings she'd given them, just make it hold people up. Run some extension cords to the room with the fireplace. Just drill a hole from the living room. Just get the room clean, get it working. Now, she said. Go. She said her daughter was coming home. This was after Em got her good job. Before Ad went missing and no one could find her. Supermarkets were ramping up self-checkout, and more and more forms were being filled out electronically, instead of giving information to a person whose job was to take it. Everyone struggling to come up with a secret language of passwords. Writing them on slips of paper, taping them to the sides of desk drawers thinking, *give me a break no one's remembering this shit.* According to major media outlets, either it was about to be all about India or it was about to be all about China. Domestically, people supposedly clustered on the left and on the right desiring compromise. But compromise was beside the point because no one felt represented. No one really felt depicted anywhere as soon as they stopped to think about it. The country continually bombed some countries transparently and some countries covertly. *Transparent* was about to enter the discourse of romance, as in, *I have been nothing but transparent with you.* People didn't even know who all was being bombed every day. There was a percentage of people whose identity was wrapped up in knowing who all was being bombed. Who *made it their business* to know—at least, to wonder. Even those people almost always forgot to wonder.

It took a full day for Benny and Tasio to build a sturdy riserless staircase to replace the ladder. Tasio had never been up there before. They ran extension cords. From one window in the enormous room you could see the woods and from the other window you could see the driveway splitting the field. The mother brought pieces of a bed and they put that together. The finials were pegs; it had been a bottom bunk. The mother and her husband left together in the car, which had never happened before. The dogs were really excited about the stairs, going up and down until Benny put them outside. They patched some seams in the drywall. Benny said, "There's really no way around drywall." They couldn't think of anything else to do.

"Okay, good night," said Benny.

"Okay, good night."

Around midnight Tasio heard a car coming up the drive. He stepped outside his shed and watched the mother and father walk a shape in a blanket into the house. He held his sleeping bag around his shoulders as if it were cold. He watched the light change in the house as people moved around in it. Voices came through like when you are a child alone in bed and all the grown-ups are in another room.

For some days, the father and mother went up and down the stairs with trays and the mother seemed to forget about the house so the men decided what to work on. Once, though, she came silently to where he and Benny were doing a yard thing. She turned off Benny's radio and took it away. Benny said, "That was uncalled for." She left and after a little while he said, "I know how to turn off a radio."

Eventually, the girl started coming downstairs with her mother, wearing her own flannel nightgown with snaps like an old person, eating in the kitchen. She eyed the things she must have grown up with. *Oh, you, there, saltshaker from forever. Oh, you, woven potholder, you photograph of me with my sister in a pharmacy frame, you pinchpot one of us made, you spice rack covered in grease from the stove, place mat with a hole from a cigarette before I was born.* This was sort of what the girl was thinking, sort of what Tasio thought she thought, and sort of what she later told him she'd been thinking. Dogs seemed to come through only one or two at a time, to flop on the floor and sleep flat nearby, or put a chin on the girl's knee for a moment and then leave. The girl didn't touch anything unnecessarily. She went back to the room and into the bed, forgetting to close the door behind her.

From Benny he learned that the girl had been manic "and I don't mean *busy*, I mean out there *psycho*, like that's how you end up shooting Jodie Foster," and was found catatonic in her apartment— "Catatonic, let's see, lying there like she's dead but it's just she can't move, but it's not paralyzed (mimes stiffness), it's the mind (pointing at his head, making explosion motions around his head with his hands), it's the mind slows down (train chugging mime), and then the mind stops, so the body stops, right?"

Tasio shrugged. "*Catatónico*," he said. The girl had telephoned a friend to say it was so hot in her apartment her potatoes had liquefied. She said, "I'm having trouble with sentences," and then nothing for weeks until they went and found her.

Tasio would walk by the room before he realized he was walking by it. He'd forget having found a reason to go up the stairs. He asked Benny what the original plans for the stairs had been. The answer was: a proportion of tread to riser that gave the illusion of floating. The mother had provided schematics for this. It could be accomplished with turns. "Are the stairs possible?" he asked Benny. Benny shook his head and shrugged. When he found himself at the top of the stairs at the door to the room with the girl in it, Tasio thought, what would it take to want something impossible so much that you could make it come into existence? The girl was pale, silent, angular. Her hair short, ragged, bleached. He thought if he touched the skin on her face it would leave a mark. There were some marks on it, healing. He couldn't tell how they got there. The circles under her eyes looked fake. The air in the house had changed. The frenetic aspects of the mother had fled. As the girl spent more time awake, the mother stationed her where she could see her while accomplishing some small task. Socks were mended near the girl, books balanced. The mother had never been kinder to a phone tree. Tasio invented reasons to pass near the girl. Looking for a tool. Getting a drink he left. Carefully phrasing a question for the mother in the interests of quality craftsmanship. Mother so set and earnest, father insomniac and then sleeping, carrying bowls around the house and staring into the changing face of his computer behind a closed door. The girl, a person so far away and in such darkness that it seemed impossible for her to remain visible to him.

He went into the kitchen and got a Gatorade from the fridge. She was at the table, looking at him so strangely that he just did the tiniest goofy jig, wagged his elbows for a second. Her face softened, lit like a tiny bug, and then went out again.

He said he was going to Wendy's and she said, "I could use a Frosty." He still didn't have a car, so when his uncle came he just had him drive to Wendy's and right back so it wouldn't melt.

He started peeking into her room where she lay in bed when the mother wasn't home. He couldn't tell what she was doing. A dog burst by.

A dog burst the door open and the girl looked at him standing, caught in the doorway. The dog pranced around the room with a corncob in his mouth like a cigar, then settled into a corner and ate it. Special moments accumulated that demonstrate the crossing of lines, the sparking of—

He came into her room in the evenings when people might think his uncle had picked him up. Adeline did not like the lights on after dark. She said he should imagine life before electricity, so much more of time lit by internal image, the bulk of reality what we now call imaginary. He said he thought the paw by the door had powers. She said, "My mother says you can go to Pompeii and see dog prints in the concrete. Not that she's ever been anywhere."

She said, "All of our words for fucking are stupid."

She said, "I don't want to talk about my mother." The house, Ad said, was a prison.

They said to each other "I know" or "okay" in a dozen ways, some of which included words, but also him kneeling beside her tiny bed, placing his head near her hip, moving his hands over her body, some crying, the stirring of memories. When she pulled him toward her by his belt, a dark dog curled in the corner looked up once and then tucked his head away again. Good dog. On television the camera backs away from the room because of censorship, wait, no, because of decorum, wait, no, children, wait, no. But here, what's in the room is not yours and not mine. It would be an invasion to go in there. In fact, it can't even occur if we go in there.

On the roof in the sunlight Tasio imagined that the mother had plans for elaborate contraptions to animate the house. The house on chicken feet is from where? He pictured force fields. He pictured mechanical spikes springing from walls, scales snapping over the structure below him like a superhero's armor, scales extending out over the fields and flattening the forest. One day he told the mother he was going to take Ad to listen to poetry.

"With your uncle?" she asked, and when he nodded she pulled her chin back and flattened her mouth in the way that means *you must be joking*. "Drinking, I gather. Out all night." Like, *you are such an idiot*.

"She's a person, not a baby."

"You think I'm overprotective. Well, screw you, I want my daughter safe. I am trying to save my family."

"Safe from *poetry*?"

She took him by the wrist and yanked him down the stairs into the kitchen, into a chair at the computer. He let her do it because she was so angry and he'd been fucking her kid. She was limping.

"Why are you limping?" he said.

"Hank ran into my knee."

"Who's Hank?"

Hank was a dog.

He said, "I don't have things for you to break."

She let go of his wrist when they reached the computer in the kitchen. The computer provided a perfectly reasonable explanation about how a puff of pot, a glass of wine, disrupted slumber can tip a certain kind of person into psychosis, which is not an insult, it's a condition. "That is what happens to Adeline. If you care about her, these are the stakes."

He said, "Okay."

The mother said, "I know what I'm doing. Don't forget it."

He didn't promise anything. He still felt that he should take her to the fire, but then he didn't take her.

In the dark with Adeline he did not try to understand, when he felt something, how he was able to feel it. He said something like, *He perdido el tiempo en mi mente. En mi cabeza, ha desaparecido el tiempo.*

She said, "What?"

He still did not understand why the mother's husband was such a ghost. He experienced sex with the girl as a pressing through dimensions, the girl moving toward him not merely with desire for him as a man or a person, but to prove something real in life. He said, "You confuse me with happiness." He gave himself in a way he could not take back. He thought those words or words like those—giving himself in a way he could not take back. No one from here—and by *here* I mean the consciousness of this place Tasio entered—no one from here gets to know—*here* as an aspect of nation, region, history, race—this place, space—no one from here gets into the room of him. No one here gets to know—crossing over from Chiapas when you're seventeen, your family ruined by poverty and illness, your uncle completely trashed, telling stories about your father before he disappeared. How great he was, what he used to do to your mother, why your mother is counting the days until you lose your mind, and that's what she means every time she asks how you're doing. No one from here gets into the room of this teenaged boy feeling it coming, madness his mother warned him of, and this twenty-something girl who's already in it, human contact like another country, another time in history on another planet. No one gets into the room of flora and fauna of the five zones, conquest through the nineteenth century, in Chiapas the people, the history, the food, culture, artifacts, the postperennial rain forest agriculture, whatever bananas near the Pacific you heard on the radio, read on the idiot internet. The four millionish, the mostly peasants and many Mayan. The pre-Columbian, continual occupation and ruins. In Chiapas the weather and industry, the people, the haircuts, the way the clothes are worn, the way they are ever-changing. Chiapas like and unlike its neighbors to the several directions. Humid and tropical Chiapas of the average rainfall of more than three thousand millimeters. Recent ranching and several parallel foggy sierras with resplendent quetzals and horned guans, with monumental remains of Palenque, Yaxchilan, Bonampak, Chinkultic, Tonina for one's stay near waterfalls of today's society. The ecological wonders and stunning colonial towns rocketed to fame by Zapatistas, the storming and occupying tumultuous years, the well-lit streets lined with intriguing international cafés, delicious sugary churros and safe places to stroll, the fair-trade coffee, indigenous and commercial flavors, the shopping galore for the modern shoe lovers, the paradise of cowboy boots the likes of which you have never. The lionizations and *ejidos*. Seizures of cities, jungle strongholds. The paramilitary. The escalation, reescalation, capital *O* Other campaigns and declarations. The population pressures of Chiapas. The quick deforestation, Ladino landowners, mestizo campesinos, migrants and fleeing Guatemalans. The US-made tear gas. The obstruction of movement. The living lives and the constant fear. The razed villages. The rising of the cases of torture and disappearance. The lawless exploitation. The fivefold increases. The small elite. The expropriation. The suffering chronic unemployment and below-average literacy rate of Chiapas, the infant mortality rate of Chiapas. The southernmost state. The expert opinions of UNHCR. If you are where you're from, if it takes one to know one, if they can see where you're coming from, if you can only imagine. You stand at the door. You stay there.

In the hospital, Em said, "Anastasio was here one night."
    Ad said, "That boy loved me."

Adeline started moving around the house on her own. She walked with the dogs in the woods thinking about the future, even a future that at first reached only to that afternoon, then next week, then wondering if she'd ever go out to eat again, and then, you know, if she'd ever have an apartment again or if she'd live in a tower in a house built for old people to sit by themselves in separate rooms in the woods forever. So when Tasio walked down the hall by her bedroom in case she wanted him, now she was not always there. Listening at the door. Pushing the door with a single finger in case its latch hadn't clicked. I'm only the wind. I was never here. Nights after sex he drank more and more, out of her room and off with his uncle and his uncle's friends and back into her room and out again, her pale unpainted walls, surrounded by empty rooms in progress, and the living room with Benny asleep on the sofa, and the bedroom with the mother asleep among animals, and the kitchen containing the multitudes, and the study with the father awake among wall-to-wall books with his head in the internet in a part of the house where Tasio still had never been.

Tasio bought a car from his uncle that he drove fast into the countryside. He tried to explain to Ad that increasingly he understood everything. He started feeling a claim over her based on sharing something. He came to her smelling like bonfires. When she did move out, into a little apartment a few towns away, he drove more and faster to see her and get back to the woods for his job, and to see his uncle and his uncle's friends. He did not go into the house at night anymore unless he had to shit. He tried to shit in the woods, but no. Then, within days of Ad disappearing—gone from the apartment and into the unreconstructible time of Rory the club kid, Rebekah the baker, Marianne's box of ashes, Sal's souvenirs, plus Valerie, an old boss, Betts divorcing (*amicably!*), Orlando of the scary voice, plus Em's ex and that Russian manipulator—Tasio took an ax to the marquetry floor of his shed. The mother heard the noise. She went to the shed and saw what he'd done, but he was no longer there. She found him in Ad's room still holding the ax, and said, "Okay, now you've got to go."

He said he wouldn't.

She said, "Anastasio, do you have a license to drive that car? I suppose that car is registered?" She looked like hell, thin, her wrist wrapped in a bandage with a splint, and where did that come from?

He said, "Ever hear 'building permit'?"

She said, "Ever hear 'green card'?" She said, "Tasio, my daughter is *missing.*" Giant blue eyes that could hack you to death. Mouth hissing "*missing.*" So he left. A few weeks later his uncle came by looking for him, and a few weeks after that he was in the state asylum on a seventy-two-hour hold but then he was out again because otherwise, what a mess, shipping him to a detention center in Texas and someone in there must have had a medical-political issue with that, or someone did not want to deal with that paperwork on minimum wage, went for some easier paperwork that got him released, because he still had that car somehow and went by the house again, dogs keeling over with glee to see him, he had something *very important* to tell the mother that he'd figured out. Sleepy Benny in his stupid trilby opened the door and wouldn't let him in. Tasio said, "What have you done with the women!" right out of the movies that guided him in his mania, assuming that's what it was at this point, grabbing the old guy by the front of his camp shirt, why do you wear something that makes you look like that? *De mal gusto tan tonto.* (I looked it up.) Little boats sailing all over it. "Hold on there, Tas." Benny eyed the gun on the coffee table. But then he pulled a small notebook from his back pocket and a pen (ballpoint) from his shirt pocket and wrote the name of the hospital in Kansas City, tore the page out, and handed it to Tasio.

This is when Em was in an airport, attempting to orient her body in space via memory.

"Just let me touch the paw," said Tasio. He pushed the toe of his boot toward the threshold. "I don't get what the problem is, let me touch it." He could not believe he hadn't taken Ad to see that moron acting poetry. He was sure that if he had taken her, he would not be so lost. But Benny just stood there and he couldn't hit him so he took the slip of paper and left.

If you don't have to stop to sleep or eat you can make it in a couple of days—even if you don't know to go *around* the Smokies—and hell, if you are Tasio you can make it even if your car breaks down because you're such a quick study you can fix it with a couple of bottle caps and a straight razor—you can picture that—I can—you know some things, have some capacities—I know some things—bottle caps and a straight razor—enough to get to this hospital in the middle of the country, definitely a circumlocutory institution, but if you are Tasio you're used to preposterous constructions. When Tasio saw the hospital silhouetted from the highway he thought maybe that's what the house looked like in her imagination—the daughter's, he thought—but maybe mother's? Maybe that's what he'd been erecting and performing other intimate acts upon and within for almost a year, ever since not long after he slipped into the US, which talk about preposterous constructions. State line after state line invisible, one after another picture of some bird. On the radio, a patter of copyrighted material was speaking his life, the breathing and dying, the sunset eyes, certain geographic restrictions that apply, sexy ladies killing the beat and the underground, the TVs and pagers, the sudden novel Cuban rapping, the west and the east, everyone gettin' hit, everyone's drunk and high, everyone's writing the book, writing the book, taking the medicine and a crib and a condo and picket fence where all is lost and found with childish things, with rings, with someone like you, how you know, how you speak, with shining stars, fancy clothes, and cars, no telling what I'm gonna do, gonna kiss me through the phone, through the runaway train you jump on, already gone, Jesus, everything, put you first, time to live, time to die another day, him and me, you and I, through the motions, the house and the home, the devil in your future, what you're worth in all-consuming passion across a border in the back of your mind through the nothingness of life in war for destiny, dents in the fender, fit the pieces together, a QuickBooks manual, real soup with real meat in it. Over a beer in the kitchen the mother had explained to Tasio that she would never have sex again. Why did people go on with it, so self-indulgent. They were surrounded by her meaningful things. He'd been afraid she thought he was after *her*—sexually—and then afraid she thought he was after her daughter.

But then he'd thought, maybe it's just we're friends.

Near Nashville, the slow guy from the fire crossed his mind and he thought, where does that guy stay, who takes care of him, how does a poet get around?

When Tasio stood at the foot of Ad's bed in the ICU, he was still vibrating from the road. Even to himself he felt like no more than a vibration, which science says we are, which mysticism says we are. He looked at Adeline and thought, in whatever words, am I invisible? Am I dead? Am I made of tiny insects that have eaten my body? So when the woman at the window turned—a halfhearted version of what Ad sometimes looked like when she was sleeping—and seemed to see him and he spoke to her, he didn't wait to see if she would speak back to him. He had seen Ad, he had seen that she was still there, at least her body was there, at least it seemed to be under that blue blanket near her head, which he could see with the beams from his eyes.

When they moved Ad out of ICU to a regular hospital room, Brenda the nurse said she'd never done this—moved someone out. She said, laughing, that she wasn't sure she'd hooked the new stuff up right because it was stuff for people who might get better, she was going to get someone to check her work. "Not my area of expertise!" she winked. It was easy to see her with a kid, a boyfriend, margaritas with the techs after work. Em and the nurse, both giddy, guided the chair and the IV out of the blue room and into the gleaming, astringent, incandescent hallway.

"It's bright out here, right?" Adeline said.

"Miracle," Brenda said.

Adeline said, "Me?"

"You're *sweet*," Brenda said.

Later, Em and her mother occupied the new room at the same time for several minutes. Em said, "The nurses are saying Ad's a miracle." Her aunt unpacked white bags of takeout and told a story about a friend of hers in Death Valley who had a kid with encephalitis. What a blessing he was, this kid. Em wanted to shove her through the window down onto the parking lot: *My sister is not a blessing! She's a human being!* According to experts, Ad wouldn't remember much of anything from this time, if she ever remembered things again. Clocks versus time, the body of a clock, a clock sinking to the bottom of a pool, a head filled with water. A body filled with charcoal, a patio, a blue room, a new room, wherever cable comes from, a hotel comes from, a hand-painted plaque of a saint where news of the world used to come from a radio among noisy white bags where a plaque of a saint used to be. Why would they call it a *liver*? What would it be for something to matter just because it existed *now*?

Her mother said, "Miracle," but Em couldn't tell how she meant it. She could not catch her mother's eyes. Gist of the woman, mother.

"They're the experts," the aunt said, and as Em followed the green path marked by footprints on the floor showing the way to the elevators, she didn't know what that remark of her aunt's meant, whether it was for or against medicine, if there was anything else it could be. She couldn't tell if there was irony in the remark, and she couldn't remember if her aunt was an ironic type. She didn't register any of this consciously. It was a blip in her mind, something like "huh?" that ended when she pushed a button with an arrow on it and it lit up, pointing down. "You should go home," her mother had said. "Get back to your job, your life." Did she mean that? What did she mean? Em stopped along the path to the motel and looked back at the hospital to see if she could spot a window that might be near her sister, but the number and angles of windows, doors, and wings made the building incomprehensible. She was so tired. There was the motel, the path, and she just got herself back to the patio and sat for a while among the smokers.

The new room was bright in the early mornings. Em looked at her sister's face, her sister's surface. Was her sister's nose, what do they call it, aquiline? Her skin, do they call it milky? Had that stripper at the foot of the bed said anything remarkable in her interview? Did the stripper expose herself? Later, when she remembered the stripper, Em heard no questions or answers, just a couple of voices and a person's body, each more expert than the other on the subject of *her*, and what she *was*.

"Back when you . . . back when you worked with . . . you must have felt that . . ."

"Well, you know . . . let me tell you . . . for the record . . ." Caterpillar to Alice, "Who are you?" and this time Alice knows.

Em remembered what it felt like to watch the stripper speak in the dark, this light at the foot of the bed explaining her life in porn so assuredly, an origin story, as if what has been will be. Then, the disembodied voice offstage finally silent, the girl making the joke about the microphone and the phallus so you don't have to, the girl or the act of watching protecting Em from something just enough to anchor her beneath the strange floating coverlet, some girl's knowing laugh ringing bells of her past as a person with a body who could speak and make words move from one end of an idea to another. What makes a hotel *swank*? *Swank* is coated believably in fantastic satisfaction for the length of your stay.

"Your father said Tasio was here," her mother said, remaining uninterested in looking at Em, or unable to look at her as they exchanged updates on the threshold of her sister's new, lit, regular room, when the blue room held flesh, symptoms, and magic. The difference between divine and magic might be *singular* versus *multiple* in origin. News was, if her father hadn't closed Ad's eyes she'd be blind because they'd have dried up. Doctors left them open because she was dead and her father closed them because she was dead. *I told her a joke and she smiled*, Em's father had said in such earnest during a threshold exchange back in the blue room. *A terrible joke!* he'd said, brimming with wonder. Now Ad was only possibly sort of indefinitely blind.

Adeline was alive because she was an organ donor. Her eyes had been perfect, like her mother's. Eyes, experts say, are windows to the brain. Why hadn't they wanted her eyes for donation? A learned statement could go here about how eyes take impressions of the world and extrapolate to form, from fragments, a continuous reality. A learned statement could contrast the reality of the relationship between organ donation facilities and practices (deeply flawed) with what Em only now realized she'd thought (all hands on deck!). What's a nice gesture? Would an expert wanting eyes for some innocent look at dead crazy suicide Adeline's eyes and reject them because of her brain? A donation is a gift. What did the experts think of Ad's perfect eyes? *Poor soul, no one deserves this.* Why has my mother stopped looking at me? Em wondered. Because my eyes are safe. I'm not empathetic enough. I don't have very good ideas.

She remembered saying to her mother on the phone when her sister was missing, "Doctors are useless," because Ad had said it.

"I wouldn't go that far," said their mother.

"But basically, right?" Em said, and they had a back-and-forth about what exact kind of useless or not useless—almost a fight even as your mother is doing everything to save her girls' lives—their lives!—a girl with an unfathomable illness that can kill her, and another girl, a citizen who deserves to go to work and come home.

Maybe that's unfair.

Outside, someone jumped into the motel pool and the sound made Em's organs contract. She felt the halls of hospitals and halls at work versus a lush blue room and a hotel, the swank one, her desk and Frank's desk that lay next to each other with a wall between them like a burned-out married couple, as if their lamps might, when their chins lifted, blind each other with single eyes. What people say, *soul sucking*, numbing and dumbing, a hulking desktop computer at bookends, past and future, television at the foot of the motel bed, banker's lamp across a crappy veneer to the foot of the bed, where something glows. She clicked the remote so the TV went off, humming in the aftermath of the latest gunfight. She didn't know anything about Chiapas except it was in Mexico and people fled it. She didn't know anything about madness except it makes a person both more and less. Something about remote, about scratching the plans for a fortress into your heart with a brooch. Something about Ivan Ilyich, eyes weary of gazing but unable to cease seeing what was before them, golden cords and tassels polished up with metal powder, rigid limbs sunk in soft coffin cushions, him and his pain thrust into a narrow, deep black sack, the final constructed things that surround the body, and finally all that was oppressing him dropping away at once from two sides, from ten sides, from all sides. That's Tolstoy. Producers of cable programming, experts in the effect of motel bedclothes on the alienated, watching from a great distance, beaming. Tasio was in Em's bed, that is, Em's dream, holding the brain of Yorick. Heads on platters turned like clockwork: bring me her head, breakfast in bed, off with her clothes, chop-chop. Dogs brought her heads like frisbees. Some of the dogs were Jack at the foot of her bed through the night. She held the head of a dog from childhood. She followed the dog's head through the woods, tracking the body of a vanished king.

^ Invasion ^

She heard that beyond the motel, away from the hospital, was a grocery. Following vague directions, she walked up the shoulder of an overpass not meant for pedestrians. Midday, bright, cars everywhere, the brand landscape of stores you recognize from every highway. A good distance ahead of her, a figure proceeded at an odd gait. A figure is mysterious and emblematic. Weather madman, madman-in-a-box, this one was a tall, skinny white man who affected a gangsta walk. Em's pace was more purposeful than his, and soon she could see that the man was not wearing any boxers. His pants were below his ass, held up by his gait. She could feel the narcotics coming off him—exiting the hospital just as he'd arrived—released on his own—would they call it—*recognizance*? She didn't know enough to know whether he was any good at this walk. He seemed bad at it. *Echolalia*, mimicry without meaning, is symptomatic. She thought she was at a safe distance, but then he abruptly turned one-eighty degrees, so that his body, unbroken in its pace—though he was not looking at her and she had no instinct about where his decision to turn had come from—was now coming toward her. Panic rose and she wanted to cross the road, but there was too much traffic and what if he yelled something like *where do you think you're going*? He wore a netted athletic shirt, and the way it fell did not wholly cover his groin, so she could see his lion's mane of pubic hair and the base of his penis, in fact, most of his penis—it might only have been the lip of the head of his bending penis that was keeping the jeans up—she did not understand enough about the physics to be certain.

But he passed wanting nothing from her. Among the gusts from cars she tried to discern a gust from him. She thought, maybe he's going back to the hospital. She almost relaxed into a satisfied feeling of gratitude, forgiveness, and best wishes. Then, somewhere behind her, he turned again and approached at his unrelenting pace—she swung her head around to check—he seemed faster!—and there he came. Now she kept her eyes forward. She heard the sound of his advance like a distant airplane or an approaching insect. He swerved to avoid her without remark. He kept going. She automatically graphed the sound, willing it forward, a line toward absolute zero. At the end of the overpass he turned sharply around the guardrail and scrambled down the embankment. She knew colonies of people often accumulated under overpasses. A group of crows burst up like a fountain from where he'd gone, made their crow noises, and dropped, together, back out of sight. She spotted the grocery anchoring a strip mall, knew it by the visible corner of its shopping cart icon. Went for it.

Inside, everything where you'd expect it to be, every brand a brand you recognize and still so hard to find anything. Walking along the mouths of aisles hoping the signs will help and they don't. She stood mesmerized in front of Dairy waiting for a kind of yogurt she liked to materialize. In the parking lot afterward, white plastic sacks pulled her down by both hands. If there were mountains in the distance she didn't notice them, and if there were no mountains near Kansas City she didn't notice that either. She couldn't remember if the grocery store had been crowded. The parking lot was pretty full. Bits of sun, bizarrely silent, exploded on mirrors and chrome. She walked one way and then the other trying to figure out which way she'd entered, but the curbs and sidewalks were impossible to understand from the perspective of a person in the parking lot. Someone designed this. Panic returned. The clouds billowed obviously, and then every car that went by contained a person who looked a shade like Adeline. Adeline at a sequence of angles. People with sacks from the stores headed to their cars, spreading across the lot, no one looking at her, everyone a version of Adeline. The image of herself was nothing but eyes with tiny afterthought ears. Em put the sacks down, extracted her phone, and called Frank's sister, Sheila, who'd been collecting her mail. "I have to come home," she said. "What did I tell work? Two weeks?" she asked. "What is it now? More, right?"

"Trauma doesn't punch a clock," Sheila said.

Em held on to the cell phone with the dim pressure of the sacks at the outer edges of her shoes. She wasn't sure she would recognize her body as her body if she met it on the street.

Once, in a casita in the high desert where she lived with the ex before they broke up, Em opened the door to a fat rattlesnake coiled on the welcome mat. Her first morning back from the hospital in her starter home, she heard cats screaming outside while she put coffee grounds into the overcomplicated coffeemaker, and in the moment that it took her to open the door to the stoop where she liked to eat breakfast, she expected to see a cat fighting a snake. But no, they were cats fighting in such a hellish mass she couldn't distinguish their colors. When she opened the door and appeared before them, the one who turned out to be gray must have looked at her and lost his advantage. Later, she could picture him staring up from the chaos. She'd seen this gray cat lurking, looking into windows around the neighborhood. The one who turned out to be orange got away, across the yard and over the fence as if someone jerked him by invisible strings into flight. Then the gray cat, huge and thwarted, leaped the fence, pushing off it with his hind legs at the apex, angling away in another direction. In the aftermath, fur and some cat crap dotted the stoop, beaten from the orange one. It was horrible, familiar. And the sounds, horrible. She picked the bits up with paper napkins. She took the napkins into the kitchen and put them in the trash. Then she took the trash out.

Back in the kitchen, she washed her hands and then washed the sink. She dried her hands on a dish towel and then put the dish towel in the laundry. Then she put a new bag into the garbage and got the towel back out of the laundry and threw it into the newly lined trash. She washed her hands again. She tried to decide if she should take the trash out again. She cried a little over the sink, letting her hands drip into it. She pictured another version of herself who had stayed with her sister instead of running back into a structure.

What therapists say, *present in your body*. What activists say, *body on the line*. The little house was so silent, now, and still, as if it had been moving with her and then stopped with her.

She wandered the house looking for her little radio. The cats had reminded her of weather radar in time lapse, a system that gathers, tangles, and disperses in rhythms, and looking for the radio reminded her of the weather madman, incorporated him making traffic snarl, the voice of that helicopter reporter, so enthralled and confused. Her house had four or five rooms total, depending on how you counted spaces, plus one bathroom, two staircases, a basement, a back door with a stoop and a front door with a path to the mailbox. She paused under the archway between the dining and living areas, settling her hands under the hem of her shirt, making a little hammock for them. Ad had been dead and now she was more or less alive, in a state of would-she-stay-that-way, what-was-her-form-of-life-now. Em looked out the window, an involuntary action that came from movies depicting thinking, and from architecture, which put the window there, a passage for her gaze. Within her house, she thought about her sister. Through the window and beyond the small tree in her front yard—a cute nonfruiting deciduous tree—was a red-and-white realtor's sign in her neighbors' yard, which had not been there before Ad's death. All over the country places were going up, so many foreclosures, so many short sales. Sleazeballs were buying them up, bundling under the radar, about to make a killing. The bubble had mostly occurred in news she slept through. Her area had national news with local segments, *BBC World* if you caught it in the afternoon. Syrians or Serbians populated it recently. A sign of the health of an area was having something local and something international. She forgot what she was looking for, with the sign there. An arrangement of colors occupied her vision. The items found with Ad in the swank hotel had been given, by officers, to her mother, at the hospital, in a paper bag. A paper bag might be the opposite of a swank hotel. The final effects were: current and failed prescriptions in foil blister sheets dotted with a few uneaten capsules; the clothes she'd been wearing; the crumpled suicide letter among several receipts; a pack of cigarettes with one cigarette left (turned upside down); and two half-drunk bottles of fancy flavored vodka, a bottle of vanilla and a bottle of orange (to die of creamsicle, Ad later said). The packaging of pills, the clothes of a girl. What could their mother do with that stuff? With the garbage, especially? What is garbage? Stuff that used to be stuff. The aunt, wearing a floppy hat with felted violets on the brim, had suggested a burial. Em said, "But we might need it." She meant, *for clues.* She meant, *for putting what happened in an order.* She meant, *if not for meaning, for peace.* Pills bursting through foil like micro-superheroes in their bright outfits, the weapons of choice, the clothes of a girl who made a decision.

Em's mother had taken the bag to a vinyl chair in the corner of the hospital room and sat holding it in her lap, her daughter, deadish, numbers moving up and down on the machines. Em thought of her mother in that position, so small and frozen, an image pieced together from what she knew—of the way her mother was in the hospital, of the way the effects existed in a bag police gave her, of the way her mother passed her on the threshold with the bag in her arms and took it with her and Em asked, "What's that bag?" The father's shift was coming up. He was on his way, following color-coded footprints

that led from wing to wing through the hospital. Em had brought
takeout to divide among them—
   What's in the bag?
   Dinner, want some?
   What's in the bag?
   Last effects.

Once, when they all lived together, the father was waiting in the
driveway for everyone to come out so they could go somewhere
like dinner. He saw a line of ants and followed it into the woods.
Everyone came out, he was gone, and they called for him. The dogs
were confused, locked in the house with their noses to the windows.
Emilie, Adeline, and their mother stepped into the forest snapping
sticks with their nice shoes. The mother called out. "Where are you?
We're going!" The girls felt bored and anxious about sticks getting
dirt on their stockings, going into public with parents who had
sticks on their clothes. Finally he called back, "All right, all right,
I'm coming!"
   The thing about ants is follow them and eventually you'll discover exactly what they're up to and where they're going, whereas
the thing about spiders besides time and craftsmanship is you wreck
their whole life in one swoop and they just start the fuck over no
matter how many times you do it.
   In the car the parents fought about who had been making everyone late first, then they fought about who said what in the argument,
then what was more difficult: his pain, or her dealing with his pain.
It was a methodical fight and they were only moderately committed to it. Even from the back seat, Em and Ad had agreed about its
weirdness. The difference between the blue room and the new room
at the hospital was that the new room was less contained. It was
light because it was a regular room where you open the shades for
daytime, but it was also light because a realm of what's possible had
been left behind with what was no longer going to have happened to
Adeline. Em came to the blue room for her turn and there was her

mother in a chair in the corner holding a beat-up paper bag. Later, in the light room, she saw the bag again, in a pile with takeout and a sweater. She thought, *my mother is going to carry those things home like relics and embed them in the house.* What does a house mean?

Em left off looking past her little tree to the neighbors' Ryan Realty sign and returned to her kitchen, where she dug through a drawer where she used to keep a little spiral notepad. In the time it took to find it, Em had thought of a lot of questions along with *what should we do with that bag of effects,* such as: what was that stuff they wrapped Ad in for that weekend she was dead that looked like bubble wrap; why weren't her organs distributed before she came back to life if everyone needs organs so bad; if there's so much brain imaging, where are her brain images; where are the supposed video games to make a brain regenerate; if she dies again what am I going to do, just believe it, because once death has revoked its promise, what are promises, and aren't promises just facts with a certain number of promises holding them together so what are facts; is she sleeping so much because she's tired, drugs, sadness, or brain holes; where did the phrase come from "boil them in their jackets," did Em read it, overhear it; why did she keep thinking of pills in *jackets*; doesn't it ring a bell, the house of a snail that hauls; isn't there a place other than deep in her mother's construction to put Adeline, like with beautiful flowing nurses, and maybe now would be a good time for a pamphlet, right? *So Your Loved One Is Comorbid . . .* so where's my pamphlet? Thank you for the effects, she thought. Almost but not quite lining up. A shadow crossed the little window in the kitchen door that led to the driveway. Maybe it rained while she was away. Sure it did. The tree was doing great.

One night while Em was in the middle of the country in the hospital with her sister, the neighbor across the street from her starter home had come out of his starter home. Insomniac in his striped bathrobe and leather slippers, deep in anxious thought, he walked the moon-and-lamp-lit lawn. His mind ranged and when it came back he was near the center of his plot. It's not that everything's connected, though everything is. The person across the street is another possible you. The lawn in the dark seemed like a lake to the neighbor, the street just a broad current. He felt like he was standing on a convenient rock that grazed the surface. Earth and water teetered. He was afraid because he had a good job and yet his subprime variable mortgage rate rose. He'd read somewhere that in China the consumption of pesticides had become the most common method of suicide. He imagined an American field of factory corn. He recalled his own lawn in daylight, bionic with treatment, recalled the way he liked to cover it with his push mower, the pattern he'd work out in the process, and the toothy iron kind of mower that his father still used, that clipped grass by plowing inches above land. He remembered reading about China and then looking up. There was the window of his breakfast nook, his lawn beyond it.

The neighbor had gone inside to wake his wife, which he had never done, in the night, in all their years together. He touched her shoulder, she rose, and they went to the computer. They examined their options. They read up on the bubble. They wanted to preempt foreclosure. If they had to hand over their house they wanted to hand it over to people, not banks, they decided. They would need a real estate agent. They understood that Ryan Realty was in the midst of a very public lawsuit—even Em might have caught a blip about it on the radio before she let the sound sink back down—but the company had represented them when they bought the house, and they'd felt fine about their experience. They'd liked their guy fine. None of this was *his* fault. Still, together in their nightclothes at the computer they felt obliged to read up on the scandal, in which Jane Doe and John Doe, as they were identified in their suits, had filed against top local executive David C. Ryan of Ryan Realty, whom they accused of outrageous conduct constituting an egregious breach of social norms.

"The Does," said the wife in the computer light. "Like they're related, but they're not." She'd taken the chair, and her husband stood behind her, his hand on her shoulder.

"Wasn't there a punk band?" said the husband. His slippers were still damp from the yard.

The suit, they would discover via your source for local news, *wove a sordid tale of broken vows and familial deception, sexual deviance and the American dream itself, our homes and, perhaps most disturbing: technology. Have we misplaced our trust?*

In the night, the neighbor put his nose close to his wife's hair and took in its familiarity as they read. Reading is so weird, the way you believe the marks mean things, the innumerable assessments your brain makes per second, all too fast to count as choices. Video recordings had emerged of John and Jane, separately but on multiple occasions, as teenagers but in different decades, nude or only partially dressed, engaged in *private behaviors* in David Ryan's homes. The suit was only the latest development in a scandal that *rocked the municipality* when allegations were lodged against Ryan, one of the area's *top businessmen* and a *fixture in local society circles*. "This despicable conduct constitutes malice and oppression, and merits an award of punitive damages," the suit read. The investigation of Mr. Ryan had been sparked by the divorce between Ryan and his then wife, Sugarie Coffer-Ryan, who turned over recordings and other evidence to authorities that she had taken from his computer. Ryan's criminal attorney stated that he had done nothing illegal, and subsequently filed suit against a large and powerful law firm. The suit accused the firm of malpractice for allowing an attorney who had once worked for Mr. Ryan to advise Mrs. Ryan on her divorce. The neighbors had fun making puns out of the name of the firm; then they made fun of Sugarie's name. Mr. Ryan said, "He knows me. It's unethical. They know my business. We go way back." The neighbors found themselves vocalizing fragments of what they were reading. They found themselves putting on voices to point out a range of ironies. The scandal was reported to have *taken a toll on the handsome and respected executive*, who announced that he was cutting his ties to the company his father founded *as a newly wedded man* some sixty years before.

Jane had been recorded in the bathroom and bedroom of the Ryan family's primary residence; John at the lake house. Allegedly, Mr. Ryan used hidden cameras to tape them. The lawsuit and law enforcement documents included allegations that the cameras in the Ryan homes were concealed inside clock radios and other household items. Jane, daughter of David Ryan's college roommate, had worked as an agent for the company after dropping out of school and becoming estranged from her parents. They'd never forgiven their old friend Mr. Ryan for bailing her out. However, they now stated, even if they had not already stopped speaking to the Ryans, they would now, because when their daughter was videotaped she was a minor. There was a photo of the parents on the courthouse steps talking with reporters. "Look at them," said the neighbor's wife, pointing with her mouse. "Puritans." She moved the cursor to a figure in the background who, rather than going about her business, appeared to be looking on. "I bet that's Jane Doe. Look at that haircut, she's a little rebel. I bet that's dyed. I bet they cut her off. I bet they're why she dropped out."

Em's house was humble, from the forties, but still a charmer. A shadow crossed the little window in the kitchen door again, could have been a breeze moving branches. The across-the-street neighbors' was more of a rancher with some modern updates and a decade-old second-floor addition. Em's had one bathroom with a pedestal sink and a chipped iron tub. Its original furnace still worked at eighty percent and looked like a B movie insect alien. When an appliance went off like an alarm, she'd sometimes yell facetiously, "You don't have to yell, the house is not that big!" The appliances were pretty new—the real estate agent had noted it as a perk—but it occurred to Em that they were designed for someone who would want to know what was going on in a *laundry suite*. While local news outlets were keeping people up to date on the ongoing saga (*Who do you trust with YOUR home?* with a camera eye for the *O*), Adeline had been missing, family following leads, Frank following Jack, train after train. On the phone, Em's mother had been reporting how Ad was rumored to be, where she seemed to be, where she was rumored recently to have been. "I am sometimes not sure what is happening until I tell it to you," Em's mother said. "I sometimes think I am the thread between you and your sister, then I think you are my thread to her." Em sometimes noticed that she did not think anything without, at some level, wondering what her mother would think of that thought. Then the mother said something about setting Benny on the stairs, and Em pictured Benny sitting on the stairs, and then she said something about the dogs, and Em thought, oh right, setting Benny *to work* on stairs. There were some things in the girls' history that if you looked at it one way, it was individual parenting choices with all the right intentions, and if you looked at it another way, it could qualify as abuse. *Qualify.* There had been times when a lot of Ad's and Em's friends would remember things from their childhoods and ask each other, Do you think that was rape? Do you think that was abuse? Ad would sometimes come out of a conversation with a friend of hers about the friends' terrible experiences and ask Em, Do you think when Mom does this or that, Dad should stop her? Em would say no, no, that's not how she means it, she's just trying to whatever. But sometimes Em would come out of a conversation with a friend of *hers* about the friends' terrible experience and say to Ad, *I don't know, maybe.* Meanwhile, Ad and Em's mother had been raised in a situation so abusive that no one with even a smidge of information would ever say, *would you really call that abuse, though?* There was no question and it was a fact about their mother that they all relied on. The way she had survived.

"After everything," their mother said in a story she returned to with some regularity, "I went to see my mother because she seemed close to death. She was not so close to death, as it turned out. But she must have thought so because she told me she was sorry. It was so unlike her to say it that I believed her. She said, *I am very sorry*, and I was sure she was thinking of everything I was thinking of. But then she didn't die and a few years later she called to say she took it back. Just like that: *You remember when I said I was sorry? Well, I'm not. I take it back. I'm not sorry and I never was.*" When Em was cleaning up after the cats, she thought of that story her mother told. It looped right into a memory of her ex saying, "I could do this forever," about some mesmerizing sex they were having. The connection was: now the ex was her ex, so, clearly, no, she could not do that forever. Or to be precise, perhaps she could have, but she didn't. In retrospect, what would you call it? *I could do this forever.* Not so much a promise as an exclusionary clause. As Em took the trash out to the curb—the very trash that held the remains of the catfight—she thought, here I go making a graph out of real life, that is just like me. It was tacky, no, it was shameful, disgusting, garbage, worse, it denied and belittled her mother's childhood, it was cruelly arrogant to make comparisons, like you have any idea what that must have been like, like you can ever imagine, even knowing a person like you know your mother, you can't know that, there are just some things that you can't know and if you think you can, well it's what you might call disrespect-ful, you might call it *hubris*, who do you think you are, seriously, get your mind out of—

She was going to go in to work at some point. It was unclear whether her absence had affected anyone, but up that hill could be a nice place to lay her brain.

Ms. Doe, twenty-four, learned of the recording when federal agents summoned her to the offices of the Hi-Tech Crimes Task Force, a cybercrime agency, to identify herself in a video. It must have been so strange, looking at herself coming out of the shower or something (the paper didn't say), thirteen years old blowing her hair dry or something, with all those Task Force guys—probably a Task Force lady, for appearances, standing nearby as if not watching like they do—identifying herself. Wondering, is that me sexy? Plaintiff two,

John, watching himself come in from the lake, taking a shit or something, thinking, I'll never be in that good of a shape again. It was John who'd been able to list for authorities some potential "household items." In the bathroom, a vase with a flower and knickknacks, including a perfect conch shell on the vanity. In the bedroom the clock radio and a stuffed bear that seemed, as he put it, "age inappropriate." These kinds of highish-end development houses always have spacious bathrooms with lots of storage and room for display. The beds are always piled with *decorator pillows*. Both plaintiffs were suing for invasion of privacy, infliction of emotional distress, and negligence. "Dave and Sugarie were kind of role models for me, you know?" John said on the courthouse steps. "He came into our homes—crap, I mean we came into his homes . . ." It was unclear from the articles whether Sugarie's son from a previous marriage had been living in any of the homes during any documented incidents. It was unclear whether this omission was significant or incidental. "Parents kick their kids out of the house all the time," an anonymous executive was quoted as saying in a way that could apply to any number of aspects of the story. He later retracted the statement. It was unclear what Sugarie's relationship with the tapes had been before the divorce. The way the news came at them—"them" being the neighbors—they definitely felt invited to speculate even when they weren't overtly instructed to do so—which they sometimes were. *What do YOU think?* And a comments section below.

But the important thing was that the neighbors were doing a beautiful job of deciding together when they were done with an article or a clip and then picking a new one. That is just a really delicate thing for a couple to do in a smooth way. It felt great, and it also felt great to not even mention it, like smooth sailing is just what we do. At some point they had switched places, the neighbor taking the chair and his wife sometimes in the position at his shoulder, sometimes sitting with him in the chair, half on his lap, but not with her whole weight. The narrative came together in a pattern of nesting and tunneling perspectives, probably with a manmade lake at the center.

There was a rhythm to the clicking and reading, and such a quiet banter between them, across the machine and the material, that the wife swiveled the chair around, straddled him, and they copulated by the light of the peephole computer.

It was still officially morning. Beyond the stoop where the cats had fought was whatever had made that shadow fall across the window of the kitchen door while Em leaned against the countertop near the drawer deciding what to record in the notepad. What did she want to remember? Things. Things to figure out. She had no idea what she was feeling. What she wanted to do was to keep track of the things she didn't understand, and what she was feeling hardly seemed to be the point, but she couldn't remember, so she opened the door, and when she saw what she saw, she remembered the sound of her doorbell—it went off in her head—but she couldn't remember if it had actually rung. There was the pale coat in a heap, and a man in it. It was Jack the madman lover, collapsed on her stoop. Peeking from the buttonhole of his lapel was a blue bachelor's button, one of the rare true blue flowers that occur in nature. She had some in the yard. It was a little early for them, weather or climate change. It wobbled in its buttonhole from a breeze Em couldn't feel or from a man shivering beneath his clothes. She focused on the flower because after so much anticipation and then having nearly forgotten, here he was in the flesh. Or she focused on the flower because what does it mean for a figure, an emblem, to pluck a flower from your own yard? Your *yard*? Jack struggled to stand, and Em found his elbow. She helped him rise. He seemed to go up and up, and she let her gaze rise with him. He wobbled at the top, his body shifting loosely but encased, the sun clanging around his head.

He seemed oldish, he was pretty beat-up, the coat was pretty dirty. He was gangly, with admirable bones, and here was his face, so close, quiet perfect monochrome variations of skin, color sliding into the gullies that curve around nostrils, the patterning of pores, kinds of textures of hairs, sparse and silk over here and then almost distant steely sprigs of gray and soft brown beard. But mostly, his mouth: his mouth was sewn shut, lips swollen around the string, which was a butcher's twine. No signs of infection, but blood caked where the needle had gone.

Em knew this image from horror movies but mostly from queerness, the famous image of the artist David Wojnarowicz with his face sewn just like that. She jerked her eyes from Jack's mouth to his eyes. She clapped her hand over her mouth and felt moisture arrive in her nostrils. Her fingers instantly felt like string and she flung them away. She swung her eyes up and down the street but the neighborhood looked empty and silent, everyone's glossy trees, barefaced houses many pastel shades. Her own eyes were dark brown and easily accidentally mean. The yard across the street was freshly mown except for ragged strands up the post of the sale sign. She wanted a neighbor to help her, but she also didn't want anyone to know. Jack gestured with his arms and hands *gimme a break*, and then he added grunts in triplicate: uh-uh-*uh*, uh-uh-*uh*. He meant: *let me in*, like she was the door. A few bubbles came trembling through the string at the corners of his mouth. His eyes were so freaked out she knew she was thinking of him as an animal, which did not honor his humanity, and did not honor animals. "Blame the disease," advised advocacy websites. She knew just what it would feel like to touch Jack. Like a piece of perfectly seared meat. To rid herself of that image, she imagined lifting a gun and shooting herself in the head with it. The sun behind Jack's head represented the *boom*. She backed into her kitchen, found the phone, called Frank, he picked up, and meanwhile Jack came into the house behind her and started moving around the perimeter of the interior, looking at her things. It was what her mother's dogs did when they came into a house, hunting dogs, bred to flush birds from the edges of fields. His eyes leaped ahead as he traveled her rooms. His movement had an innocence to it, even as it portended a whole range of violations. Again, she shot herself. There is nothing wrong with animals, sometimes they get rabies, sometimes they were born funny, sometimes the world fucked them up.

The phone felt wrong against her face.

"You're back?" said Frank.

"Frank, you need to come and get him!" she found herself shriek-ing. "He's not mine. He's *yours*! And now he's *in my house*!"

She remained next to the phone after he hung up, holding on to the lip of her countertop. The machine blinked nearby. Jack was not in the room. The driveway was filled with stones someone had chosen from a cardboard sample to primp it to sell to her. She had a thirty-year traditional fixed-rate mortgage, not some interest-only scam. She heard Jack in the house. Her brain held the image of his bachelor's button and its pupil made of seeds. If Em went out and made it to the end of the driveway she would be some percentage of the way to work. Another shadow moved across the threshold: the gray cat through some trees. Jack appeared in the archway between the dining and living rooms. He and Em had similar builds, but on different scales. There was no sign that he was in pain. A dull-ing or inability to be aware of pain is symptomatic. He was cast-ing his eyes about, looking for something. From her spot near the wall near the telephone Em could see past him to the little tree, and beyond it the window of her neighbor's curtained breakfast nook. She silently tried out a bunch of stupid things she might say to him and dismissed each (a) for being stupid and (b) mouth sewn shut. She remembered standing over her answering machine imagining a shape looking over her shoulder, listening through birds for her sis-ter. He was going through the rooms again and touching things. He touched the carved back of the chair in which she routinely drank her drinks. He touched the phone on the mantel that anchored the house to its inception. Then he came to her. He arrived in the arch-way and locked on to her with eyes it seemed she'd been freaking out about forever, and moved, incrementally, closer. It was impossible to tell if he was threatening her or calling her out for feeling threat-ened. She wanted to throw up. She could feel her organs getting ready to turn inside out. She felt him wanting her to break open. He came so close she felt the electric cushion between their bodies. Her nose was near his chest. The pale coat was open, exposing a long-underwear top, almost childlike, almost silly. His smell came into her like smoke. She was filled with it, invaded. Maybe the backstory melodrama scenario was that Jack the madman lover—*gasp!*—knew about the night in the ruins when Em slept on a puddle of tarp with Frank, and was *infuriated*. Maybe he knew by *instinct* that something had *happened between them*, had traced across the land the residue of that proximate contentment. Maybe Frank had been *using* her, feigning intimacy under the stars and then telling the story to Jack but in a way that *betrayed her* and *served his purposes*, that intoned something *sexual*, like she *wanted it* but he put her off. *But nothing happened!* Her vision filled with waffle weave. In the periphery, the blue bachelor's button. One of Adeline's favorite examples of what it's like to be in a psych ward: flowers sent to her rejected at the desk because "they eat them." Something about stars. Something about rare blue flowers like diamonds. If she'd been able to speak or move she'd have snatched the flower. *You stole that!* She kept her eyes on the flower to avoid looking at his mouth, and then he was in the kitchen rummaging through her cabinets. He found her stash of grocery bags—the brown paper cube stuffed with squares, the white plastic ball of white balls slowly unwadding. He put a paper bag over his head. It made the sound of thunder, opening. An effect. She didn't know what to shoot, so thank god she heard Frank's old station wagon pulling into the driveway. Jack snatched the bag off his head, stuffed it back in the cabinet, and winked at her. He scooted out the door and across the strip of grass to the driveway. Frank leaned over to the passenger side and let the car door flop open, a man in a crisis who knew what to do.

She sat on her stoop. Her hands went to her mouth. She had no access to what it meant to Frank to see Jack's face like that, if he already knew or not, but she was able to feel very stupid for imagining him betraying her in such stupid ways. She could see the back of Frank's head and a hunk of his shoulders, and Jack fooling with the preset buttons on the radio.

Frank turned and cranked his window down. He yelled, "A little help here?" He'd been trying to reach across Jack to pull the enormous door shut again. She ran over and pushed it so it slammed, and quickly stepped away. Frank flung his arm around the passenger seat, churned his body, spewed rocks as he backed up. The flat-assed station wagon bottomed out on the dip at the end of the driveway, and then went on down the street like a raft. A jangly song came through the window that she thought for a second was "Frankie and Johnny" but it wasn't. She stood outside the little house she owned in the sense that she paid money to an entity. It was now bland noon. In the song, Frankie puts on a red kimono and goes downtown with her gun. When she gets there, everyone knows who she is. What could bring a girl like her to this? was the sentiment of the song.

Sugarie Coffer-Ryan ("Sugary Coffin *Lyin'*!"—postcoitally floppy, the neighbor put his hand over his wife's mouth in play to pretend to stop her joking—she was having aftershocks of giddiness as they returned to reading—shhh, this is serious! this is our life!) continued to live in the couple's four-million-square-foot Ardent Oaks home (okay, *Arden* Oaks, but, you know—) listed for sale at two point nine gajillion. The morning after her husband had its contents removed, Sugarie waited for the rentals to arrive, blinking in a corner of the great room beneath a cathedral ceiling, planks made of real hardwood veneer streaming from her feet—just stood in that corner, blinking, is what one or both of them inferred. David Ryan remained unresponsive to questions as to whether he installed hidden surveillance equipment devices in his primary and vacation residences. "I do not want to impugn my wife," he said. In addition to cutting ties with his company, he resigned as a Boy Scout leader and rented a place out of town. Eventually, according to a different article, Ryan told an investigator that his equipment was for security purposes only and that he knew nothing about the sexual images or videos that might have been captured on it, and his attorney stated that, in addition to Ryan not knowing anything, the cameras were clearly visible. The attorney for the plaintiffs, however, responded stating that the use of hidden cameras in private areas and the fact that the images were kept for years made the security camera explanation implausible, a "bad joke. I mean, there was a camera *inside* a plastic flower in a square plexiglass vase filled with marbles. I mean, honestly. It was in a *clock* at the lake." To which Ryan's attorney quipped, "Who has a clock in the bathroom?" To which the attorney for the plaintiffs quipped, "Are you calling my client a liar?" Then they each said something about *intent*, but one attorney related it to the law, and the other attorney related it to individuals' motives, and the husband said, "Yeah, but didn't he mean that clock thing as a joke?"

"I wonder what else was on those tapes," the neighbor's wife said. She'd gotten down off the chair and lay flat on her back on the carpet, letting her husband read to her from the computer, her hands folded contentedly on her stomach. "Like what people really do in the bathroom. I don't mean the disgusting parts! But it's an incredible thing we all have in common," the wife said. "We go into those rooms and interact with that same set of, what do you call them, fixtures? Wait, is a toilet an appliance? But we go in there and just like sleeping, we are all *sort of* doing the same thing but the particulars must be very different."

This is why married people share beds and bathrooms, her husband said. "Here's my theory. Those rooms are the embodiment of intimacy, because you're including a person in your most vulnerable moments. To sleep and poop together is to protect one another from invaders." He tried to draw an amusing gross-out parallel between dreams and defecation, immaterial and material insides brought into the light.

Two images bloomed in his wife's imagination: opening a brightly papered birthday present, and untying a person's robe, opening it, and all of a person's body opening with it. "In case you're wondering, no you may not come in while I'm *doing my business*," she said, avoiding the word he'd used. Even as a child, she hadn't liked using words like that. She'd watched other children use them, giggling with elation, and only felt confused, anxious, deeply alone.

"Do you mean to say," said her husband, "that *that shit ain't funny*?" But he felt her tense up, so he got off the chair and knelt. "Hey. I will never impugn you," he said softly.

"You better not," she said softly, too.

Now they were tired. They got themselves back into the chair and pushed on with their research. They wanted to make an informed decision. They learned that while several (unnamed) others who may have been employees or officers of Ryan's companies had also been implicated in the suit, there had been no reports of cameras in the bathrooms of any of the company branches. The wife said, "You know, all I really want to know is did they put cameras in the houses they sold. That's what matters, right? No one's even asking, they're all like just dancing around it like one big prick tease." He could not disagree. All they could find out about the company itself was that it was routinely rated by employees as a "good" or "excellent" place to work, the workplace environment often characterized, in the free space, as "like a family."

In fact, the federal probe finally closed due to statutes of limitation, and the internet turned its attention to the remaining details of the divorce. In the hearings, Sugarie described her husband as a man who engaged prostitutes, used and grew marijuana, and secretly without her knowledge or approval videotaped minor children in sex acts in their home. Sugarie continued to live in the family's primary residence while it was on the market, represented by Ryan Realty out of spite. She described the home as "oppressive yet spacious" and "the only evidence remaining that we were once a real family with real feelings of closeness." The neighbors were waiting to have children until they felt financially secure. On the surface, they were unified about not being secure, but on the inside, they were unified in a way they didn't even know, both secretly hoping for an accident they'd have to live with. So cute.

David Ryan purchased another giant house in another development, sharing it with a girlfriend (actually totally reasonably aged) who said it was her dream home and who was spotted helping him lug the third of three SUV-loads of recording equipment into the three-car garage. "For the record, he's a technophile, not a pervert," she stated. The neighbors watched a YouTube video of the couple snow-boarding. David Ryan's attorney released the following statement: "David and Sugarie Ryan have been enduring a painful and emotional dissolution of their lengthy marriage. Personal and business financial details—including a prenuptial agreement with Sugarie, and various holdings in his vast portfolio—have been made public as part of these trying and ongoing divorce and custody proceedings. They have a minor child and an adult son. This is the personal, private, and confidential matter of David, Sug, and their children only."

"Come on," said the wife. "Are there cameras in the houses, are there cameras in *all* the houses!" She made a move to take over the keyboard.

"Hey," said the husband. "Sweetheart, my darling. Let's see if we can find a blooper reel for the Hi-Tech Crimes Task Force." That got her to smile.

I need to do laundry, Em told herself in the driveway in order to propel herself back into her house. In the basement she held the basket and stared at the furnace, so intricate, hulking, menacing, sculptural. Grease oozed from its joints. What is that mural where the men are the machines and the machines are the men? The furnace was created for a generation of working-class family homes erected midcentury by an infant construction industry. Such houses marked a shift from those built by families to last generations—houses made from materials such as stone—to stick-frame standards of builder-driven design. As an example of how much crappy real estate was out there, though, for *this* generation, a class action lawsuit over the use, in several new developments across town, of a siding product that *resisted* but did not *repel* rain, had recently settled. A percentage of families had replaced their siding, a percentage had covered their rotted panels with vinyl, and a percentage of families had just used the money for something else. The houses in Em's neighborhood (she routinely congratulated herself) were solid. They maintained a clean distinction between the body and its neighbors. An erosion of boundaries between thought and speech is symptomatic. Adeline had described energy entering her body and moving up her spine as a snake. In *1984*, Orwell explains that history is made of documents and human memory, and without history there is no truth. The way it was going in newspapers included rapidly shifting boundaries with regard to fact, opinion, rumor, fiction, infotainment, crowdsourcing, citizen journalism, punditry, snark, and troll farms. On TV, *Big Brother*, where you can watch boring people try to win by being in a house together, had been on for a decade. Email was free in exchange, via user agreements you clicked through without reading because they were purposefully too long and obscurely written for anyone to read, for monitoring web-browsing habits. Laws prevented the stripping of the mad in hospitals, but not in prisons, where most, when institutionalized, were housed for profit. The gun lobby concertedly suggested that, rather than restrict guns, we *do something* about the mentally ill. The more outrageous things people in power were saying and acting on, the more people flung their hands around and called them insane. But say you were one of those people calling people in power insane. Slow down so you can remember what you were feeling and you can tell it came from wanting power back. So now you're like *oh fuck*, that's what happened when they made being black symptomatic. It was an example of how people say *history forgot*. History, what happened? Nothing happened. The economy bubbled, banks were bailed. People in houses in neighborhoods across the region, perhaps the country—*perhaps the world!*—began to eye the objects in their homes with a vague suspicion they were unable to shrug away—they peered into button eyes of stuffed toys and into the blinking lights on their appliances and telephone machines. They looked at a clock and wondered if a clock looked back. A teenager put electrical tape over the camera on her new laptop. A grandfather dismantled his VCR and locked it in a trunk along with his rifle and his emergency kit. "I spy with my little eye . . . ," a girl said to her brother, "your baby-hole!" Some residents *took to the internet* for spy gear in *self-defense*. A lot of families who hadn't bothered with alarm systems installed them, that hotline system where you intercom the company if you're freaking out, and they intercom you when they think you're a robber. The image on the tin flag you're supposed to stick in your hedge as a warning, which people like to steal, is an eyeball. The rise in the purchase of these private surveillance systems also seemed to parallel an increasing if still nascent awareness of the splitting into two distinct groups, people keeping their homes and people being fucked out of their homes, and this anxiety, for those purchasing systems with their monthly payments, took the form of fantasies of being robbed by figures dressed in black catsuits, ski masks, or hoodies, and for those who did not have that kind of money or for whom having people listening in to their houses 24/7 did not feel like safety, the anxiety took the form of being robbed by fatcats and other honky gringos in leisurewear with yoga mats. And it was true, people were trotting the perimeter, eying your stuff, eying you, or you were trotting the perimeter in your hoodie catsuit, eying, knowing you for what you probably had, and in that way everyone turned into emblems and figures together.

Em compared her washer-dryer combo to her furnace. It seemed impossible that they could exist simultaneously.

In bed in the adobe casita, back in the high desert days before they broke up, Em's ex woke in the night and tried to tell her a dream. Em had not been sleeping. She had been thinking in the dark, almost forgetting where she was, about ways to make and fail to make a living. The ex, from her separate sleep continent, said, "There was this thing . . . it came up sort of out of this other thing . . . it reminded me of . . . you know when you . . . that feeling?"

Em didn't say anything in the dark. She felt derailed and interrupted. She put her hand on the ex's hip. She let the ex take the gesture as she'd take it, and didn't say anything until—it could have been weeks later—she thought she was safe to plant an idea as if it was unrelated. Now they were at the ex's kitchen table, a hewn block so heavy it would probably go down with the house. Em said, "Other people's dreams are always boring, don't you think?"

They proceeded to fight about dreams and drink their coffee angrily. Can a person's dream be inherently interesting. Can it be interesting if you really know each other. Can it be interesting if it's just random or silly. Can it be meaningful if it isn't interesting. Can it be interesting or meaningful if it doesn't make sense.

The ex said, "Dreams that don't make sense matter if you love someone." Then she downed a last swig to block her face and said, on her way to the sink, "I can't believe you'll sleep with me in my bed, you'll fuck in my bed, and you won't hear my dreams." Em felt caught. She refrained from saying, *maybe I think your dreams are stupid and I love you anyway*.

In the brainstem of her stick-frame home she remembered that when she'd been pinned to her own wall with Jack approaching, she'd recalled for an instant the moment in the catfight when the gray cat looked at her, which recalled the snake on the doormat of the casita in the desert. She remembered that her dream from before the cats fought was her mother at dawn at an estate sale, wandering among tables behind a peeling, emptied country farmhouse. She's in a dress with cherries on it and has her two little kids with her, hops them up onto a table full of candlesticks. Their dimply legs dangle. Her mother says, *now you two act valuable*, and the little kids become perfectly still. The summer she'd moved in with her ex she felt in love and ready to change everything, to abandon one image of the future for another and move out there for good, be a person she'd never guessed she might be, mounds of dirt spiked with cacti suddenly possibly not ugly. If she tried hard, she could sometimes see in those landscapes her ex felt so a part of that O'Keeffes came from them. But rattlesnakes kept appearing on the property. Em and the ex learned how to use special metal hooks to cantilever the snakes into plastic garbage cans and called the humane relocators to take them away. But every few days came another snake, sometimes two, pissy, rattling, and posing among the rocks. The relocators said the snakes would die if they took them more than a mile away, that they get lost and die outside their territory. They said the snakes lived in dens with thousands of other snakes, all related and piled on top of each other.

"Why do they keep coming?" Em's ex asked the relocators. She looked fantastic. Dusty and badass.

"Probably your place is on an ancient trail." Then the relocators asked if the girls wanted to meet up for a drink later and the ex patted one on the head. The relocators went away. Em and the ex sat at the hulking table, which her ex's dad had *hewn with his own hands* (as the ex liked to say), trying to figure it out. They still didn't know what to do about the snakes. What does a snake mean? What does one after another mean?

They had a gun but couldn't decide to use it. "They're animals," the ex said, and that didn't help. The gun, the animals, the decision, all of it scared them and soon enough they just broke up.

Another easy dream of Em's went: Em and her father are in a room with a bunch of rattlesnakes, which are her sister's madness. Her father is interested, but doesn't seem to get that this is a dangerous situation. "Dad, those are rattlesnakes," says Em. "They'll fucking kill you." Her father has a machete, which he would never have in life, and goes around the room blithely cutting their heads off, glancing back for her approval. The heads cut like cucumbers and pretty soon all the snakes are beheaded. Em and her dad stand dumbly among them. "Well," she says, "before, when I saw snakes, they were a lot faster."

Where was her sister—where was her sister *really*?

After a long night of clicking across newspapers through the internet, trying to let their house go, Em's neighbors walked through their rooms as the sun nudged rays through the windows. They pretended to assess objectively, but found the house more charming than ever, that nook, the sweet knots in the floor, the humble finials, so many practical and stylish choices they'd made and invested that surely anyone could appreciate. After so many months of arguments they assessed it holding hands. They held hands opening and closing their large appliances and held hands testing a couple of creaks in their stairs. It all seemed incredibly valuable.

The neighbor and his wife decided to use Ryan Realty. It's really not fair to assume, they agreed, or to hold something against people just because they work in a place run by creeps. We all do that. Everyone does, right? So who are we to judge, right? Ryan Realty dominates the local market and we are in one serious pickle. They got their listing the next day plus the red-and-white sign to prove it, so that when Em came home from the hospital in Kansas City it was there for her to see through the window in the morning after the cat-fight when she got distracted from looking for her radio.

Em's house encased her. A plank dining table hovered somewhere above her left ear, for instance, handed down to her by her mother but, before that, passed through untraceable families until whatever farmland auction where her mother bought it. When you buy the table you eradicate a specific family eating on it, dragging it around, the thousand-piece puzzles abandoned, the pushing of one another against it frontways and backways for sex, the stacking it with gifts for the occasion. It was a good buy. All that sense of history without messy actual history, the idea of people in the intricate grain, the fetishized patina of knife marks and cigarette burns, the softly worn corners and blackened depressions. In the shadow of the belly of the furnace of her house, Em squatted and, her finger moving over the crumbling concrete floor, drew a halfhearted yet desperate diagram of the situation, imagining it in the power-point lexicon of her job, where she would soon go. She drew a wobbly circle to represent the country, and a line down its middle, making it almost a brain. She took three pebbles and put them in the ocean while she tried to decide the rest of the map. The pebbles were her job (plunk, my spot on the land in the convulsing culture) and the house of her parents where she came from (plunk, at an equidistance from where the hospital in Kansas City would be), and then she held the third pebble, because it was meant to be her sister. She placed the pebble on the house and it fell off. The methodical gray cat trotted by the slim window at the gutter. She tapped the sister pebble up next to the house pebble. She found a little piece of glass and used it to scratch a divot next to the job pebble, in order to represent the basement. Now what would she be, the shard of glass? No, the shard of glass would be something else, dangerous and sparkling, like Jack.

Em's most common thought during meetings at work, by a margin of eighteen percent, was, don't look at me, I just do the graphs. Doctors had no prognosis for Adeline, not since she came back to life. "The brain is so mysterious," they said. What is that song *stretched out on a long white table, so clean, so cold, so bare.* What is that poem, *Eurydice filled with her vast death which was so new she could not understand that it had happened.* What if she was *made for* this? Em thought with horror in her basement, looking at her foolish map. Her father with his miniature medieval people doing their symbolic dance moves on the chess grid. Her mother contained in her property, in her house, with her things filled with things covering the surface of her things. Why are you going to childhood, looking at your origins, this helplessness, this un-American choiceless American meant-to-be-destiny-ness? According to one of the books Em had stopped reading, *for the mad who overlapped the visionary, thoughts became feelings and feelings thoughts—not necessarily in the epiphanal conception of the image or the symbol, but in a friction-filled rasping of planes of different types of experience grinding on a sort of no-person's-land where concept and feeling fight it out for priority, leaving a new space where sensation lives in its glowing self.* Among the questions she was afraid to ask her sister because what's care versus invasion: *Is dreaming what everything is like for you?*

Back seat of the car—argument you can't follow—but a tenor you understand is *off*—the girls understood as *off*—onto something— along the lines of—bodies aligned—she couldn't, but if she could—if Em could shake the right things off—she might see the stark out- lines of—sisters unencumbered—in alliance—pure form—the phone began to ring, and the gray cat settled in the gutter window and watched as Em methodically put dirty things from the basket into the washer and started it, then put the clothes that had been sitting in the dryer into the basket. Finally, upstairs, the message machine picked up. Em could hear Frank's voice but not what he was say- ing. She hiked the basket up the stairs and set it on the plank table. She pressed *message* on the machine. Messages had piled up while she was away and she didn't want to hear any of them. All these people who thought Ad was dead, or back from the dead, or who felt they had been fucked with, calling to express themselves, then maybe apologizing but you can't unscramble a cat in a bag, people from work or friends from other places or the far reaches of what re- mained of the family. She'd listen just enough to know a voice was not Frank's and then brutally hit *erase*. She bushwhacked messages to get to him, and when she arrived, the message said:

"Frank here. We made it fine to my place. He's on the computer. He's calm." Em thought, yeah, right. You with the magic touch. The voice halted and the machine sounds swelled, filling in. Then Frank said, "I guess you're not picking up," and after a few huffy breaths, "What's with you anyway? Why are you *here*? Why aren't you with your sister? Who's going to listen to her if not—" Her hand shot out and hit the machine like she was biting it back. Tape rewound or fast-forwarded but the voice stopped. The addict-madman hopped over the guardrail and his penis wagged. The can for coins bounced by the madman-in-a-box. The weather madman held out his hands, palms up, and in each spun a tiny tornado. Em looked from her soft living room chair to the machine and back. She thought she heard an echo, a spasm from the machine, a foreign body in the house like a cat upstairs, having curved in from the roof, dropping from a sill. What the hell happened to that little notepad? She scrambled around in the drawer but didn't find it. She had some more questions. Plus, why would a person like her ever listen to a person like Frank? He was not even management. He was ex-management. He *lost* power. He was not even the straight-white-old from a dollar bill, he was a cheater who didn't know why he fucked who he fucked. Why had she and the ex kept getting stuck at a measly level of *depth*? What is it about *exposed* people that makes viewers jack off in their secret spaces? Doesn't *somebody* have to go to work? Em scanned the surfaces of the room, noticing a series of places a bird could alight, then stopped herself by clapping her hand over her mouth, and then tore her hand from her mouth and stood there gaping.

Why wasn't she with her sister?

What had sent her running was seeing Ad, prismatically, in every face in the parking lot of the grocery in Kansas City. Not her sister, just meaning, everywhere.

She could picture herself in the blue room watching Ad move in and out of dream, memory, hallucination, safe from any need to understand. It was—it was some *kind* of intimate. Now Adeline was some kind of *back*, and Em could only see herself sitting there and sitting there, not understanding in perpetuity, proving to her sister moment after moment that she would always be alone. Now Em imagined Ad imagining her as symbolic of what it meant to have options. Also, being an option. *Why don't you stay with your sister this time around? It seems like a natural option.* She didn't like herself as an option. If she stayed away from imagining other people's imaginations perhaps she could stay safe from them. If my sister is not a blessing, maybe I am not a real option. No one would suggest that this was admirable.

Also, she had seen her parents moving through the hospital, interacting with the institution in resolutely parental ways. She knew that if her sister ever left the hospital, she would end up back in their house because for Ad there were three places in the world—missing or about to be; in a hospital; and in the house they came from—and

Em knew exactly what that house was. It was her parents' brains. You came out of their bodies into their brains.

She bathed, dressed, didn't register her neighbor and his wife standing in their yard regarding the Ryan Realty sign as if it had bloomed from a spore overnight, and walked up the hill to her job in a state of not being dead, wallet and keys in her pockets, phone in her fist, leftover ideas of suits and cases bouncing along behind her. She spotted the entrepreneurial custodian behind the bushes outside the building, but it turned out he was just removing graffiti with *The Solution* and a putty knife. She picked up a clipboard from her office and slipped a legal pad into it, clutched a ballpoint, arrived late to a meeting, took a chair on the outskirts of the conference table, which was loaded with colleagues, watched the agenda move, watched hands fly up and be counted, watched the debate over whatever issue degrade into a debate over procedure. She watched a male colleague with a pointy beard and then a female colleague with earrings like drawer pulls slap the table for emphasis, watched a different male rise from his seat and then sit, the edges of his jacket grazing the table, the female colleague's slaps creating a layer of vibration over the layer of vibration that the table always picked up from the AC, watched a woman with heavy glasses rise and lean in with a pointed finger. Something about the nature of contribution, something about corporate vision, something about nepotism.

"Guys, guys, what really matters at this juncture—"

"Juncture? Can't you see the writing on the wall?"

Stakes rose and fell in the rhythm of whack-a-moles, then just rose. Em perched on the edge of her chair with her pen poised, trying to pick out something she should record. The women's dyejobs were vivid. Ties swung from the necks of multiple men. Gray cats. Orange cats.

Then Mac, a guy who had been hired not long after Em but whose evaluations showed promise and drive, a guy who always used a black pencil to write and kept two or three sharpened next to his

pad at meetings, said something that made the room wobble to a
halt—whatever it was, Em had been listening to the wrong thing
(Janice saying in singsong, "*Hello-o*, some people would like to get
a word in *edge*wise . . ."). In the stillness, Em stood and reached behind her for the doorknob. No one noticed. They were watching
Mac the sack, lack, tack, back, knack, and then watching Pauline
the mean, teen, preen, scene, lean, who, from Em's perspective, was
nothing but a strawberry-blond cloud that floated across the room
and then stopped as if to dump rain on the box of croissants. By
the time Pauline snatched and then snapped one of Mac's pencils,
Em was out the door and had shoved it shut. Behind her, imaginary
puffs of dust from an all-out brawl pulsed under the door.

When Adeline was dead, a single clean and shining strand of thought
slipped out from the tangle of Em's mind, which was that her mother
might die of this grief, and her father, too, but she knew she would
not die, and she did not want to die, and although she continued,
like occasional punctuation, to imagine a gun sidling over and blowing her head off, she did not actually want this to happen, and experienced the image more as an emblem of death than a desire for death.
Moments with the gun were just unsophisticated efforts of her imagination to make something of the situation, maybe even a signal to
stop trying to imagine the impossible. When Ad was alive again, Em
had not thought, thank god, she's alive. She'd been angry and frightened. One thing that scared her was the proximity of newspaper-
saga-plug-pulling situations in the courts. One thing that infuriated
her was having believed so unconsciously in the finality of death and
the usefulness of knowledge, and, now that the problems with those
assumptions had been so vividly exposed, not having discovered any
alternative beliefs. She had settled into a state of prolonged uncertainty,
perhaps the opposite of the epiphanic.

   "A house is a machine for living," famously wrote Mr. Le Corbusier,
so excellent at his chosen profession. In that second, brighter, post-
ICU hospital room, Em's sister had blinked in a shaft of sun that kept

moving in a small way because something like leaves in wind was be-
yond the available view, which was of the corner of an adjacent wing.
Amidst light, motion, shadows, visions, something was registering.
Her face, in moments, in the shifting stream of sun, had looked, to
Em, in flashes, almost coherent.

"Adeline, I'm so glad you're not dead," Em had said. She'd already
decided to leave.

Adeline said, "Thanks, Em. I'm glad I'm not dead, too." It felt like
a promise, something forever.

That evening, Em had dinner with their mother. Someone had
brought takeout eggplant parmesan at Adeline's request and they
were eating the leftovers on the hospital patio. The patio was vacant.
Em said maybe Ad should come stay with her until they found a
place that would take her with all the comorbidities. But saying this
was only a gesture. She knew Ad wouldn't end up at her place. It
was her mother who'd done the hardest work for Ad over the years.
Her mother read the histories of mental illness, searched for therapists, wrestled psychopharmacologists, engaged the antimedication
advocates, bought *so much* fish oil, vitamin D lights, infusion pots,
tinctures from exotic locales, went to all those meetings and police
stations, court dates, joined all those internet groups, got her ass to
NAMI conferences, cooked according to chemistry-specific nutri-
tional guidelines, picked Ad up from wherever, toted Ad back to
the house, woke her up in the morning, woke her up again, negoti-
ated, got her to take meds, got her to play Scrabble, got her to watch a
movie, put her to bed, read her mood, kept reading her moods, looked
for signs, kept looking for signs, got her to take her meds, meds, meds,
visited please-kill-me-now halfway houses and posh zillion-dollar-a-
month facilities for the more-approachably-fucked-up-than-Ad. She
knew more than all the experts except the one she was currently cit-
ing. Their mother was a spectacular member of the club of women
who measure value against self-sacrifice and still Ad killed herself.

On the patio, Em and her mother each balanced half of the styrofoam container on their knees. Em had tried to tear the container

neatly at the hinge but that is impossible. Her mother got some paper towels from a bathroom because back in the room Adeline had used the single napkin from the packet of utensils. Em used the plastic fork because her mother insisted on taking the spoon. They went back and forth with the tiny white knife.

"I don't know if you know this, Em, but I was stillborn," her mother said. Em had not heard about this before. "I was born in Grandmother's house, her maid attending. Born dead. When my grandmother died, after all her social climbing, do you know who was there at her funeral? Me and the maid." She said that at her birth the grandmother had two tubs of water, one steaming hot, one icy cold, and dunked her from one to the other until she cried.

"What's your point here, Ma?"

"I don't think I'm being mysterious with my point. My point is I know what she's feeling."

Back in the lit room, at the end of a yellow path, the father was taking his turn bedside, probably trying to get Ad to laugh.

"I'm thinking about going home," Em said. "Home to my house."

"You should go," her mother said. "You need your own life." The remark seemed generous, and maybe it was, but there was also rejection in it. Em knew that one of the things her mother meant by no longer looking at her was, *you should have been with me saving your sister.*

Adeline had told Em, "I'm glad I'm not dead." But on a different day in a moment just as real, she said, "I know I said that, but things change."

Em's ex consulted a Lakota neighbor about the snakes. Something about transformation (duh), something about big medicine (okay), something about you ask the snake something. One way they stayed at a measly level of depth occurred to Em when she was back in her kitchen, some mechanical hum from the house at some pitch linked to the voice of her ex on the phone in the night in the motel near the hospital with the blue room. How did she put it when it turned out

Ad had been in the desert with her when she was missing, in some state of madness, getting high? The two of them had *really connected*, the ex said—about *magic, sadness, and hell*. The ex took meaning from a mishmash of some kind of Catholicism merged with some pre-Columbian native something that Em didn't have any reference points about other than TV depictions of voodoo, which she knew were racist not to mention from a whole other part of the world than where her ex's family was from, but she didn't have anything to replace the images with, working against so much passive mainstream living that the images just sat there being racist, not to mention about a totally different—if perhaps overlapping because of migrations in history that she didn't know?—belief system—plus the ex was increasingly into tarot, hypnosis, and astrology—and Em thought it was all equally *fine*, but fine like when you're thirteen up all night fortune-telling, like what was that story with the wife, the lover, the hut, the boatman, every generation of girls has stories like that, probably every culture! But soon enough you're piercing each other's ears with ice and nails, you're about to go septic, you're obsessively pricking into your wrists with pins the symbols of solemn oaths you made together in order to prove something, to sustain a rush of feeling and connection. The paranormal, Em thought, could have kept her and the ex at that measly level, their real feelings about it. Her sister experienced ghosts, spirits. It was unclear whether she only experienced them in madness, or if she experienced them in madness in a way that confirmed what she was unsure she truly experienced *not* in madness. More than once Ad had let Em know that she felt meds cut her off from the truth as much as from delusion. Ad expressed this in madness and in not-madness. Em wondered: Did she not believe in the things her ex believed in because they were stupid or because she was afraid, mistaking fear for certainty, for rationality, for sanity? She had pleaded with her sister, when her sister was in madness, "But so what? So what if there are ghosts?" Ad ignored that question, didn't have a retort. But when Em thought about it herself, she knew the answer. If there *was* something both true and supernatural, paranormal—she could only think of it as *magic*, an aspect of that encompassing concept—it meant that it was pretty stupid to try so hard to find beauty and meaning in going to work and coming home to your house of things because there were real options, even without babies. If there were real options, then everything she did every day was irrevocably stupid and based on lies. It was, in fact, pretty stupid regardless. Anytime she thought about it, she knew it was based on the lies of the powerful here on earth. She knew that without believing in anything other than what she already believed in. She could tell from the news every day, if she let it in.

Em left the cats fighting in the office, walked with purpose back to her adorable house, and, without going inside, got into her car. Her job did not feel harmless. Her bland success was a horror show. She parked a few houses up the street from where Frank lived on a dead end, walked along the curved shoulder, and, when she reached his property, slid into the hedges. She'd gathered pebbles from the driveway and now fingered them in the pockets of her skirt. She wanted the men to be in there with a jar of honey, doing something dirty or corrupt.

She wanted to *catch* them.

The men were in there. A man and the madman he loved. It was afternoon. It was a living room. They had tea out on the coffee table with cubes of sugar. Frank was in a big leather reading chair and Jack was on the sofa with a colorful afghan over his shoulders. Em couldn't see the state of Jack's face, but they must have cut the strings because she could hear the timbre of his voice through the wobbly glass, and see Frank listen and respond, just as audible and inaudible to her as Jack was, the two of them talking back and forth like a couple of human beings.

(Voyeur)

Somewhere between 9/11 and our first black president, Ad was on and off the streets in Los Angeles and their mother hired a private investigator to follow her and report on her level of safety. She'd been released from a hospital with a sack of pills that made her sick, plus voices in her head saying, "Those pills make you sick." She tossed them in the trash as she stepped through the glass doors into the city. Osama bin Laden would turn out to have been, at this time, building a compound for his family in a field in Pakistan. *Beasts are by their dens expressed, birds contrive an equal nest*—that's a poem. Two stories with four bedrooms on each floor, each with a bathroom and a third floor added without a permit, which had windows along only one side. Some of the windows were slits and the normal-sized ones were blacked out. It had a terrace with seven-foot walls because he was so tall. The private eye was so expensive. Their mother bought her first cell phone so he could reach her at any time. She held it like a walkie-talkie. She had the holster for it and everything. The PI, following Adeline, made reports and sent videos. Here she is on someone's porch with her makeup on like a clown. Here she is driving around and around the FBI building. Here she is disappearing into a crowd in the daytime. Here she is disappearing into a crowd at night. He lost her in another state. He found her in a different car. Ad left a message on Em's machine, "I know you're going to think I'm crazy but I swear to god some fuckhead is *following me*."

The reports from the PI evolved. "She's safe, Mrs. Preliminarily safe, in my estimation. I don't know about the element she's taken up with, which is of concern. Don't worry, I'm on it Mrs. I'm building a rapport with some peripheral figures. I'm laying the groundwork for moving in. Your daughter is a very special and remarkable person, Mrs. I want you to know that I don't come to this profession by accident. I come from a long line of people who have a need for truth and engaging their perceiving capabilities."

Em said to her mother, "Maybe if you watch someone long enough you just fall in love."

"What a stupid idea," said her mother. They were in Vegas. The private eye had tracked Adeline down there. They were at the Venetian. The goal was to find Ad and try to get her to go to another hospital, this time maybe New York, where the laws might help more. The mother had not been out of state in twentyish years. She did not like to leave her property except to replenish supplies, sent her husband for groceries and hardware when he'd go. She said, "I've never been to Venice, but the light seems well researched."

They were both a little high on the oxygen they pump in. They leaned on a railing on a bridge over the famous river. You couldn't tell whether you were seeing the bottom of the river or not, it was so expertly lit. This forced pause in deceitful air, steps from acres of stomach-churning overlapping casino sounds, each uglier than the next. The sound representing money clanging when chips representing money fell into state-of-the-art video slot machines in the shape of old-timey registers. Dayless, nightless, carpeted, mapless Vegas. The PI, her flight, the room had been heaped on a credit card. Em's mother had not won money from her principal since the batch she spent on a span of roof, and now this private investigator. At the fake river, her mother had a cast on her arm, always hurting herself in response to crisis. High school, Em came home drunk, her mother snapped a finger in a door. High school, Ad failed a class, her mother slipped on ice and cracked a rib. Car wreck on the way home from intake at a psych ward, ran a light, spun, just fenders. The flight was on a credit card, the motel near the airport was on a credit card. The cast was on a credit card, Benny was working for room and board, her father had taken early retirement ("it's not the work, it's the *politics*") and his pension bought groceries, utilities, he did some substitute teaching, nodding off at a stranger's desk, all those kids trained to expect nothing. Em flew herself in.

They didn't find Adeline in Las Vegas.

Their mother went home. She'd lost the cell phone but didn't notice for days. In the bathroom, three dogs managed to crowd around her feet as she undid her hair, which she'd been wearing lately in two braids like a child. In the bathroom with the wallpaper half peeled off, she changed into her nightclothes, a flannel gown with a sleeve torn up the seam for her cast. She rounded up the other dogs by walking through the rooms in the house patting her thighs. In the living room, she paused to look at Benny sleeping on the sofa and thought, *that one has no idea what it took for me to go to that fake place.* Not even her husband, overhead, had any idea what it had taken for her to leave her house and go to the land of casinos. So much waste. She'd returned to a message on the landline that her husband had not erased so she could listen for herself: *You want me drugged. You want me in prison. You're a demon.* Her daughter Em, leaning with her on the railing of the fake bridge, pointing out the light fixtures in the clouds, she also had no idea. It was the loneliest she remembered feeling since childhood because she relied on Em to understand her, and she knew, at this level, the level of mother, mother with *lost child*, that it was impossible for her to understand.

When the mother's father died, she and her sister had fought because she would not go to the funeral. The fight was about forgiveness. "Not this time," the mother said, and her sister said, "You don't forgive for *him*, you forgive for *you*," and the mother said, "I *refuse* for me." After the funeral, the aunt called to report. She said it had cleansed her. The aunt had studied to be an opera singer and ended up with a good job at Bell Atlantic before it merged with Verizon, which came with perks like the coupons for car rentals she'd sent for the trip to catch Ad. Their little brother was a genius dyslexic who couldn't learn to read and killed himself at fifteen. The mother said, "But what if I went and it didn't cleanse me, that doesn't make much of a story." Her sister said they served potato salad and ribs at the memorial because that's what he would have wanted, and the mother said she'd tell the story of standing over him, gnawing on bones.

Back on the bridge in Las Vegas, Em and her mother had been planning a trap. Em said, "Say she's still here. Say we find her. Say I go up to her because she thinks you're Nazis and the KKK. Then what? You're down the block in the rental with your hazards on? I mean someone has to be driving the car, I mean even without that arm how would we—she's your *kid* . . . Do you think the PI guy's being legal anymore? Like have him hop out and grab her and stuff her in the trunk?"

Her mother said, "He said something and I had to let him go."

"Oh," Em said. "What did he say?"

Her mother shook her head. "Something creepy. Something wrong. It crossed a line."

Em said, "What are we *doing*?"

She said, "Em, I can't give up on her," which is an incredibly reassuring thing for a person to say, though there's also a line between *giving up* and *letting go* they did not talk about because her mother assumed they agreed and Em was afraid they did not.

In the Venetian in the perpetual twilight, looking at clouds, Em and her mother had agreed about Las Vegas. "This place," her mother said. "Who wants to go outside, you can't go outside, it's so hot outside, it's death outside. Who wants to go inside, inside you're trapped inside, you go inside, it's the machines, you go away from the machines it's *this*. I knew I would hate it here. How can people—I'm not here for this anyway. I used to be curious. People always going to Vegas. Everyone's such an idiot."

Gondolas gliding through chlorine. Her mother's hair wet from the shower and in braids. Em did not want the true terrors of her mother's childhood to inhabit her—to have been raised by a mad-woman and an addict, to have run away from and toward who knows what untold atrocities. She liked to think of her rebel mother, who stood, with the dog by her side, between her mother and her younger siblings, *you'll get to them over our dead bodies*; who put a bra on the statue of the Virgin Mary in Catholic high school; who marched on the right side of history in the sixties; who pulled a knife on her own father when he went after his next wife, who liked to scandal-ize her in-laws by wearing a bikini without shaving; who looked so young when she had a baby that people thought she must have been abused and came over to admire the two of them, this innocent girl with her innocent baby named Em.

Behind a hedge in the upscale community of established homes where Frank lived, Em took her glasses off, rubbed them with the edge of her shirt, put them back on. She counted twice—using her fingers to be sure—and discovered it had been twenty-four hours since she left her sister. There are surely instances in the data of indifferent sis-ters, even enemy sisters, but a sister who comes through childhood with you is your witness, is what Em thought, in her way of turning vaguely to numbers for comfort. My sister is my witness.

Did you see that*, sister? Did that really* happen? *Am I making it up? Oh yes it did, your eyes did not deceive, sister.*

The distortion from the window glass was minimal. Jack had a garish crocheted afghan draped around his shoulders and leaned his elbows on his knees. In a matching leather chair, Frank leaned for-ward as well, but intermittently lifted a piece of a sandwich from a cutting board on the coffee table and took a bite. It had been cut into small squares, but it did not appear that Jack was eating any of it. The strings that had been pulled from his mouth lay in the saucer like signs of life in a petri dish. She could see that they were talking, but she couldn't hear anything. They had more tea. So gay. When her sister died Em had waited in a cab in that driveway (currently stage left) while Frank went inside for drugs. She peeled back the sheen of dumb shock that had characterized the moment, and could remember running her eyes along the row of garage windows methodically while she waited, and that an imaginary person seemed to have been staring back from inside—a person who must be tall in order to see out that window, and multiple to see out of multiple windows. An imaginary perspective, a thing stored in the garage, vibrating from it, or taking on the vibrations of an idling car, running its eyes along the series of windows. From his leather chair, Frank leaned farther forward until his seat lifted, and took Jack by the elbow. He had something fervent to say, and his new position revealed the window on the other side of the room, beyond the coffee table, where his head had been above the chair. There was a woman in the window, a woman also outside the house, like Em, looking directly across the room at her. It was not a reflection—wrong light, wrong woman. She wore a pearl necklace with a man's button-down shirt, and Em could never pull that off. The woman was potentially in Jack's line of sight, and within her own confusion, Em wondered if he, too, saw her, and if he was keeping it to himself, taking her for a ghost or a hallucination.

"*I know,*" said Em to Ad, or Ad to Em.

"*I know!*" said Ad to Em, or Em to Ad.

Em thought she could hear a branch snap from all the way on the other side of the house, but was that even possible? She ducked, her heart going bananas, and pressed her back against the chimney outcropping. She flattened herself and craned her neck—and the second she noticed her body responding in sync with a thousand airing cop shows, she crouched, humiliated, put her head to her knees, and squeezed her eyes shut. Several times Em alternated between being sure that she had been seen and being equally sure she had not been seen before it occurred to her that—*wait a minute*—as much as she might have been caught spying, she definitely, absolutely had *caught someone else* spying. Spying! She could just march around the house and—but when she opened her eyes and stood up, the flattop box-wood came to her chest, and the woman in pearls was already striding across the lawn toward her.

She had a pale face and a dark bob.

"Is that your husband?" the woman asked in a stage whisper, stopping across the hedge. They were about the same height, a couple of busts on pedestals. "The fat one? I mean the *big* one?" she said. "The skinny one's mine. In the granny blanket. I knew those boys were kinksters."

It was so strange, like looking herself in the eyes in the mirror, but without any mistaking of the eyes for her own. "Jack's wife?"

"I am, yes I am. And that's your asshole? Oh, don't look so pathetic. I'm not calling you names. Can you hear? Is Jack talking about being raped in some stables? Comes back every year or two. He runs around telling everyone. He says *listen to me, listen to me.* Well, let me offer you a corrective. Young Jack was not raped in any stables. He was very moved by the film *Equus,* with Jane Fonda, and *I* was once raped in a stable, though my rape was not a horse stable, it was goats and pigs. Less picturesque. And it was my prom date not my father, and I wasn't very emphatic in my protestations, just sort of dribbled forlornly in the straw. My mom's a comedic actor, and my family had a friendly acquaintance with some of the Fondas through her but that was it for a connection. Now, I'm not saying anyone likes a rape, but it's interesting to me that Jack is never upset by *horses.* He likes horses *especially,* of all animals, but he doesn't like stables. The bars, maybe. On the stalls." She made a gesture of bars in front of her face. "I can imagine it's the bars he doesn't like." Em had been vacillating between wanting to hear everything the woman had to say and feeling she should stop her in the name of violating a madman's privacy, but she got sidetracked with the business about bars, thinking immediately of the strings, then the row of windows across the garage. Isn't the secret wish of every diarist to be read, even in violation, and *understood*? Also, she had no sense of whether the woman knew what Jack had done to his face. The woman was in an elevated state, definitely, but Em wasn't scared. She was feeling a little charmed. Also a little protective. Of herself. For feeling charmed.

"To be clear," the woman said, confidentially, "I'm against all rape, I don't want to diminish rape, I don't want you to get the wrong idea here. I'll tell you what I know, though. What am I—I'd say about halfway between the two of you, you and Jack? Ah, I see, he's your father, am I right? Your asshole father. Not to be a homophobe. Well, Jack and I watched that film in the theater as puppies, a special screening, and I told Jack this story on the rainy return to my car, marquee receding. About me! *My* personal history. It was a moment of closeness between us. But he was not raped. Not Jack. I was raped. Me. My life. Mystery solved."

"I'm sorry," Em said, "that you were raped."

"What a relief," she said, and winked. "I'm Josie Bell. I am Mrs. Jack Bell. I am the man's wife. Having filed taxes with him—or for him—lo these many years." Mrs. Bell reached across the boxwood and wrapped her fingers around Em's shoulders on either side of her neck, peered at her with dark, precisely lined eyes encircled by the haircut, dyed too dark, possibly on purpose. It just seemed hard to believe that a woman like this would make a mistake with hair color.

"Poor thing is so far gone he can't keep his universes straight. He may be phoning me, talking about 'rape, rape' because somewhere deep inside he knows that I know what's not true and something inside him hopes that I can set him straight. Straight! I am full of it today. Well, you might not know how it all goes, with crazy people."

"He's just—in love," Em said.

"You don't hear from them and then you're back in their scribbly brains and they're after you, 'listen to me, listen to me, only you can understand!' and you're feeling so special and dreadful. Could be Jack hardly knows the difference between people anymore. That really happens—it's a known symptom at a certain depth. But what do I know, there are many rapes. Run the numbers and surely every-one is raped, on average." That's sort of my job, Em almost said, run-ning the numbers, but before she could, Mrs. Bell pulled her hand off Em's shoulder, flashed the ring on it, and then put it back. "See that? Married."

The ring was huge, beautiful, and shining from Em's shoulder. She turned her head to look at it. Bush branches pushed into her stomach. She'd never understood the fuss about diamond rings, always held herself above it, but now she thought maybe she'd just never been around a really good one, because this ring was plain old beautiful. She looked at it and thought, *it really is pure.*

Mrs. Bell said, "Damn right it's a fine rock, and I am long-suffer-ing." Then she pushed through the hedge, brushed leaves and twigs from her slacks—whatever they were, extremely nice pants—and patted the ground for Em to sit with her, which Em did. "We should talk," she said. But then she popped up again to look in the win-dow. "Great. I can almost see part of one of them." The men must have shifted positions, inside. "This ring—" she said, wiggling her fingers behind her for Em's benefit "—this ring has spent some days and nights suspended in hock. And did you notice what's on my fella's hand? Did you see? You could see, right?" She didn't seem wor-ried about being heard. From her spot near Mrs. Bell's legs, Em re-called what she'd been able to see through the window. She hadn't seen much of Jack's face and body, only the god's-eye afghan and most of the back of his head, scruffy like a child's in the morning. But she remembered him from her own house, not so long ago, and she could picture his hand from back then, with the stone on it, the round rock. Opening her cupboard and putting the hand with the stone into it. Traveling lightly across her mantel. "So, so ugly," said Mrs. Bell. "They take turns wearing it. You noticed, I'm sure. It's atrocious, you can't miss it. Jack picked it up on a beach in Howth and had it mounted. *Mounted*, oh my god kill me, please make me stop. So in case you were wondering about that ring, there's another mystery for you—solved."

"I'm not married," Em said. "I was just standing here not hearing anything."

"So you *are* his daughter, yes? No? His ex? He has a sister, right? You're his sister?"

"Sheila?" She just felt overwhelmed. Mrs. Bell turned from the window to look down at her. "I'm nothing, no relation," she said, working hard not to cry. "Frank told me a story once, with pebbles."

"I'm not Sheila, sweetie. I'm Josie."

Em said, desperately, "*Sheila's* Frank's sister. She leaves casseroles."

"I know the type," Josie said, and winked again. Jack had winked, but this was different.

"Frank's a guy from work. He took me home when my sister died and now she's come back to life." Em stood so that she could push her hand into her stretchy skirt pocket and hold in her fist some of the pebbles she'd put there. She must have known at some level that she'd made them into symbols, and she must have suspected on some level that they were meaningless outside the meaning she'd assigned them. But she still wanted to pull one out and—something—pass it along. To a woman with a rock like *that*?

"So wild," said Mrs. Bell, turning again to the window. "Well, at least we all know who we are, now."

Em joined her at the window. She felt more invisible with Josie beside her, and that calmed her. She let the pebbles fall to the dirt at their heels. They watched the men for a little while. Jack tore a piece of bread off a square of sandwich and slowly put it in his mouth.

Em said, "Is Jack usually talkative?"

Josie said, "It's hard to say what's usual. But sure. Sometimes *very* talkative."

"Do you think he's talking now? Or is Frank doing all the talking?" What she really wanted to know was if Jack had ever been in prison, because data suggests that women kill themselves in madness and men become aggressive toward others.

"Sure he's talking," Josie said. "Looks like it to me."

They watched this show with the sound off, sparrows rustling and chirping a few bushes away. Separately, the wind picked up and dissipated. Frank taking a sip. Jack taking a sip. Back when Em had friends, she had a Chinese friend who told her that in China when you go to the doctor—these were her words—*they give you a drink and that silences you.*

Josie yawned. "Let's get around the other side. We need a better angle. I can't hear anything. Look at you," she said, brushing a leaf off her shoulder and picking a stick off her knee sock. "Poor thing." Em followed Josie through the hedges. She did not like being called a poor thing. At the next window, they could see the men had taken a book from the shelves. Frank was holding it and they were looking at it together. One page appeared to be filled with text and the other with a bright illustration. The book lay open on its own but required both Frank's hands to support it. For a moment all four of them were still, silent, and looking at the book. In the stillness, emotion pushed up Em's throat and all her effort went toward not disturbing anything. You shake a snow globe not to shake it but to be with peaceful aftermath.

Josie exhaled a burst of angry, miserable air. "Let's just go in," she said.

"We can't go in!" said Em, and just then, Jack turned and crossed the room, enveloped in his garment, filling the window with those colors for a bright blurred second, making the women duck. "Ack!" Josie cried.

The men exited together into the kitchen, so that when the women peeped in again, the room was empty. In the kitchen, though, beyond their view, it could not have been prettier. Afternoon light through trees made shapes like enormous grape clusters blink along the surfaces of the wooden cabinetry, streaked floor, and marble countertops that were beautifully scarred from the decades.

Em followed Josie Bell around the side of the house. It turned out that two of the kitchen windows looked onto the screened area of the wraparound porch rather than directly into the yard, and a third, because of the grade of the foundation, was well over their heads. In the yard was a garden bench they thought they could drag over to stand on, but on closer inspection, its rotting legs were cemented into the ground.

"We could go up there," said Josie, suggesting the porch. "It's just screens."

"Maybe we weren't meant to see," Em said.

"Weren't *meant* to? You're kidding, right?" said Josie. "My shrink says if you did it you were meant to do it."

"I'm nervous they can hear us," Em said.

"So what if they do?" Josie said. They were having the conversation at the edge of a garden pond that held koi. There were happy hostas everywhere, and a cute shed with clapboard siding and a window with shutters. "Yeah, Frank's so *Zen*," Josie said, and kicked a stone into the water. The koi came in and out of visibility with their solids and patterns.

"Maybe there's a ladder," said Em, and they went into the shed. It was stupid to ask about being *meant to*. Every time her sister had been given a new diagnosis, she'd gone back through growing up together and could see teleologically how it explained things.

Inside, Em wasn't afraid of being heard anymore. There was a dirty little window and she looked out of it at the splotchy house. What was in the shed was tools, like different kinds of saws and hammers and screwdrivers on dusty pegs on dusty pegboards, hoes and gardening stuff, old roof tiles piled on the warpy plywood floor, things Em didn't know the names for, and things everyone knows the names for that go in a shed.

"No ladder," said Josie.

"My mother has a shed like this," Em said.

"Wowie zowie," said Josie. She dragged a fat coil of rope from under a folded tarpaulin. "We could scale the roof," she said.

"Mrs. Bell?" Em said. "Seriously. Why are you sneaking around?"

"Why are *you* sneaking?"

Em thought about it. Doctors and parents were busy doing their jobs adequately and inadequately. She said, "I just want to see them in their natural habitat."

"So you're an *anthropologist.*"

"Do you think—is it a *loving* thing to do—to make a person go to a hospital when they don't think there's anything wrong themselves?"

"It is if there's a magic pill."

"So you think, *no?*"

"I think it's one of many shots in the dark—not pitch dark, but pretty darned inky." Josie brushed off a paint can and sat on it with her arms falling around her thighs. The change in her affect was both abrupt and believable. She did not quite cry. "I once performed an experiment," she said. "I had put up with a great number of things over the years, trying to hold this marriage together, to protect the life we had set out to make. Thank god no kiddies. But one night I came downstairs and Jack had piled everything from the kitchen into the hall closet—dishes, food, chairs, pans, garbage, like a poltergeist, all tangled with the clothes that had been in there and balancing, when I opened the door, like those sewn-together yarn animals by that artist what's his name. I went to museums when I lived in a proper city.

"Once the closet was full, I discovered, he had opened the kitchen window and pushed everything else out, everything that fit through the window. Into the closet, then out of the window. Hole in, hole out." She made the gesture of penetration, sadly, sticking her index finger through a ring made with her other hand. She rolled her eyes. "Jack was talking about the pipes in the house. He'd cut his hair off and pushed it into the sink drain. We'd established a very civilized marriage, except for the insanity, the *illness*, so sorry. I really think—I mean it's different when a diagnosis yields a solution, but not for us, right? Not for our people. A diagnosis is very good to have when you want something to fling at police so they'll try *a little* harder not to beat the fuck out of someone. I'm sorry. I'm just *spilling.* I once knew what it's like to feel dignified."

Em said, "You are dignified." Then she said, "Mike Kelley."

"Hmmm, right," Josie said.

"I only know from my sister."

Josie swiped her finger through the dirt on the floor and drew an *X* on her forehead. "We fought, but we had careful fights, with no name-calling. In his manias I could feel him protecting that sanctity. He could be very cruel, but he did not direct that cruelty at me. I don't know why this one got to me, pushing everything into the closet and out the window. It's not *so* strange. Pushing against the home we made together. Signs of a culture he couldn't fit into. And Jack would say, what's so wrong with *strange*? People get all up in arms about *strange* to distract from *evil*."

"Is that what Jack says? About evil?"

"That's what we both say," said Josie. "It's the truth."

"I thought the problem was pain," said Em. After Tasio took an ax to the floor of his shed, Em's father had told her about it on the phone. Even before she saw him in the blue room in the hospital he'd become so real to her from conversations with her family that when her father related that piece of news, she pictured containers all through the house—all the vases, cannisters, bowls—even sinks and toilets—imploding. She knew the vessels contained her mother's feelings.

"No," said Josie. "The problem is evil. Everyone has pain." Saying this made Josie stare for a moment at her ring. She exhaled with a tiny shrug, and continued.

"'So what if I emptied the kitchen, is that against some law?' He said that to me later, when I tried to talk it out with him. As if there are no stupid laws. But I mean the bulbs from the ceiling light were broken off and swept away. The refrigerator was empty, on its side, shoved into the parlor. Its door had fallen open and ice had melted into the rug.

"I am more or less a housewife, except I don't cook, clean, or have babies. I come from a little money. I might be staying at the Days Inn now, but I know *exactly* what I'm missing. I had wanted a baby. I still do, probably, want to have a baby. But I don't know, what do I think, *babies* is what we need right now? A baby from *me*? I just do want one. Maybe not a whole person who could turn out to be anything, but a *baby*, you know? Oh, that's not fair. I should give myself a little credit, don't you think? A baby would warm me up to want the whole person.

"But Jack. It was not okay. I stood in the kitchen in these particular old slippers I hang on to, I wore them even on my wedding night. There's my Jack in the kitchen he's emptied, and I stood there in these slippers, and for my experiment I called my husband *crazy*. I'd never said that before. In all our years of turmoil, I had never called him crazy or any of those words. We did not name-call. It was a line we did not cross. I know, *rape* this, *rape* that and I just met you—I must not be very convincing—but that line we did not cross. Now I say it all the time. Crazy. See? What happened? Nothing happened. But I'm careful—because of what happened when I said it to him— which I *will* tell you—I mean sure I say 'crazy' to people who have no clue because fuck them, who has the time? But I don't say it to crazy people. And I also say it to people who know *crazy*. Like you. Because you know what I mean." She had gotten up off the paint can and was going over to things in the shed and brushing dust off them. "I can say certain things to a person like you. I can, right?"

Em nodded. Maybe Josie still thought she was Frank's daughter or something, or maybe she just knew the truth. She didn't care. She felt so many things she had not felt since she couldn't remember when—believable, trustworthy, knowledgeable, and outside herself. Josie had been living in an actual house with *crazy* versus Em with it over the phone, unfurling in the distance. Okay, there had been some face-to-face. That time. That other time. But the distinction didn't keep Em from feeling that she heard Josie loud, clear, like nothing was between them and nothing was disturbing the integrity of their distinct shapes.

It really gave her a sense of possibility.

"I keep testing it out in private," Josie said. "I'll be standing alone somewhere and say it to see what will happen. I'll be in a line for some bullshit and whisper it to see what will happen. Nothing happens. Jack was standing there with the butcher block full of knives under his arm. When he saw me watching he started throwing one after another out the window like darts. Not *at* me, right?—don't get too shocked. But he was doing it pointedly—*pointed*, dear god, make me *stop*—I just mean it was about me. Anything could have gone by that window, and collateral damage. I was the audience. Anyhow, so, 'You're crazy!' I said, pointing at him, and swear to god: he *disappeared*." She snapped her fingers and the ring somehow found light in the shed to flash. "I was in the kitchen, all by myself," Josie said. "No knives, no him. No noise. I was so alone. I wouldn't want to call it a nice or happy feeling. Believe me, I don't feel good about it, but it was some kind of nice, some kind of happy that I was feeling. My shrink assures me," Josie continued, "that feelings are feelings, not right or wrong. I wasn't doing anything. He just wasn't there."

Em stopped herself from deciding what kind of true this could be.

Josie said, "It was horrifying, doing nothing, feeling nothing that was wrong to feel. Jack is a pain in the ass. He *ruins* things—things I care about and things he cares about. He makes wonderful things and then he ruins just as many as he makes and it never evens out. When he got kicked out of school—I mean, that was a long time ago, I don't know exactly what transpired, violence and humiliation to go around. And a little niece he loves very much who he is never allowed to contact again. His family was never a day at the beach, but they are done with him, they are *through*.

"Anyhow, it was a relief for five minutes when he disappeared. Then wormy ideas kept crawling back in my head, ideas about the future, and there he was again. In the kitchen again. With me."

Josie stopped talking. She returned to her paint can and sat primly. She'd been wiggling her fingers to demonstrate worms and now they lay upside down in her lap.

"What ideas?" Em asked a woman in a shed in a garden near a house.

Josie shrugged.

"What about the knives?" Em asked. She'd been standing this whole time, resting one hand on the windowsill, fiddling with the chipping paint. The other hand had the ability to make contact with Josie, if she leaned or crouched. Probably her knee. Let's just say it had been a long time since she'd touched someone or been touched in a memorable way.

"Gosh, I don't know. On the floor, out the window. Nothing happened with the knives."

"And Frank? Such a betrayal."

"Small potatoes," Josie shrugged. "Insanity always trumps." She fingered her pearls. "You know, you're young. I bet you clean up just fine. You can do better."

She thought about reminding Josie about who she was and who she was not, but then she just thought about doing better and cleaning up. Josie said, "I've watched them in bed. I prepared myself by looking at Picasso's gravures that he did when he was a famous disgusting shriveled old man and then I just went for it and bought a bunch of DIY guy-on-guy porn. I can't trap him, you know? My shrink says I only control my own behavior. She keeps acting like a crazy person has volition. Is Frank crazy, too?"

"Why would you want to watch that?"

"I heard it really gets straight ladies off."

"But—context!" cried Em.

Josie leaped up from the paint can and it rolled away. "I want to know what I'm *dealing with* here!" She caught the paint can and sat back down on it. "Do you not find it *significant* that words like *glucose* and *serotonin* are in the popular vernacular? Not to mention they're trying to make us choose our own health care plans in the name of educated consumerism and guess what! There's no education! I'm starting to doubt there's any *health care* in there to find! There's just stuff! Words and stuff! Novels and novels of tiny print! Corporations are people! Lies that *no one* believes! *Pro forma* everything! I bought a step stool for the pantry and it was covered with stickers showing you in seven languages as well as pictograms exactly how a child could die climbing this device. Who is being kept safe here? I tell you for sure it is not little children! You know, I'm out of money. *I have no money left.* I am living in a goddamn Days Inn and I am likely to skip out on my bill. I am hoarding supermarket mini muffins from the continental breakfast. I mean it's great that nowadays I can sue my dentist if he rubs his dick on me when I'm sedated, I call that progress, but I appreciate my exhibits curated! My news edited! I believe in a powerful citizenry and the public good! Infrastructure! We are adrift!"

Em pushed herself away from the sill, found her own paint can, pulled it near Josie Bell, and sat on it. Now they were knee to knee. A lot of dust had gotten on Mrs. Bell's pretty clothes.

"Back there in the bushes, I couldn't see much, but I could hear a little," Mrs. Bell said. "Frank telling a story that featured a *sudden explosion of understanding.* He flashed his hands. Bullshit."

"Frank is a Romantic," Em said. Josie and Em were not touching, and they did not lock eyes, but Em said, "My mother doesn't know how to relate to me since my sister's death, like lines got cut." With her finger she drew three dots in the dust on the floor, and lines to connect each dot to each dot. Then she drew another dot like a satellite, on the outskirts, for her father. Her image of herself was a parrot with its mouth sewn shut, falling. She could almost believe that Josie had used a magic word and made an entire person disappear.

"I forgot your name," said Josie, kindly.

"Em," said Em. "My sister's eyes are damaged but they might come back," she said. "Her brain is damaged. It might come back. She's in the hospital. I guess she could be out, now, I don't know."

"Like the printer's measure. I know from Scrabble," Josie said. "Jack and I used to play."

"Yeah," said Em. "I am a broken-off useless bit. I'm space for something."

"Me, too," said Josie. They were surrounded by tools. Josie picked up a wrench that happened to be near her foot and turned it over in her hands. "Poor us," she said. "It's not our fault. You know, I used to be so annoyed when I'd say my name and people would say, 'Oh, I knew a Josie,' or some association, 'Where are your pussycats?'"

"So annoying. So random."

"And yet not. Someone gives you your name. Names come from somewhere, whether you know it or not. People like to make their lives make sense."

"I hate talking," said Em. "I always feel stupid after."

"I feel smarter for about five minutes and then I plummet," Josie said.

"Are you plummeting?" She was trying to think of a story to tell Josie about Adeline, even something next door to Adeline, like Frank's story in the ruins with Jack. The honey. *You know how when—* she tried to start herself off in her head—*You know how when—? You know—?*

"Let's look in the house like the cat on the pig on the goat— remember, for kids, with the musician robbers? I could climb up you. I'm tiny."

"We could knock on the door," said Em.

"No—he'll run, I'll lose him."

"Maybe, maybe not."

"You're not my shrink."

They were energized but they could not leave their shed. In a beloved story by Flannery O'Connor, a guy who is going to get shot is "squatting in the position of a runner about to sprint" yet unable to move.

Em said, "Tell me about the porn."

"You perv, get your own porn." Josie said it with real annoyance, then caught herself and winked.

"Did it help you?" There was a way that she was asking in order to keep them both in the shed, but she was also asking because of the conversation, because of how she was feeling in it, which was *mutual*. What a rare thing, what a gift, to want something for yourself that is also for another person. Look in the window of the shed and there they are, two women on paint cans, talking.

Em. Know what I'd probably do with Joan of Arc? I'd put her in a hospital. I'd put her in a prison.

Josie. You'd burn her at the stake?

Em. Well, I guess not that. But I wouldn't believe her. I'd want to, but I wouldn't. What about you?

Josie. This exercise is a little . . . I mean, context, right?

Em. Do you believe God spoke to Joan through visions of the archangel Michael?

Josie. What do I know? Maybe.

Em. But do you believe it?

Josie. No.

Em. Well, do you believe that the English should be driven from France?

Josie (*laughing*). I don't know.

Em. Would you join her army anyway?

Josie. You know, I think I would.

Em. You'd follow her not believing her and not even understanding the politics?

Josie. Yes, I think I would.

Em. You'd just follow her because of, like, charisma? Force of character? To be part of something? Even commit violence? What about the porn? Did it help you?

Josie. Wouldn't you?

Em. I'm kind of a prude.

Josie. I mean follow Joan.

Em. It would probably feel fantastic. (*Beat*, how people say.) Did it help you?

The video of men fucking that Josie Bell watched all the way through began with five of them—five white men with tribal tattoos—gleaming in a dark abstract space. Four of the men wore minimal leather appointments, mostly boots. Three sported conspicuous piercings. Two were bald-headed. One wore a cop's hat to indicate top BDSM. The night she watched it, Josie wore her slip and a hooded sweatshirt. She sat on the pillow leaning against the headboard, ready to learn. The sun had recently set. The four men marveled through the credits over the fifth, suspended vertically center screen, encased in saran wrap, lit reddish, bloodish, only his head and boots sticking out, a sweet strip of white socks between the boots and the clean edge of the plastic's sheen. For a while, no cocks were visible. Josie knew there were going to be a lot of cocks, and that she could recall the tube socks anytime she wanted to adjust her relationship to what she was seeing.

The four men lowered the fifth from an invisible grappling hook onto a platform and gathered around it in a not-quite-closed circle, visible from the waist up. The platform itself appeared to be made of an industrial machine run through a car crusher. The platform suggested, moment by moment, an altar, a sacrificial rock, an embalming table, a catafalque. The men's attitudes ranged from animal interest in suspiciously available meat, to reverence as for the mummy of a king, to scientific intrigue in a remarkable specimen. Josie did not register whether each man embodied a different emotional realm versus the various attitudes slid from one man to another.

This opening sequence also established hierarchy: if One, Two, Three, Four, and Five represented the men, then One would be the man in the cap, and Five would be the man in plastic wrap. Interactions among them revealed a coincidence of dominance and muscular bulk. One through Four moved across the encased body with their mouths, with Four lingering at the body's boots, sometimes with One guiding his head. Two and Three, in the background, came in and out of view. When they weren't making out, Two, who wore an empty cock harness across his chest, would move Three's head across the top part of Five's body and push his fingers in and out of Five's mouth. One moved around the table in a supervisory role, placing his hand on the back of each man in turn, and then began gently fooling with the pocketknife. As One moved his pocketknife along the plastic and then Five's tongue, cocks began to emerge across the tableau, within methodical camera movements that matched the pace of the pocketknife. Why not a medieval dagger or a scythe? Why not the kind that pops out with a surprising click? Why not a good old set of chef's knives in a butcher block? Well, Josie thought, the golden chalice was a banged-up cup according to *Indiana Jones*. Not all of the men seemed to be very hard, though they all had huge cocks. She wondered, am I bitter, am I bored, am I a cold fish? What's my psycho-sex drama? A breeze came through the window, absolutely pleasant. A gun, Josie thought. My psycho-sex drama has a gun in it, none of this flimflam.

The pocketknife scenario culminated with One slicing open the chrysalis along Five's cock, which turned out to be the biggest of all and pierced with six barbells crossing the shaft (it's called frenum) and also with one barbell vertical through the head (it's called apadravya). There followed a survey of penis-centered activities and types of camera angles: in close-up, Four sucking Five; a wider shot, artfully angled, revealed One holding Four's neck and Two in the background, jerking off with his back turned; a still wider shot revealed Five sucking One; a still wider shot and Three was doing something with One's ass but it was unclear what exactly—oh, just supporting it. Then they gathered around the body: One pushed his hand into Five's mouth, and then he pushed his cock into Five's mouth, with Two guiding, or maybe Three, meanwhile Three and Four (or else Two and Four) sucked Five's balls and cock, respectively. Then One came around the body and into the shot in his cop cap, slapping them. Then the camera backed up and he fucked Four's ass. Then Four had a solo with Five's boots. Then One sliced the rest of the plastic casing off Five. Later, Josie could not remember the music. It must have been ambient. She tried to think of it on the drive to Frank's house. Marvin Gaye was on the radio, singing "Sexual Healing," which she'd been too embarrassed to listen to when it came out except by herself in her bedroom tucked in with headphones and her hands on top of the covers, and even then it was a risk, emotionally. On her way to the hedge she listened to Marvin Gaye and wept.

Opening the second part, two of the guys are bound spread-eagle against a stone wall, side by side, one frontways and one back. One of the guys is Four from the first part, and the other one, facing the wall, Josie's not sure she's met yet, because she doesn't yet know how tightly contained the system is in this plot. Two other guys come in: One with the cap and Two with the suspenseful chest harness. Now she knows the other guy must be Three, who just hasn't stood out as an individual yet. One goes to Three, Two goes to Four. There's pushing around, being pushed around, backside smacking. The aggressors berate. They lob rhetorical questions (do you hear me, do you understand me). They each go after their own guy and then they team up and harass Three together, then they harass Four. It may be that Four gets switched out with Five at some point . . . it's hard for her to tell what's part of the intended continuity, and what might have just looked best when they filmed it so they put it in. Then the sound of a distant siren. Josie looked at her bedroom window and then back at the screen—couldn't tell where the siren was from— her world, their world, a soundtrack, a real siren outside the pornography studio, a neighbor letting the dog out with the sounds from their television—and then it went away.

Josie thought, maybe this is enough. I've seen their bodies at work, I've heard what they have to say. Frank and Jack had not used props and so on when she watched them. Which she had. She had not looked at Picasso, and then pornography, and then the men. She had been to Frank's house before. She had looked at Picasso, then she had followed Frank and Jack to Frank's house, and the porn was, rather than part of her preparation, a debriefing. She'd climbed up a ladder that someone had left after not finishing cleaning the gutters (Sheila's husband), she'd crab-walked around on the slippery roof of the porch until she could see into Frank's bedroom, and then she'd waited for them to get to it, and when they finally did, she lucked out and they made it to the bedroom. Now this. She'd simplified the order for Em because it worked better in the conversation and one of the things that gave Josie the capacity to be a good friend was her ability to be in the moment with someone. Frank and Jack had been loving, with all its clumsiness, real and anxious laughter, and other unpretty, unmanly noises. She'd seen them like that and it didn't help.

She checked the DVD case and there were going to be three parts plus the intro and an "epilogue" and she was only partway through Part II. The spread-eagle guys were alone again, men on a wall, waiting for the other guys to come back. The camera observed their fingers touching with tenderness and solidarity. Josie thought, okay, great, now you have feelings, too. She thought, it's just people. I will muscle through. I am going to watch the fuck out of this video.

Naturally, things escalate. Five—now it's definitely Five, out of his chrysalis and into the dungeon—endures some punishments filmed from a new vantage behind a black chain link grid to reinforce the geometry theme. Four sweats and cries, and then One compliments and kisses him. One and Two approach Five, but Five is defiant. It's hard to make out the dialogue, but they seem to have a conversation about Five's incredibly pierced cock, and after an angry exchange, Five is left alone. The camera offers a lingering close-up of the cock, which bows and sways a little. Nothing significant has happened to it yet.

That was the end of Part II. Josie felt sad and frustrated. She was not sure what she was supposed to be feeling about the lone cock. The men in the video all understood. Was the cock lonely? Was the moment suspenseful? Shouldn't a grown human American be able to watch a movie about people fucking and follow the action? Bad filmmaking or cultural difference, she could not decide. She'd recently received a bill from a hospital that was so overwhelming she just took every envelope that arrived with a plastic window after it and put it in a drawer in the little desk area in the kitchen. She'd paid the plumber when she'd needed a plumber. There he was with his tools and his fat hand. She paid the housekeeper. She'd paid *a lot* of hospitals, lawyers, and psychiatric professionals along the way. When she started letting the bills go, though, she let the abstract ones go first. She missed Jack, and missed him and missed him from the time when he was a man with a bunch of attributes that challenged and delighted her instead of a man who was definitely, in retrospect, beginning to go crazy. She paused the video on the elaborate penis, close-up and dejected, went downstairs for a bowl of ice cream, and brought it back up. She broke the seal on the last Tuesday bedding and arranged herself again against her headboard, set the laptop on a pillow near her knee. Maybe she was warming up to them, these fucking men. Maybe she wanted to know what would happen to their cocks next.

Part III opened with an aerial view of the void, no walls, no visible platforms, no nothing around. One in the central, reclined position, still wearing his cap. Two sucking his cock, camera shifting to reveal Three and Four first looking on, then pairing up similarly, then Three dividing time among different men, sometimes bridging two of them by using a hand on one and his mouth on another, really he was doing whatever he could that was within reach. One's hat, through it all, remained remarkably stable, and was featured at a wide range of angles, giving him more personality than the others just by tilting one way and then another. Now One gets a wave of happiness—there's been no orgasming at all, she realizes—he just sits up, puts his arms around Two and Four, kisses Four on the mouth for a second, with great gusto. Then he's grinning, beaming in the void—true joy, Josie thought—and pulls the men into a close circle. Three kisses him. Four sucks his nipple. Two returns to sucking his cock. There is no music, just sex sounds, and an energetic levity that hasn't been present before. This is when Five arrives, and One, still reclined, reaches across the shoulders of the bent men to put his fingers in Five's mouth to draw him close. He looks into his eyes with meaning.

When the camera returns to One's genitals, Four is no longer sucking, he's standing, and the other men support One's legs as Four penetrates One from above. Everyone's looking inward. One is where the table used to be, the set piece that looked like a crushed industrial machine, and everyone is working together, so that if a machine can be proud of itself, this is it. The camera swoops in, and along with the sex sounds are methodical, encouraging words from the group. "All right!" "Go! Go!" "You got it!" Aerial view, again, starkly composed: two cocks, one in the act of penetration, one cock free with a hand on it, and the back of two shaved heads.

Then something amazing happens.

Josie recognizes the free cock by its piercings. She knows it's Five even before the camera backs up to let us see that it is no longer One who is being fucked. It's Five. She narrows her eyes at the screen and sets her ice cream down on the nightstand.

Four comes.

One appears, licks the come off the ass, then fucks it.

She knows that something is happening with the social order, something is *changing because of the social order*, and that something is making a lot of people happy. There is a relationship between Jack and the world as she knows it being abstracted in this cinematic moment, and it's the reason, besides plot, that she continues watching—to make herself look at what she couldn't understand and was afraid of, the goal being not so much to understand it but to look, which is what a person ought to do, generally, with the world around him her them and it.

This sequence is presented at several angles. When other cocks are in the shot they are being masturbated. When the camera backs up one of the other medium guys is doing the fucking, and others are spanking him encouragingly. Someone's put on chaps at some point, and no one has a chest harness anymore. When Five, who has been fucked and fucked and fucked, is finally flipped over so you can see his face, Josie can't really tell what he's feeling but she's pretty sure, during the awkward fade that follows, that he's probably, in real life, a little overwhelmed with the amount of fucking and not really focused on projecting his feelings to an audience. She understands in that moment that he's the protagonist, and that he always has been.

There's a fade-back-in for a sequence of fucking in smaller sculptural groups. She can imagine Jack as one of the guys, then remove him with no problem. The camera moves along gently, it's panoramic, it's treating the void like a landscape. Then we hear a voice: it's a disembodied voice, because no one's face is visible—and then clearly it's One's voice—you can tell because he's just so happy—saying, "Good fucking boys! Good, good fucking boys."

The film concludes with two ceremonial acts. First, One through Four gather around Five, who remains on hands and knees while the others masturbate themselves with their free arms around each other and then rub invisible ejaculate on Five's back. Then it's just One and Five onscreen. They are face-to-face. They are incredibly happy. One kisses Five and puts the cap on him. Credits then roll.

In retrospect, there were parts that turned Josie on and parts that didn't, but she knew that was normal—you're supposed to leave it on in the background or else fast-forward to the particular thing that gets you if you're a porn kind of person. Much of her ice cream remained, soupy lumps on the nightstand, so clearly she'd felt something. She did not want to get out of bed to take the bowl downstairs to the sink. She did not want to push herself out of her bedclothes, the tucked sheets. But then she felt a little stuck in there. She dragged the little movie icon into the little wastepaper basket, and the disk slid out. She didn't get out of bed. She didn't masturbate. She thought about their happiness. She was tired, but she thought maybe the real reason she didn't masturbate was spite, and in the morning, she called her housekeeper and said, "I'm sorry, I just can't afford you anymore," and her housekeeper said, "Oh. Okay, then. I have other jobs." Maybe she did.

Josie told herself she was ready to abandon the house and confront the Frank situation and then she booked a room at the Days Inn not far from where he lived. It gave her a break when Jack went off with Frank, a few weeks every couple of years, let someone else feel responsible for a while. This time longer than usual. But who were they all kidding? It hurt.

Josie said to Em, "My shrink got burned-out on Axis I and II in residency. She said she started bringing it home. In fact, one guy tried to break into her house with a meat cleaver. Now she likes to help people who won't mess up her life. She told me this in therapy."

Em said, "Is she supposed to say that?"

"I appreciated it," Josie said.

"Where'd the diamond come from?" Em asked. "Is Jack rich or what?"

Josie perked up and went back to her stage whisper. "He has practically no money at all—he stole it! It's terrible but kind of fantastic. My baby was reaching for that brass ring and thought, I want the diamond!" Then she said, "I guess I could sell it."

Under the shed was dirt. Ad had said the bodies of Kurt Cobain, Elliott Smith, David Foster Wallace, and *who knows how many others!* were buried under the shed at their mother's house. *My people*, she said. The dirt was made of sand, animal shit, infill and the chemical residue of processed potting soil, bones and shells from all over the world, treated seepage and a set of china smashed to bits and buried by long-ago neighbors for some family reason, bugs and fish protein, rotted bulbs and sterile seeds, bacteria and the gristle off steak, thorns, and berries. The dead and the dirt and the dead in the dirt are shapeless. They kept going with their conversation, like what is responsible versus held responsible invasive versus understanding versus freedom versus your own good versus good for culture versus good citizen versus good for the man versus natural versus clean, individual versus way of life versus nurture versus illness, data, martyrdom, giving up, red herring, peace, comfort, productive difficulty, banging head against wall, stabbing own foot or the feet of others, toeing lines, growing up, agreeing to disagree, triggering the latent, copping out versus interior life, options, abandonment, persecution, legal necessity, human rights, worth living, control, deceit, purpose, intent, pursuit, and left the shed and approached the house without having made any decisions. They passed the koi pond that Frank would never think to maintain, so who was keeping those spotty foreign fish alive? They went up the steps to the screened-in porch. Frank opened the door before they could knock on it. He was alone in the kitchen and Em considered, for a moment, the prospect that all three of them had made Jack up.

Frank, wiping his hands on a checkered towel, said, "Hello. Come in," and returned to what he'd been doing at the sink. Em and Josie just stood in the doorway on the porch. Jack appeared in the doorway across the linoleum from them, still wrapped in the afghan. It was so garish—pink, yellow, and orange bursts with black centers of the god's eyes, black borders to each square, and a black frame around the whole ugly thing. Just for background, god's-eye pattern comes from peyote mandala, and is symbolic of the power of seeing and understanding that which is unknown and unknowable, the four points representing the elemental processes of earth, fire, air, and water. It wasn't Jack's fault that this blanket was the one that Frank kept draped over his sofa, that his mother had made it in a crafting fit not long before her death in 1978. He may have been unconsciously drawn to it. The blanket may have been significant because there is order in the universe after all. Or I did it. *Voilà.* I put it there for *good reason*. It is such bullshit to go around collecting evidence to confirm what you already think, yet here is a bed that made you. Some translations of Ovid have this to offer: that He who was the world's artificer, author, architect—whichever god it was—created man from seed divine or else by mixing earth with rain, and so was the earth, which before had been so rough and indistinct, now organized to wear the human form.

"Why is everyone looking at me?" Jack said from his doorway. The perforations around his mouth were red with soreness, but not gory. Josie stepped toward him, into the room.

"Oh babe," she said. "Your face."

Em put her hand over her mouth where she stood, tears pushing at her eyes. Frank leaned with his back to the sink and observed from there.

"That's right," Jack said. "*My* face."

"But I loved your face," said Josie.

"This *is* my face," said Jack. His thin clothes, that undershirt with limp sleeves, soft cotton pants darker at the knees like a gray horse is darker at the knees. He had come into Em's house, silence-equals-death and looking for something he had reason to believe was *in there*. Or was he all echo? You're queer, you know the image, you feel something, you try to apply it—and then he'd flown into the house with no more purpose than to get out again like a bird or a bat or a bee with all the mysterious inapplicable mechanisms of those brains and desires.

Everyone stood there blinking from their corners. It was a shoot-out with their eyes.

Should Em go into the house? She could not. She just turned on her heel and ran.

During what would turn out to be his final days in his office, swiveling in his chair, waiting for Jack to return, Frank had discovered that it was possible to change your desktop screen saver to something other than looping stars. Same stars, one computer after another, since the dawn of computers in his life. Right before he changed his to the image of the vacant golden condo that he'd thought, for a time on the train, might have been their destination—that obscenely expensive thing born dead, profound and tacky, consortiums of creditors already suing each other—Russian investors pulling strings from the other side of Alaska—he squinted at the stars one last time, jiggled his head for final psychedelic trailers, and then Jack was at the door. He came in joking about the ugly office, "Does this room make me look fat?"

After the women were gone from the kitchen, after what was going to happen in his house had happened and the officials were gone and the two of them had cleaned as well as they could bear,

Frank and Jack climbed the stairs and went out the bedroom window onto the porch roof to look at the real stars. It was such a good, old, neglected, mossy roof. They didn't think about the speed of light versus the size of space, the life and death of stars over which, together, they'd blown their minds as young men in a developmental phase, debating the concept of destiny. It's a scam, they agreed in the end. In the future, when he thought of it, Frank wondered if it might have been Trump Tower with its missing floors that they'd been destined for in New York City, because by then he didn't remember that he was the one—not Jack—who thought the whole quest might have anything to do with architecture.

What a lucky clear rare night. Reddish lines materialized and dematerialized between stars, optical illusions. Familiar images of brain neurons have been derived from moments like these to help us imagine beyond fleshy coils. On the roof, Frank remembered the night in the hills outside town with Em, and he remembered the terrible train, abandoning Jack. With these stars, he submitted to the sentimentality of imaginary lines drawn from those bits of light that we believe are things to one another to form pictures, and then to people on their earth sphere who see them. He just took it, like a child who yields, finally, to his parent's arms.

Driving herself home after what was going to happen in Frank's kitchen, there was a stretch of road where you go up very steeply, and Em saw stars through the windshield—they struck her—and that's just the way it went because some of the stories we tell stay true. Her image of herself was: floating in a mystic circle with mother, father, sister, and in the center of their circle some giant newspaper, some Sunday edition, everyone yanking a page, wadding it up and stuffing it into one another's mouths like wedding cake. Later, later, when she slept, she and Adeline floated, fetal in space, and then Ad was pregnant, there were going to be new babies, and tiny babies floated everywhere. Infant means languageless, ontogeny sort of recapitulating phylogeny. Em ran from the house because the mad see the unseen—what the collective suspects but can't express, a perpetual frictionless swing from object to subject—and woe unto the mad-man who fails to speak to us and woe unto you if you want to know what is happening to you. The mad wake with extra arms and a kick in the eye, a terrible mathematics shining, a terrible semantics, planes knocking, incompatible grammars, frequencies, waves.

So Em ran from Frank's house past the koi and the shed to the back of the property—not far, but this was an older neighborhood, gener-ous parcels, and you could build some speed. She had never made the transition from being young to exercising, and her heart hurt by the time she hit the rubbly brush where invasive species can have their way with a few yards of earth. A bartender who had one eye and an eyeball ring had once handed her a drink, a festive Manhattan, his red socket sealed, and made a joke he'd made a thousand times to relieve customers who were anxious about his face. It may be worth mentioning that Em had always had two eyes. Eyes are small, con-tained in their places in faces, but they reach endlessly in their phys-ics and their symbolic history. In the near future in relation to this moment in this rubble beyond this house, Adeline's eyes did come back, good as ever; they stabilized on their own about a month after her release. The rest of her brain remained mysterious in its abilities. She spoke, now and then, from her bed in the unfinished room in her parents' house, from a great sleepy distance, in words, phrases, and some sentences. Once Ad could see again, Em was able to won-der why she'd been so fixed on that one vitiation. The part of her that considered herself a coward knew it was to protect herself from the idea of a brain in the flux of damage. So a person is blind, so you have to learn some things. So your language and culture are over-invested in the visual—shift your perspective—

So by the time she abruptly turned around in the brush like a windup toy and headed back across the lawn she was telling her-self this, in these exact words: You are going to march right in there, young lady. She passed the shed, the pond, and then she heard a lot of yelling coming from the house. The door was closed again so she went without guile to the window next to it and peered inside. Josie was standing on the table, with her back to Em, wagging a chef's knife in one and then the other hand like a lounge singer. The cadence of her speech ramped up, turned erratic. Her body lashed. Her boots were beautiful—soft gleaming leather with a graceful heel, and they did not seem to have gotten dirty from any of the day's events— and then she slipped. She lost her balance because of the wildness of a thrust or her speech or the facts of the furnishings and their arrangement in relation to her body. Both men reached for her. Em tore herself from the window and hurled open the door. She had seen the knife flashing like a ring. Josie hit a chair on the way down, which skittered for several feet and then stopped. She lay on the floor with the knife pointing to where it had cut her neck. The scene was incredibly bloody. The clipped strings from Jack Bell's mouth lay in a saucer on the coffee table in the living room, just visible through a doorway. In an empty teacup remained evidence that someone had been crumbling sugar cubes into sugar. Beyond the teacup, a stairway going up. A tiny sound arrived like thread, and grew. When Em first registered it, she thought it was a kettle, but the noise came from Jack and grew into something unmistakably organic.

Frank went to Josie. He told Em to bring him a phone. There was the mustard-colored one on the wall with a long curly-cord stretched stiff. Em handed the headset across the table to him and returned to the body of the phone to dial. Even though the noise Jack was making had become piercing, Em had no trouble hearing Frank tell her to go.

She didn't want to go. She wanted to know if this was death or not, was this going to be death or not. She just wanted to know. She thought maybe if she was there to wait for it to happen or not she'd know.

Another terrible thing in that moment was the way Josie stopped being this person she had liked instantly without even noticing, a person who could be her friend if not her sister. In the moment when Em was moving from the window to the door as fast as possible, Josie had transformed into a figure who had arrived in her life as if to have the very conversations they'd had, and now that they'd occurred, was moving out of the picture at the speed of light, symbolic, obscene, and that seemed to Em to be a kind of radical injustice if not true evil. Every form of storyteller is implicated—the one who's done with Tasio is implicated—and there's an emotion that goes with that. Em recognized it from childhood, a primal sense that claims your body but doesn't stop you. Frank sat with Josie's head in his lap holding the dishrag to her neck with both hands and the phone cricked against his neck. There must not have been anyone on the line anymore because he kept telling Em to go, that they were doing what could be done, there was nothing for her to do, there was no reason for her to be here, no one needed to know she'd ever been there at all, it didn't matter if she had been there or not.

Where was Adeline?

The suicide note of a person resolved to action in the moments before suicide settles into plain speech. There is no sign of madness. There's a palpable absence of anger and bitterness, and without those things, an exhausted longing for beauty. This, in any case, is how it was with Adeline and the note she wrote with death in sight. In it, only the certainty that what was beautiful in her was inaccessible to others, that what was beautiful in others was inaccessible to her. It expressed a desire for death and regret for causing pain, and even though words were created to be repeated, repeating the words would violate the words and their writer and the entire swank hotel.

II. Voices

Loki the Jokester

Among the blondest gods lived Loki the jokester. Deep in the night, he snuck into the queen's bedroom and cut off her hair, because if he could take her hair he could take anything. There will be no more female people in this myth. The gods were so pissed. Loki needed gifts to appease them. He went to a pair of dwarves for help. They were master smiths, and Loki convinced them to forge amazing gifts on his behalf. The pile of gifts they created included a skein of golden hair that would take root in the queen's head, which was impressive and creepy. There was also a spear that never missed. You could kill people or animals, or you could maim them strategically, or you could just poke a hole in anything you wanted from any distance you could think of, sending a message. But the best of the things the dwarves made was a magic boat that came with favorable winds, that could contain and carry anything you put in it, and folded up to fit in your pocket. A different pair of dwarves heard about all this and bet Loki and his dwarves that they could make gifts that would please the gods even more. Loki took the bet, and set the stakes: the loser's head.

The new dwarves set about crafting, and Loki turned himself into a stinging fly to annoy them. A fly must mean *puns*. The dwarves made excellent gifts regardless. Loki even stung one of them in the eye while he was working on a magic hammer, so the handle of the hammer ended up a little short, but it didn't matter because the gods liked the hammer best of all—better even than a golden armband that dripped miniatures of itself in case you want an endless source of shining circles symbolizing unity plus real exchange value, and better even than a boat that could actually *fold space* if you want to discover the universe or tell an amazing story. Well, that shows you something about the development of the culture of these big pale blond people. They like the hammer. They like to tack some stuff together and also they like to crush it. So Loki and his dwarves lose. The gods prepare to take Loki's head, so Loki points out that while they *do* have a claim on his head, they do not have a claim on his *neck*. The gods are exasperated by the semantics, but they concede. Something about life before small print. Something about controlling the narrative. How it moves from one voice to another and transforms. How it transforms, yet traces of its history remain in sounds and shapes. When a story is in your mouth, wield it while you can. That may be the lesson, because even gods can lose at words. The winning dwarves took their tools and lashed Loki's mouth shut, sealing his jokehole, and to this very day, you can find an image on the internet of an ancient stone into which has been chiseled the tragic, goofy image of what happens when you are only one guy among many dwarves who all want to get somewhere in life.

FRANK WRITES A LETTER

Before Josie with a knife in the kitchen—before Josie even existed for Frank—when he was busy with his second wife and Jack was in Tasmania, in Maputo, in Medina, and he was boss at a middling company on the decline in a time of decline—when he wanted to know what being boss was good for, after all—(people in the office said that when Frank said "very nice," he meant "not impressed"; people said, "He called my idea lame then changed it ten percent and used it himself, and I will always wonder if he knew what he was doing because I *did* get that raise"; people said, "He used to make me feel special and then I disagreed with him in that meeting which I never would have done if he didn't make me feel special, and after that he never noticed me again"; people said, "He's like my damn father and you know what, life has been a lot better since that man died")—when he had not seen his lover for too long, Frank snuck out of bed, pulled on some old sweatpants, chose a reliably inky pen, took a hardcover book of paintings by Lucian Freud from a shelf for a lapdesk, and a camp lantern from under the eaves, and a box of monogrammed stationery, stepped out the bedroom window onto the porch roof, and began to write a letter. He started it on the roof, but he didn't finish it there. Over time, he wrote at his desk in an alcove of the bedroom, at the kitchen table, and with the book of paintings in a chair in the living room. He tried to write on the computer at the office, imagining that he'd transcribe, later, onto the stationery, but he found that at the office he couldn't access the feelings that lead to words.

> *Dear Jack,*
>
> *Where are you? Having a fine old time I hope. Perhaps I will write this letter and perhaps I will not. I am remembering the summer you practically lived with us because your home was too much. Perhaps I will write this letter and send it and perhaps I will write*

*it and feed it to the dog. You do not even know if I still have a dog.
That is the great joy of the missive.*

I do not. I no longer have a dog.

You will have to take my word for it.

*You stayed with us because our house was more stable than yours
and I have been remembering what you let slip about your father
that summer. I think your mother was gone. I think, now, that
she was in an asylum and you didn't know or wouldn't say it. I
think of her nodding out on a veranda. I know that's not possible,
I know there were no verandas for your family. Did I ever tell
you about my uncle in Philly? I have been thinking of a different
summer, when I had a position interning in this uncle's offices in
Philly. My father's brother, a judge. Law, politics. These were jobs
I had heard of. My mother was several years gone, and my father
pronounced me "at sea." You will soon understand the irony of that
declaration. I was twenty. We were twentyish. I hadn't seen you
for a long time. I will write you the story, and then I will send it to
you or not. I have the power! Ha, ha! You will have to wait to find
out. Meanwhile, I will not cross out a single word. That will keep
me honest. Even back then you seemed younger than me and wiser
than me, and even back then I didn't think it was right. Younger
in terms of vitality while I was pudgy, repressed, oversexed, bracing for disappointment. I thought perhaps away from my father
the world would be my oyster, my father who felt he had not made
it so good, and this was true, in comparison to his brother, though
we had a large lovely home, took vacations, and so on. I know now
that my father did very well but was unable to see it. My mother
liked to blame his anger on this sibling competition he'd lost.*

*Time has passed. What a funny thing that if I did not write to
you that time has passed you would never know it. See? You can
trust me.*

*My uncle's house in Philadelphia was canary yellow with clas-
sical pillars so white they were something like teeth, fangs, I remember thinking, that had emerged shining from the boxwood a*

moment before my arrival, swords from sheaths. My uncle's house had many rooms, occupied by an array of children, my uncle's children, mostly girls, born every two or three years. There were also rooms for their nanny, a housekeeper, and his wife's elderly father, who was paralyzed, and for the old man's nurse. I went to work with my uncle in the morning and came home with him in the evening. I'd wait for him in the empty offices until he returned from social engagements in town, and often he would let me accompany him to restaurants or meetings with other blowhards. These were the legendary smoke-filled Edwardian leather-bound landscapes I'd hoped for, but once inside, I had no idea what to do. We stood in packs among packs. We gathered in mohair club chairs. "Take note!" my uncle would say, always in a moment when I happened to be contemplating the many shades of nut in a dish, or considering a change in my brand of cigarette. "Take note!"

Did he mean for me to write something down, literally, to have a pencil in my pocket, which I did not? What if he expected me to quote something back to him? "Frankie, you remember that case, let this fucker in on the details, will you?" What to remember, what to let sail by. I purchased a small notepad but was too afraid to take it out for fear he meant mentally. Take note. Late at night, in my room, I replayed the day and made lists in the notebook in tiny handwriting I hoped only I could read, but I also hoped that anyone who saw it would marvel at its precision. I remember the braided rug in my room in the yellow house. I remember odd shapes that the shade on the window cast at night. I would think I was so clever one moment, putting ideas into relation with each other, and so foolish the next. I would doubt the tiny handwriting I had worked so hard at. My uncle never had to write anything down in order to produce at will. He was one of those men.

There was a year when I ascended the department ladder, here. You were traveling in a cold white place. I received a single floating postcard from you. No return address. I was a whiz in the biz. I scaled the ranks. I led for a time. I felt powerful. I could walk into any room and speak off the cuff as if from the heart. He died—my uncle—shot, in fact, by the wife of a man convicted in his courtroom of a massive embezzlement—she of course was losing everything—this was not long after the summer I lived in his house—you may remember the case—I'm sure you were busy—where were you at that time? Austria? Siberia? I identified with the indirect fallout aspect of the case, and for those years, rising through ranks such as they were, I felt a bit of his ghost in me.

Another young fellow started in the office around midsummer. Somebody's project. A sailor called Jimmy. Navy. Bright and able, from the other side of the tracks, returned from traveling the world while you were gone into it. I missed you.

This kid came into the office and put everything I lacked into high relief. Naturally my uncle loved him, and swiftly I was displaced. My uncle made a few efforts to pit us against each other but I didn't make enough of an impression on Jimmy for him to take the bait. He gazed only at my uncle and down I tumbled into the basement with the legions of file clerks. Mazes of pale tin shelving. A smell you will always know, the smell of real information made uniformly manila. Increasingly, I returned to the house at a reasonable hour while Jimmy joined the men with cigars. I couldn't think of what else to do. And in a way, that was fine. Now I knew I was not my uncle's mentee, and though I still would not admit to being my father's son, perhaps I was closer to that terrible yet potentially liberating knowledge.

We had difficult fathers, Jack, you and I.

When I fuck you, Jack. When you fuck me—

Okay, I'm back.

In the evenings, at my uncle's, big and little girls flew about the house chased by maids. Usually everyone had eaten by the time I arrived and I made a sandwich of their scraps and ate it on the sofa leaning over the coffee table in the parlor in their company. They called it a "family room." My aunt read magazines in an upholstered rocker and her ancient father nodded in his wheelchair in *the corner by a window he never looked out of. I sat there eating across the room from him. As the long summer dusk proceeded, the nanny and the housekeeper and some of the older girls disappeared into their rooms with their secrets. One evening just like this three small girls were ostensibly working at a puzzle on the other end of the coffee table—something I found very creepy and I do not know why, because what is so creepy about little kids doing a puzzle? They worked on this puzzle while I ate my sandwich, which contained a wedge of lamb with sopping greens. I was very immersed in the pleasures of this sandwich. When I looked up, one of the girls had traveled over to the old man, unzipped his trousers, and was flipping his flaccid worm right and left in her fist. "Girls!" I said, because I couldn't tell one from another.*

But I was ignored completely, as if I hadn't spoken. Then one of the girls at the puzzle got up and stomped over to me, sock-footed, and looked right into my face, jutting her chin with her arms akimbo, this audacious mock-up of a bratty child, and then spun on her heels and stomped over to her grandfather, looked at me again—swoosh, swoosh over her shoulder to make certain she had my attention. And when was the last time anyone had looked at me? I remember wondering in that moment, a soft pulsing place inside me saying "she noticed me—me!" And right then she spit on the old man's face. She hit the corner of an eye. "Aunt Sarah!" I cried out. She looked up from her magazine.

Now, perhaps her father was obscured from where she sat. Perhaps it looked to her like two little girls gathered around their grandfather in some granddaughterly way. Perhaps she couldn't see what was going on in the old man's lap? Perhaps she couldn't see the wad of mucus crawling down her father's cheek? "Mind your business, Frank," she said. "You can judge when you have a family of your own."

Frank let the letter sit, not ready to finish it, not ready to send it. The letter lay for a long time in the top drawer of the bureau, one floor down from the small framed picture of a tree in spring. He'd take it out to read and reread his own words. He could not find anything wrong in it. He laughed with himself at all the right moments. He felt for himself. He evaluated his prose style with objectivity and found it downright admirable, and he felt sadness at the isolation it conveyed, bird in a room with only people. But he was afraid that if Jack read it he'd see right through to something. He didn't know what, only that he didn't want it to be seen.

> *Time has passed again. Time passed before, at least twice between sentences, without my mentioning. As I write and then do not write, my wife, who may not be my wife for long, seems to me to be in motion like a cloud turning from one thing to another, always up there in my peripheral vision. She is not even my wife, she is my second wife. I have also been thinking about my son. His mother no longer even seems to have been a person, merely my wife. When I began this letter, as I remember, he seemed to be seven, just as he is in the photograph I keep on display. He is by a boat in the photograph. Just now, however, as I write, he seems to me much older, a man who might have his own young son. The image is vivid everywhere but the face. I see his clothes and I see the bracelet on the wrist of the woman's hand he holds in the picture I imagine I'm looking at in which he has a son, this grinning towhead. I must have lifted him from a catalog—standing with a man's hand on one shoulder and the woman's other hand, bare-wristed, on the other. The image, naturally, develops as I record it for you. And now that I do the math, I know the image is from an imagined future. My son is not old enough to be the father in this picture.*
>
> *Enough.*
>
> *There is the second part to this episode in my life as a young man in the house of my uncle. I continued to go to my internship, such as it was, and in the house I made myself fastidiously polite to every member of the household. I took my supper into my room, ate*

it reading comic books, and went to bed as soon as I could. Lo and behold one day I came home from the office and my uncle and the sailor Jimmy were not out on the town; they were in the house already, and my uncle's driver was hauling Jimmy's steamer trunk up the stairs and into my room. My belongings had been moved into a chest in the terrible family room. My uncle said I was welcome to sleep on the sofa in there or, alternatively, there was a trundle in Connie's room—that I remember—that nasty girl's name— whichever one she was—and when he said it, sure enough, one of my cousins nearby glared at me, so I said, "That's all right, the sofa will be fine, Uncle." I began to try to think of places I could go until the fall semester. I wondered where you were, too. Thought of you bounding lightly across the earth and oceans. I was afraid to ask if I still had my position at the offices. I couldn't tell if I had done something terribly wrong. I was terrified that the girls might have made up lies about me, and I ran through what I might have said at work that could have been reported back to my uncle unfavorably. I sat at the dining table with the family that evening. I followed them into the family room afterward and placed myself on the sofa, a red beast with gold tassels. I sat engulfed in it, as innocuous as possible, and the adults drank scotch or brandy depending on gender in special glasses. All evening I watched Jimmy perform. Really, he was just being himself—easygoing, naturally warm, affectionate with the girls, as if actually interested in the work and in the workings of the family, asking what Aunt Sarah did with her time—who knew? She ran several charitable organizations, for the poor, for immigrants, for the insane.

I continued to show up to the internship where I floated uselessly among endless shelves of folders, other grayed-out people moving their fingers across them, and then when the office closed, took to wandering the city spending my meager earnings in bars until it was late enough that the family would have gone to bed. Then, along dark streets, I made my return to the yellow house with its bared teeth. I kept a candle stub in my pocket where I'd once kept

the notepad. By its light I scavenged food in the kitchen and fol-
lowed its singular glow all the way through the house into the fam-
ily room and the sofa so that I would not have to look at any of it
on the way to my anxious sleep.

Eventually it dawned on me: I had done nothing wrong. I was
wrong. I did not suit; I did not belong. Not to the bold outer sur-
face of the family, not in the land of movers and shakers, and not
in the dark and contorted inner workings of those worlds. Though
I should clarify: this insight of profound displacement did not
"eventually" dawn on me. It was revealed to me in an explosion
one night, a week or so after I had been dislodged from my room, a
night when I had drifted from bar to bar through the city of love,
walking off what I drank so that when I arrived back at the house,
I was hungry and it was dark, but I was somewhat sober.

As I approached the door to the room where I was expected
to sleep, there crouched my uncle, without hat and coat, peering
through the keyhole. Upon hearing my steps he made mute gestures
with his hand for me to stay quiet and then peeped through the
keyhole again. He was laughing, silently. The flesh around his hips
and thighs pressed the fabric of his pants into shapes like brain mat-
ter. "Come over here," he said in a whisper. I approached on tiptoe.
"Just look!" he said. "Take a peep!" He was giddy. "There they lie.
Look at the old man! Can you see the old man?" He shifted aside so
that I could look, and I looked. I could smell his old gravy breath
on my neck, and I could hear sounds from within the room that
only materialized in my consciousness now that I looked. Upon the
red sofa, directly below an ornately framed portrait of my uncle,
aunt, their children, and two dogs I'd never heard of—in fact,
I'd never noticed the painting, even though it was enormous, the
family depicted on the very sofa it now hung above—and I had sat
below it for how many torturous hours?—and it had been looming
over me as I slept! Now, beneath the painting, on that sofa, I could
see two figures, fused: my aunt and the sailor Jimmy who had been

*allowed to take over my room now that my uselessness was clear
to everyone. Her legs gleamed white like broken pillars against the
dark upholstery and then they flapped like wings as he went at her.
In his corner across the room sat her father, the paralyzed gray-
beard, in his chair, looking on, hunched over his hands and curled
up as usual like a boiled shrimp, without being able to speak or
move. I turned around to my uncle. He had the greatest difficulty
keeping from laughing aloud. He was holding his hand over his
nose. "Did you see the old man?" he whispered. "Oh lord, did you
see the old man? The way he sits there looking on!" He put his face
to the keyhole again, and when I was able, I backed away. I fled
the house, leaving in it everything I'd brought with me.*

*I think you were in Alaska. Or Norway. Or a Mongolian
desert.*

*Doesn't it seem so strange to you that I am here in this fourth-
rate city, this second-rate town? Why is it, people being people, that
one's family, acquired by happenstance, means so much? I wondered: What exactly did I flee? My cruel uncle? My virile rival? My
dismissive aunt? Their nasty brood, the future? The grotesque itself? Truly, when I looked through the keyhole it was the vacant
old man from whom I ran.*

Time passed again. Then Frank signed the letter, *Yours*. He put
it in an envelope, addressed it, sealed it. Imagined the hands of
Jack's wife receiving it. Could not tell if he liked or did not like
the thought of her hands on the letter. Found stamps, recklessly.
Chose, between an image of the flag and an image of a tree, the
stamp with the tree. Wished for a stamp with a boat. Left it on the
bureau in the room he shared with his wife. Days, and he had not
decided whether to send it. He indulged fantasies of Jack reading
it. Jack sitting in a tree in a field, reading it, Jack on a yacht in the
ocean, reading it, the trifold making a zigzag in the air. Usually sun
bloomed through the page and wind ruffled it. Part of not sending

it was to preserve the fantasies. Jack in the Southern Cone, helping indigenous people do things, accessing their *ways*. Mail would have arrived in a sack on a raft. He looked at the letter and decided again every morning, and looked at it every evening before getting into bed, to sleep on it.

One evening the letter wasn't there. His wife was in their bed, reading a book. He asked, immediately, "Have you seen the letter that was here?"

"Mm-hmm," she said.

She kept reading, he thought, passive-aggressively. "Did you take it?" he said.

"You kept forgetting to mail it."

He yelled at her: "Why do you make these *assumptions*?" He swept his hand across the top of the bureau, and the change he always dumped from his pocket flew off and clattered amiably to the floor.

"Well, it's gone now," she said.

"That was not for you to do," he said. He sat on the edge of the bed and then got up again. He fumbled around on the floor, picking up coins. While he was down there he said, "You mailed it, yes?"

"Yes." She'd taken it and put it in her purse to mail, but she hadn't mailed it.

"That's all?"

"What do you—" she said, and then realized what he was asking. "Maybe I read it, maybe not. Suck on that, Frank."

She hadn't read it. Instead she'd carried it around, forgetting to put it in the mailbox at the end of the driveway and then forgetting to put it in mailboxes around town. Eventually she pulled something else out of her purse, the letter slipped out, and it landed in a puddle. When she picked it up, Frank's handwriting through the wet envelope was so earnest that it made her angry. Never had it occurred to her to read the letter. A seal is still sacred, and breaking it was never an option for her. But when she saw the handwriting she dropped it right back in the puddle and left it there.

My Strange Addiction S03E08—Urine Drinker
by Emily Hochman

Carrie is fifty-three years old and lives in Colorado Springs, Colorado. The show begins with shots of gorgeous snow-topped mountains and Carrie in a snow flurry walking a little white poodle wearing a pink jacket. It's part of the show's format for the subject to introduce themselves and then say they are addicted to whatever strange thing it is. Carrie says she is addicted to drinking her urine, but it's quickly apparent that she doesn't really consider it to be an addiction per se, she believes it to be a legitimate medical and beauty treatment. She holds a glass of honey-colored urine up to the light, she sniffs at the mouth of a jar, she sits at a table sipping it while she reads a book.

She explains it has a wide range of flavors: sometimes lemony, sometimes grassy, sometimes like champagne. She says her eating habits changed when she realized how much diet affects the taste. She had to stop eating asparagus, for instance, and she loves asparagus. She uses it for many things, not just drinking. She brushes her teeth with it, washes her eyes with an eye cup, strokes it through her hair. She has found that aged urine makes the best lotion. They show her preparing a bath and pouring a glass of pee into the water, and then while she soaks, drinking it through her nose with a Neti Pot. Urine is good for everything. And you know, she looks radiantly healthy. Her eyes are bright, her hair is thick and glossy, her teeth are strong, her skin is clear. She also has a captivating presence. There's something graceful and bewitching about the slow, musical way she talks and the thoroughness of her facial expressions. I would describe her in reference to astrology and tarot: She's watery. She's the Queen of Cups.

The use of urine for health and cosmetic benefits, called urine therapy or urotherapy, goes back millennia. The earliest records are from ancient India. There is a section devoted to drinking urine in the Vedas, and it is also documented in ancient Chinese and Egyptian medical texts. Records of its use in topical, bath, and mouthwash treatments can be found in many global cultures. Doctors inspected urine by taste and smell to aid in diagnosis. As the field of medicine evolved and modernized, the practice became largely obsolete. There was something of a revival in the early 1900s, when a British naturopath named John Armstrong published a treatise in which he argues that all ailments, except those caused by trauma or bodily abnormality, can be cured with urine. The book was widely read and he prescribed regimens to thousands of patients. He cites a Bible proverb: "Drink the waters of thine own cistern, and running waters from thine own well." This verse is almost exclusively interpreted to mean "one should only have sex with one's own wife," but he places a lot of importance on it. Urine therapy is still not uncommon in China, where it's estimated three million people partake.

Six years ago, Carrie was diagnosed with stage three malignant melanoma in her lymph nodes. The doctors told her that with chemo she had a year to live. She decided to try alternative treatments, began drinking her urine, and four years later she was feeling healthier than ever and credited urine therapy for her recovery. Intermittent text from *My Strange Addiction* appears on the screen to insist that not only are there no benefits to drinking urine, there can be adverse effects. That urine contains toxins that can cause dehydration and kidney failure.

Carrie has found a new mole on her back. Her three teenaged daughters sit together on a sofa while she sits facing them. Except for having similar nondescript long haircuts, they don't look alike and they don't look like their mother. They implore her to see a doctor, have the mole looked at, and verify she is not hurting herself with the urine. You can see by her face that she really, really doesn't want to go, but that she is moved, and as they all wipe tears from their cheeks, she consents. The doctor tells her the mole looks irregular and that she should have a biopsy. Carrie says she is averse to knives because if you cut into the surface of the body, it signals the inside for the sickness to come out. The doctor tells her the blood tests have come back somewhat abnormal, the levels of toxins are higher than they should be, and it is likely attributed to the urine. She explains something I am sure Carrie has already heard and read many times and doesn't agree with: that she is reintroducing toxins into her system that were intended to be expelled. Carrie looks skeptical, like she had made her decision before she walked in. The doctor appears genuinely sympathetic and asks Carrie if she has lost faith that conventional medicine can help her. Carrie's face contorts and as she cries she says she totally has. I recognized her situation and really felt for her. Sitting in front of doctors who think they alone have the right answers, prescribing treatments that sound invasive and inhumane, dogmatically promoting exclusively Western medicine with willful disregard for its deficiencies. And she's sitting there, taking it for her family. I've been there, and I cried too.

I drank my urine once. I was psychotic and as a result of primarily delusional but partially justifiable bad thoughts about my husband, we were at war. I had sequestered myself in my workroom, and, to avoid bumping into him in common spaces, peed in a glass. That one went into a potted plant. A second one was on the windowsill in an IKEA glass, a pale yellow, when my sister called. She had been alerted to my psychosis. That's something that drives me nuts every time I go crazy: all the significant people in my life sending group emails to each other imparting everything I say and do and colluding on how to handle me. Being excluded from discussions that are all about me feels incredibly disrespectful at the time, but I guess there isn't really another way. I insist they CC me and they don't, but what's the point? I would just send incoherent diatribes in return. Every time I talk to my sister at these junctures she sounds incredibly far away, in outer space. She always asks me to tell her what I'm thinking and feeling but when I do it's like my words hit an iron wall, it's like she doesn't understand English. I know it's because I am saying things that are coming from an alien dimension. I don't really expect her to agree or understand, but the feeling of being on a distant planet is very upsetting. I know when I am talking that she is writing stuff down for potential use in a piece of fiction and that she might be distracted. That's what writers do. She often stops in the middle of whatever she's doing to take out a little notebook and jot something down, and this is good material. I always amp the crazy up a bit.

I was spinning around my room, arms flailing for no one but the ghosts, phones tapped, talking loudly with the windows open for my neighbor to hear so she could testify in court on my behalf. I saw my glass of pee, thought of Carrie, and drank some. It tasted totally fine, like water but a little bitter. And I told my sister, "I'm drinking my pee right now, what do you think of that? It tastes good, do you think that's disgusting?" She didn't have much to say about it, she didn't really care. I accused her of being the Salieri to my Mozart, referencing *Amadeus*, and she said she didn't remember anything about it. It's my favorite movie. I meant I was a Mozart and she was squeezing my genius for her own use. One of the symptoms of mania is grandiosity. I always think I'm a genius. A couple of weeks later, when I was in the hospital in the same psychosis, I was talking to dead David Foster Wallace, who was telling me how wonderful my writing was. I said yes it's much better than my sister's, she's crap (I was pissed), and he said, "No no no, she's quite good. Not as good as you, but she's good." I think the hardest thing about becoming sane and the squelching of the delusions might be the eradication of my belief in my own greatness. Imagine you are convinced you are a revolutionary, a prophet, a Van Gogh, a priestess, and then the meds kick in and what you really are is a nobody, and even worse than that, a psycho. It's even harder than saying goodbye to the spirits, maybe even harder than the humiliation.

Recently I was on an extended visit to Lucy's house. I'd spent the day working in her study, and it was getting dark. I'm primarily a visual artist, but I sometimes write as well, and I was working on a companion piece for the drawing I'd done of Carrie, years ago. I was perusing my sister's impressive bookshelf when I spotted the manuscript for this book, which was in its almost-final draft. We had agreed I would read it when she was done. There it was, sitting in a giant stack with "Em" all over the top page. It's my nickname. The first passage I flipped to was the urine drinking. (Near the end of the second chapter.) What I'd been working on was this essay about Carrie. I'd gotten to the part about being on the phone with my sister and drinking my pee, and took a break to look at her books. That's a synchronicity. I like talking to resolute nonbelievers about synchronicities. What I say is, "The definition of synchronicity is *meaningful coincidence*, you believe in *coincidence*, don't you?" This usually stumps them. But I secretly think they are also magic, evidence of vast unseen soul networks, an interconnection that means I am not alone even though I am usually alone.

I flipped to several more pages before I felt like I might be crossing a line. What I saw was my life. It was my suicide and my coming back to life and my psychosis and my hospitalizations. In case the question comes up about how she has such intimate knowledge of mental illness, that's how. And I felt like this is *my* story, it's *my* book to write. But it's her story too. The loved ones of people with serious mental illness go through their own torment and learning curves, and artists process their emotions and refine their thoughts with their art. A lot of fiction writers depend on events and characters from their own lives and I know exactly how that is. I rely on photographs and other source material for my painting. Almost always, except when I am in another dimension. So I can't fault her for that.

Yes, when I was drinking my pee she was taking notes. And perhaps she was a bit distracted. But I sounded just as far away to her as she did to me. And there wasn't an iron wall, she was hearing me. She got the nuances and the complexities, the deeper questions I wish our culture was asking. She's using her career and her audience to advance discourse around SMI, and in many ways, on my behalf. I don't have a career, I'm a psycho. The networks I was building were with the unseen, to the detriment and destruction of the seen. She's using her sanity to deconstruct insanity, applying her organized thinking to disorganized thoughts. These issues are critical now and I haven't written a book.

Homelessness, suicide, incarceration, discrimination. Cruelty, ridicule, isolation. A voice, anonymous, once told me that I was "a not insignificant member of the revolution," which was tempered enough in its grandiosity and unpredictable enough in its wording to echo as honest and encouraging later on. Since then, I have been asking myself what I would be doing if it were really true. The subject of mental health is so profound and multifaceted I don't actually know what I would advocate for in terms of acceptance and infrastructure, magic and meds. It's something of a relief that I don't have to figure it out in order to be an artist.

Update: It's eight years after the show and Carrie has a YouTube channel. She has not been back to the doctor. She does not look eight years older and she's still glowing. The irises of her eyes have lightened to a paler blue and her teeth are whiter. It really made me play with the idea of trying urine therapy myself but I'm sure I take too much medication. Most of the videos are about the therapy. The others express her unequivocal belief in the Flat Earth Theory. In one video, her feet, in different-colored socks with opposing viewpoints, debate for ten minutes, and the Flat Earth sock wins easily. I thought, "Nooooo, what are you doing?! Now nobody is going to trust your opinion on urine, people are going to think you're crazy!"

THEIR FATHER VS. BOBBY FISCHER

Soon after Josie failed to make it safely out of Frank's house, Adeline was pronounced stable and established down the hall from the father's study where he stared into the light of his computer, insomniac, the perpetually incomplete house surrounding him, Benny and the mother asleep in rooms below, stars above because so far even when we can't see them, everyone appears to agree they're there, his desk surrounded by crammed bookcases, lurking on websites where the unmedicated advised one another about how to get off your meds (*safely!*), holding in his mind his daughter's breath, telling himself that just because he couldn't hear her breathing from his room didn't mean she wasn't. It was the father who had been at her bedside when her hand moved. Now his task was to search the internet for suitable residential facilities, but he kept returning to these sites. He would read about a facility and try to picture what it would be like for a patient there—not Ad—but "a patient"—and then he would read, scrolling, accounts of the madness-experiences of the unmedicated as expressed to the medicated. He listened to radio archives from the American West of people recounting their paranormal experiences. He was trying to imagine what it was like for people to believe things were real when they weren't.

Once, when he had the flu as a young man, he woke from fever dreams thinking he'd really fucked his mother. All morning that idea of himself lived within him, and he was a man who had fucked his mother. Shaving, looking for socks, a man who had fucked his mother. A man who had fucked his mother drinking coffee black from a cracked mug. Was it like that? Just *more*? He knew he would not be able to understand what being them was like for *them*. Still, he thought he might be able to imagine what it would be like if he were *like* them. Maybe some more than others. Some of the unmedicated were excellent writers and some were really bad writers. He tried to listen to their voices and what they were saying. Then he tried to listen just to the sense of their personalities. Some of the clumsiest writers he felt most acutely. Some of the voices, he couldn't hear past a sneering or desperate tone. He thought, *I wouldn't like you medicated or unmedicated. I wouldn't like you not insane.* Some of the voices had him thinking, you have a way with words. He listened to his own inner voices. He heard his reading voice and thinking voice. How writers say, *finding your voice.* How activists say, *our voice must be heard.*

His wife and Benny set upon the house to get it ready while he drove Adeline from the airport. Dust the mantel, fresh sheets, dust the lampshade, little bed there vacant. Benny found a condom in its packet under the cloth on the improvised nightstand. Put it in his pocket, why not, you never know. The father led his daughter into the house. Her mother said, "You sit. Benny and I can take her upstairs," and she and Benny took her upstairs. He just let them take her, as if his wife were saying, "darling, I'll do this difficult thing for you," when what was happening was just what it sounds like was happening. From the living room, the father listened to the sounds of them up there. On the full-sized chessboard was the game he'd been playing with Benny when Ad died. A game can sit stopped in time forever, and you can just pick it up. The paperback book he practiced against had floated around the house since his daughters were babies. It had spent over a year on the back of the toilet, but usually it lay next to the sofa on the coffee table that held the chessboard with the current game. He'd brought it with him to Kansas City. Now it was missing. It was by Bobby Fischer, known for ways of being missing. On the cover was Bobby Fischer across the board from you. While Benny and his wife were installing Adeline, he went around the house looking for the book. It can become irrationally important to find a certain thing. But he could not find the book because the truth was, while tiny chess had made it home, onto a shelf with other games in the coat closet, he'd left the book somewhere in the hospital in the middle of the country.

First you hold the book, and then you just hold what the book gave you. In movies, chess takes place conceptually, in fog on the beach, in the desert, in outer space, and in proto–virtual reality. In the house, the father played Benny in the living room while Benny's handgun lay on the coffee table surrounded by pawns, and he'd played against his paperback in Ad's hospital room surrounded by blinking numbers flowing in blue, and he played on the computer in his study, a room that floated darkly in the house of bare studs, pink insulation, and wafting plastic sheeting. In the computer, human electronic opponents moved familiar pieces from around the world. Since Adeline's death, when he moved a piece he sometimes saw the chambermaid who'd found the body in the hotel room. He imagined the chambermaid in that outfit hotels know you want. In her apron she cries "eek!" when she walks in—slapping her rosy cheeks with her hands, mouth round—pointing at the body. Adeline, little sister, baby.

Bobby Fischer remained undefeated world champion of chess because, he explained, chess was pure, in a corrupt world there could exist no pure chess, therefore there was no chess, and so he could not be beaten. Some men escape madness by making an effective argument.

Family joke: When the girls did something right, their father liked to say, "Great game, Bobby!" And they knew to reply, "How would you know?" because that's what Bobby Fischer said.

The human ear is shaped to catch a human voice. In his room, the father struggled to imagine a difference between the recounting of visions and the recounting of dreams, and his ear was open for the sound of Adeline breathing, though breath would never carry that far. He thought about hearing voices, and tried to become aware of his own experience as a person who *heard things*. He tried to remember hearing a voice. He picked Ella Fitzgerald, because he knew her voice so well. He tried to remember her voice in a way that would sound real to him in his head, but he was unable to do it. Trying was harrowing work. After many hours on the internet reading, listening, and imagining, he sensed patterns, threads across synchronous words and rhythms, conflations of brainy shadows that mapped the landscape of where he'd been on- and off-line. People moving on and off their medications said, "You have to get on, you have to get off, believe me, your life depends on it!" Where are their families, he kept wondering, among them, or lost to them?

When the father moved away for graduate school, his mother experienced a bout of creativity in his absence. He came home for winter break and she'd wallpapered the apartment: halls of octagons textured with sand, kitchen of springy embossed plaid, a bathroom splotched with gold and silver mylar, TV room burlap over earthy orange. This was after a grueling semester in a special program for young men with the potential to make notable advances in mathematics. It had become clear, that last week of the semester—his adviser, chair of his committee, had said it to him explicitly—that while he could certainly complete his degree if he wished to do so, when it came to *significant* work in the field, if he was going to do it, he'd be doing it already. Of course the wallpaper geometries mocked him, every room decked out for a different party. She had not been a warm parent, but bumbled dutifully through the narratives of wife and mother in the time of Doctor Spock, don't pick the baby up. He drank burnt percolated coffee with his father at the kitchen table while she went to and from the refrigerator. Do you want juice, do you want this from the deli—"Ma, I'm fine—Ma, sit down—" searching for the courage to tell his father that he'd failed, when his father had always referred to graduate school in mathematics as "a stupid life path."

The weekend Adeline was dead he'd sat bedside with the machines in the hospital, data of a dead girl scrolling, blood still made to run, her mother approaching and then receding, unable to be still. He sat with his hands to himself. Most of his daughter was concealed in a compression bag, but he could see her face and her arm. Otherworldly blisters had risen from her knuckles, higher than they were wide, from her body weight on them for so many hours that had passed between the body and the carpet before the chambermaid arrived. He imagined the carpet had been elaborate with patterns. Hotels are almost only decoration. He'd waited by the bed for strangers to take her organs.

When he lifted his consciousness from the computer and shifted it to the feeling of the house, he didn't know if he was hearing the right kind of quiet. He left his study, entered Ad's room down the hall around corners, and pulled a chair to her bedside as he had pulled a chair to her bedside when she was dead, and as he had pulled a chair to his wife's bedside when Adeline was a newborn. Now he watched her body for the movement of breath, her eyelids for the flicker of dream, remembering his wife sleeping postpartum, body sewn back together in the aftermath, and their sleeping baby with indigo on her belly button and silver nitrate swelling her eyes.

Now, during the day, his wife moved as silent as ribbon up and down the stairs with liquids and solids, hot towels and ice. Sometimes Benny, too, went up and down the stairs, carrying something heavy, thumping after her, sometimes dogs clattering after her, too. The father hung back. He liked the dogs, but sometimes an aura of the monstrous emanated from them. It was not their fault. He even loved the dogs. He went into the internet. He'd peek out, see his wife moving through the house at her consistent pace, confirming life like pulse and breath. On and off meds, people were saying, "you're not listening to me! You may think you are but you aren't listening! Is anyone out there? Knock knock, anyone home?" In the quiet of the house when his wife was sleeping he became afraid that Adeline had died again. In the chair at her bedside he touched her shoulder until she opened her eyes and aimed them wobbily at him. "It's me, honey," he said. Her eyebrows moved across some expressions. Her mouth moved. It was not yet clear if her vision would resolve, or what exactly happened with her eyes when she tried to use them. "I've got a joke for you, honey," he said. "Are you ready? It's very bad. You'll love it. I found it on the internet." It was strange to hear his voice in the air after so many hours of others'.

He went back in his study. He read up on more facilities. When he'd try to picture Adeline in any of them, he'd retch, so he went downstairs and pulled his chair up to the TV, sound low, Benny sleeping on the sofa, to catch up on the news. Osama bin Laden tittered across deserts and mountains, beard streaming like a wisp of smoke. Newscasters who were clearly assholes went on and on. He went back up to his computer, and according to the internet, bin Laden was of uncertain age, height, and weight; he had an uncertain number of wives; his money was inherited from his father; his father's wealth was from construction; his father and brother died in separate uncertain plane crashes.

Nobel Prize winner John Nash, whose madness is depicted in 2001's Academy Award–winning *A Beautiful Mind*, designed a series of games based on theories about predictability in poker that presumed rational behavior dictated by self-interest—including one called "Fuck You Buddy," which is hilarious. Based on these games, popular psychiatrist R. D. Laing theorized that as long as players behaved in their own self-interest, a state of equilibrium would be reached. Known at the time as Nash equilibrium, when applied to the larger culture, it suggested that *stability* requires constant suspicion of other people. This concept crossed the father's mind more than once over the years, as his marriage deteriorated, as his daughter went mad, and as he watched *Survivor*, where people are always freaking out and trusting each other for no reason. When Adeline developed an interest in tarot, he'd thought about *cultural climate* as what's in the air when a child comes into the world. According to R. D. Laing, Bertrand Russell once remarked that the stars are in one's brain. The stars, as described by Laing extending Bertrand Russell, were no more or less in his brain than the stars as he imagined them. To paraphrase: The relation of experience to behavior was not that of inner to outer. His experience was not inside his head. Stars were not in his head. Stars as he imagined them were not in his head. His experience of the room was out there in the room. To say that his experience was intrapsychic would be to presuppose that there was a psyche that his experience was in. His psyche was his experience, his experience his psyche. Many people (Laing continued) used to believe that angels moved the stars. It now appears to many that they do not move stars. As a result of this and similar revelations, many people, like him, do not now believe in angels. The girls' mother had discovered upon reading philosophy, becoming an atheist, and losing her guardian angel that a guardian angel no longer existing does not mean that a guardian angel never existed. The window in the father's study afforded a better access to dark sky and stars than most people have, but still, because of the Anthropocene, you could only kind of see them, yet you were sure they were there because they always had been. He remembered sitting at the bedside of his baby, who was of his body, and her blue belly button. He looked up "ether," as in *what's in the ether*, on the internet.

When he looked at his daughter, he had to wonder what had come from him. He felt that his wife had history *in* her body, and that history came *at* him from all directions. His father had been in the war: married his mother, shipped out, and they both stayed true. They were not nice people, but they were not unusual. They lived in one of the first planned communities for families just like them. People do terrible things to people all the time and to children everywhere. As terrible as you can imagine, they do it. His was a childhood in the age of the Skinner box. Most of his family was killed in the Holocaust. In a passage from Elie Wiesel, soldiers tossed babies into the air to shoot like skeet.

He'd been to protests with his wife when they were students. On the internet, he poked around archives he found from that era, and paused on this poster from 1968:

The silence of the *jeunesse*, the bandage gag, the diaper pin, her target eyes spiraled through time, from his own youth to Adeline. A rough translation is *a youth that the future too often unnerves*, which was not what the internet translation robot came up with, which he knew could not be right.

At Ad's bedside at the hospital when she was dead, he'd told her a joke. He did not remember any other language being present for him during that time. Sound was there. Smell was there. Light was there. He told the joke because it came into his head formed. He must have said it aloud. He didn't remember actually saying it. It was a terrible joke. In his study he tried to remember what the words must have felt like in his mouth and throat, but he couldn't tell the difference between what he might be remembering and what he could feel now, in his study, as he said a sample word into the air. He said "baby" and felt it vibrate his mouth, maybe a little in his throat.

"Grosser than ten dead babies in a barrel is one dead baby in ten." That was the joke. And then her hand moved, and he told a nurse, and he was afraid that she was still dead, just moving, and afraid that she was alive and inaccessible. He thought he could feel her synapses leap and make contact.

A unit of time occurred between when her hand moved and a new reality of her being alive in which the difference between a watermelon and a dead baby is that a dead baby floats. Jokes appeared as if he'd accessed them with a new sense—sixth?—seventh? Medical personnel and family members were around and not around, though everything remained astonishingly quiet, notes taken for charts, adjustments made to machines, the reading of vitals, the difference between a dead baby and an onion is you don't cry when you chop up a dead baby. It was as if the jokes appeared to sustain the change, or to sustain him in it, a sacred state of terror and bedazzlement, a formal compression of the space between things, diamond from dirt, narrative poles of death and life, where the difference between a baby and a bagel is you can put a bagel in the toaster but you have to put the baby in the oven. What about a bun? A baby on a stick is a kebabie. A preemie is an appetizer. You can get a dead baby out of a blender with either Doritos or a straw. Vegetarian ogres eat Cabbage Patch kids. The difference between a bucket of gravel and a bucket of baby is you can't gargle gravel. The difference between a dead baby and a styrofoam cup is a dead baby doesn't harm the atmosphere when you burn it. A good reason to put a baby in a blender feet first is you can see the expression on its face. In his study, with the memory of the blue room, he understood himself to have been looking down the throat of his country. He was in its kitchen, its carport, its yard shooting the shit. A baby with no arms and no legs hanging on your wall is Art. A dead baby with no arms and no legs lying on the beach is Sandy. A dead baby with no arms and no legs lying on your porch is Matt. The dead baby fell off the swing because it had no arms and no legs. What has four legs and one arm is a Doberman in a playground. The difference between a pile of bowling balls and a pile of dead babies is you can't use a pitchfork to move bowling balls. The difference between a dead baby and a tree is one is legal to hit with an ax. The difference between a lamp and a dead baby is it's really easy to turn on a lamp. More fun than strapping a baby to a clothesline and spinning it around superfast is stopping it with a shovel. Worse than a dead baby in a trash can lid is a trash can lid in a dead baby. Worse than smoking pot with a baby is making a bong out of the baby. Funnier than a dead baby is a dead baby in a clown outfit sitting next to a retarded baby. You can get a baby out of a tree by giving a Mexican a stick and telling him it's a piñata. The difference between a Cadillac and a pile of dead babies is I don't have a Cadillac in my garage. How people say, *our way of life*. Worse than finding a dead baby on your pillow in the morning is having fucked it when you were drunk the night before. He understood the babies to be pink and genderless. He understood them as a dirge of babies.

What's grosser than gross is a garbage can full of dead babies and grosser than that is the bottom one's alive and grosser than that is he eats himself to freedom and grosser than that is he goes back for more. Harder than nailing a baby to a tree is nailing a baby to a puppy. Sicker than driving over a baby is skidding. To change a tire it takes two babies: one to prop up the car and one to replace it in case it explodes. At her bedside and in the waiting room they must not have been aloud, but they felt aloud. Or he moved his lips and no one was bothered because he was the father, he was probably praying. Or no one noticed because who was noticing the father when his daughter had come back to life? Sometimes they didn't seem to be words in a row, just pure iteration, just access to the knowledge of the existence of a field of these jokes alive in the ether. It's difficult to tell how many babies it takes to paint a house because it depends on how hard you throw them. The dead baby crossed the road stapled to the chicken. The dead baby crossed the road chained to my bumper. The way to stop a baby crawling round in circles is nail the other hand to the floor. Babies and old people are both fun to throw from moving cars. The way to make a dead baby float is two scoops of dead baby in a glass of root beer. Or take your foot off its head. If you want to spoil a baby leave it out in the sun. The toddler dropped its lollipop when it was hit by a truck. You know the baby is dead because the dog plays with it more. The babies had a life of their own. The babies mantled and dismantled. The babies moved in and out of the jokes, figuring and reflecting, real and unreal. What you call a dead baby with its skin peeled off is sexy. The best thing about Siamese twin babies is threesomes. A dead baby with no arms and no legs in the middle of the ocean is fucked. Worse than fucking a dead baby is fucking a dead baby filled with razor blades. Use a coat hanger to prevent a baby from exploding in the microwave. When you cut a baby with a straight razor you get an erection. Most sexless when fucked to death, most white when hate-crimed, words floated far from their makers, hairless and pure. When you burn a baby's face off it makes weird noises and crawls into walls. A bum calls a baby in a dumpster a freeloader. If a tree falls on a baby in the forest and no one is around to hear it, it is still hilarious. The best time to bury that baby you killed is when it starts talking to you again. The way to get a baby to run faster is chase it with the lawn mower. There's always hot water at childbirth so in case of still-birth you can make soup. Babies have a soft spot on their head so you can pick them up five at a time. What's small, shiny, and blue is a baby with a plastic bag over its head. A baby playing in a plastic bag thrashes about on the floor. A blind, deaf, quadriplegic baby can get cancer for Christmas. A homesick abortion is red and creeps up your leg. Four and a half dead babies can fit in a barrel. What wiggles, spits, and is covered in shit is an inside-out baby. A baby chewing on razor blades is pink and red in a pile in a corner. Green and sitting in a corner is the same baby, six weeks later. A baby in a casserole is brown and gurgles. A peeled baby in a bag of salt is purple, covered in pus and squeals. *Plop, plop, fizz, fizz* go twins in an acid bath. Small and red and full of holes is a baby on a bed of nails. Pink and red and silver and crawling into walls is a baby with forks in its eyes. Pink and chunky is a baby with leprosy. Pink and spitting is a baby in a frying pan. What you get when you fuck a pregnant woman is a baby with a black eye. White and bobbing in a baby's crib are the asses of pedophiles. Bright and sizzling is the baby nursing an electrical outlet. A baby combing its hair with a potato peeler sits in the kitchen getting smaller and smaller. A baby playing with a chainsaw is red in four corners of the room. A baby on a barbecue is red and dances all around. A baby with a punctured lung is blue and flies around the room at high speeds. What gets louder as it gets smaller is a baby in a trash compactor. Revenge is a baby with a dog in its mouth. Shot through a snowblower is a baby: white and red, and hanging from a telephone wire like a million shoes. A baby of color and light is incantation. The dead baby came alive and died again, then came alive. Jokes moved through the father as Adeline came back to life.

    In his study, he found a website that was an archive of dead baby jokes among archives of other kinds of jokes. He knew where they had come from in his life—a few of these jokes—from a drunken night with other promising mathematicians in graduate school outdoing one another. In the dorms, he had not been able to contribute a single one—they were all new to him. The feeling of being unable to contribute to the game was a layer of the horror of the jokes, and over the years, if one of them popped its head up he swatted it away. He was with Ad in the hospital room when she spoke again. Her voice surprised him, because it didn't sound hoarse. It was her voice as it had been before her death.

She said, "Why didn't you let me stay?"

The father went down the placeholder stairs to look again for his Bobby Fischer book (maybe someone had shelved it?). Chess is not, according to aficionados, about math, it's about memory. Em, as a kid, refused to learn, would not think ahead. Adeline played and wanted to learn, but it didn't stick. Mostly the girls liked to use the captured pieces for dolls, which they were allowed to do, but not to take the pieces out of the room. He remembered explaining that the pieces could come back from being captured in extraordinary circumstances, they were not dead, and needed to stay nearby for the game. Bobby Fischer had three beds in his apartment. Beside each bed was a chessboard, and he slept in the beds in rotation. Bobby Fischer fantasized for *Harper's* about what he'd do after he won the world championship: "I'll build me a house. Maybe I'll build it in Hong Kong. Everybody who's been there says it's great. And they've got suits there, beauties, for only twenty dollars. . . . I got strong ideas about my house. I'm going to hire the best architect and have him build it in the shape of a rook . . . spiral staircases, parapets, everything. I want to live the rest of my life in a house built exactly like a rook." Was Adeline a rook? Was she in a rook?

At the bottom of the stairs, the father saw something glint in the dark. He thought it could be the eyes of a crouching dog—but the dogs were all asleep behind his wife's shut door. Maybe it was a different animal, one from the woods, in the house, glinting. He made a sudden move he thought would scare it, but it didn't move. It just glinted and glinted. Then he thought it could be a ring, and approached it. He felt the excitement of potential discovery, and also the fear of nothing being magic, what it would be like if he got up to the glinting and it was crap, just some shard from the constant construction. But also what if he'd spoken magic words and brought her back from the dead?

What if he just wanted his stupid book about chess, and not a new copy, either. What if he wanted his own broken paperback with his own illegible notes in it and the grubby marks and tears from the sweet fingers and grotesque drippings of decades of his family—

So he pretended he hadn't seen anything glint in the dark. He proceeded into the living room and stood over Benny, who kept sleeping and sleeping. He picked up the gun that lay on its side next to the chessboard. During the day, as their contractor, Benny liked to be all boss. Mister *You tell me your dream for this space I'll take it from there*, Mister *Everything is possible with the will and the know-how*, Mister *I'll just stay here on the couch during these trying times for the family*. What did Benny suppose was going to come into the house at night that he would use that gun? The father thought, Fuck you. He thought, *I'm* the father. He picked the gun up the way you pick up a rodent, and he took it to the front door and flung it toward the woods the way you fling a dead thing that means nothing. He heard the gun go off. Dogs barked from behind the door.

He pictured everyone in the house sitting up in their beds and listening. Adeline, too—he pictured her sitting up in her bed, listening. Even her sister, states away, upright in her bed, listening. Had she heard an alarm? In the distance? A false alarm? Benny muttered and turned over. Dogs settled down. No one called out. The father stood on his own threshold and tried to feel the difference between inside the house and outside the house, inside himself and outside himself. He remembered, when Adeline had come back to life, calling from the hospital and leaving a message at the hotel for the chambermaid who'd found her. "Just tell her—tell her the girl she found is alive." Then he went back upstairs to see if she was still alive.

III. Magic

$ Money $

In your job you like to walk into a situation prepared. You've got a better shot at it here—being prepared—than anywhere else in your life. They send out an agenda, for one. And you can fall back on that job description. When Em followed Frank to the ruins, part of her thought she knew better than him, and part of her hoped he knew better than her. Now Josie looked back from her state and winked. What were they supposed to be in on? In the end, whatever that means, you are on your own, is what Em thought. How people say, *you live as you die.*

"You know what doesn't help? Hospitals," Ad once said, having called with urgent news from her delusions. This was years ago when Em was in love, packing up to move to the desert with her ex. She was surrounded by boxes during the call. Some of the boxes were going into storage, but some were coming in the car to drive across the country with her.

So then, some weeks later, remedicated, "You know what doesn't help? Hospitals. The only way they work is they take everyone's money and you don't have a choice." Em was in the desert still trying to find places for the things from the boxes in a way that would assert her presence without ruining what made the ex think of her home as her home, which was going to turn out not to be possible. The first thing Em felt when she arrived was hurt: the ex had shown her the drawer she'd cleared out, the shelf on a bookcase. "You can put your steamer trunk here," she said, and *here* was the guest room.

"Hospitals never look at the content of your experiences," Ad said. "They only want to *stop* them, they never allow them to *mean* anything." When Em tried to talk this through with the ex, the ex told her a story about a black friend of hers who had a white girlfriend. She called them Black Girlfriend and White Girlfriend through the story for clarity and also with a vaguely ironic tone that Em caught but couldn't parse.

The story went, Black Girlfriend and White Girlfriend were in a very intense graduate program together. White Girlfriend was doing a lot of reading and writing about race, lots of heavy theory for her project—and oh yeah White Girlfriend was German. So they're about five years in, just about ABD, and White Girlfriend starts getting increasingly crazy, that region where maybe crazy, maybe just really into your work, maybe just really stressed out, maybe just learning things that are blowing your mind, revolutionizing your perspective on everything.

On the break between semesters, Black Girlfriend went home to see her family on Hilton Head Island, where everyone was in awful turmoil about deciding whether or not to sell their land going back generations, a family earthquake, chasms of heartbreak every-where, so she wasn't having a lot of contact with White Girlfriend, mostly just "ugh, this is hard, I miss you," "me, too," etc., partly be-cause of the awful turmoil being not so easy or fun to communicate, partly because the opinions of the German family about the gayness and cross-racialness of the relationship were unclear and already an undercurrent in the relationship that they usually just ignored be-cause the continents allowed them to. When she got back to school, White Girlfriend was not there, and she'd expected her to be back. So she calls the house in Germany, and finds out from the creepy mother that she's not coming back because she's had some kind of breakdown. White Girlfriend is in the hospital.

Black Girlfriend calls but she hardly ever gets through (the schedule for when you can call the ward is so confusing, plus the time difference, plus her German is mostly reading German, and even when someone picks up and says, "Yes, yes, I understand perfectly," because Germans all think their English is perfect, she doesn't know if they really do understand because she'll ask whoever picks up to go get White Girlfriend, and usually that person—some other patient—wanders away calling for her with the phone off the hook and no one comes), so she calls, but if she's honest about it she knows she could call more. She just feels like she's talking to White Girlfriend as much as she can handle because even though they're half broken up already, she's confused about her feelings in a lot of areas, even doubting her project on top of it all after spending that time with her family.

So they're on the phone at some point and White Girlfriend says that both her creepy mother *and* her doctor believe she was pushed over the edge by *thinking too hard about race.*

And that's when Em said to the ex, "Wow, that's the reverse of Adeline," and told her about no one caring about the content of her sister's delusions and how she'd just chalked that up to no resources, slap people back together, get them out the door.

The ex said, "Exactly," but Em kept thinking about it and bringing it up.

"Some of Ad's delusions definitely have race in them. I mean they have to, right? We're American."

The ex said, "Sure."

Later, still thinking about it, Em said, "So I guess what we have in common with Europe is the goal of stop thinking when it comes to your health?"

The ex said, "Ha ha."

Later, Em said, "Did the black girlfriend hear that thing—how did you say it? *Being pushed over the edge from thinking about race—*

did she hear that from the white girlfriend when she was still in the hospital, or later on?"

The ex said, "I don't know, does it matter?"

Em said, "I guess I was wondering if she was on or off meds when she said it."

"Like if you should believe her?"

"I don't know, just for the information."

"No such thing as *just information*," said the ex. "You think it matters, so why?"

It may be worth mentioning that Em's ex was, as the ex sometimes put it, "a brown mutt," while Em was, as the ex sometimes put it, "just a faithless Catholic Jew."

In the end, Em lay in bed next to the ex, reading her magazine, remembering Adeline quietly sadly asserting, "Some of the things I experienced are real," and in *that* moment—wherever they'd been—on the phone? In some room in some hospital? Let's just say they were in the woods walking along a pine needle path, passing a stone hand to hand—

In *that* moment, the content of Ad's delusions seemed pretty clear: disconnected from people she loved and longed for, animals and the dead spoke to her, objects in the world told the future.

The road from the disaster at Frank's back to Em's starter home was black and curvy, same as the road out to her parents' house. Em kept pushing the image of Frank's kitchen away, but it was only replaced with her mother's kitchen. Both rooms had big square tables, though Frank's was neat and her mother's was covered with things and clogged with dust. All along the curving road, Josie remained, in Em's mind, on the kitchen floor. Low afternoon sun poked dramatic holes through fluffed-out clouds. Frank, one knee on the floor next to Josie, kept reaching up for the mustard-colored phone. Em kept feeling herself in his body reaching toward where she'd been in the doorway, holding the headset out to him. Within the shapes were feelings. Like, put your hands up—you feel that. Even in Frank's body, she felt uselessness, *the kitchen is such a mess*, and right at the moment she had herself approaching Josie with a bucket, lowering herself to a knee, submerging a giant yellow sponge, raising the sponge, soap gushing down her arm backward into her shirtsleeve—she hit a wet patch in the road, and the road did exactly what her father always warned it would, oil rising to the surface of the pavement, and the car slipped out of her hands, hydroplaning over the shoulder into a ditch. It turned over once and landed right side up with a lush vine wrapped around its antenna. The door flopped open and Em got out after a brief struggle with the button on her seat belt. Her loafers sank into marshy earth. The image of her sister was her sister spotlit in a white nightgown floating over a tiny bed with her limbs floaty, the gown floaty, is there or is there not a man in the shadows in tacky formalwear conducting.

A noise came out of her. If she were a creature in the throes of true powerlessness, the sound would pierce with its emotional clarity, but Em was a just crumpled-up person at a still relatively safe distance, so it was not much of a sound. Anyone alive in the car would never hear it, but Em felt it come out of her and then heard it outside of her, coming back. She connected it with Jack. It was not the guiseless noise he'd made, but it was something—a sign of a new phase, of coming into it. I don't know why one thing becomes another, only that it does, and you can look back and see how, and you can look back and see how another way. If it's not predictive, what does it mean. If it's not predictive enough to control, what does it mean. If it is predictive enough to see yourself in relation to others, is that something. If it's a better understanding of one person in one situation with more contingencies than can be beheld, can there be some fruitful comparison, is that something, or what if you just leave it alone, what if I leave it alone, a song anyone could sing, even someone like Em, in a vacant lot in a half-built and possibly abandoned development, houses wrapped in Tyvek. Stalks and husks of crops were still strewn along the earthy border, what was left of a field. She wondered if she could use her Nokia to call for a tow, if 411 still existed, but instead she got her never-out-of-its-case-except-to-see-if-it-really-had-all-that-stuff (yes it did) Leatherman from her glove compartment and took the license plates off the car, an old Toyota. She fanned the flat wrenches of the Leatherman and one fit the plate bolts perfectly. Here's a cheer for standardization. The grass in the field was high enough that when a breeze went through, she could hear it, and it made the houses, one after another into the distance, seem even more inert. She had never been able to skip a rock, and had no hope that she could throw the plate any distance, but man, she thought, wouldn't that feel good, license plate skimming over the field and then smashing right through the stillborn eye of one of those piece-of-shit houses? Then she remembered about VINs, so she just tossed the plates into the ditch, climbed back up to the road, and walked until she felt disassociated from the car, which happened the moment the pavement was dry.

Behind her, the car was a blotch of red in a slant of light. She wore a black knit skirt with pockets that sagged lumpily with anything in them, a blue blouse, an ivory cardigan, knee socks, and the loafers. Little thorns and round leaves from Frank's hedges burrowed in the fabrics among smudges from any number of places dirt comes from, plus now a little blood from a scrape on her brow. She came around a curve and there was a defunct country gas station with a phone booth and a ragged phone book dangling between plastic covers. A bench. Tin sign for Coke. The big plastic sign that would have a yellow scallop or a red winged horse was missing above the tanks. She flipped through the phone book for the number for a cab and called it with her phone, walked along the road until the cab caught up to her and stopped for her, which was a little magic that she didn't even notice, though she felt a small surge of freedom when the driver whose face she never saw said, "Where to?"—that she could say anything and put it on a credit card and then toss the credit card out the window. Like a can, she thought. But backward. She memorized the surge, hoping she could call upon it later. Then she started to cry and told him her address. Thank god he was not an advice-giving cab driver. Brown back of his head.

The taxi pulled up to Em's adorable house. The driver said, "No machine," so Em paid in cash, cut across her yard past the young tree to the back door, went in, and did not press play when she saw the tiny red bulb blinking. She took a shower, drank half a bottle of wine, went to bed, and in the morning got up and put on clean clothes, walked up the hill to the good job, tie-swinging pencil breakers, anemic personhood parade, truncated potentials and potencies, Mac the sack, Pauline the mean, tromped up the stairs, down the crappy hall, opened the lurking door, hung her whatever on the coatrack, pulled the chain on her banker's lamp, which shocked her because she had forgotten to pull the edge of her sleeve over her wrist to defuse it, stupid cosmic ventilation fuckup, the stairwells always damp and the offices always dry, no relation to actual weather, and holy shit, her crap computer was gone. She stuck her head into the hall and looked up and down it as if she'd catch the thief. There went the carpet, rolling along. She knocked on Magda's door, sexy retro Magda—not home—then went knocking on doors down the hall. She pulled the phone from her pocket. Nothing wrong with the time. Tried to remember if the light was right, walking up the hill, and had traffic been normal? She could not remember the state of the sky or the contents of the parking lot. She'd awakened hungry, but not *abnormally* hungry, not you-passed-out-for-a-month hungry or whatever it would take for things to come to this.

What had that meeting been about anyway? She remembered a storm of people's heads and office supplies. She remembered croissants.

What could have happened *overnight*? Approaching Josie with a giant yellow sponge. Oil rising to the surface of pavement. Car slipping out of her hands.

Now here came her office—one doorknob after another as if moving through time, and then her door. Inside she saw that the pink leaf from a triplicate floated on the desk where the computer had been. It turned out to be a real live pink slip, and it came paper-clipped to a memo on xeroxed letterhead. The company had been sold for scrap, there'd be a severance check in her box if she didn't have direct deposit. Was that possible? It did not seem possible. There it was in writing, whatever that means. Evidence. She glanced around her office as if it might look sold. The writing did match the situation of no one around, not the weekend, and a couple of checks. The date on the memo made sense to her. Yesterday. What must have happened did not. Back in the hallway, clutching her leaf, she tried to imagine *collapse*, but here the building was, surrounding her, damp then dry then damp, quiet with occasional slaps of her feet down the stairs, the door closing behind her with a *hush* followed by *bang*. She strode purposefully and, along another hall and then through the cubical sea, down more stairs to the copy room and her mailbox, she imagined the building collapsing behind her with the sound off. There would be a stack of three mail-order DVDs for her at her house. Outside the mail room was a large black-and-white photographic portrait of a guy who might have been a donor for the building, the architect of the building, or the founder of the company, from the '50s, looking mild, feeling excellent. If a pack of twenty-year-old artsy drifters from Berlin came across this place, could they turn it into a dance club? People are so inventive with paint and everything. Was it possible for her place of work to have been so wholly extinguished so suddenly? But she missed so much. Anything could be—well, maybe not anything—well, what did she know about the possible.

Most of the mailboxes were empty, but her pigeonhole had an envelope in it. Along with a paycheck, prorated plus severance for a total of just about $5,000, was a folded sheet of paper with an invitation to *Everyone!* from Irene for a Saturday BBQ at her apartment complex. Now it would be some kind of wake. Em scanned the other boxes, and it appeared that only Frank, Barb on maternity, and "Max Regal," whoever that was, had failed to pick up their mail. Em had been to one of Irene's BBQs, arrived late and left as quickly as possible. Five thousand dollars was more money than Em had ever held in her hands, and holding a check feels pretty close to holding money when normally you have direct deposit to your bank followed by direct deposit to whoever holds your mortgage. She looked at the number. It stumped her. What does $5,000 mean?

She took a different set of stairs up, as she often did for the minor amusement of changing her route. When the stairwell dumped her into the hall she encountered the custodian coming toward her in baggy green coveralls with his cart and a wheeled mop bucket. The cart was piled with computers. When he saw her, he stopped the cart with his boot and grinned. He had narrow teeth.

"Headed to storage," he said, before she could accuse him of anything. He patted the hand-sized ring of keys at his hip. "Security."

"Yeah, that's a real handful," said Em. "I mean, of keys."

"Just me. Last man standing."

"Yeah," said Em. "Except now there's me."

"You know what will be living a million years after the nuclear bomb?"

"I hear roaches?" she guessed. He narrowed his eyes even narrower. "Yeah."

"So you're a roach, is what you're saying? We're roaches, you and me?"

"What?" he said. "I'm keeping on for a week. I've got some seniority. Doing the once-over." He took a fat green sponge out of the cart and gave a squeeze, then put it back and grasped the handle of the mop. She knew a version of that sponge.

"Was there embezzlement?"

He peered at her, deciding whether he could trust her, or maybe just peered. "Only in the end," he said.

"How do you know that?"

"Everyone knows."

"Everyone's at Irene's." It didn't make any sense to say it, it was just association, he wouldn't know the difference. He didn't even have a pigeonhole. "Do you know what's happening with the building?" Em asked. "Do you think they'll sell it or demolish it?"

"My guess? It'll sit here for rats and vagrants to move in," he said.

"With the roaches," she said. "Good thing you're cleaning it up."

He remained implacable. She almost produced a follow-up question but then stopped. She hadn't wanted to know the details when the company was alive and she didn't want to know the details now that it was dead, didn't have room for it, didn't want the information shaping her.

"Did you get a check?" Em asked, holding hers up as a visual aid.

He nodded. Narrow everything.

"Hey, maybe your ticket to ride! You could start your business, *The Final Solution*?" she said. Maybe he didn't remember telling her about his business plan. It surprised her, in fact, that she remembered it. Absently, the custodian revved the cart handle with one hand. His other hand clutched the handle of the mop leaning out of its bucket. That reminded her of something she couldn't place. She didn't want him to leave.

"Is this building hard to clean?" she asked.

He said, "What?" It wasn't clear if he didn't understand the question or if he was insulted, but she was definitely annoying him.

"I mean such crappy materials—" She used her toe to peel back the rubber bumper that was coming unglued from where the wall met the carpet. When she released it they both watched it very slowly but not completely return to its place. She touched the slick paint on the spray-textured wall. "When I was a kid there was this book," she said. "All the kids loved it, but I hated it except for the part when someone had to take an eyedropper and use it to move an ocean from one place to another. I liked that part a lot."

"You can't do that."

"Exactly. I must have felt validated because I used to take a stick and pretend to vacuum the woods behind the house."

He said, "I'm not a big reader." Something moved across his face, pain or an itch, but she wasn't done. Her voice had become stupidly loud. "This paint—you're really only supposed to use it on trim. It's so plasticky. Feel that—is that grease or humidity? It's both, right? That's disgusting. Feel it." He made a move to orient the mop bucket for departure. "What was it like here yesterday?" she asked. She realized that the way she was holding her hand could look like she was feeling for drops of rain.

"Yesterday was like this," he said.

"Was it just crazy in here? Were people just *losing* it?"

He shrugged. Em thought he was lying, drawing a line in the sand. He did not appear to have any eyelashes. She thought, I bet he really is stealing those computers.

"Clear your office," he said. "Anything you don't want, leave. Truck's coming." Then he shoved off with the precarious cart making metal and plastic noises down the hall, around the corner, past another stairwell that led to another tower that held an elevator. He had not used the mop to push the mop bucket along, he'd just held on to the mop handle and let its soggy end drag along behind him, leaving the bucket in the hall like something else that reminded her of something. A suitcase, she realized, when for a second she expected it to explode. She flipped on the fluorescent overheads in her office and looked into her wastepaper basket to see if she recognized everything in it. She knew she was looking for sperm.

She snuck her sleeves over her hands to discharge static while going over her personal items. Her Van Gogh coffee mug had gotten into the file drawer with her gallon of water and slid around in there on the ziplock bag containing three bent tampons. Maybe she wanted the coatrack. There was the ancient telephone. The morning of the catfight—before the catfight—she'd sat up in her own bed after weeks with the motel bed, taking in the familiar things that her bedroom housed. The bedclothes, the lamp, the way light fell at that time of day in that season, the way the wall could use a coat of paint but nothing urgent—they were *hers*, and she fell for it: feeling at home with herself. Then she went downstairs to do her cereal thing, but there was no milk, no milk gone bad, either— someone had discarded it—and then cats were fighting on her stoop. Her stomach was sore from crying. She'd thought, I should not have left. I've made a terrible mistake. Not like she'd come up with some way to solve problems by clinging to the railings of her sister's hospital bed as if that's what they were there for. Handles. Loved-one handles.

Sheila, she realized in the fluorescent light. Sheila had discarded the milk when she came by for the mail, and now, Em was sure, now she'd be dealing with the whole mess of dead or not dead Josie—police, coffee in styrofoam, official forms—not to mention sudden knowledge of her brother's gayness or whatever it was while she ran around taking care of everything for him, scatterbrained yet *on it*, because this was Frank's mess and she was that kind of person, that kind of sister. Sheila was going to be very busy with people materializing in her consciousness as she notified them of this terrible news. She'd be on the phone with Josie's mother the comic actor, her father whatever he was. Sheila was going to clean the remaining blood from the kitchen floor and decide whether to throw away that good knife, put it back in its drawer, or donate it to a thrift shop that benefited the infirm. She'd ask Frank what to do about Jack Bell, and Frank would be so fucked up Sheila would have to decide for herself about Jack Bell. This stranger. And if he hadn't disappeared, when she tracked him down, she'd likely find him suicidal enough for a hospital to take him. She'd likely have to dump him at one.

I could call Frank, Em thought. *Hey Frank, want me to pick up your check?* She picked up the receiver, held it to her ear, dead already in sudden efficiency. *So, speaking of money, I mean speaking of severance, how's Josie? Dead? Not dead?* Impossible. She could feel the lost part of losing her job, the paycheck part, the part where you have to be somewhere and if you're not it's a problem, but then the loss transformed into a surge, a taxi driver saying, "Where to?"

Em pulled her key ring from her pocket and tossed the car key into the wastepaper basket. She tossed the office key into it, too, but then took it back out and put the office key back on the ring with the keys to her house. Closed her hand around them so the keys stuck out between her fingers, which is how keys can be a weapon. Asked herself if she felt armed. Put the keys in her pocket again. She snatched Frank's check and party invitation from the mail room on the way out. A truck had indeed pulled up. The custodian and a couple of other guys were loading it with office furniture, electronics, a Xerox machine, and several plastic potted trees. It was not an official-looking truck, just a long-bed pickup with nothing painted on the side. Employees or criminal masterminds, so hard to tell. She went back up to her office, got her coatrack, and carried it like a guitar down the hill. In her living room, she set it near the window that looked onto the smaller hill in her yard with the young tree on it. Because of her angle, the tree appeared to be exactly the same distance from her house as from the neighbors' house across the street. Those people were so uptight they were uptight about *garbage*. Em kicked her shoes off and left them at the base of the coatrack, got a glass of wine, sat in her chair, and read the letter that came with her check. It was midafternoon. Soon it would be however many hours, days, since Josie had, whatever, fallen. In the letter, every few phrases came a numbered reference to employee contracts and handbooks, and by the end of the letter Em was reasonably convinced that if she looked up these passages and assembled them properly she would understand the terms of her employment and how it had come to be over. She understood that her contract, which was so long she'd never read it, or her handbook, which was so long she'd never opened it, would explain everything that she should have known all along. The documents were also available online if you typed in this enormous address. She was made aware that any possible class action situations would be handled in case-by-case arbitration as per what they'd all signed upon arrival when all you're thinking is what could possibly be in this document that could make me not need this job. Following praise for the integrity with which they all performed their sensitive and important duties (Em pushed down a burgeoning fury by reading *harder*) was reference to a company-wide meeting that had, apparently, been held by convening small alphabetical groups in the conference rooms because there was no single room in the building in which large groups could assemble, the large areas being taken up by cubicles.

The humor of office memos is well documented. The letter concluded with thanks to everyone for their grace and professionalism in the difficult alphabetical meetings and then Em looked around. Now what. She compared the coatrack, which had ended up next to the living room window, to the tree outside. The tree had a good number of leaves. She took out a piece of paper and wrote "Free" on it. She stuck it on the coatrack by stabbing the paper with one of the branching prongs. That almost made it a hatrack, but not quite. Then she took it outside and set it on the sidewalk. The "For Sale" sign in her neighbor's yard had tilted so she went over and stood it upright. She gave it a pat, went back inside, and returned to her chair, trying to decide how she wanted to handle Frank's check. She kept an eye on the coatrack as she drank the wine and watched out the window to see what would happen next.

House pets can do this all day.

Maybe the neighbors would come out and shake their fists.

Money. It just makes you want to lord it over people.

What does $5,000 mean? What is it good for, what use is it, what could it *do*? If a CEO at a top corporation makes three hundred times what a person with her kind of job makes—made—suppose her halfwit company was only half that bad, and suppose Frank was, like half a CEO, okay, give him a third, give him a third of a third. Point being, any of that would be a pretty big check. Frank would have negotiated for severance at time of hire. His check would be something that could do something like actually pay for a pretty nice hospital for any number of comorbidities for an amount of time that might mean something. Of course, she hadn't negotiated anything. So what was her check supposed to be? Hush money, she thought.

She got up for a refill.

On her way back she rounded the corner through the arch to the living room, and saw that the coatrack was gone. She let out a little noise, a kind of squeak, ran to the door, flung it open, looked down the street—and saw the back of a person in yellow pants trotting lightly away down the block with prongs high. Just before the person disappeared around the corner, the person, at the apex of a step that was so light it was more leap than step, glanced back. She appeared to be a woman, and she had soft brown hair that levitated as she descended. At that same moment the industrious old lady can collector appeared at the corner in her yellow pants with her arms outstretched. The young woman rose into another leap, raised the coatrack like a torch, released it, and in the moment the coatrack was in the air, its prongs became antlers, and then in the moment the can lady caught it—snatched it from the air—*that* moment—it was just a coatrack again, both women scurried away, and then the street was empty.

The "Free" sign had fallen off along the way, and from her doorway Em could see it, halfway down the block, rise and then settle on the pavement as a plane in space. She felt a shiver of undeserved happiness, and that just made her want to finish getting drunk.

Even alone in the house Em would keep it together and try not to act drunk. All the universe but for a soft tunnel vision fuzzed out, and she could set herself to the essential tasks of walking from one room to another, dragging her clothes on and off, not losing or breaking her glass. Time was an imaginary airplane that carries you at sunset. In her airplane, Em turned the radio on, low. Protesters in Hong Kong demonstrated outside a shop selling Apple products. She let apple pies turn in diner cases for the tiniest second before they resolved into machines. A distant bullhorn condemned the company and its suppliers for a spate of suicides. A cartoon princess lay in a coffin in the woods, childhood when death is just a chunk of white fruit like a frog in the throat. She leaned over Josie like a prince. Eleven factory workers had killed themselves so far that year, and four more, officially, had tried. Apple remained silent but the supplier announced a pay raise. The phone rang, and Em let the machine pick up. It was Sheila. The machine let out a whine and then her voice came through.

"Hello, this is Sheila. Where could you be? I hope you are not going to work. I hope you are taking care of yourself. Are you sleeping?

Maybe you've gone to be with your family. That would be natural. If there's anything I can do, be sure to let me know. I'm here for you." Em wrenched herself out of the chair and stood over the machine, took a fork from the drying rack to lift the plastic cover of the cassette, and pulled it out. It caught and she had to tear the tape. On that tape were piles of condolences and probably the video store and the dry cleaner, *return our stuff, pick up your stuff*. She wound the loose tape around the housing, put it in her sweater pocket, and tapped it with her hand a few times. She called Sheila back.

"Oh, it's you, it's you," Sheila said.

Em said, "So is Josie dead, or what exactly?"

"Gone, gone. They came in the ambulance and it left with no lights on."

Em winced at the rhyme and could not, would not, register the content. She told Sheila about the pink slips. "When I took Frank's envelope I think I forgot I wrecked my car," she concluded.

Sheila said, "Okay, okay, just hold on to it until I see you."

Em said, "What do you mean, 'okay, okay'? I'm not a child. I'll put it in my mailbox. You can pick it up whenever. You can pick it up at your convenience." She said *convenience* like an accusation. She said it the way Ad would say it, the way she had, in fact, said it, ". . . so I'm a little *inconvenient*!"

She might not have been sensitive to the extra sheet of pain in Sheila's voice after that. Also, she kept tapping the cassette in her sweater pocket, and finally thought, it's broken, I should just put it in the garbage—so she did. Sheila went along describing errands she was running for everyone, which meant Em had been right in spirit, the way she'd pictured her with the blood and everything. But being right was not remarkable to her, this time, the way being right about Jack had been in the ruins with Frank, which verged on magic even in memory. This was frustrating, mundane. It was just sad. *Insight* is the medical term for when a mad person understands herself as mad.

Down the counter, the radio made a report from a new aftermath, always taking you to the scene. She shut it all the way off. Sheila's voice was comforting even with the hurt in it. "Do you know how hard they make it to cancel a dating service? I can't even tell you. And I can't even tell you—the *bureaucracy* around an accident like this—" Frank was going to care about losing his job, she thought, even with a fat check. A guy like that would care, right? She did not want to face whatever wound that severance would make. Feeling for a person who'd sat in a plaid chair through the night at her bedside, yet holding back vindictive cartoon sniggers at his loss. Or had he been transformed by madness into a person who didn't feel loss or fear for something like a job? Even a month ago, she'd have been able to tamp down the contradictions. Now she thought, I bet I can get Sheila to break the news, and wondered why she'd worried at all. Of course Sheila would tell him. She'd pick up the check and she'd give it to him. Em didn't have to prepare for any of his feelings. She'd put the check in the mailbox. She didn't really have to do anything she hadn't already done.

"You dumped my milk," she interrupted.

Sheila said, "It was past the date."

"You can give me my key back," Em said. She did feel the utter lousiness of everything coming out of her mouth. Comforting, familiar, domestic obscenity. She knew what she actually wanted to say—she wanted to talk about the young woman in yellow pants tossing the coatrack to the old woman in yellow pants, and what had happened in midair to that silver-pronged object, and she wanted to talk about the nature of antlers, layers of living and not living. But who did she think Sheila was—Josie?

"You know what you are, Sheila?" she said, softening her tone as if apologetically. "A fixer-upper." She knew Sheila would take it as nice if there was even a chance that it could be nice.

"I suppose I am," Sheila said, so Em was right again.

Sheila described a form that required a signature from the deceased. She said she was sure Frank would love to see her and if she would like to come over, there was casserole. She said, *support one another in trying times.* Em kept making the little phone noises of hearing and listening, of being about to break in but letting someone finish, and when Sheila said *from the deceased*, Em just thought of Ad, who she knew was no longer dead, so it was a kind of *stab-unstab* feeling, and if Sheila heard these noises as more than amplified background interference, she ignored them, a crying person recognizing a drunk person for what she is—remote, i.e., unavailable, i.e., useless.

After her best lousy effort at a polite hang-up, Em proceeded to the sofa and watched most of a movie during which a doctor resignedly lifted the paddles of the heart-shocker machine from the body and said, "Call it," meaning, "Call it death." This after *not* calling it for the whole emergency room scene. "Call it," a nurse had said. "It's over, you have to call it!" and the doctor could not, he could not bear to call it because his heart was overrun despite all he knew. But in order to end the scene he had to say the magic word, and that is death.

She fell asleep that night to a breeze that came through the half-open window by her bed. It carried a scent that some notorious flowers have, a tricky garbagy sweetness that is a phase of rot. Overnight, it coalesced with her mind returning to Jack coming into her house like a hunting dog, trailing his own scent, and how when you smell someone you are ingesting him because smell is the particles of what smells. Facts. Great. The next day, she was still in bed, letting the sweeping motion of her mind fade, when the doorbell rang. She opened it to an enormous basket of fruit wrapped in plastic.

"Let me see that card," she said to the delivery guy. The gift was so huge she could not see his head. It was from Sheila, and the key was enclosed. "Fuck," she said, and left him there while she grabbed Frank's check from the kitchen and ran it out to the mailbox where she'd forgotten to put it. The delivery guy just laughed, standing on the front stoop as she darted across the lawn and back, the gift swaying above his legs in their uniform. He carried it into the house for her and set it on the table. She took in his face as she signed for it. An easy, open face.

She said, "But what if I hadn't been home?"

He said, "But you are!" and his voice rang through the house.

When he left, she realized she'd liked him, she'd gotten something like a *good vibe* off the guy, and when he left, she felt his absence. She looked around. It was really a house that had been appointed with a spare hand. The white basket piled with fruit was garish and monumental in it. In the days that followed, she'd catch it in her periphery and spook. She gave it a wide berth, but felt she had to live with it.

Without work, she sat in one room and then another through the day. In a way, she was waiting for something to come to her. In a way, she wanted to call her family, but she'd only just left them, and now there was even more emptiness. She didn't want to tell them about the car or the job and she didn't want to evade explaining, either. She thought, this is when a person would take care of things around the house while they were looking for a new job. New washer for a sink. New window screen where a cat clawed one. Put a picture in a frame and hang it. A person would *nest*. She thanked god she wrecked her car or she'd have to go to a home improvement warehouse. Within a week she'd eaten through the food in the freezer and done what she could with rice, olive oil, and condiments. She'd taken the plastic off the fruit, which shone with wax and had no smell at all, but she had not eaten it. She understood that the fruit was food, and that her body was in all likelihood craving nutrition, but she'd look at it and think, there's that gift, instead of thinking, I could eat that. She used up a jar of capers for perhaps the first time in her life. She used up all three kinds of mustard, almost for the hell of it. She finished the alcohol in the house, including plain Drambuie on ice. She thought, in a terrible Russian accent, everything must go, and still didn't eat the fruit. She watched the three mail-order DVDs and sent them back, flag up on the mailbox. She watched the three videos she had out from the strip-mall video store, including the one she'd watched before the hospital, and leaned them, in their alluring cases, on the windowsill by the back door—the way she used to, she thought, back when she did things like run errands.

In her bed at night, Em listed the things visible in each of the rooms of her home because there was a clear end to the list, it was like counting down. Then if she had not blasted off into sleep she'd list the things *inside* the visible things, and if she still could not sleep she'd place the things from the lists into their places in the last place she lived, sort the things that had been there from the ones that were gone now. If she still could not sleep she lingered on each long-lost drawer and the sound of its pull, knocking, moving backward through the songs made by toilets flushing in one rental before another. It was almost impossible not to be asleep before she got all the way back to high school and stepped into her mother's house as it had been when she lived there, four simple rooms not unlike the ones she lived in now, except that in this one, her own house, almost nothing disturbed the surfaces.

After a night of trying to tear her mind away from carpet fibers in the swank hotel blowing up huge in her sister's dead eyes, and a day of trying to block the image with television via whatever bits of PBS came through the bunny ears, Em's father called. He said that he and her mother both had cell phones now, and gave her the numbers. Then he relayed a scene from the hospital in which experts explained Adeline in terms of drowning. She'd drowned chemically, and a drowned body is not dead until it is warm and dead. The chemicals kept her cold in a way the experts took for dead, and the weekend on life support inadvertently warmed her. Good thing, said the experts, so lucky. In her galley kitchen, on her white cordless, after the dinner of bouillon cubes she'd eaten, the image of Ad was the outside of Ad's body translucent like a shell and you could see symbols for the chemical elements that made up her existence clustered into the shapes of her inner workings and color-coded in a way that began to resemble a digital depiction of a pile of fruit. Now she was out of clinical danger. It was time for her release. Family should get on the horn for a long-term facility. There might be special programs in an area. Many innovations in development every day made it a good time in history to have this illness. So Adeline was home now, her father said in a tone of triumphant conclusion, *and that is how the leopard got its spots.*

Em thought, I know this story, just add brain damage.

He said she was sleeping a lot and her mother had already slipped off the roof and sprained her ankle.

"The *roof*?"

"The low one, off the kitchen. A slow slide, she didn't land hard." Her mother declined to come to the phone. Some reasonable reason about dogs. Her father said he knew Em wanted to come help (she didn't know that she did) and that he agreed with her mother (which sounded unlikely) that just because one person is struggling shouldn't mean another person can't make her way in the world (which sounded like something he would say that no one else involved would say). He said, "I am very proud of you," and she knew he was doing everything he could think of that a father should do because he had no idea how he felt about anything. Em did not know how to ask about Adeline's brain. She kept looking at the fruit in the basket on the table, worried that it was going to go bad before she'd be able to make herself eat it, though it remained shiny. She found herself imagining a doctor lifting a bright organ from her opened belly, as if by cesarean section, lifting it for all to admire. Feeling a stranger touching a part of you that is wrongly outside yourself. Jack had come into her house and touched her *things.* She imagined the space left in her body with an organ removed and her stomach turned so dramatically she wrenched her concentration away and dropped it onto the handset— *nestled,* is the word, right?—between neck and shoulder, listening to her father. The position activated a part of her that wanted to be bionic despite technology, and for a moment she felt tenderness for the whole situation, and for herself. She got a paring knife and returned to the table. Sliced a piece of fruit. Doesn't matter which fruit, they were all out of season. She put a slice in her mouth and it was disgusting, so she spit it into the sink. She said, "Okay, Dad, well, give everyone my love, I actually have to go—" put the phone down—it had felt *alien* against her body, now that she thought of it—maybe she'd only been remembering liking the phone—something left over from childhood when the thing practically went around your head, and it had weight, and there was the voice of your friend from school on the other end, a miracle of intimacy—and took the basket of fruit outside. She had to circle it with both arms to carry it and use her elbow to unlatch the back door. She set it down in her yard under the moon and the stars and threw one piece after another as hard as she could at the side of the next-door neighbor's rotting garage. Unlike the neighbors across the street, those people were never home.

She woke very early the next morning, still dark. People on the radio in California were *occupying* places. People on the street on the radio really used the word *solidarity*. They said they were *being in* it. Em wondered about *feeling* versus *being*. They all said *being*. Do you just get to *be* it by saying it? By saying it in a *place*? Are you *in* it when you are in a *building* in a certain way? She joked to herself about whether or not she *bought* it, this strategic fleck of language, imagining a *movement* at the edge of the continent, imagining *activists*. She put something on and checked the mailbox barefoot by porchlight. Frank's check was still there, which meant Sheila had not come by, and also that the mail carrier had not gotten confused and taken it, stampless, when picking up the DVDs. When she folded and stuffed Frank's check into the tiny butt pocket of the gym shorts she'd pulled on she found that her check was already in there, still in its envelope with its film window. She folded them up together and stuffed them back in the inappropriate pocket, flipping through images of her sister like a deck of cards: sister crumpled on hotel carpet, sister flat in shiny compression wrap, sister among machines in blue room, sister blinking in bright room with takeout, sister in the room of childhood. What are my options? thought Em. What's in the cards, pick any card. If she did not walk up the hill to the job, perhaps she could walk *down* the hill, she thought in her wet feet.

Down there was the city part of town. She'd walked through it with Frank, coming from another angle. Banks were down there but not her bank, which was several miles away, a low brick island surrounded by strip mall. Inside, she plucked a few strands of grass off her feet and found some socks. She forgot even to make coffee and walked down the hill. The coatrack had gone that way. Light feet, live antlers, yellow pants, generations. She followed the dirt path worn along the busy road, which wasn't busy this early, so early that the sky was fuzzy and pink. Soon it got a little businessy, with a few structures that had been zoned one way and then a few that had been zoned another over the decades, crappy paint decisions, a sidewalk that came and went, some fences board and some fences chain link. A couple of big signs informed the public of teardowns and warned about loitering. A place that someone had fixed up had a handmade laminated sign on the garage door that read "This Is Not a Public Bathroom." A few doors down, where mixed-use buildings began, so did tents. What's surprising about people in tents is that many of the tents are so bright, sign of the newly houseless, tents still looking like *gear*. Em walked past enough tents that enough time passed that she witnessed a man get out of his tent and prepare to shave, and a block later she witnessed a similar man zip his shaving materials into a small satchel and begin dismantling his tent, and in another block a man was completing the rolling-up process for the day. She was afraid to stop and watch him complete this task, though that was what she wanted to do, she wanted to slip into a shop entrance and watch him through the corner glass of a display window. But all the shop entrances were taken by sleeping and just-waking-up men. Some were not getting up for work. Some of their bodies were rotting, and you could smell it. Together, they were demonstrating phases of destitution. She passed a man with chemical eyes and a beard and a cart and a neck brace and a tiny dog pointing its head out from the man's piles of stuff and before she knew it, she was walking up a new hill, away from the city part of town. She was coming at the building she used to work in from the back, not that it made a difference, it was just as ugly as it had been when she'd had a job.

What she'd put on along with the gym shorts was a very large Oxford with the sleeves rolled up, and thick leather boots with the damp socks. Josie had worn a man's shirt but did not look like a clown. Em was starting to get a headache. When you get a check the next thing you do is extract the money from it, so she felt stupid for walking through town for no reason and ending up back at work, not to mention what it had taken for her to leave the house at all. Around the front of the building, the custodian and two other guys were smoking near the glass doors to a corner stairwell. One of the other guys was black, one was East Asian, and Em's custodian was solid hillbilly. Like *Charlie's Angels*, she thought. Sabrina, Kelly, and Kris but in the final season when one of them was a redhead—and that's what you get—reduction—when you don't think there's a chance to know anyone, when you don't think that's what a person is for in your life.

"Oh good," she said. "You're still around." She could see through the entrance into the wide switchback stairwell with its stacked windows that must have been supposed to be an interesting architectural feature. If the paint inside were fresh and some nice color and if the railings were clean, if the ventilation issue didn't make everything smell like a cheese cave, if it were a clear day so light came in, or if the square sconces next to the windows had bulbs in them, and if the glass in them were also clean, and if you looked up, and let's just say there was also something up there you *wanted* to get to so your attitude wouldn't suck—say all these things, then the shapes carved by the stairs winding had an off-kilter but still elegant geometry that made the negative space in the center—anyhow, say all these things were all the case, then Em could imagine that, for somebody, that shape might once have held an appeal.

"Are you going to be able to get at those spiderwebs?" she asked the group.

"Spiderwebs?" said the Asian guy.

"Yeah, and wash the windows. Maybe open them so it can air out for, you know, whatever's next."

"If we open the windows, dirt and pollen gets in," said the black guy.

"And spiders," the Asian guy said, nodding at the black guy in reference to something.

"I guess I was just thinking," Em said, "like, you put someone in a nice suit in their coffin."

The Asian guy laughed in a way that seemed genuine enough.

"Do any of you guys have a car?" Em asked. "I wrecked mine but I need to go to the bank." The custodian's hand floated into a pointing position with its cigarette, indicating a sun-bleached hatchback lonely in the lot. It turned out all of them could use a trip to the bank, so they squished into the car, a Civic with bubbling purple sunshade film on the windows and parts of the wheel wells patched with riveted sheet metal. The black guy's name was Jerome and the Asian guy's name was Charlie.

"No way!" said Em. "I was just thinking about *Charlie's Angels*." She also thought Vietnam.

"Funny," said Jerome. Em followed him into the back seat. Jerome had such long thighs he had to physically pick up his legs and stuff them in sideways. The process made all the guys laugh. Jerome also had one long fingernail, but it was on his ring finger, which didn't seem right for cocaine, and he didn't seem the type for that anyway. Em couldn't think of anything else people had one long fingernail for, maybe a musician, but it looked so brittle, and she thought maybe he'd been going for a Guinness record and it broke off and he just tidied up what was left, and that's as far as she got with that mystery. By then, Charlie and Jerome were laughing at something else she'd missed and the custodian was turning the engine over and winding them out of the parking lot. The custodian was just eyes on the road, driving along. What happened to Mr. Chatty Entrepreneur? People had moods. She tried to compare race anxiety with movie-suspense anxiety with sexual stimulation with walking by a madman on the street. I'm processing, she thought. And I have a headache. The custodian had taken a back way and they passed a power station, so apocalyptic at night but in the day just a diagram of something. She compared memories from childhood with memories of dreams, the urge to treat them as cyphers. She remembered Ad calling to list the signs in the world she was about to crack. She missed her ex. Someone to think you are getting to know, someone to think you are some coherent knowable thing. Someone to continue seeing over and over indefinitely through time. But she also missed her ex as a particular woman who was not an example of anything—she missed the particular woman she was, and wherever she was, barring madness, continued to be. In the car with Sabrina, Kelly, and Kris, Larry, Mo, and Curly, Tom, Dick, Harry, Amos, and Andy, Em really wanted her money.

At the bank, Charlie went to the ATM and the rest of them got in line for the one teller on duty in her slot in the expanse of walnut veneer. There were no banker's lamps visible. The woman in front of Em wore a simple white blouse, jeans—expertly cut, precisely distressed—and heels that exposed her feet, revealing consistent pedicure. The woman's hair, too—long, straight, blond, you could just see the scissor work that made it land on her shoulders the way it landed, its gradations of color distributed in a mathematical way meant to appear not mathematical. Em wanted the woman's clothes, even if it would never work for her to wear the pieces together, how people say, *that outfit is wearing you.* She wanted hair that would fall just so, but in a way no one looking at her would think was accomplished through money. Hair that would appear to have come from good stock. Most indeterminate for Em about this woman was did she want to look *natural*? Did she want to look *expensive* in the words of Isaac Mizrahi on TV? It was some layered combination that she did not understand.

Jerome and the custodian stood behind her. A few more people came in right after them with audible expressions of frustration at the length of the line. Most branches had closed altogether, leaving only more or less scarily exposed ATMs scattered everywhere, as if to break people of an addiction to tellers. Then it was the woman's turn, and as she crossed the moat between the "wait here" sign and the teller's slot, Em could see that her handbag was flashy, patent leather with big designer initials. Em knew vaguely that women these days were obsessed with *bags*. The woman also wore a ton of jewelry, thick gold bangles, a honking sapphire ring, a necklace mostly obscured by her shirt collar, a watch faux disguised as another bracelet—all of which had been, at first, invisible to Em because of the angle and the way the woman had held the handbag in front of her body.

The woman crossed to the counter, opened the purse, and dumped it out. Some stuff slid off the edge, mostly necklaces, but also coins, lipsticks, and a key ring with a miniature boxing glove, stitched of (probably) endangered baby animal leather, which fell and bounced, anchored by its three keys. She started pulling the jewelry off her body and plopping it onto the pile and then started sorting it—pieces of jewelry this way, other stuff that way—checkbook, wallet, sunglasses, phone. Now Em could see on the woman's face that she had been freaking out inside the whole time Em had been assessing her. She could tell through all the tension in it and all the makeup on it. Her lips pulled back so that her teeth were partly visible and her professionally shaped eyebrows kept twitching. She was a gilded tower in radical precarity.

Beyond the rich woman's head, the teller's face remained professionally vacant. She was probably twenty-four years old, trying to raise a kid and pay off college. She had no excuse, working at a bank, for thinking her own financial plan made any sense at all, or maybe you work at a bank and you just start believing it, or maybe, Em thought, the teller was like she, Em, had been back when she had a job, bent over her one section of conveyor belt as if it weren't encircling the planet in a cinch—and yet there she was, upstanding teller, pretending the falling-apart rich lady who had dumped a heap of jewelry onto the ledge was not attempting to engage her in a game of emotional chicken. That was Em's read on it. The whole pleasure of people watching, after all, if you can stomach it, is deciding for yourself who another person is.

Em turned to check what Jerome and the custodian might be thinking. Jerome had his arms folded, his hip cocked, his head tilted, and he was demonstratively looking away from the woman. The custodian seemed not to notice. He stared into the slip he'd filled out on the provided surface area with the plexiglass slots, attached pens, and placard thing with the date slid into it. He held the slip with both hands, almost ceremonially. A fat ring with a teardrop solitaire sat like a toad near the rich woman's trembling hand. She had finished making her piles. A tubular bracelet slid down the jewelry pile and then off the ledge. From behind Jerome and the custodian, a man said, "Can I get that for you, miss?" He said it too quietly for the woman to possibly hear as she bent to retrieve it, brushing the heap with her sleeve so more stuff slipped off the ledge. A lipstick rolled near Em, and she picked it up. If the woman had looked at her, she would have handed it back, but she didn't. She put it in her pocket where the checks had been. Jerome said under his breath, "Okay . . . ," so she knew he'd seen her do it.

The teller put her hand up to the people in line, a "halt" gesture, and then came through a secret hinged area in the—what's it called? isn't it called a bank? *a bank of tellers?*—so that the people are the architecture, the entity is the people, the people speak from the depths of the entity, money talks—banks, fortunes, counters, tellers—and silently helped the woman retrieve stuff and put it back on the ledge. Someone else from the back of the line said "helllllpppp"—it took Em a second to realize the cry was meant to animate the sliding bracelet. She swung her head around to see who had made the joke, but everyone's face was inscrutable. The teller, so good at her job though its days were numbered, used an even voice to speak with the woman, low enough that those in line could hear only rhythm. The teller had the woman wait at the far corner of the counter, and went back through the hinged section, returned with some kind of official tray and swept everything into it. The rich woman's face, now that Em could see more of it, looked a lot older than her body had seemed, and she had been crying for so long, apparently, that it had given her a rash. Em touched her face. She didn't know if she had a rash. Then the woman and the teller disappeared together into the backstage regions of the bank.

When Em was a child she once visited the safe deposit room. A man in a suit and a tie with miniature fox heads had escorted her and her mother and then held the drawer in his arms like a box of roses. Em's mother, in a dress with life-sized cherries, let Em place into it the things they had chosen earlier that day from around the house. A plastic horse, a silver dollar from her father's father, and her birth certificate. She'd been so surprised to see the little drawer pull out and reveal such depth. Just like a card catalog at the library, but here she put her things, and just as each card in a library catalog represents a volume, and volume turns two dimensions into three, she placed her things into a space in the grid in the vast secret room that suggested the way the world worked. All these people, she'd thought as a child, have their special things in there, safe forever. The safety was identical, as she remembered it, because the safes were identical. When Josie called her diamond a rock, what happened to it? It seemed like a real question. The ugly expensive toad of a ring, the ring Frank and Jack passed between them, and Josie's ring went mouth to tail with one another. She wanted Frank to give her his severance. She wanted it with an intensity that made her feel faint. She clutched the lipstick in her pocket. She didn't want to deal with Frank and whatever he was going to think about madness and money. She wanted Sheila to get him to sign it over to her.

A new teller appeared in a slot in the walnut veneer, a man this time, country club handsome but a couple of clicks toward Frankenstein. Did he even need this job, was he putting in time to prove something to his father, would he be managing hedge funds in a week, would he tell his kids he earned *every penny*. He switched the brass-tone nameplate. Em went up and showed him Frank's check. She said, "Can I deposit this for him?" The only thing that allowed her to ask the question was how habituated she had become to acting in ways that were absolutely unrelated to her desires, which at that moment were to get one of the guys to forge Frank's signature and cash it for a kickback. I'm losing my chance right now, is what she thought.

The teller said, "No, that's not possible."

She said, "Doesn't he have an account here?"

The teller said, "It's not possible for me to give you that information."

A tiny particle of herself seemed to sit up, right through the head-ache. "Of course it's possible," she said.

The teller said, "I can respect that perspective."

Em said, "You lost your credibility the first time you lied. Now I don't believe you about anything." She cashed her check and the teller didn't blink when she didn't deposit any of it. She'd expected to have to fill out a bunch of things for approval with a sequence of managers, but the teller just got out an 8½ × 11 envelope and put stacks of hundreds in it. He didn't even look at her like *I dare you to walk through the parking lot with this and not get mugged*, didn't ask her what denominations she wanted her bills in (she would have said twenties but whatever) and by the time she was walking out to the car to wait for the others, she was completely baffled, she had no idea who was defying what rules, or who was in alliance with who, but— especially when she reached the hatchback and it was just Charlie there, sitting on the hood breaking out a new pack of gum—she felt elation contained only by the headache, a kind of high that was part whiff of freedom and part fooling yourself. She held her envelope like a schoolbook and felt its lumps. She remembered the sound of the woman's things sliding and hitting the counter and sliding again to the floor. Everyone in line with Em had flinched. "You can really hear the math," her father had said to her, placing Bach on the turn-table when she was little. Then she had a terrible thought, which was: We'd be rich from orchard money if our mother would give up on the goddamned house. If she would just move with her husband into an apartment like other people who don't have good jobs anymore we could take that money and trade it in to get Adeline's brain and body reunited with the planet. Even this stupid one, this stupid planet.

"Want a piece of gum?" asked Charlie. The bank had a drive-through and was surrounded on three sides by parking lots for the strip mall and on the fourth by the six-laned road for box stores. It wasn't fair to call the planet stupid. There's nothing wrong with the planet. It made her sick that she'd thought it. She took it back.

"What I really want is a cup of coffee," she said and trotted across the six lanes to the Burger King to get one, holding the envelope of money in one way and then another at the lights, over curbs, into and out of the sphere of fried smell, then setting the coffee and the envelope down on the pavement to switch hands periodically because the cup was so hot. Back at the bank, she drank her coffee and Charlie chewed his gum. Even that level of coffee managed to crack the headache and give her an endorphin sparkle.

"Want a hundred dollars?" she asked Charlie.

Charlie said, "Yeah!" so she fished a bill out of the envelope and handed it to him. He stuffed it into his pocket without looking.

When Jerome and the custodian emerged from the bank they all got back in the hatchback again and dropped Em off at her house.

By then, both the headache and the elation were gone.

So Em had cash, the mortgage and utility bills on autopay, plus a rich lady's lipstick, which was now rolling around in the house somewhere. The image of Frank's check was it folded into an origami bird winging her sister away. Then it was one figure riding it, one figure dangling from its talons. She watched the DVDs, sent them back, more arrived, but she was building up her tolerance and there were not enough movies. PBS did not make up the difference. She called cable and signed up for the premium package. Within a week a guy came and did his thing with the lines and then she had cable, because it's not that hard to meet a cable guy if you're always at home, and it's not that frustrating when he's however many hours late if you're steadfastly ignoring time, and it's not hard, when you realize your TV will not accept cable, to call up a department store and get them to deliver a new TV COD. This harkened back to the glory days of a postal service redolent with gallant ponies. Then get a new appointment for cable, voilà. If you walked along the dirt shoulder of the road going not toward the job and not toward the city, there was a mercadito within a mile, and what do you know, a liquor store next to it. She bought some wine and a gallon of scotch and carried the bottles in her knapsack. At the mercadito she bought some food along with the one book in English from the rack. At home, she read the book and listened to news on the radio while napping. She played a game guessing how many days she could go without ever setting foot outside. She played a game about how long until she could smell herself without changing the position of her nose and another game about using all her dishes, even the deviled egg dish, before washing any of them, and another about waiting for dust bunnies to reach a predetermined size before doing anything about the floors. *Real* bunny was the size she waited for.

Somewhere in there cable started up and she just fell into it. On TV, people watched TV when they were depressed. Her picture was so clear that when the depressed people watched static it sparkled. Over time—hours—days—she let her sense of morning, night, and season flop around with their onscreen depictions so that her awareness external to the TV felt scraped of specificity. She got up for a refill and as she rounded the corner through the arch into the living room with her freshened glass, she could see the vague shape of the little tree in the dark through the window, and she could see a glint off her mailbox, but something—oh! *fog*—obscured everything beyond the street—it obscured the neighbors' house and yard entirely. She experienced a flash of fear before she recognized the fog as weather—that it was she, in her house, that had disappeared—and then the flip side, that the neighbors' house had sold, and that what happened to a home when it sold was that it disappeared. The new cable danced in the corner on mute because she still tried to save herself from commercials. If the addict madman was a reflection of society and the man with the new liver was a charismatic storyteller, the difference involved a lot of money. She called the house with her

family in it. Her mother was busy. Her father passed the phone to
Adeline. Em glanced around for her little radio. She'd left it somewhere in the house, maybe near the bathtub for when the time came
to bathe.

Em said, "Hi, how are you?"

Ad said, "I'm okay."

Em closed her eyes and tried to let her sister's voice take on
dimension.

Ad said, "I'm sorry. I can't think of sentences."

Em said, "I could come visit you."

Ad said, "I'm not any fun."

Em said, "I'll visit as soon as I can."

Ad said, "Okay."

On cable, as a girl ran from a deformed guy with a scythe, Em
played a game where she lifted herself in and out of suspense, brain
engaging and then releasing distance, *she's me, she's not me, I'm her,
I'm not*, which may be the action of attempted empathy if not empathy. That was horror. She watched a guy she didn't like humili-
ate himself frame after frame and played a game of feeling bad and
then not bad for him. That was comedy. Network crime shows
replicated—Richard Belzer, David Caruso, Mariska Hargitay,
Marg Helgenberger, Melina Kanakaredes, Joe Mantegna, Jerry
Orbach, Vincent D'Onofrio, Mandy Patinkin, William Petersen,
Gary Sinise, Ice-T, Sam Waterston. What people want is to feel
smug, she thought, watching the same smugness come from every
episode—felt smug, quashed the smugness with her drink, quashed
Josie. She watched low-end documentaries about how weird some
people are, like people pretending to cure people of hoarding bar-
gains or animals, then switched to an old-timey cartoon of a kitchen
cooking itself dinner, all the cups and pans come to life to do your
work for you with glee, which is about how people want slaves. If
you are Adeline, time in psychosis had accumulated into years over
the years, add into that your normal time dreaming and imagining,

multiply that with dreaming in psychosis, chart that and what small slice of her is gold and true? As Em moved through time via television, her idea of Adeline rose and fell within her awareness of watching. She'd watch imagining her sister watching. The kind of truth or falseness of the lessons from television rose and fell in not quite alignment with the truth and falseness of imagining her sister watching. Whereas sometimes you have to beat the truth out of someone, which is an admirable self-sacrifice. Whereas clearly, no one should ever, *ever*, do that to a woman—for example, this to a woman, this to a woman. Whereas if you don't understand a person, they're probably an animal. If a person is an animal, they are probably evil. If a person is evil, they're not a person anymore. If you are not a zombie yet, a zombie will come at you and you'll realize this is your loved one who is not themselves anymore. "That's not a person, it's a thing!" your nonzombie gang of people from an emblematic selection of eradicated cultures and social stations keeps telling you. If a madman is a character, once you decipher what they mean you can finally stop their killing spree. If you decipher what the madman means, you may yet understand yourself and what it is you must do. You have to look through their eyes to do it, which may make you crazy, too.

You're so brave, though, if you look.

If you want to avoid all literal and figurative madmen, you will have to watch sports, though who knows, announcers probably invoke madness as a compliment and if you are willing to watch sports you are going to have to think about race, money, war, so why does anyone watch sports?

Cameras were trying very hard to convey action by cutting back and forth between two people wearing headsets typing into computers in different work environments, so Em decided to visit her mailbox. She tucked the remote in her waistband and brought her drink along, squinting in the sunshine, getting her socks damp cutting across the grass. She rested her free hand on the little flag. Frank's check was still folded in the pocket of those gym shorts, which had made it back into the laundry basket along with the final pebbles from the pocket of the skirt she'd worn to his house so many plots ago. The only thing in there was coupons, which she left to save herself a trip to the garbage. Not even bills, ever since billpay. It was hard to justify checking the mailbox when the worst thing that could happen would be three DVDs sitting in there with no one playing them because you were busy with cable. She just went because it was about time to go, it was in her body to go to the mailbox, push her hand into darkness. But on the way back across the lawn to the television, she tried to think of something she could send to Adeline, because now that she wasn't psychotic, maybe something could arrive as intended. She went through a list of things Ad used to like (certain celebrities, animals, bands, books) but how current was her information? Send her a little heart locket on a chain, maybe. Ad appreciated the sentimental, she appreciated cuteness. On television girls were always fingering their heart-shaped lockets. But she could hear it already: How could you send me a *body part*? How could you send me a *chain*? How could you send me a *hollow heart*? And how did it get that way? Hollow? Did you ever wonder about that?

"*Ad, you can put anything you want in there.*"

"*Like I have choices.*"

Em pulled a sweater from the laundry basket, put it on, and went through the day too warm with it on, too vulnerable with it off. When she'd closed her hand around it in the basket, it was like a sponge. When she lay in bed at the end of the day, she was still wearing it, and Josie was still on the kitchen floor with a lot of blood and the blood was moving, or was it the light in the memory? When she dreamed, her custodian appeared looking pink and folded. On TV, after a family goes through crisis, they just have to find a way to sit near each other, hold hands, and right as they start to talk everything through, scenes fade because it's not in the words it's in the meaning, besides there really are no words, and that's healing.

She watched TV as if she could finally finish it. People kept finishing each other off. Taking care of each other. Wrapping up. With cable, she lived through one thing after another. I need you alive, you're no good to me dead. Bring me his head, eek, a thumb in a box. Perhaps the mad are transformed beautifully on the inside, because on the outside, just look: we are the same. We hope so—we hope they are transformed—and with that hope we CGI many beams of light.

Em called her father's new cell from a stair with a view of her sofa and the television on mute. She said to her father, "How's Mom?" and he told her she had been busy with some mechanical situations with the house, hands full, could not come to the phone. He brought the phone to Adeline in the single bunk that floated in the bare room. Em's stairs went around a corner behind her back.

"I'm sorry, I'm trying to think of something to say," Ad said. "I don't even dream. When I'm on this medication, there's no dreams."

"Maybe you just don't remember them," Em said before she caught herself diminishing her sister. The difference between dream meaning and paranormal meaning is whether it originates in an individual psyche or an external force. Em had often been jealous of the beauty and complexity of her sister's dreams. She could not imagine going to her sister in a way that would not be fucked up. She was pretty sure she was waiting for something to come to her—or to emerge from inside her—that would allow her to go to her sister and not fuck up. When Em and Ad were kids and did something wrong, their mother would explain to them at great length the nature and implications of the things they had done wrong, then leave them in their room to think about it. Em remembered reading books and drawing pictures with her sister while they were thinking about it. Their mother would return to check: *Do you understand now?* Usually Em would say, "Yes," and Ad would say, "No!" If "yes" was convincing, you could go downstairs and feed the dogs. If "no" or "yes" was unconvincing, their mother would provide more information to think about, go and come back, check for believability, go, come back crying or yelling, with new explanations to think about. The mother had not been believed as a child. The mother had been dismissed and ignored and she was going to be believed by her children. She was going to be heard and understood. Maybe they both gave in, "I understand! I understand!" and everyone could go downstairs and clean some dishes. Maybe she would not believe them when they said they understood, and there is nothing worse than a liar. "I'm *not* finished yet," she said when she had more ways to think about it.

I'm in my room, thought Em, thinking about it. I'm waiting for someone to come to the door. I'm waiting for a great voice to come from my culture through the sieve of the television and say, *that's right, now you understand*. Not everything comes from childhood.

On the phone, Em said, "How's Mom?" because time was passing.

Ad said, "We talk about what's in me."

"What do you mean?"

"We talk about her mother and her grandmother. We have to learn from our history."

Later that night, after cable, Em was awakened by a single can tumbling down the hill past her house. She listened to its prolonged call. Can People were hidden in the shadows of the underground. They darted across quiet streets in yellow flashes. The houses she dreamed of contained trash chutes, laundry chutes, cage elevators, dumbwaiters. The metal sound of the can included the image of a single head rolling. She sat in her sheets and as dawn came over her surroundings a single bird flew up in a straight line past her window. It seemed to be green and to come from green trees and land below, even to bring a lush stretch of earth up with it—beauty!—from a unity between what happened outside her and what her mind produced in its frictionless setting when she wasn't looking.

She got up and took a bath. She put the radio on the edge of the sink, played it low. It was Chopin, not news. She looked at her face in the faucet in the tub as she had when she was a child. So funny. Sometimes at her mother's house you'd wake up and have dog noses coming at you from multiple directions, *Come on! Let's go!* At the end of the bath, she was glad to see that enough had come off her to make the water dirty. She felt incredibly warm from the bath and her bathrobe. She flossed her teeth and instead of using just enough floss to grip she was wasteful about it.

"Such a priss," Em said to herself, spitting. "Such a prude." She'd recently watched a knockoff of *Poltergeist* with a house that implodes and is swallowed by a chasm with lightning flashing. She told herself that the building where she'd worked was not haunting her, though it absolutely was, and she pawed through the basket of clothes checking for smells until she encountered Frank's check folded and bent to the shape of her butt. "There you are," she said, as if she'd been looking for it all along instead of avoiding it. "What am I going to do with you?" What, she wondered, would be *brave*? She put on that huge Oxford shirt again, and those ridiculous running shorts, green with white borders like gym uniforms of the late '70s. Could have been a gym uniform from the late '70s. She must have done at least some of that laundry because the items smelled fine. What happened? Nothing happened, but she put her keys in the vestigial shirt pocket that was once for pens or cigarettes. She found a pen and stuck it in there, though it was too long to fit securely. She picked out some good cushy socks that would still fit into her boots. She looked in the mirror and pulled her hair back with a rubber band. Pieces fell out around her face in a way that she could live with. Then she left the house.

She used the mailbox as a writing surface and scrawled a message on the bent envelope and pushed it into the darkness thinking, *crematorium*. For a second, she understood people who like to chuck their coins into fountains where they can glint celestially. In a celestial economy, there'd be a system beyond the one you're in all the way to dark matter. Maybe, she thought, she was just too thrifty to escape. Too conventional to steal. Too fearful to connive. Too healthy to transform. She looked around for signs of any Can People. I could never be one of them, she thought. The yellow pants of the Can People would be cheapy-thin vinyl, elastic-waisted. The Can People would have piles of extras stashed in the cars they were always fixing and kept hidden in municipal landscaping. They had each other to rely on. Sometimes the things they brought home to their cars would blossom into other things and scamper into the brush, creating ecosystems. Things with a new texture of life, with minds of their own. Where to? She turned right where the head in the night had rolled left into town, and walked up the hill.

The message she'd written on the envelope was, *Dear Sheila: I could really use this money. Think about it. Love, Em*

Then she'd added, *P.S. Not kidding. Tell Frank I know where it comes from.*

! Sexy !

Other companies had transitioned to card readers, but not this one.

"Don't worry," she muttered, drawing her keys. "It'll only hurt a little." She jammed around in the hole even though she was sure it wouldn't work, and it didn't. She'd lost her chance to know if her office key ever worked on this lock. The handle was the same handle but Em couldn't tell by peering and poking whether it had a new core. She set out to try other doors, recalling what little she knew of Josie's body as she walked the perimeter of the building, feeling her footprints, feeling its footprint, shaking a door, poking, considering her options. She recalled Josie methodically, how people say, *from the bottom up*. The boots. She did not know what Josie's feet would be like inside her boots. *Cared for.* Maybe in recent months *let go*. What would their underlying shape be—delicate? Craggy? She kept the boots as the image she had of the feet, moved along, up the leg and there, too, hardly anything to remember, a texture of trousers, an eternity of a single outfit. She'd never know, why would it matter, she had an overall sense of proportion, what is the body of a person you only wanted to know? She remained unable to think of Josie as dead and thought of her instead as *out of reach*. She remembered saying "you know how when?" and she remembered Josie saying "don't I know, sister," which absolutely didn't happen, and she remembered what it felt like when Josie touched her on the knee, radiating possibility, which didn't happen either. She shook three or four entrances, five if you counted the padlocked one to the basement. She'd once spent a meeting doodling the floor plan of the building on her legal pad, unable to work out the relationship between the outside of the structure and where she was, on the inside, at the table in the conference room, where spaces kept bumping into each other as she drew them. Supposedly, Frank Gehry takes a sheet of paper and crumples it, then tosses it to his team and says, "Build this!" She was back at the main entrance. It looked like all the others, was only *main* because it faced the parking lot. The footprint of some prominent churches is a key to heaven. Her custodian would have a skeleton key.

The lowest window to the stairwell was open a crack, and she managed to jam it upward. On her first attempt to mount the sill she banged her head, her second attempt was just general clumsiness, and the third she found herself actually penetrating the structure, supporting her body weight with her arms in the way she hadn't done since parallel bars in gymnastics when she was a kid. Her legs dangled outside the building, and inside was the portrait of the architect, donor, or founder. She looked him in the eye and said, "*Hushhhhhh.*" If she had a third hand she would have held a finger to her lips. If the architect of the building had designed her, she'd have had that third hand. It would have been a good idea at the time but where do you put it when you sleep? She was wearing the exact right amount of clothing for the temperature, which was the same inside the building as out. It was a bit of a drop into the stairwell, and she scrambled the rest of the way through remembering to soften her knees as she landed, but she still scraped her knuckles on the concrete floor.

When she righted herself, she was surrounded by shards of green glass, the lip of a bottle still intact. She looked up at the stair railing coiled around her, then picked up the lip and slid it onto her finger, smooth side in. She'd never owned a ring because whenever she'd put one on, all she could think about was whether she'd ever be able to get it off. She wasn't drunk, but she was hung over, still deeply under the influence of cable, and also a little high from the note she'd left—from her own audacity, snatching the narrative elements floating out there, wielding their ambiguities in order to make something *happen*. The pressure from the ring and the minor threat of its edge created a reassuring locus of awareness. It was probably like that with cock rings. She went up the stairs fiddling with it. Diffuse evening light caused no shadows.

At the top, she leaned on the metal railing and looked down through the geometry. She was remembering being a child, butt to butt with a friend on some stoop trying to catch the moment when streetlights flicked on, what it had felt like to finally catch it, when her custodian appeared on the ground floor, craning up at her. With his face foreshortened, in the second before she recognized him, he looked like one of the types of men on TV that she always got mixed up, actor-looking men that made you ask, "Is that the cop or the other guy?" She darted off the landing. Her body had responded to being caught, but she wasn't sure if she was actually scared.

She followed the hallway that presented itself, passing a sequence of offices, hardly any light coming in, just enough to put a shine on the door handles so that they sketched three-point perspective, just enough so that passing the fifth office door on the right she felt an allegiance because her office had been fifth on the right on a different floor. At the end of the hall, she could go one way, the other way, or into a bathroom. She chose bathroom. Inside, she rinsed her hands, then brought water to her mouth, then went into a stall with a wonky latch to use the toilet. She sat there tilted forward so that her finger could hold the door shut. She looked at her finger with the ring on it, thinking about dogs who know to look where you are pointing versus dogs who look at your finger. Thinking about the blood diamonds of Congo, pure and evil. When she emerged from the stall, the custodian was there with his hand on the lip of a sink.

She said, "This is the women's," which despite the sign on the door, it wasn't anymore. Like her office was just an office, this was just a bathroom. She was not scared. She was something else.

He said, "These are an independent system," and flipped the light on. Half the length of the fluorescent tube in the ceiling fixture was fizzled out and wires she could see through the plastic shade lay alongside the bulb.

She said, "You've come to help me turn on a light?" He made a kind of sneer or sheepish smile, completely unreadable to her. "Your guys here? You still making rounds? Isn't it past time to knock off? Grab some beers?"

"Hey now, hey," he said, backing up. She thought about threatening him with calling someone, but she hadn't brought her phone. I'm on a roll, she thought. She tried to put together a mean joke about hillbillies changing light bulbs but couldn't figure a way to land it. She took a step toward him.

"I didn't see your cart out there," she said. Now they were both in the hallway. "I don't see your cart. Where's your cart?"

"Your hand," he said. There was a ragged trail of blood down her finger. As she looked, a drop fell.

"Crap," she said, and pulled at the ring—which hurt, and stuck.

"What did you do there?" he said.

"Don't you have tools? Help me get this off!"

He took out his giant ring of keys, opened the office closest to the bathroom, returned with a tool kit, swung through the ring, *swish jingle clunk jingle*, and found the key to the narrow door in the alcove that connected the bathroom to the hall. While he was in there she snuck a look into the office he'd opened. There was a tall army surplus thermos on the desk with the paper remains of lunch, and a sleeping bag in a lump in the corner. He returned with a first aid kit in a flat white tin.

She thought something terrible then. She thought, *swank*.

He said, "That's an unusual injury." She closed her hand into a fist in order to feel the controllable increase in pain and blood flow.

When she released it, the finger throbbed halfheartedly and then went quiet. He propped the door open with a chewed rubber wedge. She followed him into the lit bathroom and lay her arm over the edge of the middle sink in the row of three. The mirror had fine circular scratches right where it met her face, as if someone had tried to clean it with steel wool. The custodian placed his tool kit and the first aid kit on the floor and opened them. He took out a hammer. He drew a paper towel from the dispenser and lay it on the floor. "Put your hand on that," he said. She knelt and lay her hand, palm up, on the bent paper towel. She put her weight on her other hand. She got into this position with deliberation, unable to escape its sexual aspects. He stood over her with the hammer for just long enough to seal the dynamic, though if she ever thought back to the moment she would not be able to tell if the charge came from him or from geometry, the fact of a woman on her knees surrounded by a grid of pale green tiles marking three dimensions, holographic. She lowered her head and her spine fell into a sloping line. He squatted next to her and held the hand in place while he cracked the ring off with a light, precise, and unadorned blow. He helped her to her feet and returned her hand to the sink. He rinsed it for her and patted it dry with more paper towels. He riffled through the medical kit and muttered a few words from the backs of tubes. "Not in or near eyes. Numbs as it disinfects. External use only." He added, "I usually like a spray."

She didn't ask if he lived in the building because clearly he lived in the building. With her eyes closed, she leaned into the sink, holding her own wrist and paying very close attention to the pain. Sadness was rising, about to make tears, and she pushed it away with her breath. She let him make decision after decision. He made the dumb sounds of thinking to himself, narrating the task: "A little of . . . now I thought there was a . . . here we go . . . now if I . . ." He returned to the closet twice, once right before he began to wrap her hand, and again, arriving with the clang of a dustpan, to sweep up the shards of her ring from around her feet with a brush. She felt the brush cross the tops of her boots. He tapped the pan against the plastic of the garbage pail that was in the corner under the paper towel dispenser. His caretaking was gentle and elaborate. When she opened her eyes, her hand was thickly wrapped in white, the hand of a polar bear. He'd overturned the medical kit in the bowl of the adjacent sink and was now trying to get the pieces back into their spots in the tin. She shifted so that her lower back was against the lip of the sink and crossed her arms. He gave up putting stuff back in the right spots and just threw what he couldn't fit into the trash. He saw her watching and said, "Sorry." His arms hung. The kit in the bowl of the sink was also geometric. She put her polar bear hand on his shoulder and her other hand on his hip. She let it close around the loose fabric of his coveralls. This shocked him—he took a step back and put his hands up, surrounded by tiny green tiles. "I didn't touch you," he said. "I didn't touch anything. I didn't do anything," he said. She pulled apart two snaps at his midsection and stuck her bare hand in. She closed her eyes and imagined his dick as connected to a person, and then as a warm shape in space surrounded by the fabric of the coveralls, which was a kind of crinkled sack, plastic yet embryonic.

The floor, when they lowered themselves to it, was all these things: cold, a grid but slightly sloping and warped; sort of clean but you could see where dirt scooted into the rounded corner and the details of grout, and around a drain with its brand stamped into it. She told him to take his jumpsuit off—not to be funny—nothing felt funny—she just used the word and he just did as she told him to do, decision after decision. She reclined and he unsnapped it, lowered it, took off the plain undershirt beneath it. He wore pale blue boxer shorts—perhaps his regular clothing system, perhaps what he wore only since he had the building to himself. She saw no shame as he removed his clothes, and no betrayal of lust other than the erection, which everyone knows is related at best indirectly to the emotions of a human man. He dropped to the floor and she didn't have to say "remove my pants" or "take off my bottoms" or "help me out here," or "off with your whatever." He just did these things like she'd pressed *go*. He was a lover in perfect tonal balance, no awkward smiling on the trek toward skin, no effort at grace or guile. The removal of half her clothes—the necessary amount—was a cooperative disassembling. Just let her do her part. Just let him do his part. He crawled onto her. They tested out their mouths and their mouths prefigured their genitals. Her wrapped hand floated safely nearby. He turned away to yank on himself and then pushed into her. It felt certain. It felt like relief. He humped like a boy so surprised that he gets to fuck a girl that he's back alone with his pillows, and then his face lights up when he sees it's really a girl, and then he forgets her again because he's overcome with his body, and then he remembers her again like she's the one coming and going. His skin was so loose around his bones that she felt it drape against the sides of her stomach, but when her eyes were open his face surprised her by being old. He kept his gaze over her shoulder except when he stretched his neck out with effort and his vision went internal. When he pressed himself up on his hands and curved over her like a leaf she took it as a sign that he was about to come, so she had them flip over.

He did have eyelashes, they were just pale.

She brought herself to an orgasm that was big, internal, and groaned through her like a single animal that broke into many as it clawed through earth. She let no sound out. She kept her face flat until she let it go mean. When she was able to, she got off him and went to the sink. She knew what his angle was as she washed herself with her one hand. The bandage on the other was already coming loose. She knew she got water on the floor and probably some drops fell on him, too, which she wanted. She used her bandaged hand to dry herself. Then she undid the bandages and threw them in the trash. She picked bits of cotton off her finger. The bleeding had been sufficiently stanched. It hurt but not that much. *You'll live*, says your mother, your sitter, your custodian. She leaned back against the sink. She still had her top on and no bottoms. She had clipped her pubic hair with scissors but shaved nothing. He sat on the floor with his ankles crossed, brown bird in his lap, faint pinkish imprints from the tile reaching over his shoulder. She thought, don't worry, nothing happened.

She located a staircase and outside found the moon incredibly expressive, one of the middle shapes on the way to full. A few stars like droplets of water freeze-framed around it, a dog midshake postswim. On the walk down the hill she carried her hand by resting it in the crook of her other arm. At home, she found a band-aid in the linen closet and then went back into cable. She had felt something. She had felt several things, actually, along the way through the building and into the custodian—*into him* is how she thought of it—but she could only take so much. She slept on her sofa. Somewhere in the night she was startled to find her white wrapped hand next to her face, staring back. A phone rang nearby, with the sound of a phone ringing, which was the ringtone she'd chosen for her cell phone. She pawed around and located the sound on the floor near the sofa. The ID told her: Mom. She picked it up and heard rustling and bumping.

"Mom?"

Just rustling, bumping.

"Are you okay?"

The phone hung up. She called her father, certain that someone had died, and headed up to her room with the phone ringing and pulled a suitcase from the closet. She was going to have to take a cab somewhere. She pinched the phone with her shoulder because her cut hurt and she needed her other hand for the suitcase—and cell phones were never even meant to be held like that. Her father picked up.

"Is Mom okay?"

"She's fine," said her father.

"Okay. Is Ad okay?"

"Everyone's the same," he said. "How are you? Are you okay?"

"I'm *fantastic*," she said—angrily, sarcastically. "No—I'm sorry—I'm okay, I'm fine." She pushed the suitcase back into the closet and righted herself. *Fantastic* was a word her sister had used on the phone in madness to describe herself. Em was horrified that she'd used it, even if her father would never make the connection. "How are you?" she said, back to the tone and pace they both knew as their dynamic.

"I'm okay," he said.

She sat on the edge of her bed. He caught her up on a couple of things. A famous facility would take Adeline and not lock her down, but he and their mother were in disagreement about whether they could afford it. They were in disagreement about what counted as affording something. The facility said that, with the brain injury, brain chemistry, and possible addictions, a good estimate was a year to know where you stood. The mother said money was meaningless, cost was a construct. The father said they didn't have the money, they didn't have a way to get it, this and that about his pension, what a sub gets paid at the high school, they didn't have the money. Em could hear panic in his voice.

"She says when a kid comes back from the dead you do not give up on her," he said.

"What does Ad think?"

"She promised me that she would never, never do that again." He meant kill herself.

"Oh," Em said. "What did she say about the place?"

He said he hadn't wanted to bring it up unless it was an option.

It was trash night a block up, where the routes changed. She could hear someone rolling bins out.

"Well, what do you think, if she went there would they help her?"

"Who knows?" said her father. "I've been led to understand that some people have been helped."

In the morning Em woke and ate a bowl of cereal on her stoop. She didn't think she had ever heard trash bins from the next block before. It was the hill, she thought, that had made it possible, sonically, even if she'd never registered it before. She had not checked the mailbox or allowed herself to second-guess the note she'd left or the math she'd done with no actual numbers or the ideas about human beings that got her to it. She had not added imaginary threat money to imaginary family money in relation to a year to know where you stood, but there were imaginary piles. She still didn't have any milk, so she ate the cereal with her fingers. Otherwise, breakfast was uneventful.

She did some more cable, mostly guns and cars. Then she walked back up the hill. The custodian was smoking at one of the entrances with Charlie and Jerome. He both leaned back against the rail and slouched forward. Charlie sat on a step like a mushroom. Jerome stretched out crosswise up the stairs with his hands behind his head as if he were in a hammock. The pickup truck was there, empty, half up on the curb. They all raised their chins in acknowledgment as Em approached. She went through an internal "what if they are, what if they're not" conversation regarding whether they were talking about her and was fine either way. She said, "Hey," to them, generally, and then, to the custodian, "I want you to let me in and help me with something." He nodded at the guys, stubbed out his cigarette, which was close to finished anyhow, and used his keys to let them in. They headed up the stairs.

"I haven't seen your Civic," Em said, and he said Charlie was selling it for him. She wondered briefly if he'd ever lived in the car, and if he had drug connections, if he sold drugs. His eyes still looked to her like the eyes of a user, active or dormant. But if he didn't have drug connections in the way that gets a guy a mansion, she couldn't see the upside. It's not like she wanted drugs. She tried to picture her father dealing drugs. Meanwhile, light came through the windows and finally something pretty happened because of the architecture, nice golden late-afternoon light with blue edges where it settled on the floor.

"I want you to show me your room," she told him. She thought she saw him make just the faintest shrug, but mostly the request clarified who was leading. They went up two flights and then down a familiar hall. They passed her office without her noticing at all. He led her to another stairwell and up another flight. There was the bathroom they'd used, and there was his room. He opened the door and let her go in first. He leaned in the doorframe, supervising her inspecting him, or, more likely, just being there, benign. The walls had been stripped of shelves, leaving the metal brackets sticking out of their slotted standards. He'd laid a long flat cushion on the floor that she recognized from a lounge sofa and was probably the source of the distant smell of microwaved lunch kits. His sleeping bag made a lump on it, and on the floor nearby was a lump about the same size, made of clothes, and then another slightly smaller lump of clothes. One clean, one dirty, one hoped. His thermos was on the desk, army green, and that was it. She wondered if he'd ever lived in a tent.

"You could put a microwave in here, or did you get rid of them all?"

"Last power was yesterday," he said. He opened the file drawer, pulled out a huge flashlight, and set it on the desk.

"Very hip," she said. "Very *now*. Does the bathroom still flush?"

"Um, yeah," he said. Maybe he was not so much benign as vacant, contentless.

"You could run your *Solution* empire from here."

He just squinted at her. But when she reached for him, he was surprised for only a second and then went with it, fine. He even had condoms. Rubbers, she thought, and then, galoshes. Her exes had been girls for a long time.

They used the desk because the cushions disgusted her. She felt the thin flat side of his nose pass along her hip. She moved her tongue in and out of his small mouth. After the desk, she led him into a breezeway on the fourth floor. The cinder blocks were perforated at an angle that allowed no view, but she recalled the projections of light they let in at certain times of day. She wanted to see if there was enough streetlight to create the effect, but there wasn't. He had his sleeping bag wrapped around him. She said, "Never mind." She touched his penis to see if it could go again, but he wasn't ready. The walk back to her house in the dark was a corridor. She'd heard him say, as she left the breezeway and entered a stairwell, "Really?"

Em's sex history included an early stretch of promiscuity intended to cover a broad range of kinds of sex and kinds of people to have had sex with. She'd enter a social community, assess hierarchies, and go at the man who achieved the highest value likely accessible to her, primary variable being accuracy of self-perception versus perception of self by others. Win some lose some for sure, but what started building up was a sense of *injustice*, that when she was rejected before, during, or after, it was for reasons she could not have known or prepared for, that seemed to defy group standards in a breach of contract, and any stated reasons from the individual rejecter ("um . . . it's just that . . . I don't know")—usually a guy who'd called her a "breath of fresh air" and "funny!"—were so innocuous they had become gibberish in her memory. Anyhow, for a few years when she was at her official hottest in terms of body parts, she invested herself thusly, dumbly. She learned nothing, but a particular feeling built up over time that turned out to be anger. That emotion overtook everything, so she stopped, and for the rest of her twenties, focused on sensory desire. When did she have it—sensory desire—was the question. For a long time, the answer was *not in relation to people.* The light, the weather, the mood of a room or a vista could arouse her. It was *around*, but for a long time, it was as if people were giving off static that prevented her from locating any specific origin. When, eventually, she did, desire led to a few women for a few scary nights each and then it led to a couple of exes she rarely thought about anymore, eventually one ex whom she really went overboard about, followed across the country, it was stupid, it was a disaster, she came back, and then The Ex, whom she only followed across half the country and still thought about with mathematical regularity. Their sex had been good right away, in the sense that it was rigorous, enthusiastic, by all evidence skillful, and they really immersed themselves. Maybe, how people say, *lost themselves.*

Soon enough, the ex wanted to give Em secret signs at parties, tiny adjustments of eyebrows, a head tilt, and have her *know what she meant. Check out so and so; save me I'm dying here; I'll tell you later; let's blow this pop stand* . . . But Em was obtuse. "Why are you kicking me under the table?" she said. "What? What?" she called across the crowded room. She confused her ex. She embarrassed her. Em really liked being party to a secret code, but even when she did understand she'd often withhold admitting it. Why would she do that to a person? She and Ad had done some high-quality secret coding at parties, so she knew it was possible. She knew it felt good. "Watch out for those two," some guy said. "Sisters." There's nothing like getting the message. So why wouldn't she do it? What was she withholding? And what could be more cruel, she thought—as she walked up the hill, looking at the astonishing progress of her finger, healing, healing—what had it been, a few days? a week?—in a world of madmen who cry out and nothing comes back, or who are subsumed by silence—than to pretend you don't understand when you actually do.

She returned to the building, and then she just kept returning to the building. At first she didn't take it for granted that he'd be there. She'd traipse the halls wondering what she'd do if it was now all hers. She pictured many stupid scenarios involving her own secret empire. She'd imagine that the people who'd populated halls as employees had just been noise and there was no reason she should hold anything against the building. Maybe she just didn't understand its architecture. A peaceful collective could arrive with bandanas tied to sticks and induct her into their utopian squat. *Thanks for letting us use your building. You can only go so far with encampments.*

Then she'd come across the custodian, always also in transit or smoking. Let's do it. Let's do it in a closet. Let's do it on the roof. Let's do it in a cave. Let's do it upside down. Do it, let's do it in the way back of the bus till the cows come. The building did not seem to sell or get looked at or marked for demolition. Charlie and Jerome either stopped coming around or she always missed them. She remembered the custodian going on and on idiotically back when they were employees, and she was relieved that she'd managed to silence him, more or less, with sex. Sometimes she tried to think of something genuine to ask him, but she couldn't conjure more than a quirky, minor, perfunctory, insulting curiosity about who he was or where he came from. Meanwhile, they performed the undulations of becoming ordinary and then strange again in a wide range of rooms and interstitial spaces. She found him once, for example, smoking on one of the stoops in the shade cast by the hedges so they did it in the hedges and encountered no problem with the weather, thorns, insects, or animals. She could see how absurd it would all look from the outside, but from the inside, it was just people doing what they could with the available materials.

At her house she got a bill from her insurance for COBRA, which she did not remember signing up for. She got bills for the bills she hadn't been paying, and bills for the fees for having been sent multiple bills. This is your final bill and here is your final notice. There were a dozen websites she could go to and invent passwords so that she could send money. She could send checks if she could find some checks and stamps. She watched some more shows and then looked up how much it would cost to pay for Adeline to go to the facility her father had located that was supposed to work when others did not, and then looked up the comps for her house and subtracted title fees and what she'd owe the bank. The money that remained would pay for ten days, cost of which the facility's website was refreshingly up-front about. They promised a graduated funding structure, but still. Could a person, in effect, take a mortgage out on her sister? If she defaulted they'd never be able to sell her. If the place didn't work, what about the down payment? Not to mention what does it do to a person to have a mortgage taken out on her? Like people surely mortgaged people during slavery. And what about the severance check that, for all she knew, was a one-dollar fuck-you from the son of the mild man of excellence in the black-and-white portrait, for something Frank had done to piss him off that Em wouldn't know about, too busy searching for a wallpaper-colored blouse to match the wallpaper. Ugh and the *threat* part. How had she put it? She could not remember. It was probably *veiled* when she didn't mean it to be veiled, and you can't *veil* with a person like Sheila or she'll just interpret in a way that keeps the world the way she thinks it's supposed to be. Em looked at some less reputable facilities until she was so sad she moved her computer—which was starting to freeze when she turned it on, anyhow—into the basement and snuggled it onto the utility shelving between the bunny-ear television and a giant box of laundry detergent. During sex, she felt herself as an organization of shapes, as something with legs, as an extraction of senses. She felt her skin as a container. It occurred to her less often to go home. In her dreams her clit grew into the beak of a parrot, waxy and bright.

"Do you have a dream house?" she asked her custodian at some point, and immediately forgot his response.

"Do you have any Advil?" she asked, shaking him in the night when she woke with a headache, and he did, he had a brand-new bottle and handed it over. In the bathroom, after a mortal struggle with its cap, which had become tilted on its threads and needed to be slammed back into place before she could wield the child-protection mechanism, she had to break through the seal. There were no more lights in the bathroom, either, by this time, so she had to balance her flashlight on the edge of the sink. It was a mini piece of conference swag meant for a keychain that he'd found and given her for short trips. It held what she was doing in the bowl in a limp beam— washing hands or splashing face or *whorebath*, a term her ex had employed lovingly, or now, trying to get at an Advil. She pushed her finger, which was better except for a rosy indentation, into the seal. It made a depression, and she tried peeling the foil layer around the lip, but only scraped a strip off with a fingernail, and by then she seemed to have cramps on top of the headache. *Look what's become of me*, she muttered in half sleep over the sink. The sink had a screw-in plug, so she unscrewed it, washed the glop off the screw end, and used it to pop through. It was her favorite Advil, translucent blue.

At some point she woke up and he'd laid coveralls over her as if they'd be comforting.

At some point he emerged above her in his underwear eating a tuna fish sandwich ambiguously.

In a hall, the imaginary voice of her mother said, *you're being a real pill.*

One of the custodian's ears was larger than the other, and sometimes they lay flat when he was speaking, actually tilted in a way she'd never seen on a person before. His fingers were spindly with large knuckles and surprisingly tidy nails.

He often used the phrase, *I'm game.*

Tenderness, at some point, had emerged in their sexual efforts and there cannot be anything wrong with that.

Leaning with his back against the wall and the bulky flashlight shining straight up, the custodian said some things about his family one night or afternoon in his office where sometimes you couldn't tell the difference, it was so deep in the architecture. He said some things about where he'd been raised, which was not far. Mostly in the mountains, he said, where he still had people. He'd suffered a few cruelties Em hadn't heard of before, and he found pleasure in things she'd never known anyone to care about. So maybe she hadn't silenced him so much as activated in herself a curiosity about her surroundings, of which he was one of many aspects. Maybe she was just relaxing into the weather, like when you just tell yourself to stop shivering and it's cold, but not *that* cold. Mostly, the custodian was poor in a way that she'd always been afraid of but couldn't actually imagine except in the form of images from sources she knew not to trust, like newspapers, books, magazines, videos, car rides, conversations at parties, pithy anecdotes that stuck and you forgot where they came from. He was poor like in documentary photography about California farmworkers, Ellis Island, the Dust Bowl, floating out of context. She listened to the custodian as if through water, and while the cadence of his voice was clumsy, it was entirely within her power to keep it from bothering her. She found she liked letting it wobble nearby.

At some point she woke up and he was utterly one hundred percent familiar to her.

At some point they woke to an electronic sound. Two short beeps followed by a long one. She sat up in horror. Again, two short beeps and a long one. He raised himself to his elbows and cocked his head. "That's not the fire alarm. I don't know what it is," he said.

"It's some *appliance*," she said, clamping her hands over her ears. "You have to find it and make it stop!" This time it didn't go back to its two short beeps, just the long one kept going, and she expected Jack to come flying down the hall in his pale coat with that sound coming inexplicably from him because this time he'd have *no mouth at all*! The door to their office was shut and Jack would pound on it nonverbally, *let me in*, but it was an interior office with no egress, so they were as good as at the bottom of a jug with nowhere to go but down the hatch.

Her custodian left the room with his enormous flashlight and a hammer and she sat on a cushion like a raft, clutching the mini flashlight in her lap, and waited for him. The sound would seem to have stopped and then start up again. It went back to short beeps plus flatline. Then it faded out. Then another series of beeps, and so on until it didn't come back, and kept not coming back. When he returned, Em said, "Did you get it? What was it?" He shook his head.

"I don't know, but I don't think it's coming back." That was a line from many movies but she didn't notice, she was too frightened, waiting for the flatline sound.

"How do you know?"

But it didn't come back.

She had a clingy hangover about the experience for a day or so but fought it off. She even took a few Advil for good measure, as if the discomfort were physical, though she knew it was not. I'll take care of myself, she thought, a threat, a promise.

They were smoking in a hallway two floors away from the custodian's room, sitting with their backs against the wall like a headboard, ashing directly onto the carpet. She was feeling especially uncorked after sex. "Let me bounce something off you," she said, taking a deep breath and launching in without waiting for his attention. "Now, you're *a lot* older than me, right? So I'm guessing you remember the thick golden waxed paper that used to contain breakfast cereals within their boxes, also, the crimped sleeves of crackers. Pulling the seams apart—remember?—you could feel a *ticking* of release, and then fold it back into place once you'd taken your dry food out and it would sort of stay." When she glanced at him, she could not tell if he was listening, but she wasn't sure it mattered. The words felt great coming out, just on their own. "I've been remembering the grocery, back when I had a car, before the mercadito. You probably know it— the one on that side of the hill?" She gestured behind them with her thumb, but kept her gaze on the expanse between two doors in the dull daytime-but-no-window-in-sight atmosphere. There were two main groceries for the area, both in the same chain, but one was trying to be upscale and the other was crappy. People she knew called it the ghetto grocery. That's the one she meant. "Last time I went, I bought my last box of cereal. Perhaps even my *final* box of cereal. Used to be you could buy a half pint of milk but not anymore, have you noticed? Now it's only cream in half pints. Let me give you an example of how upstanding or fearful I am, by nature. When we were children—people of my generation—at school lunch, plastic crates arrived filled with half pints of plain, chocolate, and strawberry milk to choose from. What kind of choice is that? Well, I was the child whose mother told her to drink white milk, and so I did. Children everywhere, drinking their sweet pink and chocolate. I drank mine and I imagined theirs."

He said, "I had those milks."

"Do you think we have choices," she said. "People like you and me? Or do you think I have choices but you don't because you're poor? Or do you think something like this (grand sweep indicating their habitat) can force a transformation? Do you think a true transformation is possible? I saw something transform into a deer. At least, something with antlers like a deer." She couldn't say coatrack. It was embarrassing.

She paused to let him respond, and when he realized she wanted him to, he said, "Deer come into town because we encroach their territory," so she did not pause again for a while, and she did not ask if he knew anything about Can People.

"Well, I decided I was not going to buy a half gallon I could never finish in time. No more throwing away bad milk and paying for the privilege. So I just stood by the magazines and watched the rubber conveyor with my box of cereal under my arm, tried to let it come to me how to eat it. Not that I wasn't prepared at that point to eat it plain. I wanted to come up with something. There is definitely no yogurt I would eat from that grocery, so something else. By the time I was outside trying to figure out where to put my change because I was wearing stupid work pants with no pockets, I was a little hungry. I'd been going through a sort of depression—not like some people, not like maggots-in-the-potatoes depression—but you may know that it's symptomatic to disengage from your body and I'd been eating more as a habit than for sustenance. So I was a little hopeful when I felt hungry in relation to the cereal. I put my change on the top of a garbage can, warpy, plastic, bleached-out hood, you know how shitty that store is, I know it's gross but money is so dirty anyway. However—before I tell you what happened next"—she shifted toward him a little, as if she believed he was right there, listening, taking everything just the way she meant it—"I have something to tell you about *change* and *transformation*. Now, you may have noticed over near customer service there's a machine where people come in, dump their coins, and turn them into dollars. Not before their very eyes, but within the machine like a magician's scarf. I took my box of cereal and my little handful of coins to look at it before exiting the store. I expected the machine to sort the coins into kinds of coins and spit them into those cardboard fingers. But the machine skipped all that. It took your money, put it down a funnel that counted it in a barrage, and then gave *part* of it back in the form of bills. You know what that's called?"

"A fee schedule," he said.

"It's called degradation," said Em. "God," she said, almost to herself, "it about crushed me. It was just the most pathetic thing. If I could invent a machine it would sort everything, *everything man-made on earth*, into glistening tubes arranged by size and color and every human mind, equally, could find *anything*, just by wanting to. Mark my words," Em said, another expression—it caught in her throat— that her sister sometimes used in madness, a phrase she might never have spoken before in her life, "mark my words, in six months those coin machines in the ghetto grocery are going to be minus commission and fucking store credit only. Loyalty cards my ass, you pay *not* to play. All this opt in, opt out. Do you think the Appalachian wilderness is ghetto?" She turned to him demonstratively, willing him to consider this, and he did.

"Ghetto is more *buildings*," he said, putting his hand just over his own head.

"*Any* buildings? As long as they're taller than you?" She looked around, innocently. "Is this building ghetto?"

"Ghetto is more which *people*," he said.

"Are we ghetto? What about nature? Are we bad? What do you think has value in its *nature*?"

He said, "God, right? God is value in His nature. Em, you're too much for me."

"What about the Appalachian wilderness? What if we're activists? Okay, never mind," she said. "I suppose I have to tell you what happened with the cereal." He'd brought one of his boots into his lap and was examining the condition of its stitching. "I opened the box of cereal as soon as I stepped outside the store," she said, "and I haven't paid attention to it for a long time because, you guessed it, there's no more golden waxed paper, it's a kind of whitish plastic that you can't possibly open with any grace, it's like it's *designed* to create a mess. Like it *exists* in order to—" she felt simultaneously stupid and urgent "—I know it's been that way for ages, but it *snuck up on me*, I couldn't believe I never noticed before. Once you rip it open— and it *wants* you to rip it—there's no cartoon pair of scissors with a dotted line—or—I just realized—it's like it thinks that once the cereal is *in there* it's over. As if no one is going to eat it, so why say anything? And then—and then!—even if you tear it open against its will, it won't even pour straight the way you have to tear the bag, it's that plastic that warps, it ends up all over the counter and floating around the box. Look, it's not like I haven't been eating my cereal in these circumstances for years now. I just felt really sad about it. It snuck up. I was standing by the garbage can and I wanted to throw the whole box away but as I said with the milk it's all such a waste, so I left the box on the top of the garbage can along with the change, which I couldn't bear to bring with me." She searched him for something that would school her, but he was still deep in his boot. She said, "Even if it was already gross, it was grosser now. I left it for the ghetto," and when that changed nothing in his affect, she felt a maw open up inside her. She felt it fill and swirl, and when she could speak again, she said, "I left feeling really hungry, hunger all out of proportion. Hunger that was not even mine anymore."

During her feelings, the custodian had set his boot aside. Now he shifted his eyes from the wall he was sort of staring at to Em. He said, "A large family eats cereal fast."

She looked into his beady eyes. They seemed concerned, but she could not tell what for, or if it was just narrowness again. "Why do you think the company failed for real, like beyond bad apples?" she asked, and then before he could respond, she said, "Oh never mind, I don't care." She'd become aware of the vibrations in her throat as she produced sound, and it was making it difficult to hear what she meant above the sonic contours of the words as shapes in her body. There was a lag time between making a word and being distracted, in one direction, by the feeling of having made it, and in the other direction by only half knowing what she was saying in the present. Language was getting chopped up by her interior—a kind of digestion unrelated to absorption. She wondered where he kept getting cigarettes from. She thought about asking him, but surely the answer would be a letdown. "Look," she said through the cacophony, "I just want to bounce some things off you. Just try to be a wall. Do it for me. I don't know what to do. I have to think of something. I don't like my options."

She expected him to say, "I'm game," but he surprised her, held her gaze, and said, "Okay, shoot," at which point the image of a gun sidled over, which had not happened in a long time. She surprised herself and pushed it away before it could blow her head off. Language and her body settled into their separate corners. The carpet still crept up the walls in corners that had never been square and she could see where it buckled nearby.

"How about I go into packaging," she said. "I'm a virtual packager for this job we lost, so why not? Not decorative packaging, though. I'd specialize in the stuff *inside*. I'd make bodysuits for objects. Those intricate plastic tray things where the gadget sits in a shadow depression and its cord has a little coffin with a twist tie and the whole tray thing slides perfectly into a square shell. I'd work in cardboard because I'm against styrofoam, like any decent person. Cardboard may still have a soul. Have you ever seen that guy downtown in the box? I like that little tab you have to slip out of the toaster oven door, have you ever bought a toaster oven? I like how you take something out of the box and you can *never even imagine* how it would go back. I've moved a lot, so I've kind of been in training. If I think about it, I was probably made for a life of packaging. Both my parents have characteristics. You know what's the most important art of our time? I'm sure you stay up at night over that. It's those drawings of how children can kill themselves with everything you bought. Plastic bags, window blinds . . . I know, I am really backing myself into a corner, I may as well be waving a kitchen knife around like a microphone. It's just the thing that makes me so sad about packaging"—and the maw opened again, and she stood at its edge—"is that I can't help thinking that it affects the things inside, *and* the things outside, like I open the poor crackers and they're so sad to have been packaged that way, and then I eat them and they are in me, I am the package, and they are in there seeping into me and changing me with the sadness of where they came from.

Never mind. I know what I wanted to ask you. You'll understand this as an entrepreneur. You must be going through this with *The Solution*. But, like, if I were to do something right—really right and valuable— with packaging, I'd have to understand how an unconnected person overturns an industry. It's probably locked down like big oil, right? Like water, right? Locked up? Locked? Do you think I'd be able to hack it at a factory?" she asked. She immediately forgot his opinion, though, because along with it, he explained that at plastic bottle factories you take a mini bottle the size of your thumb and put it in a machine that blows them up into the size you see in stores, and that was amazing to her. Because of the idea, and because it came from him. She just looked at her fingers for a minute as nascent bottles. She said, "Do you think the last person on earth to smoke a cigarette will know it? Of course they won't, how could they?"

"People I know, we smoke," he said. "And the Chinese smoke."

"The roaches will smoke. All that will remain, smoking roaches and the beeping of a thousand unattended appliances."

"You're a strange girl," he said.

"Maybe, maybe not," she said, but she appreciated the remark. "Let me put it this way, I put a coatrack on the curb and it *escaped*. Just for a second—a flicker—but I saw what it could do."

"Someone took it."

She didn't mention the way one day she went in for a meeting and the next day everything had changed.

"Look, you dropped that bottle down the stairwell, didn't you?"

"A bottle?"

"The one on my finger. During my high jinks. The ring. Remember? It cut me." She held out her finger so he could look at it. She was looking at her bare feet in the distance. There was a funny mark on an arch. She took her hand back and pulled her foot up over her knee—she had scars on her Achilles tendon from back with Frank, the kind of scars that would have healed ten years ago, but now she was at the age when even minor injuries start to stick. Along with the finger maybe it was starting to look like she'd really been *through* some things in life.

"Yeah, right. The bottle. Wasn't me," he said.

"Who dropped it then?"

"One of the guys?"

"Why would someone do that? Did someone try to drop a bottle on someone?"

"I didn't see it if they did."

"Well, why would someone just drop a bottle down a stairwell?" she demanded.

He did a now-familiar thing with his face, sort of sneer, sort of sheepish.

He said, "For the explosion."

They had an argument. Later, she thought the lesson was that as soon as you take a literalist seriously just because you're fucking, you're going to ruin whatever it was that had you fucking them to begin with. The fight was about 9/11. She really wanted to push it at that point, she really wanted to see if he had anything in him of real use to her, so she told him how she'd been standing at the top of the stairs just the other day ("Which stairs, those?" "I don't know—any of those stairs—how could you think that matters to my point?"), thinking about the cooks and stockbrokers all reduced to their common humanity standing on their ledges, making their choices. She described a woman she'd read about, this young widow saying, "My man would never abandon me." She described the woman's absolute certainty that he'd gone down with the building, as if he were some captain and it were some ship. She described how wrong a response that seemed to her, to Em. A moment you really should give to another person, of all things, right? There's a guy—a man you supposedly love so much, and he's in this impossible situation, a situation more impossible than anyone left alive can possibly adequately imagine—and she won't even give him that.

"Give him what?" the custodian asked, really going for it, ripe or primed at last for a true back-and-forth after their long morning, afternoon, whatever-time-of-day-it-was, of warm-ups, false starts, talking past each other. They'd even shifted their positions in the hall so that they were turned toward each other with their legs folded.

"Like there you are," she said, "with fire at your back and city below and sky everywhere else. You are at the core of a historical moment. You are the embodiment of it. Pain that extraordinary—a choice that is *so completely* and by *all rights* your *own*—and this person, in the same breath proclaiming love, means to take it from you. How could anyone begrudge a person that choice, to choose sky if only for a moment? Come on, look up," she said. They both looked at the ceiling.

He shrugged. He said, "I guess her man was just different. Not everyone jumped."

That killed the whole thing for her. "What do you know?" she said. "You've met like three people in your life you're not related to. You're from the woods."

He said, "I'm not from the woods, I'm from the mountains."

Later, she lay in his arms anyway. She did not want to give him up. More precisely, she lay near his arms, was aware of the limbs nearby, and missed her ex. The time when. The time when. She got up to wander the sea of cubicles. She tried to think through Adeline's options, her own options, and her options with regard to Adeline's options, the difference between a person like her making a choice and a person like Adeline making one. She tried to do this thinking in a direct and concrete way, but she'd come up with one option and it would slide away when she thought of another. "You're a bright girl," the imaginary voice of Magda said from the depths of the cubicle sea. Em heard a phone ring and realized that she'd accidentally brought her cell. She checked the ID, which said, *Mom*. She let it ring and watched it until it stopped ringing. It gave its single bleat.

She picked a desk and sat at it to listen to the message.

Rustling, bumping. Radio sounds.

Then her mother starts talking, mixed with the radio. Then her aunt's there, apparently.

They're driving in a car, sisters of their generation, happy chatting clams.

Em stayed on the phone, listening to her mother's life persisting and the inside of her mother's purse. Something about her uncle and her cousin. Something about dogs. The voicemail cut off at its default setting.

Em found her custodian and led him back to the bathroom, got him off while sitting behind him in a driving position she liked a lot, her front to his back, her legs around his, her hands reaching around his waist, her hands around his penis where she couldn't see it, her face pressed against the knobs of his spine. She pulled her hand from the sink after washing with the mini flashlight though who knew what time it was outside. Her fingers smelled funny, and not from the terrible pink soap she still would not use and that still hung stickily in its wall dispenser, a medical contraption for aliens. Her hand, when she wet it, had an immediate body smell like a napkin, which, when you wet it, sometimes smells like wood again. Also, it was hard to tell in the dimness, but when she touched the surface of the mirror, she could feel them, the scratch marks where a face would be. She'd noticed them when she injured her finger, but not since, which made her wonder if she'd been using a different bathroom. As she drew her hand back from the surface she could almost feel someone over her shoulder with their hand making the circular motion that would have created them, washing, effacing, erasing. She remembered her hand wrapped, an embryonic puppet, and touched her little scar. She lifted her hand, a wave from an automaton, then started to collect her clothes and realized her custodian was still in there with her, reclined on the floor in an awkward feminine way, wedged against the wall.

He reached out his hand. "I could use a little—"

She felt violently interrupted. In a way, she had been sharing a wave with Josie. It was private, and it might not have happened, but in another instant she might have known. She felt the interruption as committed by the custodian in continuity with how the bathroom stalls were laid out in such a way that left a gap at the wall for him to get stuck in. Like the stalls came in a standard size and the room did not, or someone ordered the wrong number of toilets and just shoved them in anyway. It made her go back over the sex and try to pick out the moment when he had been in the process of getting stuck and either didn't notice, or, more likely, was too something to just tell her they were too close to the wall and he didn't have a place for his fucking leg, and rather than act on whatever measly level of trust it would take to avoid it, he simply stuck his leg where it should never have been, into an architecture that should never have been.

"Did you do that? To the mirror?" she said. Pissed. "You call that cleaning? More like rubbing one out." Furious. She approached him with her hand out, which he knew better than to take or else couldn't see. She went right up to him with her hand disingenuously outstretched and he just looked at her and looked at her, blank with *she just could not fucking read him*. She brought out her other hand. She crouched and peered at his face. She thought: What is the difference between working for a place of business and putting your fingers into the nostrils of another person and clamping your hand over the person's mouth. It was unimaginable, unimaginable, unimaginable, and then something darted by the propped door in her periphery in yellow pants. Her hands fell away—they seemed to her, in fact, to disappear and then reintegrate with her body a moment later—and she managed to use them to gather her clothes into a wad under her elbow.

He said, "When a man—" but couldn't finish. Em thought she could hear a buzz, as from a fizzling light, but there hadn't been electricity in a long time. She remembered a sex moment when she'd been, privately, with him but not with him, an undocumented animal, not quite fox, not quite bird, not quite salamander; and another moment when she'd been an animate piece of furniture, hilariously something not quite a table and not quite a sofa and not quite an armoire.

"I get it. You're embarrassed," she said. She did not know if she was saying this with compassion or scorn.

He called her several cruel names that anyone can think of as he unwedged himself, shifted on his elbows, bared his ass. She'd so recently turned him in space, her hands, cartoonish in the weird light, flat on his ribs. He'd not so long ago stood over her with that terrible sandwich in a way that—how could it not have been *upsetting*? When she'd opened her eyes to find him looming he could have been preparing to squat lewdly, or, she thought as she removed herself and the wad of clothes from the room, to crush her with his steel-toed boot.

He called after her, "You used me!"

On her way out, a white calla lily lay on the top of the hedge like a lady's glove after a party everyone had called *divine*.

"I did terrible things," Ad said on the phone between hospitalizations, some years ago.

"Where are you?"

"Out."

"Like at a bar?"

"Driving." The connection didn't sound like driving.

"I thought you lost your phone. Who's with you?"

"No one, I just needed some privacy." But really, Ad had snuck into their father's study and was looking through printouts from the computer about a million places all over the world where they put crazy people at different times in history, nice and nasty, including now.

Em said that whatever terrible things Ad had done were done in madness.

Ad said, "But they must be *in me*." She said she'd felt she had to kill some people and went about trying to get things to kill them with. She said she felt obligated, because of the evil they'd done.

Em said, "But you didn't hurt anyone."

And Ad said, "But I was supposed to. I felt it. It's in me. It's real."

Em said, "Feeling isn't doing. It's in me, too. You're just like everyone."

Ad said, "No, I'm not. I'm really not. I'm something else. I mean I'm smart, I'm white, I'm attractive, why don't I have what I want? And while we're at it, why don't I have any money?"

"You're hilarious."

"I'm not."

"Was that the time you went to the FBI? When you felt that?"

"No, that time there were murderers I needed to report."

When Em woke up on her sofa, it was midday. What a slew of dumb movies and show episodes begin this way. She'd come home—it was already night—and gone immediately into cable, arriving partway through a movie whose plot—it was a movie she'd seen before and forgotten—hinged on cell phones, the first, she suspected, of its kind. This struck her as both a significant document of cultural change and very, very stupid. When it was over, she pointed the remote at the TV with one hand and reached the knob on her radio, which was on the floor by the sofa, with the other, and made a simple game of trying to turn TV off and radio on simultaneously. She had to turn them off and on a few times to feel out the timing, got pretty close, and the smooth transition helped edge her toward sleep. When she was almost there, almost asleep, observing from a great distance the sense of suspension in that *almost* state, she tried to sneak her hand back down to turn the radio one more click to silent. It took three tries before her hand could creep to the ridged, shining knob without backtracking her progress, and then in the morning she sat on her stoop in the broad sunlight watching a flock of small black birds take over the giant tree in the backyard of the next-door neighbors who were never home. She kept planning to go inside when the birds left, but they outlasted her, incredibly noisy. She turned the television on. When she turned it off, the birds had gone. She couldn't hear them in the silence the way she had been able to before, which gave her the sense that television had wiped them out. She tried to sit in the silence. She thought she should change her clothes, so she took them off, and then there they were in a pile next to the sofa with nothing else to put on, so she turned the radio on and left it clearly audible because there had been a hotel bombing. She could not think of a hotel without thinking of Adeline in it, or being in it as if she were Adeline. We were taken to the scene. "Take us to the scene, if you would, please," said the national anchor to the international correspondent, and of course she would, it was in the international correspondent's contract, and her contract in this special moment co-incided with her ideology; her job was to look where others could not and see for them. Here, the rubble of grandeur. Leftover rich people and employees in tatters stumbling about, half-blind, ears blown, and at the outskirts the riffraff peeking from behind I beams across the new field of concrete chunks spewing rebar.

Em lowered herself to the floor, beyond limbs' reach of the sofa. She went to take off her glasses, but she was still wearing her con-tacts, so she took them out unsanitarily and let them get lost on the floor. Blurry, blurry, the blobs of her breasts, the layer of belly, this floor compared to the grid floor of the sex bathroom. She turned her pink soles toward each other. She could feel the tips of her labia peeking. So graphic with the floorboards streaming from her in both directions into infinity. She thought about her body hairs, arrowing, and her pores, sound getting in and cruising the parameters of her purple organs, into glistening tunnels, into the sweetness and gore of her own luxe corridors, shivering among senses and senselessness.

She blew her nose, pulled her sofa throw around her, found her glasses. Her house was so dirty.

Her landline rang and she brought the radio along with her, set it on the counter, and turned it off as she picked up. She just picked up the phone instead of letting it go.

Sheila. She learned that Sheila was staying with Frank at his house. Her two sons, thirteen and seventeen, were enjoying some man time with just their father.

Sheila said, "You know that sitcom with the puffy pink lettering? The mom and her neighbor who's funny? There's three kids in it? The neighbor is played by *Josie's mom*. Did you know that?"

Em was tired. She was listening, but as Sheila described the sitcom, she was still letting go of a man version of Sheila stretched out on

Frank's sofa with dishes of food piled on the coffee table, two teen-aged boys drinking beers, Sheila coming in the front door, *What a disaster area! This place is a pit!* She had a distant urge to say something derisive, but she was so tired.

"I didn't know that," she said.

"Her dad's even famouser. The boys know who he is. They can't *believe* I don't know him. But it's sports." Sheila paused for some reason.

"I don't watch sports," said Em. "I'm sort of . . . against it."

"I just find it so interesting," Sheila said.

"What's interesting?" She couldn't tell if she sounded mean or if she meant it in a mean way.

"I don't know, honey. The turns life takes. You forget celebrities are people."

"I don't forget they're people," Em said. "I don't. Everyone's people." She realized that she'd been hearing the jangle of a shopping cart across pavement behind the conversation, and that now Sheila must have stopped.

Well, it seemed like a shopping cart. It seemed like pavement.

Em said, "What happened to Josie's ring?"

"I don't know, I imagine it's with her family."

"She has no kids."

"There's a husband."

"Seriously?" Em said, then stopped. She didn't say *gay adultery* and she didn't say *crazy*. "Sheila, the thing about Jack, he'll just—who knows—but Jack can't take care of a ring like that. I should have the ring."

"Oh, Em."

"Yes. I should have it. I could really use it."

"Well, couldn't we all?" Sheila said in a folksy way.

"Some people more than others, Sheila."

"I don't know about a ring, honey. I just don't know."

"What about the *check*, Sheila? When are you going to pick up the *check*?"

The jangly noises stopped. "I got it weeks ago," Sheila said. "I rang your bell. You've been somewhere."

"Well, what about the *message*? Did you get the message? Did you give him the message? Did he get the message? What did he say?"

When Sheila spoke again she seemed to put her mouth more directly at the mouthpiece because she sounded louder, though she was likely speaking very softly in real life. "You didn't mean that, honey."

Sheila was fat but not that fat, just enough fat to keep her—what was this word people had started using—people said it at work—*relatable*. It went with the shopping cart, Em thought, which must be paused in the shadow of the nice grocery on Frank's side of town, piled with all-American nostalgia comfort and ethnic gourmet adventure. It went with Frank, who with just the slightest bump in the space-time continuum would have been her assessor at work. It went with Sheila's apron, which she was almost always wearing in Em's imagination when she wasn't wearing the wide-legged jeans and the softly flowered tunic she'd had on the one time they met at Em's house when Ad was dead. Em's image of herself was an amphibian moving through sewage. "Listen to me, Sheila," she said. "I know you want to be a friend but you have to stop saying *honey*. You just have to."

The sounds started up again. Sheila was rolling to her car. Now she was there. Cart noises subsided. Keys jingling. Trunk or hatchback opening, bags rumbling, doors shutting, some other way keys jingle. Jangle. It was a little hard to hear her the next time she spoke.

"I think you are giving Frank maybe a bit of a hard time," Sheila said. "You know, Em, I just have to tell you, and I don't want you to take it the wrong way, but Frank was there for you in your time of need. I'll just come out and say it. I don't understand why you haven't been to see him."

Because I hate that guy, Em thought, which had not occurred to her before, not in so many words. She thought, you can really harm a person, romanticizing an illness like he did with Jack. Traipsing along after a person in that level of trouble trying to find yourself, like you're protecting him from the system. Like that is even possible, fucking reckless, throwing your weight around, your leftover authority. Mister *I was boss*. Sheila could be anywhere, Em thought. Well, not *anywhere*, but who knew what those noises were. Maybe it wasn't even a shopping cart in a parking lot.

"I have something for you to consider," Sheila said, and took an audible breath. Em braced herself for the story it was now apparent she'd been working up to tell the whole time.

Sheila said: I had a little thingy about the size of a nail or a screw, a little piece of junk, part of a mechanical thing that probably my brother might have taken apart out of curiosity and it was left behind when he put the machine back together, probably an old clock, always wondering why it didn't tick anymore, I was just a kid, our mother was sick, she was often sick, it was terminal, it was unspoken, we all knew it, I used to sit on a stair where I could hear them talk about everything I was too young for, I carved secret marks into the underside of the bannister with it, with the thingy. Carved a perfect heart, the name of my friend I wanted to be my best friend (she never was), counted the days until my birthday, four marks then a slash, all these things a child wants to think about. I put *I was here*. Our father traveled a lot, and he was traveling this time I want to tell you about, when Frank had to be the man of the house, when he was fourteen, fifteen, but kids grew up faster then, I fixed breakfasts for the family already, though we had a girl come when my mother started to go downhill, she was in the hospital quite often, we got a different girl, an uglier girl because my father thought my brother was after the first one, I don't think he was, it was projection. My mother was in a lot of pain for a long time. She would come to a level of pain and there'd be medication, but the pain would get to another level, and up and up. I know my brother was connected to her pain. I remember playing at a puzzle on the floor near her bed and looking up for help when I was stuck, she was asleep or awake with her eyes closed and Frank was standing over her with his hands in his pockets, looking and taking her in, feeling her, he would often stand near her, feeling. She started talking. I don't remember any words but her voice was all wrong, it was not the way I knew it, he leaned into her, listening. I imagine at a certain level of pain, I imagine you just can't help yourself, you can ask a person for anything, the way he leaned into her with the light from the window, for a second they looked like— they looked like lumps—they looked lumpy. Then Frank was angry, whatever she was saying, he picked me up, messed up my puzzle with my feet as he lifted me, carried me out of the room and outside. We had the garden shed set up as a little playhouse with straw bales. He set me on a straw bale and said, "Play." He went back into the house. Our father was out of town. Well, I don't have to say it. She had asked her son to—she had asked my brother to—because of the pain. I don't have to say it—okay, Em, I will say it for you— she died—Frank did what she wanted, he did it for her because she asked, and it was a gift. But a gift you have to live with.

"What about the little mechanical thing? What was that all about?" Em asked.

"What?"

"You started out with a little mechanical thing. A broken-off useless bit you used to carve stuff into the bannister."

"I suppose I did."

"Well?"

"I was just mentioning—I just mentioned it."

"No reason?"

"I was trying to tell you about my brother."

"You just put it in the story for no reason? Well, what were you wearing?" Em asked. She heard Sheila jangle and gasp.

"What was I—*what*?" A rumbling of bags or whatever it was— unicorns—and the static of elaborate telephone headgear or whatever it was—stardust—followed. Em almost began several sentences, some apology or fake apology, but she couldn't spit anything out. She was refusing to receive the story the way it was intended. She knew that. She sure didn't know why. As far as content, it was a pretty affecting story. She was resisting its teller.

Sheila said, "Listen, Em. Frank recently came into some money. Not that—that *bullshit* from your mailbox—real money. He had an aunt, a widow, well, *we* had an aunt, but that aunt has passed and Frank came into money. Not me—she had no use for girls—she had a pile of daughters and disowned them all. Frank is a generous man. He is taking care of that woman who died. He is dealing with that and her things, her finances, her family, and with *his* money he has set something up for the husband, who is not well."

"What did he take care of? What did he set up?"

"Well, I don't press. Frank's exhausted. He says he set things up. Perhaps if you went to see him—"

"What? An island paradise, gay boys running along the beach in tiny suits? Ghost of Liz Taylor in her prime waving from a balcony? Say what you mean, Sheila. You mean a fancy hospital? He sent Jack to a fancy hospital with that money and now he's forlorn at your place watching football?"

Em didn't even believe in hospitals, it had just started, along the way, to seem like the goal. But what does it even mean to believe in a hospital? A fantasy of safety. A ton of banks were failing right about that very moment. The *big* bailout was back when Tasio was living in the house, progressing the family's narrative, but look at an FDIC chart of *small* bank failure rates in the bailout aftermath—prettiest bell curve you ever saw: in 2007, 3 failed; in 2008 it was 25; '09, 140; '10, 157; '11, 117; and into the future. This conversation with Sheila was during the time of highest rate of small bank failure in the lifespan or knowledge of anyone involved.

"I don't press. I'm tired, too," Sheila said. "My back hurts. I have to go."

"No—don't go—wait—come on—don't go."

Meanness isn't evil, but it's related.

"What, Em. What do you want?"

"I want to know what happened to Josie," she said, because she

still somehow thought there was a chance Sheila wasn't simply gen-
erously, sisterly-y running errands for her brother to support him
through some difficulties, that she would say, *you'll never guess where
I am—I am here at the Days Inn with your friend Josie, do you want
to talk to her, she would love to catch up* and hand her the phone. The
image of her own sister was Ad in that single bunk but the bed and
the body both made of earth, of *lay me down to sleep.* "I didn't mean
you should say your mother died, Sheila. I meant you should say
your brother killed her, because that's what happened."

"Josie is dead, honey," said Sheila. "It's disrespectful to act like
you don't know the difference."

Money, like dirt, can be anything, has been everything.

"Where's her body? Why would I believe you?" Em said into the
phone, very quietly, because words can be so hard to move around
and people make mistakes, but Sheila had hung up. Em sat there
at her plank table, fiddling with the place on her hand where a ring
seemed absent. She was in her bathrobe, which she must have exchanged, along the way, for the sofa throw. Her image of herself was
no longer swimming through sewage, it was swimming through a
sludge made of drenched ashes as far as the eye could see. A great
white boat surged by with a thousand portholes—two for every
cabin—and the figure of Jack at the bow. At the end of that set of seconds it was like the phone was taking over her hand, so she walked
directly to the kitchen sink, put the headset in it, and turned on the
water. She found her cell and called her mother. Her mother picked
up. Her voice sounded fine when she said "Hello" but terribly frail
when Em didn't say anything immediately. She said, "Em?"

Em said, "Mom, your phone called me."

"No I didn't," said her mother. Now, unlike from the bottom of
her purse, she sounded resigned to the great heap of life.

"I feel like since Ad died you don't talk to me."

"Em," she said, "I'm sorry, but you have no idea what I've been
through. I'm the mother."

"I feel like at the hospital you didn't look at me."

"What are you talking about? I am always looking at you."

The water was still running in the sink so she turned it off.

And went outside and faced her house with her arms folded: *let's have a look at you*. She assessed it, then crossed the street and knocked on her neighbors' door. When it opened, the husband and his wife were both in bathrobes, too, his saggy brown terry cloth and hers a chambray quilted thing. His nice striped one, the one he wore to chase after innocent can collectors, was, she supposed, in the laundry. They clutched matching mugs of coffee and invited her to sit with them in their kitchen nook.

The wife said, "Here, I just poured this," and handed Em the mug she was holding. Then she poured another mugful and joined them.

From the nook, the three of them could see past the yard sign to Em's tree and the glaze of her living room window. The wallpaper that surrounded them in the nook was enormous green foliage with yellow fruit peeking through, almost the exact wallpaper she'd imagined. Both neighbors had beautifully textured hair—his cut close in silver waves with a strong side part, hers pulled back, with rosy ringlets that didn't reach the rubber band bouncing around her face. Their names were Andrew and Isabel. She asked about the sign in the yard, so they talked about money. They'd been through the letter of hardship process and something called a straw something. Andrew explained about "the equity stripped from our home." They'd put on a credit card the cost of an attorney whose task was to decipher the offers that came in the mail. Isabel said, "We sat in pretty chairs in his office. I felt like a kid in trouble." She told a story about what it had meant to her to own a house. She said, "I am a first-generation homeowner. Now, Andrew, on the other hand—"

Andrew put a finger to his lips and said, "Careful. TMI."

But Em didn't feel shut out at all, or embarrassed for anyone, the way he said it. Maybe it was the foliage, or the delicious wrong-time-of-the-day-for-coffee-in-bathrobes coffee. She said, "What about I sell you my place for a dollar?"

"You wouldn't do that," Isabel said, laughing. But Em saw it so easily: the three of them together at a title company in a strip mall, the title company lady supervising in a maroon suit—the three of them initialing the last of a thousand pages of documents and Andrew taking out a dollar and letting Isabel hand the title lady the dollar, who handed it to Em. Then Em would say to her neighbors, "There's just one more thing to do," and she'd take that dollar and buy them a Coke from the vending machine in the hall.

"Oh, no," she said, shaking her head. "I really, really would."

"But, so, how much do you have left on the house?"

"A lot but probably a lot less than you. Do you have a job?"

"Yeah," they both said.

"Well, I don't."

They said sadly their credit was still their credit, and the laws were different now, they don't just give a mortgage to anyone, and they said she was sweet and funny.

"I just really want to give it to you. There has to be a way," Em said.

They all sat there thinking.

"It's on autopay," Em said, finally. "There might even be some money left in my account. You know, they have to send a *bunch* of notices before they can take action. That could be months and months. That's a few thousand dollars, anyway. It's some time. Maybe there's a way. You can squat, meanwhile. But, you know, nicely."

"You mean like a guest?"

"No!" said Em. "I'm giving it to you."

"You mean caretaking."

"No—you just take it and do what you want until the bank does whatever."

"Or the police," they said.

"Come *on*," Em said. "It's a leap of faith. Just take it. Use it up. Just use what you can."

"Okay," said Andrew.

"Really?" said Isabel. "Do we have to tell Jeff?" She meant their realtor.

"We'll tell him if we have to tell him," said Andrew.

"Okay," said Isabel.

"Good," said Em. "Okay. It's a done deal. It's yours."

Em wrenched the television away from the wall, unscrewed the cable, and pressed its little brass head through the hole in the wood floor that had been drilled for it and then thought, god, I'm such an ass. I give them the house and then dismantle the cable? Just because I'm done with it? but the head was gone down the hole. Right before she did it, she'd watched one more show: a documentary about the struggles of the albino community in Tanzania. They intended to organize and be recognized as human within the dominant Tanzanian culture in order not to live in fear of being harvested for the magic used against illness and other aspects of poverty. In Tanzania, apparently, people will sneak into an albino's hut and cut off as many pieces of an albino as they can, then use the parts to catch fish. Albinos, a nonalbino Tanzanian explained in voiceover translation, don't die if you kill them; they vanish. People sneak into your hut, dealers going for a complete set. "If we can collect all the right pieces, what *power*" is a quotation from this translated nonalbino Tanzanian. Em had heard about this documentary on public radio before running across it on cable, so she figured its message was intended to comfort a person like herself by giving them the feeling of being informed and right thinking. She lay on her sofa, watching the Tanzanian speak through the voice of a person who was not onscreen. White limbs glowed underwater, so beautiful, white fishes among reeds. Certainly evil was in the water, too. It was there as a layer within the desire to be free of pain. An albino lay with Em in reeds along the river, slipping fingers into every available crevice like smoke, and what would that feel like, for sickness to vacate, what would that feel like to be sick and then the person—or not a person, just the idea of a person—slips in, and you are no longer sick, you are no longer in pain, you are going to be fine.

And then she wondered, what if Adeline is going to be fine?

What does *fine* mean?

She gave up, reduced the idea to *alive*, and found that it meant something to her that it had not meant since before Adeline had gone to the swank hotel. Life and death now permeated one another in perpetual motion. How do people say, *when the smoke clears*—well—Ad was alive.

As long as she'd ruined the cable, Em lettered another "Free" sign and hauled the flatscreen into the night. Then she cleaned the house, picturing the living room encased in enormous green foliage with yellow fruit.

Sure, she thought, I could live with that.

She made herself imagine her neighbors' asses in her chairs and their hair in her drainpipes. She filled two suitcases, a big one and a little one, with clothes, toiletries, a phone cord, and tucked the rest of her pile of cash in the outside pocket of the little one. The last time she saw live art was on a visit to the Whitney where there was an exhibit about a guy—white guy—who lived out in the swamps for decades preparing to perform self-surgery to redesign his sex organs into something that was no longer a human sex organ, but beautiful as sculpture is beautiful, and he died in the act of documenting doing it. Em thought if her sister was going to evolve into a madman like that, just a person acting out private, symbolic, potentially culturally resonant acts, well, she'd just tell Andrew and Isabel she needed the house back and she'd get another job somewhere downtown among the tent people and runaways, who are more like escapees than runaways, and just start payments back up on it or sell it and buy a shack outright in some swamp and live there with her madman sister.

Look at that. Bet hedger. Hedges are sometimes said to be humanity's first property lines. Some of the first phonograph recordings are Victorians sitting around in their gold-encrusted mansions, gazing over their giant hedge mazes, imitating birds whose numbers have now declined by billions. Em could have put a sack of cash on the stoop with a sign saying "Free," image of bills like autumn leaves and dust to dust. Maybe "free to a good home," but no, a gift is only a gift if you're willing to let it go no matter what financial entity will eventually track you down and make you pay forever. She hoped Andrew and Isabel would enjoy the thermoplastic anvil of a telephone that had lived on the mantel since the beginning of time and she folded the antenna of her radio down into its slot and, because it was practically a pet, stuffed that into a suitcase, too.

She checked the mailbox, and the envelope for Frank was gone. She looked up and down the block and the block was blank, but lights were on in the house across the street. Andrew and Isabel were making out in the living room. She trotted over and put her house key in their mailbox like it was nothing.

The first night Em slept with her ex they'd had some drinks on the town and Em said, "Come home with me," which meant her rental apartment. She unlocked the door saying, "Let me show you around," which everyone knows is a delay tactic that can go either way, foreplay or cop-out. Inside, the ex picked up the vase Em kept on the little table near the door right as you walk in where you can drop your mail, and held it appraisingly. The ex said, "When I first came to this country and someone gave me a house tour—some lady my mom told me to look up—I mean, it was so weird. Not everyone does this, you know. *Oooh, here we go, the kitchen, you are such an awesome designer, look at that stove, you must be a great cook,* you know? Into the living room, *where did you find that piece?* What's a piece, you know? Like piece of ass? Here we go down the hallway, *ooh, look at your shit on the walls, who is that, what a cool dress she's wearing she looks just like you but black and white, that's so clever how you did those frames*—closer and closer to the bedroom—*ooh, I think I can see your true heart now, I think I can feel your soul . . .*" She put the vase back and turned to face Em, who was still standing in the narrow entry with her coat over her arm. The ex walked right up to Em, backed her against her own front door. She walked her fingers up her leg—Em was wearing jeans, but still. Joking and not joking—

"Like I'm supposed to tell her how her bed is so—what, *tasteful*?—and that's how *she's* gonna know that *I* really know just how *great* her husband fucks her."

Em laughed, "God, let the lady have her house!"

The sex was great. It felt deranged and by the end turned sweet. She could remember a lot of moments of really good sex with the ex—sensations and emotions with very little left of their context. It's true, Em had almost ruined it that first time, because even then her impulse when she felt a lot was to shut down, but then she didn't.

When they were breaking up, they took a last-ditch vacation with their whole pot of savings, just to see if there was anything to salvage. They both really cared. Em had been driving them around the island for a week. Now they were late returning the rental to the airport. They'd been fighting. She'd had to pull off the road to cry and gasp. Now Em was driving as fast as she could along the most dramatic highway on the planet, surging along raw cliffs, the ocean on the one side, lush hills of green against a vast earthy distance on the other, infinite depth of sky and range of color made explicit by the dynamics of clouds. Poor people lived there, invisible from the road, sunk in this beauty. Em thought she saw a metal shed explode into fire, but it was the sun leaping from behind a cliff in the rearview. The dark russet mountainsides shimmered with something like mica. Sun spazzed across the surface of the sea. There was a goddamn rainbow around a curve. It was outrageous, ridiculous, over the top. Then zooming around another bend in the cliff there was another goddamned rainbow. Em thought that if there was a third, she'd just give in, just implode in the Fiat and then, around another cliff, there was another one diving into a cove behind crashing waves.

She kept telling her ex, "I have to drive, so you have to look *for* me!" and the ex said (and was she even moved? Or was she still too angry for even this to break through? Or so angry she was keeping her access to the beauty to herself—withholding? Or not even angry, but resolving, in this very moment, that it was over, that she was truly done for good—), "Keep your eyes on the damn road, you'll kill us!" But beauty! "Slow the fuck down, for real," the ex said. "You think your *sister's* insane?" And when they got to the airport to the car return she said, "You slam a door in a person's face," and opened her door and got out and said, "like this," and slammed it.

They made their flight.

Adeline was psychotic during 9/11, driving to one and then another 7-Eleven, on a quest that made perfect sense at the time, and then no sense for a while, and then perfect sense in a different way well after the fact. Later, along with many psychotic people around the world, she thought she'd done it—made the planes fly and buildings fall. *But I remember!* All those people feeling what it felt like to have done that. If you can feel something by belief. If you can know it by feel.

Watching her neighbors make out, Em had felt a surge, like her sister was not about to die again. She experienced a moment of not bracing herself. It was a feeling she'd had as a kid who was just good enough on a bicycle to sneak the bike outside and set her little sister on it, wobbling, falling, wobbling, wobbling, and then there she is, going, going, maybe falling, maybe going.

When Mr. bin Laden finally fell in a newscast Em didn't hear because she was cleaning—or come to think of it, depending on the account of his death that you believe—when Mr. bin Laden fell in a newscast Adeline was saying to her father over full-sized chess in their living room, "I don't even remember how the rook moves," and Em was shaking a glass near her ear to hear the *clink, clink,* or Ad was calling the last known number of a guy who'd traded her a guitar for sex and babysitting because she thought he might also have given her a gun (she was going to ask him: When I was staying with you, did you give me a gun? Do you remember? But he wouldn't pick up)—while Em was dreaming of a hole in the ocean—the body of our enemy possibly slipping off the edge of a boat, possibly pushed in pieces from a giant helicopter. Em heard some clips from the president's speech in the taxi on the way to the airport with her roller bag on the seat beside her, her big bag in the trunk helping out with the suspension, her job, her house, the town, and the people in it that she knew and didn't know, all receding.

When she heard the clips of the president's speech is when Josie, too, seemed finally to die.

Animals

Their mother said, "I heard a noise." Ad and Em's mother, hearing a noise.

She was a little girl. She came out of the room where she slept with her littler sister and even littler brother. Her father was wasted, and what that is to a child—funny, frightening.

She stood at the top of the staircase, is how the story went. Her own mother lay on the floor at the foot of the staircase, an arm on backward and her legs in the shape of running. Her father had placed an empty bottle near her mother's hand, and as she came down the stairs into the room, he crouched over the body with a roll of tape.

"Nothing happened," he said when he saw her, and put up his hands. Then he made a strangled little laugh. "Hey. Get your sister, get your brother." He was breathing hard, moving in his crouch, heavy in his feet. Little mother went back up the stairs, woke the littler kids, and led them halfway back down the stairs. They sat one, two, three and watched their father finish outlining the body with the tape, and also taping around the flowing hair, and also the bottle. From her stair, little mother was eye level with her father. It was a story their mother told in so many words because she was against secrets and believed in the intelligence of children. Sometimes a dog was in the story, standing between the adults and the siblings. Sometimes a crash, a bang, or a yell preceded the stairs. But in every version of this story that she told, this moment of being eye level was present, and in every version he said, "Look. I'm an artist. Mama's a drunk," and that was the story of why they didn't know their grandparents and how their mother was making a real family with her girls.

"Here is the house that had four small rooms." This was the beginning of another story, the story of the photo album, treasured primary source that wielded power over the imaginations of the era. This photo album had black pages pressed between white covers with photographs held in place by perfect supplies called *corners* that you licked the back of and collected from the bottom of the photo drawer when they fell off.

The story went: I lived in it with my mother and my father. I loved my father because he gave me my dog and took us fishing. He was usually away. The war turned him into a druggie. I did not know how to love my mother. My mother turned into a lion and ate us. We had to stay in our room when she was looking for the Russians who put the wires in the walls (turns a black page), and here is the house I loved because it had *three wings* and was incomprehensible to me. I lived there with my grandmother and grandfather in the orchard where the money came from. I abandoned my sister and brother to be there. Girls, my girls. You would not believe the terrible things I did as a child.

The girls tried to picture having three wings.

"I became a teenager," the mother said. "I ran away from the house with my family in it. I slept on the beach." This began another story, and she told it as they were driving through the countryside, a countryside story, Ad in the back, Em up front because she was just that much older.

"We want to go to the beach!" the girls said.

"Not on this coast, you don't. This coast, the beach is disgusting. People cover their bodies in oil to sex each other up. A beach should have coves and whales. My grandmother found me. She took me in. The house had wings and was surrounded by orchards. At the edge of the orchard was a fence and beyond the fence was a dappled gray horse. I would sit in a tree that overhung the fence. When he came near I jumped onto him, and that would make him run. Dappled gray means a horse that looks like clouds. My grandmother made beautiful pies, and now I can make pies, which you will not be able to do, because it skips generations. She and Grandfather came from a fishing island off Portugal. We go back to smaller and smaller islands. Catholic school, nuns taught me to brush my teeth. They showed me the backs of my elbows, which I had never seen, taught me, like this, to clean them."

She demonstrated and then put her hands back on the wheel. Ad leaned into the front to watch and then plopped back.

"Put your seat belt on," said their mother.

She told them the stories to protect herself from being misunderstood.

"Father gone, Mother good as gone," is how she began a story about origins and beginnings. The girls were chopping vegetables at the kitchen table, home from their colleges, surrounded by the wallpaper and the meaningful things, a story about home and away from home, which began with the mother at her college. "Grandmother drowned with her money locked up, and the very next day in painting class he pushed my hair aside—I almost said, 'to read over my shoulder'—of course I mean *see*."

"'He' who?" said Em.

"*He who* my *teacher* is who, my girls. This hair—my hair—was honey then." She touched Ad's hair, which was not quite honey, but more honey than Em's. "Boxes in the drugstore long for it. I was nineteen. It was wonderful. I was a painter. I just mean I painted then."

Ad, in recent months and those to follow, was keeping to herself the surprising things she'd begun to see and hear. She had a sense—something told her?—that what she was experiencing was dangerous, that she wanted it, that people might want to take it away, that

it might kill her, and that if she were brave enough, it might transform her into something revelatory and nothing would ever be the
same. Em, during this time, was halfway packed for San Francisco,
it was about to be a disaster, keeping to herself her plans to ditch
everything for an early love it turned out would leave her when she
arrived.

This story went: I copied George Stubbs, who stripped layers from
real horses, skin, to muscle, to bone, which is how he came to understand them. I copied the anatomical drawings of da Vinci. On free
days I went to the zoo, where the motion of animals was contained,
and I drew them from life. I studied and worked. I was an excellent
student in all my subjects. I had always kept my painting secret from
my father, who would never have approved. I kept it from my grandmother, the only family who ever loved me. Before I showed her anything, I wanted to be *magnificent*.

But now she was dead, and no money coming for me.

I knew when I walked the campus that I would never be more
beautiful and my body would never be as whole. I had this foresight.
You have to consider the times. I wore my dungarees and smoked
my cigarettes and did not wear lipstick like my mother did. Lipstick
makes the mouth a cunt. The moment my grandmother drowned
I felt power in my body, power that comes only from grief and loss,
the necessity to make my own life. I was broke. It was spring. When
life is everywhere, death is too. When you've got nothing you become receptive.

This is what Nick saw in me. He watched an awful lot of Antonioni.
I did not call him Nick yet. This is not about true love. True love is
what I have for you. And not because I am your mother. True because of *who I am* and *who you are*.

(Here, in the story, she touched Em's face. There are still moments
when Em will make an expression with her face and suddenly know
by feel that it is her mother's.)

I was walking the campus after class, considering where to sleep.
I had some friends but they made me uncomfortable. I appreciated

the politics but did not like the drugs. I knew about drugs from my father the druggie. And naturally my mother was away. Asylum.

(Here, Ad said, "What kind of asylum? Was it state? Was it nice?")

As I walked across the verdant campus, the sun went down. I was thinking about the nature of color. I was looking at the grass in the dark to see how much green was still in it. I was trying to predict how wet it would be in the even-darker shadow cast by a concrete bench near a lit window, then I touched it to confirm my prediction. I devised a test in which I closed my eyes, turned in space, then opened them: How fast could I discern, in a new view, sources of light? What the moon had to do with anything. What the city beyond had to do with anything. I was not full from my supper of diner coffee, saltines, and ketchup. I hopped over a low stone wall and crossed the street. In a row of buildings where I'd never had class, a basement light shone. I could see him painting down there. I crouched and watched him paint. Looked down on him. There was nothing sexual about it. Just serendipity.

Well, okay. There is always something sexual about surprise connections. A potential for satisfaction. I must have been nicely lit. Well, he saw me and did a gesture I didn't understand at first meaning "come on in" in Italian, like this (she made the gesture for their benefit, and the girls agreed, it was upside down), something that had crossed the oceans with his family. He turned the gesture around, waving me in so that I could understand it.

Anyway, he was very seductive. (From the way she paused, the girls knew she skipped something here. The mother liked to say nothing should be hidden from children, out of respect for them as people, but they knew she hid. Was she a liar? It couldn't be.)

He told me a story about drawing as a child and experiencing the miracle of two-point perspective. He put lines on a page just to put lines on a page and then look what they did. They transformed reality. I only remembered being taught perspective in school. I thought, *this must be genius, this man.* When a man tells a story about his childhood, hang on to your pants.

We are wrapped in white sheets on his white sofa where I sleep at night and he screws me in the afternoons. There are paint spatters everywhere so that life and canvas blur. He wears his coveralls in class and everywhere because an artist never ceases to be an artist. In class he lectures on authenticity. ("A carrot is a carrot," said Ad, holding a carrot up like a long wagging finger. "Unless you made a carrot soufflé.")

In class (their mother said), we walked a circle around the life model before returning to our easels. He said, first walk the perimeter and see the soul of the thing that is there. See the soul before you exert your will. I thought of my father's dog who ran the edges of fields to flush birds. I thought of birds shattering the boundaries of a soul. I sealed the boundaries of my soul and walked the perimeter of the naked girl. Da Vinci looked for the house of the soul in the dissected body. I sometimes picked up some cash as a life model. From my position, I would try to be a shape and not a person. I tried not to look at her as a person. I tried to look at her as a shape with a soul. Here is how the light hit her. Here is how her body met the light. He was going to Florence at the end of the semester. He had bohemian friends there. I said, "Can I stay here in your studio?" and he said, "Come with me to Florence where they keep all the paintings."

Fantastic. He had a cousin who worked for Pan Am. He had another cousin with space in Florence. He said, "You will love it." Then he said, "No! It will love *you*," and slid his painted hands between my legs. I thought, I can do anything! Like jumping onto the horse in the field next to my grandmother's orchard. You remember. (They did. A horse made of clouds.)

The novelty of flight. Yes, I wore a shirtwaist dress as I'd seen in movies. He gave it to me for fun to wear. Audrey Hepburn went to Rome and listened at the mouth of truth. We arrived in Rome, with a plan to spend the night near Termini and continue to Florence—forthwith! We arrived at night. The hotel was nice. Hotels came cheap. You know Rome was founded on rape. In the room was his wife.

It was not a surprise that he had a wife. It was a surprise to find her there next to a window that, like doors, opened *in*.

That was the first and last I saw of the room—it has disappeared from my memory. But there is Nick. He'd shaved for the flight, already looking a little not like himself to me. There is his wife. What she looked like. Not pretty like me but pretty. Tough-pretty. Wild, dark hair that seemed to be in motion, curling. What he looked like next to her.

I look at her but I can't tell what she knows. She's standing, not touching anything, a small dead tilt to her head. And there's Nick striding around the room—striding around the room with his mouth twitching. I've seen this before. He has a lot of energy. He doesn't contain himself. Emotions flow through him. His body, his way of moving around is exactly the same in the Italian room as when he's teaching, when he's painting. Using his hands, using brushes. Except now I don't like it. I can see him just poking at the air around him—what happens if I poke like this, what happens if I poke like that? He's anticipating, holding back anger or joy. I think, you are not a caged animal. I think, a real animal would tear you up.

He says, "My girls, my great girls. You are going to love each other." He begins to list our desirable attributes. He cites my talent, my hair, my untapped . . . and so on. Apparently no one has an ass like his wife, no one is so liberated, no one more brilliant and nurturing. When I start to cry he says, "What is *wrong* with you? Look where you *are*!"

(Their mother became still. Em put down the knife that she'd been using on mushrooms. She put it down out of respect for the silence that protects emotion.)

I don't remember everything. There's wine, of course. We drink the wine. I forget what else until the bed. I don't remember how we got in there. He got in. She got in. I stood with the end of my wine and then I got in. Thought about the white sofa in the paint. Listened to him lecture about what Florence was going to be like. A monastery of arches filled with monks' cells each with an arched door and a single arched window, and in each cell a single painting either of arches or in the shape of an arch, and, inside each painting, people in holy acts of contemplation. Of people. Of paintings. Of memories.

In the bed I think about threes and twos. I wonder why one is better than another. I think about composition. The stability of triangles. About making motion. I think about the last time a nun smacked me. It occurred to me that Nick was old enough to disappoint himself. In the bed, from my place on his left side, I can feel his hands moving around, on her, on his right side. Why did I feel like a child in that bed? Just because of the shapes and the numbers?

When I thought they were sleeping I left the bed and passed the black window refusing to look out. I went into the blackish hall and followed, with my fingers, textured silk embossed like braille all the way to the bathroom. I couldn't find a light. I felt so clumsy, working foreign mechanisms by feel. I followed the patterns to return but stayed in the hallway and pressed my back to the wall outside the door to the room. I looked up. I could make out the hanging fixture above me, one in a series, none lit. I thought, I am in the Eternal City. All roads come here, so all roads must leave. I looked up because I was lost. It had become very important to me to renounce God after losing my family, and so what I saw was the particulate darkness, the quiet difference in density between where there was an unlit lamp and where there was not. What happens first in history, the praying or the looking up? And what if I knew, then what, so what? Skies painted on ceilings. In the hallway I thought I could be looking at a nice night sky beneath an unpainted ceiling. Then I thought, no I'm not. It's just a ceiling in the dark. I thought, is this timeless?

Why couldn't I make it mean what I wanted? I'd looked at the sea from the descending airplane and imagined the peaks of water first as endless mountains and then as endless roofs of churches, their crosses exploding off their tips like the distant droplets that must be there in the spray that must have been there. That airplane, memory already. What was I going to do with all those churches? I had promised, in my heart, to wrench them from their artworks. Nick's wife appeared in the hallway in her white ghost nightgown. The light changed or my eyes adjusted. She was like a letter someone dropped from the sky. So much taller than me. Her voice low and controlled. She seemed to consider sizing me up and then decide she didn't have to. She already had me pegged. It happened in a breath, her taking me in. She handed me an envelope. Inside was a pair of tickets. One for a steamer, one for the train to take me to it. To take me. It left one day and one night away. Steamers were cheaper than jet planes, my girls. People still took them, but they were on their way out. My grandmother went on deck to see a hurricane coming. Her third yacht trip around the world. They helicoptered her body back to California. What did it mean, the envelope? That she'd expected me? Did she know about the sofa in the studio? What if I were a different girl, would she have torn the tickets up? Or did she want me to insist, on my own, to stay? What does a coward do, and what is brave? I am not afraid of him. I am not afraid of her.

But I was an excellent student, and I wanted to know.

I slept a little, on the edge of the bed. I did not clutch the tickets in my hand. I put them in my suitcase. It is possible to take up very little space, to convince yourself you are not in evidence. When the light shifted, I woke as if it'd touched me. It did touch me. It came through a clear window, through a pale curtain, and by the time it reached me it was colorless. I took my suitcase. I do not remember the hallway lit, as it must have been at that time of day.

In the lobby the hotel people in their uniforms were not at their posts and I did not ring for them. I took a map from a box of maps at the concierge desk. I put sugar cubes in my pocket from a silver bowl in the bar. I took a warm roll from a pan half unloaded into the display case. I took two apricots from a basket. I put the fruit and the bread in my suitcase and left.

Outside, first thing, I looked for the sky. I had never seen real clouds with silver linings. So many kinds of whiteness. Particular pinks. Like the sky was faking it. Candy-green parakeets with beaks like berries swooped in pairs and landed in budding trees, I *swear* to you, and behind trees, massive monochrome buildings getting dirty as they approached the earth. All those paintings I studied, frosty flesh among swirling fabrics, the human faces of dark animals grimacing truthfully from corners. Old Nick admired the grace of my stroke, at once restrained and assured, my sensitivity to the dimensionality of my subjects. I was on full scholarship. He said I had a gift. I said, this is not a gift. I said, I work for this. I touched the sugar cubes in my pocket, each wrapped in colored paper. I had not understood that the colors in paintings I studied were literal. I felt a little let down. Saints fading in stucco frames on exterior walls, sculptures leaning midair from the facades. I walked through an inside-out city. I saw a cardinal high above me crushing the head of an infidel who searched out my eyes from underfoot. I saw a fish inside a bubble. People woke and left their houses as if to decorate streets for my benefit. I worked out ways to tote my suitcase. This hand, that hand, both, front, back. By midmorning it was getting crowded. I did not want to touch the people. I did not want them to take my suitcase. Italian men will really rake their eyes across you. I had to push through a chaotic market. People who don't form a line or speak in turn, handling everyone's meat and vegetables. I felt hot, though the weather was irreproachable. At the edge of the market, water streamed from the mouth of a wolf. I put my suitcase down, cupped my hands, and drank from it, then shook shiny droplets from my fingers. On buildings I saw keys and bees, mountains and crowns. I knew these were codes for people in the country's history. I pictured the city without its people, and I pictured the people without the city. I was testing my powers of perception. I knew the statues we know as white were once painted. I imagined being painted, asleep on the sofa, Nick pulling back a sheet, then pulling back my painted surface, and marble beneath.

I sat on my suitcase at the base of an obelisk. Water slid across the backs of rising turtles. I resisted the desire to hug the toe of a colossus. I turned to look down each of several boulevards that stretched like electroshocked tentacles. A snake stared his own toothy face in a stone mirror. I saw a dolphin turning into a dragon turning into a horse turning into someone broken off at the shoulders. I saw where Mussolini changed a neighborhood into squares crammed with modern weaponry. He made the wolf mother look *up* at the babies she raised, when everywhere else they suck at her and squirm. I wanted to know my potential.

I stood on the bridge lined with angels. I walked across it so I could see them from one side and then the other. Then I walked right back because I knew from my map that they led to St. Peter's. And you remember how I was feeling about God. I was transforming my feelings. I was choosing an understanding of my experience. I pissed in a bush that was shaped like a staircase. I looked into windows that were paintings of windows. *I can see right through you!* I imagined saying to the dumb joke of a window, having spoken to no one since my lover's wife. I let my joke with the wall bounce in the space between us. On display in a real window, a cappuccino was just a paper napkin stuffed in a cup with cinnamon on it.

But almost anywhere you can go in Rome is a church, and that is to show the single source of power employed architecturally. Where else can you go to escape cacophony? I wanted a quiet place to eat my piece of fruit with a piece of my bread, and so I drifted into a gray cobbled cloister. The food was good because I was hungry. The arms of the church reached out and clasped the arms of the arched colonnades, pilasters, and loggia. Another sort of hunger, a nun would likely tell me. I was resting in those arms. Could I go in there and remain safe from God? Ways that *yes* and ways that *no*. The face of the church bulged in a game of concave-convex. Come in, don't come in. I felt both at once. But its doors were open, and inside, an unpainted universe of soft white glowed. I put a sugar cube into my mouth. Bells rang. Dogs from inside houses all through the neighborhood surrounding the cloister began to howl beautifully. I looked up at the sky in this frame. At my feet: star patterns in the cobblestones, concrete things in the shape of stars in the ground. I stepped from one to another, and stood in the doorway of the white church, and stars tiptoed from big to small to increase its dome.

Come in. You can't come in. Come in. You can't come in. Over alternating doorways white angels crossed and uncrossed their wings. Abstract crowns with points that replicated the points of the stars, suns that wiggled, suggesting fire, and then more crowns turning into those white ideas of flames. I committed the name of that church to memory, though I didn't know the language. Now I know that its name means knowledge though I've forgotten the name itself. The master designed the courtyard to present the work of his student. Screw you, Nick. You're from New Jersey.

"You liked it because it was white?" asked Em. Or empty, thought Em. Empty as a baby, as a child can seem to be.

Adeline asked, "Did you go in?"

Grandmother stepping onto the deck of the yacht, crossing the line. You know who was at her funeral? Me and the maid. No, I did not go in. I went to a palace that was a museum, but I had no money to enter. Two entrances were at the tops of stairs. In the left wing was a square staircase and in the right wing was a round staircase. Up the stairs, galleries behind doors. Ahead, galleries behind doors. But you could go up and down the staircases. I carried my suitcase up and down the staircases. In the square one a lion led and then followed me gently through rhythmic rays of slanting light. Then the round one digested me in its coils. Come in, you can't come in.

At dusk I stood in front of the Pantheon and let it put me in my place. Comfort me with its thickness, its guiseless, skinless surface. I traced the line between the conceivable and inconceivable, setting the curve of the Pantheon in relation to the curve of the universe. Anyway, the moon was full, white hole in the sky. Isn't that enough? A bum was already asleep among the colossal columns of the portico. I was not going to sleep. I was going to keep walking the city until I had to walk right onto a train that would take me to a boat and leave.

The Tiber was lit with yellow lights that looked like heaps of ancient coins pouring into it or glowing up from under the water. Either way. I found a lit fountain in an empty piazza and put my feet in it. I did see some paintings. I saw ceiling paintings through windows at night and thought of the animals I drew in their cages. There's a line in a Marvell poem, a sly nun says it's actually the men who are caged *outside* the nunnery. It's true that, from outside, I could see that they *were* paintings more than I could see the paintings themselves. But I know what the pictures were of. People in heaven having a grand time. People suffering on earth.

I have been told that there were no green parakeets in Rome until decades later, but I saw them.

Not a single Italian heard my voice for the entire time I was in Italy. Look at me. Come in, you can't come in. I'm glad I didn't open my mouth to any of them. I made my way. I took the train. I took the boat. Third class, no portholes. Thanks a lot, wife. I was not afraid of hurricanes. My grandmother's favorite flower was the peony. She had hedges of them, and when my grandfather was discovered, suicide in the pool, someone had clipped dozens of enormous blooms and set them floating. Bobbing cherub heads, so pink and white.

That's what you're like, thought Em. You're always *come in, you can't come in.* That's what everyone's like.

"When he killed himself in the pool," said Adeline, "was it grief for his wife?"

The queen died, and then the king died of grief. Em had been taught cause and effect using this sentence in school, but she didn't know if Adeline or their mother had been taught it or if this was just the stuff of life clanging around a room.

Their mother said, "He died first. You have to take care of yourself."

Ad said, "Was it *guilt*?"

The king drowned himself in the pool, and then the queen stepped onto the deck of a yacht in a hurricane.

"This is not a love story," their mother said. "Are you even *listening*? I am *not finished.* This is *my grief.* Mine."

She said: When we crossed into American waters they rang a bell. People crowded outside. It was a bright day. I felt gratitude for the head on my own two shoulders. The world is in a blade of grass, the universe in a single grain of sand! You don't have to go anywhere if you know how to pay attention. Don't look at me like that, she said. This is not why I married your boring father. This is not why I don't suck his dick. I don't care that I'm not a painter. I have you girls as mine forever.

Their mother left the room. She returned with a stack of papers that included restaurant place mats, napkins, and legal pads, and plunked them on the table among the onions. Annotated floor plans filled and covered the papers. "In any event, you should see what I'm up to with the house. You're both away so much. Have a look at these. It's really going to be something."

So. Em. Airport. She waited for her plane at the gate, early flight, stores still closed, shining, expansive, hard, vacant; obvious, unnecessary, bouncy broadcast sixties pop.

So, airplane. Last-minute purchase, middle seat. The woman on the left said she was a painter. The man on the right said he was a composer. The woman had remarked on his violin while they were in line, and now they stuffed their legs, bags, butts into the same row, remarking on the coincidence, settling, purposefully casually incorporating their credentials into the conversation. *So where are you headed, oh that's a nice venue, have you worked with—*

Em had a view directly down the musician's ear with its evocative canyons and sprung, eager hairs. The artist's ear was broad, flat, and almost ridgeless. Soon enough the artist and the musician found a person they had in common and the musician, who had the aisle seat, said to Em, "I'll tell you what. You can have the aisle." So they switched. A few rows ahead a round gray-haired woman in a pink sweatsuit, hair slightly Einstein, was attempting to hold court. Madwoman, talking, talking. Talking so weirdly, face weird, posture weird. Guy across the aisle playing along, "What's that you say? You don't say . . ." and guy next to him overtly videotaping them with his phone. The pink woman's hamming it up, making animal noises back and forth with the one guy, who's already flipping through imaginary responses they'll get when they post, doing the fake-flirt young guns do with old ladies. She definitely has them by decades though probably fewer than it looks like because of pain. The guys look even younger because of lives rich with positive feedback. The pink sweatsuit is a result of how she's been *through it* and how she's *off*, but right now she has access to happiness, and if you paid attention you could feel the wonked cilia of her consciousness wiggling toward that good feeling. People shoving their stuff into overhead bins caught a sense of the scene through the geometrics made by arms and roller bags in motion. People in neighboring rows, organizing themselves for a disgusting flight, began to tune in.

The woman in pink sweats engaged several people in turn. She'd sense someone uncomfortable, latch on, and push. The look on her face like *I'm so sly*, but if you're paying attention, translucent down to the nub of fear. After a couple of these engagements, target passenger escaping by sliding deep into a row—"have a good flight, nice to meet you"—the madwoman began to vocalize the private part of her brain. "So I guess I'll just keep to myself here," she said. "Keep keep keeping it to myself, sing it with me now, all you children, now." The guy with the video buddy at this point leaned over the arm of his aisle seat, across the blue carpet, to her aisle seat, pushed her elbow like a saloon door—and said, "Hey, so what do you think about flying the friendly skies?" and when she didn't look up yet he said, "How do you feel about the first black president? Ah, don't like politics? Okay, how about this one, are you for or against *rodents*? You know, rodents!" The woman looked up, then, and he held a pretend microphone at her, raising and lowering his eyebrows. Then he mimed eating a nut, encouragingly. Then back to the eyebrows and microphone, "You can tell *me*, never mind all these lovely people," with as grand a sweep of the arm as was possible in the confines. "They only want to get to know you as a person. Come on, how do you feel about *nuts*?" The woman narrowed her eyes and shunted her head toward him with skepticism, like an ancient tortoise, and said nothing. The guy gnawed his nut at her while his friend filmed.

Em tried not to watch the show but sound and other scraps of sensory information kept informing her—a person moving past her down the aisle having passed between the interviewer and his subject, whatever air delivers through your clothes to your skin, whatever scents of anxiety and contained adrenaline deliver. Finally with a gulp of air she pressed the service button, which lit up with the little guy and levitating cup. She tried to think of what to say when someone in uniform came wanting to know how she could be helped. *Those men are being unkind to that woman. That woman is experiencing a medical crisis.* Then she wondered if the button had worked. It had made a *bong.* Then a flight attendant arrived on the scene, and, ignoring the video guys, said to the madwoman in pink, "Come with me?"

"What is it now?" said the woman.

The flight attendant said, "It's private," and the woman allowed the flight attendant to take her by the arm and lead her. "Hey— hey—" the interviewer called after. "Don't go—I only have a few more questions—who are you wearing? That color—it really brings out your girlish—"

Em could not discern the madwoman's affect as she allowed herself to be led, if she was resigned, suspicious, begrudging, afraid, perplexed, immune, anxious, detached, enthusiastic, grateful, amused, deflated, pensive, sour, defensive, righteous, forlorn, deadened (though there were plenty of things it was definitely *not*). Two officers in uniform waited at the ramp. Parts of them poked in and out of view. They had arrived on Segways. Em was guessing about the Segways based on seeing officers on them in the airport earlier. They thanked the woman for cooperating and the flight attendant for her assistance. She guessed that, too. The attendant looked too young to have been hired before 9/11. She wouldn't know the difference between danger then and danger now. Em decided the look on her face indicated that she felt important and underappreciated. The passenger who had been sitting next to the pink madwoman tapped the flight attendant on the shoulder and handed her the knapsack that the madwoman had tucked under the seat. The knapsack was also pink, a lighter shade, and the flight attendant tried to act like she knew what to do with it, though clearly she did not. She walked it toward the front of the plane and stuffed it in an overhead compartment. The interview guys, meanwhile, acted outraged. "She wasn't doing anything wrong!" they'd called after a different flight attendant, one who hadn't been involved. "Power down that device!" said this other flight attendant, and they hit *post* just in time.

Em tried to shake the feeling that she'd pressed a button and made a woman disappear.

The plane took off. The more disgusting airplanes became, the more the air seemed conditioned to make everyone a little high. The artist fell asleep reading *SkyMall*. The musician fell asleep reading instructions for in-flight entertainment. They floated through clouds in stupidly curved seats in a plane newly retrofitted for more seats in economy so that none of the windows lined up. Direct flight, though, then, *thunk*. Goodbye painter one direction, goodbye musician another. Go, go, make art. Sleepy eye see the future take form. Sleepy ear hear echoes of the past ring, ing, ing. It was hard to picture that painter and that musician making anything important. Perhaps they were just professionals and who knew where art would come from or if anyone would notice when it came. Still it would exist. The video douchebags looked like anyone filing out. The cameraman spoke sweetly to a child on the very cell phone that held the video. The interviewer retrieved a scrap of paper for a woman with a baby, who had dropped it intentionally because she couldn't spot a trash can. If you are among the people who want to matter in the world, there comes a time when you get real with yourself and see that you won't. It's a developmental phase, probably evolutionary, that makes you want someone *else* to try already, simultaneous with a need to be distracted from your sorrow. Let a baby take a shot. What a cellular ball of potential, plus cute outfits. This one at the airport had on a hat with furry ears.

Americans are excellent at proceeding in and out of planes. In some countries people clump and push because they have a different relationship to space. Taxis are likely equally out to get you every-where, but in your home country you can feel like you know what you're doing. There are a lot of books and movies where you go back to the house you grew up in or revisit the site of a prominent trauma, find the place abandoned and drawn with the passage of time or, alternately, innocuous and inhabited by innocents, just a place, it turns out, and not necessarily anything. There you are, and nothing bad is happening. Just because before doesn't mean next. You close its door, close it behind you. Look at that door close. What is that poem, *there are no doors in the house of sleep*. You know what sleep is, it is just yourself without all the doors, how people say *opening up*. At baggage claim Em stood with her carry-on among definite strangers and the vaguely familiar. A person she knew from the plane as *near the bathroom*. A person she knew from the plane as *rude to seatmate*, as *inconsiderate sneezer*, as *holder of sleeping child*. Also a surprising number of people who might or might not have been on the flight, so strange to have been shoved so close together so precariously, to have experienced something so unlikely as being thrown across the land in a tubular machine and still not know each other at all. Also now, milling around baggage, some people she might as well have gone to school with or had a job with if she'd stayed, people she'd pumped gas near for years, familiar sorts of faces, ways of wearing clothing and moving limbs. Suitcases rose from the tunnel, teetered, and fell. She watched people reunite with their belongings until she had seen a few distinctive luggage pieces rumble by more than once, and no more were coming out, and now it would be time to locate the dark office or call the airline or dig for an encoded slip or fill something out, so she left the conveyor belt with just her twenty-one-inch roller bag following her amiably, and found the taxis. This driver's country of origin was Sierra Leone. Within minutes he wanted her to have his private number. He explained that he would take an unusual exit to avoid the unrest.

"Unrest?"

"Since yesterday."

"A lot?"

He explained the court case without condescension. The people were right. "Good for them," said Em. This was the city with the airport, mall, and courthouse she'd grown up with, and she knew many of the ways that lines about race and money went starkly across it. The taxi driver had sharp cheekbones and a darkened patch of extra-smooth skin sliding down his neck behind his collar that could have been a scar or a birthmark. The driver didn't indicate what he thought of her response. He said, "We'll go around." She looked out the window as if she might catch the distant comet of a Molotov cocktail. It would be beautiful. She rolled her window down and the night was balmy. Rushing air filled her head with abstract sound, nothing from any humans out there beating at one another or tearing at the structures around them. The airport had of course been climate controlled, then crossing from baggage claim to the taxi stand through the smokers it had been hot and wet, then the taxi was climate controlled. "It's okay if I open this, yes?" after she'd opened it. What would happen when she enacted this ritual of return? Taxi, taxi, all the way out of the city, she wondered, and she wondered through countryside that she knew by feel, the tune of the road from childhood, the fields that were flowing along hills as extra densities, built up more than before—more lit windows, streetlights, more dug up, more shoved around, but moving by at a pace and rhythm she knew, with a way about the air that she knew, all the way to the house by a river in the woods. Time for the driver to tell his story, for her to offer him some clucks, ohs, hmmms, follow-ups, and what-abouts, time then for some soft silence, for the shape of roadside woods to look like mountains, black on black sky, for the rhythm of white dotted lines that shift to double yellow and back, and back again, to lull her into something like an unfolding, some plump receptivity.

And nothing like a wad of cash you don't know how to give a shit about.

"Thank you, good night."

"Thank you, good night."

She stood in the driveway as the taxi departed—up the dirt road that split the field that ended in woods. Something like a periscope poked out of one of the three mounds of construction debris. The inside of the house was lit up. Her mother's house. Her father's, too. Bits of shine came off plastic that sheeted the current facade. The light from the guts came off yellow as if from age. Wind rustled plastic. This moon, far from whole, was clearly spherical. Ways light's contained, ways it slips and bounces. A cloud of sound rose and surrounded her from the creature family of crickets, cicadas, and tiny singing tree frogs, bare beasties whole-body vibrating from the crevices in bark and the undersides of leaves. In that encompassing hum, humidity dropped to the ground around her ankles. The suitcase bobbed with her across the roots of trees until a plastic wheel lodged on something. When she yanked it, an object clonked against her boot, and when she felt around on the ground, there was a gun in a clump of dirt, leaves, and needles. She'd been across the room from guns, but avoided learning anything about them. Popular culture suggested that near the trigger a secret lever operated the safety, but she wasn't going to guess based on that. She lifted it by the wooden butt and used her finger to poke mulchy earth from its trigger area. She understood, fussing over it, why people say that a gun wants to be in your hand. She kept holding it by the butt to prevent it from sneaking into place, set her suitcase by a stack of doors that leaned against the side of the house near the stoop. Her cells were still winding down from the plane and then the car, but the gravity of the gun seemed to focus them. Now shadows inside the house began to move like great leaves of lettuce, and a new layer of sound rose. What lit the living room suddenly swerved, making the light dart and then settle into a flicker. It was dogs running through the house, bird dogs at chase within walls.

Even this late in history no one locked up this far out in the country, so she just turned the egg-shaped knob and stood in the foyer with plastic around her like a cheap shower. She could hear dozens of feet. The shadow of a dog shot by beyond the plastic, and then one shot by close enough to brush it. No one barked, and she didn't call out. She was in the eye of a storm, sounds of bodies crashing through the architecture. A dog burst through, bringing down a length of plastic. It was Rufus, and he skidded to a stop before her, a bird draped in his jaw, the soft mouth of good bloodlines. None of the other noises ceased. Dogs still spun through the house. They were not trained hunters, just bird dogs who lived in a house in the woods. Filmy plastic flowed like a shawl over Rufus's head and down his back. He knew to drop the bird at her feet but could not bring himself to do it. Em had managed to grow up in the woods without learning anything about birds, either. This one was a little bigger than a pigeon, and brown. She'd always been good with dogs and suddenly missed them. Rufus was incredibly high. She could feel the adrenaline coming off him, serious, wet, hot endorphin joy. Beyond, in the living room, the head of a fallen pole lamp shone wonkily from a cushy splayed chair. Dogs still trotted, panting through the house, numberless because of sound, less and less frantic, though their pointy tails were still going like fan blades—it must have been just the one bird, but they wanted to know for sure. They were going over everywhere the bird had been and balancing that information against ancient and possible new tracks. Dogs up and down stairs, their percussive nails like fat icy rain. The ever-unfinished thin and hollow everything.

Rufus was still deciding, or waiting for the command to *drop it*. Now, in the background, another dog leaped—it was Hank—he popped up from behind the sofa and over it, his ears rising in a moment of suspension at the apex—gorgeous, terrifying, goofy—and landed several paces behind Rufus, whose eyes swiveled and then returned their lock on Em. Hank hunkered down, preparing to point. Hank could make a move on the bird, or what would the girl have them do? Rufus got himself to yet another layer of stillness and issued a low controlled growl. Em yanked down the plastic to the kitchen and pushed it into a corner. Dogs trotted overhead. Two dogs watched her. Something under repair was shrouded in plastic on the kitchen table. She opened the door that used to go to a porch but now hung over the foundation. "Go on, you can go," she said, asking the dog to leap with the bird into the night, but he was a good dog and he stayed sitting, waiting for her to take it. She laid the gun on the table, took the body from the dog. It had the complete weight of a true gift. "Good boy," she said. He pranced at her side. She saw that Hank felt left out. "You're a good boy, too, Hank. What good boys." He trotted over bouncily. Other dogs arrived, speckled and spotty, circling the table, circling Em. "Look at all you good dogs. Hello, Penny, hello, Angie. Hello, hello." She had the bird. It was so soft, and warmth had so quickly left it. She didn't see a wound but she didn't look for one. A collision with a wall could have done it, or pure fear. It occurred to her that a shot could have gone off right before she arrived on the scene, and whoever fired it could be crouched in a corner right now or deep in the woods. Could be. She just didn't think so.

She found a dish towel and wrapped the body. It was yellow and green, so the plain bird lay in a nest of sloughed jungle colors. She laid the body on the table next to the gun. The bundle was about the same size as the gun, which was about the same size as whatever was under the shroud for repair. She peeked and it was a glass bell etched with leaves that she'd never seen before. She unshrouded the bell and rang it. It made a sweet bell sound and then fell apart. One more thing was on the table—a brown paper bag rolled shut. She could not be sure, because she would not open the bag, but she recognized it as the bag her mother had been given, at the hospital, of Adeline's final effects.

It was so bright in the house. The dogs were still dogs, nosing, milling. She opened the door that used to go to a porch and this time they flowed out as if leaping into a lake. In the living room she righted the pole lamp so the house wouldn't burn down. The bare bulb had already left a mark on the upholstery. She found the shade and affixed it, gave it a pat, and then stopped it rocking. For a second, she wondered why she hadn't wanted the house to burn. It was not virtue. She retrieved her suitcase from the stoop, looked for somewhere unobtrusive to park it, and slid it under the kitchen table next to a chair. She could hear the dogs outside through a dozen kinds of trees, sometimes calling to each other, onto something new.

Dogs being dogs, trees as trees.

She'd left her cell in the taxi, perhaps accidentally. If any family cars, old or newly acquired, were out there, they were lost in the dark. But you can't account for everything, you just have to move the fuck along sometimes, so once she knew no one was in the kitchen, or the living room, or behind the door to her mother's room (she looked in, she saw the bed their mother used to share with their father, wooden, quilted, she saw boxes with papers pushing at the lids shoved under all the pieces of furniture), she even peeked in the bathroom (new *Bobby Fischer* on the toilet back with beat-up *Malcolm X*) on her way to the stairs. The house was not a body or a machine. A ring was a handy circle, a key opened some physical thing. Stairs went up. She entered the bare and enclosed corridor, rough plywood and pale drywall. Step, step, step to a landing and it turned ninety degrees, and then it did the same thing again and achieved its purpose, which was that she felt a little suspended, unable to see where she'd come from or where she was headed. She did pause in the suspense, but she didn't linger, because who really cares about architecture when what you want is to arrive, and what you mean by arrive is *access* your sister, because she's yours, after all, she is your sister, you are made of the same stuff, and if you can't access her, what does that say about anyone else, and if what it says about anyone else is *no*, what does that mean for this earth, suffering such failing multitudes—

Come in, says Adeline, your sister.

As if she can give permission and there you will have it, it will be yours.

The stairwell was white, white, white—even the stairs—white.

The image of the aunt was one felt flower at a time emerging from her mouth and falling to the desert floor—(litter!)

The image of Benny was back in a shack across town reunited with drug friends. Outside, grass approaching the rusty corrugated roofline; inside, light falling in strokes over the insubstantial nodding bodies. He's just one of them. He's not wearing that shirt or that hat. He's not even thinking of his next move.

The image of the ex was the ex was doing great, she was getting married to a great girl, someone worldly yet unpretentious, they really got each other, so great.

The image of their father was following a line of naked toddlers into a field of snow. Some came along after him, too.

The image of their mother was a church burning for the insurance. Don't worry, she will never die.

The image of herself was swimming through the hallways of the swank hotel, its overwrought carpets and mirrored wall coverings, desperate bedclothes and curtains turning visceral, its elevator shafts bulging, the angles and grids of its layouts dissolving to fractal mush so that as she swam, though she'd never been a graceful swimmer, *forward* was the direction she was taking because it was the direction of her body, and the direction the body took was always toward her sister, and when she arrived—then what? then what?—the fantasy of the sacred, shared—of healing contact and insight—dissolved into the violence of penetration, inhabitation, occupation, violation.

The door to the room was open, with the bed, bottom bunk of the bed they'd shared, visible across from the fireplace, and the window next to it open, no curtain, half primed. With his feet on the pillow and his ass on the headboard perched Jack, coatless, impish, mouth circled with bright pink dots, looking happy and mean and poised for flight.

He wore one of those little white gay sailor caps. He was going to China. He described the steamer, decked-out deco, ice sculptures everywhere, last of its class. Long boats, slow boats, lovers weeping on a faraway shore. That's a song. China! He'd dug so many holes there as a child. Economic powerhouse coming up in the world. He was off for a latte in the Forbidden City, where you make your own luck, house done, time to die, the great pleasure of world travel being finding yourself in unexpected places, losing yourself in mountains that give the finger to the sky (but Jack, isn't that Japan?), meeting your long-lost true love on the Great Wall, walking opposite directions, saying goodbye forever. (That's great, but Jack—*China?*) The opera, said Jack, where a man can be a woman and a boy can be a boy. And the food—(but Jack, you really don't want to end up lost hiking and become the victim of a repressive regime—you don't want to become a statistic—you don't want to be a lone—alone—). Jack said did he ever mention the time he was *the* homeless guy they made into an internet hotspot and what it was like to be famous on Facebook and *miss it*? She said she was not the social media type. He seemed to take in the immensity of her ignorance. He narrowed his eyes with menace, hopped off his perch. He backed up a step involuntarily. She stuttered something about smokers and the air in Beijing. He said he'd show her a mountain in Japan—like, *I'll show* you *a mountain in Japan* is the way he said it, holding his hands behind his back like he had a present, meanwhile lifting one foot and wiggling it tauntingly, moving it toward her, lifting the other and wiggling it so that she gave in and said, "Okay okay, what are you holding behind your back?" as if she were just playing along. He said she had to guess, and she said she wouldn't guess, this was not a game, quit fucking around, and he said who was she to decide what was a game and what was not? He said the answer was *no one*, she was *no one to decide*. That's a direct quote of what he said. He rocked his shoulders teasingly. *Guess.* She guessed *knife* and he shook his head. She guessed *wings* and he gave a smirk, dropping his head to a side. She gathered herself for a swerve in tactics, holding her ground in the face of the dangling foot. She said, "Jack, it's amazing your mouth healed so perfectly." It had not; she said it hoping to cross a line. She said, "How does it feel to have a mouth surrounded by holes? You know what it looks like? It looks like God took His claws and touched you," but Jack was not deterred, he just stopped the sarcastic wiggling and proceeded posthaste in her direction. They locked eyes. Her ears screamed. He put his face up to her face. Where were *her* hands? She'd forgotten them. He shifted back just far enough to bring his hands around in front of him. In each he held a Creamsicle.

He said, "One for me, one for you."

Because of the tacky flavored vodka her sister had mixed with orange juice and prescriptions to kill herself, the joke landed perfectly. Comedians are always saying "You killed it, you're killing me" to emphasize, embrace, undo, and redo the pathetic, but she couldn't say anything back. It felt like the last joke on earth.

When she could speak she said she knew he knew where Adeline was and he better tell her.

He said, "Mmmm, albinos. Perfectly balanced," indicating the taste of the orange dessert items as he went from one to the other with his mouth as they dripped, vanilla centers beginning to show. "Really, you can have one. They're from this great place I know."

He meant the swank hotel.

Go suck an egg! she thought. Go jump in a lake! Go kick the can! She said if he didn't give her some useful information—stuttering—blubbering—humiliating—tears coming—snot coming—sweat—every mucus thing—she said he better serve up some useful information or she'd march right down and fetch that gun no fuckin' backsies.

"You don't think I will, do you, Jack? You don't think I know what to do with a gun. Well, I know what to do as much as anyone, a gun is no mystery."

He licked and licked.

So she went downstairs and got the gun, half hoping that by the time she returned he'd be gone, but he wasn't gone. In fact, he'd settled onto the bunk cross-legged, halfway through one of the Creamsicles while the second ran down his other hand uncontrollably.

So she shot him.

Em put the gun on the fireplace mantel. Headlights were wobbling along the access road and then up to the house where the ground became audible. She heard the doors and voices with the headlights on and with the headlights off, and she heard them, her family, maneuvering doors and plastic sheeting and into the kitchen remarking on how full they were—*I'm so full, I can't believe how full I am*—and that's how she knew it had been dinner out. She knew how nice the little downtown area had become over the gentrifying decade so she knew that the dinner had been nice, that the food had been tasteful, that the restaurant had been atmospheric, and she knew from their voices that the theater of the evening had worked. Her father and her mother laughed at something intelligent. Her sister and Benny laughed painlessly.

She climbed out the window onto the roof. Something about not interrupting, something about a *household*. She remembered her mother's grandmother stepping toward a hurricane. She had gone from her three-winged house, through the orchard, through the town that was becoming a city, to the ocean, stepped off the edge of California onto a boat, headed out the same way she'd arrived from an island off Portugal, to see the world for the third time, to see it again but different. The grandmother watched the structures made by people and then the land itself sink into the ocean because of perspective. Surrounded by ocean like an unmade bed, her mother's grandmother could turn in any direction, and did she feel freedom? Well, the story goes, no. Whatever it was, it was not enough, even though her father had been a fisherman and now she paid a captain and could pick any direction. It was not enough because the ocean was a plane forever in two dimensions. Then came the weather. This weather was a madness that could lift her or drop her, making three.

Em listened to the members of the family go to their separate rooms. The dogs settled down. Her sister turned on the bedside lamp, and she crept closer to the window to see. Ad took her dinner clothes off, put on a T-shirt that said *Tide*. Then she began twisting newspaper and arranging sticks in the fireplace. When she was ready to light the fire, she went for the box of matches that was on the mantel, and there was the gun. Em watched her sister take in the gun. Looking at it, deciding whether to put her hands on it, then how.

She said "Ad!" in a big whisper, and Adeline knew her voice immediately, came to the window.

"You creepster, what are you doing out there?"

Em said, "Just—don't do anything."

"You know, it is not okay to go spying on people," Ad said, leaning out the window with her elbows resting amiably on the sill. "It smells nice out here," she said. "Are you coming in? Stop looking at me like that. You just have to trust me. You don't have a choice. Besides, nothing happened." Em looked terrified. "Here," said Ad. She got the gun and looked it over. She opened it up and took out the two bullets that were in there. She knew what she was doing. She tossed the bullets onto the roof and they clattered away. Then she leaned out the window and threw the empty gun back into the dark.

"Anyhow, are you coming in? I'm making a fire. If it gets too hot we'll put on the AC. There's AC now, did you know that?"

Em took her sister's hand through the window and brought it to her face. She thought she could feel leftover coolness and a quiet metal scent from the gun, but also the warmth that should be there. She heard a sound, and it was Ad's cat, hopping from an invisible level of roof and coming over. Em picked the cat up and handed her through the window to her sister.

"Gimme you," said Ad, taking the cat, then setting her down inside.

Em said, "Do you feel like you're in prison?"

"Of course I do. I am in prison."

"I wanted to see you. I'm really glad to see you. I know you think you're not cute anymore but you're still really cute. I'm afraid to come in. I'm afraid I won't get out. Do you want to come out on the roof with me? It's pretty."

Ad thought about it. Then she shook her head to mean *no*. "It's just I'm trying to get better."

That's what happened. Em climbed down the house with relative ease and walked back to the road, walked along it in the night, not know-

ing how long or how late because she had no timepiece. An old guy
let her ride in the back of his pickup with a bale of old straw. She
didn't want to get in the front with him. He said, "Suit yourself."
She didn't have any pressing associations with the straw or the truck
or the way the night was being. The slider window was open so she
could hear his radio songs and she could see him drinking a beer. It
wasn't even in a bag and that all seemed fine. When she banged the
roof with her fist he let her out at a motel with a sign with a pierced
heart. She and Ad had some made-up stories about the place, they'd
driven by it all the time growing up, *I bet this goes on in there, I bet
that goes on*, and then at some point they'd lost interest and the sign
faded into the landscape for them.

It was not nice in there, nothing to admire for the kitsch. The beds
were lumpy with springs, the bedding was pilled and damp, the carpet was sticky, the room smelled of ammonia, and the windows were
bolted shut. Even the actually painted landscape in its plastic frame
had no desire for beauty in it. The glowing heart with the arrow was
definitely pretty, but it was not attached to the motel because anyone
appreciated it, it was attached because no one gave a crap and the
sign just kept lighting up every night all the same. All she had left on
her was her license and her stack of bills folded in half. In the morning she used one of the bills for the room and then had some coins
in her pocket as well. Good thing she'd been wearing her glasses for
the flight. She completed the walk to town and bumped into a guy
she went to high school with, someone she'd done something sexual with way back but she couldn't remember exactly what or why.
He'd been a respected athlete near the top of the high school heap.
Now, big surprise, he was going through a divorce. He said, "You
remember Rhonda," and Em said she did, but she didn't. They had
a beer at two thirty in the afternoon and then she went along with
him to pick his kid up from his mother's. It was a Saturday. This
guy and his life were everything she had not wanted when she left
town. The boy was seven and she ended up sleeping in his child-
sized bed, with him across his own room from her on a cot with a
Disney blanket. "I'd let you sleep with me," the guy said as he was

setting up the cot, "I mean, in the room, sorry. I mean, she wouldn't care at this point, but I don't want him to get any ideas. He's really sensitive right now."

The kid's eyes shone in streetlight that came through the plastic blinds as he watched her try to fall asleep. He held a dump truck in his hand by his pillow, and she had no idea if that was age appropriate. She just kept thinking, poor kid, the crap he's inheriting.

Who would fall asleep first? One of them did. The next day she convinced the guy to let her sleep on the cot in the garage instead, which she did for a while as she worked through her options and their logistics. It was an immaculate empty garage, the kind where the house is attached to it rather than the reverse, and he'd moved his car to the driveway, some kind of restored sports car. It was yellow. The garage had the standard row of windows like Frank's had. From inside it felt like being in a box with its lid part open. She thought of Frank's confidence and ease, approaching that madman in the box on the way to the ruins, going back and forth with him like anyone else. Why did she feel as if he'd betrayed her? But if she believed Sheila about the money and if she believed herself about a posh asylum, that's how she felt.

She thought, I should throw that feeling up. That was a line from the man with a new liver, with his new lease on life.

During the day, she made use of the public library. Even here—in the small yet gentrifying town outside a city just large enough for an international airport and to host a riot—the library had become where people get off the streets to rest. They fell asleep in plastic chairs with their faces in books for privacy. Expert consultants felt that libraries had a problem with books taking up too much space. They advised transitioning to digital, doing more with Google, and adding a cyber-cafe to boost business. Street people, was the subtext, would go back to the street if faced with people in the library purchasing muffins and drinks. But who was she to say anything, she was there for the internet because she did not want to bother the guy from high school who was already letting her sleep in the garage and hadn't asked anything more of her, not even to check on his kid, who came home from school by himself in the afternoon and let himself in the front door. At the library, she made an email address, googled around looking for people she knew from back when she had friends, found a few, and emailed them with a version of her recent history, "That job really wasn't for me, anyway, that town really wasn't for me." She didn't write Andrew and Isabel. She wanted to keep sacred the possibility of having executed a kindness, to leave them making out on the foundation of perpetual autopay. *If everything is fucked up*, went her logic, *they'll either deal with it or they'll find me and I'll fail, at that time and at that juncture, to fix things.* She emailed Ad, "Hi," and the next day when she checked, Ad had emailed "Hi" back. Then they sent proto-emoticons made of sequences of parentheses, slashes, colons. After a few days, a couple of people had emailed back from different places in the country. One of them, Lu, her friend who now worked in animation in LA, said she knew a house-sit in East Hollywood, Em just had to get herself out there.

Em worried that LA would be another homecoming. When you are making a choice about a direction for the future, it's hard to avoid the terms of moving away from your past versus circling back. She had not lived in LA before, her dalliances with the state had taken place farther north. But Adeline had. Some delusions about celebrities had originated there and some true things that doctors thought were delusions because they involved celebrities had originated there. She'd made some videos and other kinds of art there, that Em thought might be a little beyond her, or nascent, but that was—what else can you call it?—*worth* something. Also, regarding LA, not far up the coast their mother had been born and brutalized. Some of the relatives they didn't know were probably scattered around if she ever had it in her to look into that, though really, she thought, with all their genes, if the family got together they should do it to make a pact to die out.

She emailed her sister, *I've got some leads in LA.*

LA is cool, came back. *Ru gonna see dad or mom?*

She emailed her sister, *No fucking way. But I'll meet you on the roof :) ;)*

Ha, came back. *I mean if you want but maybe better not to risk it.*

It made Em think about hurricanes, and it made Em think about books. She was in the library, after all. She thought about back when she used to read, actually, a lot. The sustained private act of reading a whole book. The best part of reading a book is the moment it feels like yours alone, right before the world gets in there with you. She held on to the idea of the roof with the window, being together with her sister in a secret. It was their own kind of room, a place to stay in the sense of now if not forever.

She emailed her father and cc'd her mom. *I'm moving to California.* Her father replied (no cc), *That is huge. Talk soon?*

Her mother replied (no cc), *I guess we know who you are, now.*

She emailed her sister. *Here's where I'll be staying, and you are always welcome. Always.* She felt an emotional surge when she wrote the second *always*, even knowing the many ways things could end up, because aren't some of our ways good for something? Don't some of our ways come from the better aspects of civilization? It was a one-bedroom on the fourth floor, that's all she knew. Anyhow, she wrote emails to another round of used-to-be-friends. One of them was United Premier Platinum status and gave her MileagePlus Points.

TSA was more fervent than ever. Em watched a woman her age cry when they took away a bottle of pancake syrup that had been packaged in gingham. "You better eat that with your kids!" the woman cried. When Em went through the full-body aka naked scanner, she had a hard time making herself put her hands up like that. "Put your hands higher," the officer said. "You have to put them higher." As she followed signage to make her connection through realms of shining white corridors that housed nothing but moving walkways, she found herself marking the studio apartments that could fit.

In LA, she contacted some of Ad's old friends and a couple of them were happy to have coffee with her and hear that Ad was "a lot better." A couple of them had residual guilt over having disengaged from some chaos, and were briefly comforted by offering information to help Em get settled. "I'm glad to be a resource," one guy said. He was very helpful and Em appreciated it. He said with his wife's job he could get her into the aquarium for free if she ever wanted. He also had a code for a trial gym membership. LA was in transition. Would the kind of stupid and corrupt it was known for continue to dominate, or would some new sorts of people acquire traction as neighborhoods collapsed, some eaten by other neighborhoods, as industries and institutions fissured and rocked. What would come out of those nooks and chasms?

The giant empty weather in LA made Em remember other weathers she'd forgotten about or seemed not to have noticed in years, such as snow falling off trees, such as rain pounding with lightning and drops bouncing back up from the ground, such as the skimming kind of wind that makes a leaf move along a surface like an insect, also exotic weathers she had not experienced such as thundersnow and supercell, and onto celestial phenomena such as earthshine. The thing Em soon liked best about LA was the proximity of vast concrete and ocean. Going into the ocean, she thought, as she gazed at it from the sand, is as close a thing to going into outer space that you can do as an ordinary citizen. The thing she liked second best about LA was mountains that looked just shy of dead, because that seemed honest. It was true that her sister was doing better, in the sense that includes deep sadness and physical discomfort.

The person she was house-sitting for did not have that much to safeguard, just thrift store finds and IKEA likely bought off Craigslist. Em registered the place with the post office as her address, and some months after (though the post office was on its way out, you could tell by the way the delivery people were not going to give you your mail unless they could reach your box without leaving the driver's seat let alone nor sleet nor snow in affected regions), a letter arrived with a yellow redirect sticker on it, and it was from Frank.

Tracked me down, Em thought. She tapped it against her thigh on the way back up to the apartment. She considered cracking a window and just sliding the words right back into the ether. But you should never underestimate the desire to know what happens *next*.

Dear Emilie, my colleague,

Frank wrote in blue ink on ivory paper.

> *I understand you are now an aspiring parvenu—and that this letter is a gamble, as the only address I have for you is the one I scratched down from your mailbox.*

Not my mailbox, thought Em. The fact that the letter was hand-written was outrageous to her, willfully old-fashioned. He must have used a ruler to keep the lines even.

> *The people in your house, you may want to know, are doing something untoward with your roses.*

Not my house! (Though she felt a pang for the flowers. She had a new used smartphone by then with a dictionary app, and learned a new word, |ˈpärvə,(y)o͞o|, often derogatory, noun, a person of obscure origin who has gained wealth, influence, or celebrity: the political inexperience of a parvenu | [as modifier] : he concealed the details of his parvenu lifestyle.)

> *Sheila and I had a heart-to-heart about our history following a tête-à-tête about the future, and that event has prompted this let-ter. Sheila means well but don't they always? She is a ~~chatterbox~~ gossip. It is true that my mother was ill, that she was perhaps mad with pain, and that she asked me to do what I did do for her, and as long as you know something of that moment in my personal life that is not for you to know, I will have you also know that the last*

words my mother said to me were, "I changed my mind." Put that in your pipe. I have made many of the choices in my life in an effort not to be ruled by what amounts to a terrible afternoon.

Em tried to imagine her life as a terrible afternoon. It was afternoon, and she was reading the letter tippily on the barstool at the so-called peninsula.

Ah, well,

Frank wrote.

I may be in my final decline, but you shall follow.

The next several paragraphs contained an account of Josie's memorial, which he attended with his sister. Jack was "safe, yet unable to attend" and Em pictured him frolicking on that fantasy asylum beach, and then caged luridly in the top rooms of Frank's house, and then she thought, no, Jack could be any number of places doing any number of things and you just don't get to know and so what if you did?

Frank went on. She skimmed. At the memorial, which was held at a golf club, Frank and his sister met Josie's sports star father and comedienne mom, who politely wouldn't talk to them. According to the letter, Sheila couldn't help herself trying to make subtle contact near the quiche, and Frank concluded with a series of remarks on "our fascination with empty celebrity and its destructive potentialities." Em put the letter back in its envelope and into the drawer of some person's hollow-core desk.

She woke in the night and took it back out. She returned to the part she had skimmed. At the memorial gathering, Frank said, a young man with black hair who no one seemed to know had arrived on a junky moped. The young man, he said, was "striking, but not handsome" and went around asking people where they were keeping the body. People kept turning away from him, trying to ignore him, and eventually he left.

It must somehow have been Tasio, Em thought.

It didn't make sense. Tasio didn't know Josie. It was not the same story line. She tried out the idea that Josie had, in her life, someone enough like Tasio to transfer an image of him through the mail. She tried to think of the guy on the moped as someone who just happened to *seem* like someone she knew from another death. But aren't people so much bigger than you can know, and isn't that beauty? And isn't that magic, which is not from some singular omniscience, but from people, things, and ideas—creatures—moving in relation to each other through life?

It didn't make sense, but Em could not wrench the idea of Tasio, real, true Tasio, from the figure created by the letter. That kid changed his whole *country* for another *country*, she thought. Who else could it be?

% Together %

The moon, tidally locked with earth, maintains a fixed face on us as it orbits and librates. We gave the moon its face and call out its every likeness. Say the moon is the moon, say *face* means *facet*. Let the earth be a planet before the earth is ours, even in our imaginations. Libration is the motion that draws a Lissajous figure. Let Lissajous be a figure, let the guy who did the math pass on, meaning die. We used to go to the moon in death. On an oscilloscope, the shape drawn is an infinity with three loops instead of two. "We choose to go to the moon! We choose to go to the moon!" said the popular president John Fitzgerald Kennedy. On the internet, people making comments on encyclopedias of mythologies will explain how the mentally ill are extrasensitive, and that's why they can feel the moon pull on their bodies of scientific water.

Voices in space, Apollo 8, 1968, taking the photo called Earthrise:
Oh my God! Look at that picture over there! There's the earth coming up. Wow, that's pretty.

Give me that. (*Meaning camera*)
Hey, don't take that, it's not scheduled. (*Joking*)

(*Laughs*) You got a color film, Jim? Hand me that roll of color
  quick, would you?

Oh man, that's pretty!

Quick! Down there, just grab me a color, okay, hand me a
  color, a color exterior. Got one?

Here.

That's good, a lot clearer. I got it framed. It's really clear.

Got it?

Let me get the right setting. (*Scrambling around*)

Man, just calm down.

Well, I got it. Man, that is a beautiful shot. 250 at F-11.

(*Many silent moments*)

Very visual.

I did it. I got two up there. (*Shots. Stills.*)

In 1966, Lunar Orbiter 1 sent back data that included this same view,
but technology did not exist to produce an image at full resolution.
Forty years later, NASA produced the image from the original data
using a combination of contemporary technology and restored 1960s-
era machinery. Also called *Earthrise*, the photo both preceded and
followed the one taken by the men in space.

Earthrise shows earth rising over the moon—the earth in *relation*
to the moon, but *Blue Marble* (1972, photograph AS17-148-22727,
and/or the almost identical AS17-148-22726) shows an almost fully
illuminated earth, all on its own in space. It is among the most distributed photographic images ever. The astronauts had the sun behind them when they took the image. All the astronauts on Apollo 17
took photos and all are credited with the image, which at some point
got flipped so that North would be up. Africa is in daylight. With the
December solstice approaching, Antarctica is illuminated. The Tamil
Nadu cyclone is visible.

During the 1970s, *Blue Marble* became a symbol of the environ-
mental movement, a depiction of earth's frailty and vulnerability
within the vast expanse of space. It remains striking, however many

times people make note of it, to contrast this mode of depiction with images leading up to the golden age of space exploration, such as the March 22, 1952, *Collier's* cover showing a very penis-meets-weapon-type rocket headed for a lush and rosy planet ("Man Will Conquer Space Soon, Top Scientists Tell How in 15 Startling Pages").

In the early 2000s, NASA created *Blue Marble* composite images and animations, called them *Blue Marble Next Generation* (2004), and put them up on the internet for everyone to enjoy. At the time, 1 km/pixel was the most detailed imagery permitted for free reuse that was also functional without extensive preparatory work to eliminate cloud cover, to conceal missing data, and to parse specialized data formats. The data also included similarly manually assembled cloud-cover image sets at lower resolutions, and sets that depicted electric lights in the night. The series of photo mosaics was produced with the aid of automated image-sifting, which enabled the inclusion of a complete, cloud-free globe for each month from January to December 2004, at the even higher resolution of 500 m/pixel, and closely modeled the changes of the seasons. Would we learn from *Blue Marble* to understand ourselves as insignificant in relation to the universe and to feel our earth as lonely, fragile, in need of care, was the question.

How people say *we*.

When Em moved to Los Angeles, no human had seen the earth directly since *Blue Marble*, and subsequent images were relayed by satellite. There was some halfhearted debate about whether we deserved to colonize other planets. We knew we would if we could, regardless. Mostly, NASA was not feeling funded. A lot of people would say, *Come on, I don't even have a phone.*

Within days of her arrival in LA, Em encountered a murmuration of starlings. It's so powerful, proximity to that kind of mass movement. It feels like access to some underlying essential core pattern of existence. A crowd of identical (to you) birds in air as identical (to you) as fishes in water moving in schools. Residents of the modern city of Rome have been experiencing starling murmurations seasonally for long enough that many have become furious about droppings on their cars and have called for the city to *do something*. If you watch videos narrated by dignified Brits on the internet, they will help you out with the math: five million starlings, and to achieve synchrony, each starling shadows seven of his nearest neighbors, reacting ten times faster than *any human pilot*. The narrators will help you out with cause and effect: the peregrine falcon is after them, and their strategy is to confuse him. After they don't get eaten, they head to Siberia to mate.

Em's house-sit had come with a computer and internet. There was a wide range of ways that murmurations had been filmed. She was careful to mute the soundtracks except for the one that was just the sound of birds plus wind pushing at the mechanisms of the recording device.

In LA, Em encountered gatherings of people in like-minded groups. There were red carpet occasions, stores hyping something, this week's exciting club, today's impressive restaurant, extras getting shuffled into cordoned-off areas for shoots. Much of Em's idea of LA was fictionalized and broadly distributed versions of South-Central of the '90s combined with Rodney King and OJ combined with music videos of clubs and house parties where no one in real life would ever be interested in her, so really she should just watch videos. Also this memory from the second time Adeline was in the psych ward at UCLA and Em had flown out. After a day of packing up an abandoned room in a shared apartment, Em was returning to whatever motel, got a little lost, it didn't seem that lost, it was so sudden, it was night, she stepped into a region that was apocalyptic with destitution—*all* the buildings were unlit and abandoned, *all* the streets were empty of traffic with clumps of trash, *all* the people who dotted the dark landscape were deranged with pain, fury, confusion yet moved like lumps—no, less substantial—wads of dust, and if that seems dehumanizing, to depict them that way, well, it is. The flicker between human and figure. Em was in a soul of an architecture. She felt swallowed by what exists just beyond human senses that is human-made at its most horrible. It changed some of the landscapes of her dreams to have been in that place walking among those people, in darkness and the occasional stage of a functioning streetlight. Places she'd lived that she returned to in dreams, transformed, now felt saturated with it, with them, so something of those people must have become part of her.

She considered making a reply to Frank's letter. *Tell Sheila*—she thought she'd write, but couldn't think of what to say other than "sorry," which she knew she was but didn't know how to say why, and she couldn't figure out if that mattered or not, to know why when you were sorry. *Tell the neighbors*—she thought she'd write, but tell them what? Why? She wrote, *I can't believe you tracked me down*. That wasn't true. She thought, this will be a draft. It was on the paper place mat at a diner, anyway. It already had grease spots she had to skip over. She'd had to promise on her life she'd give the waitress the pen back. *Give my love to Jack*, she wrote. She did send love to Jack, but did not want Frank to give it for her. She wrote, *Thanks for your letter*. She was thankful for his letter, but *thud* went the thanks in writing. *Thanks for your letter*, she wrote again; *it meant a lot, but really, you don't have to write back*. She crossed out the last part because it sounded pathetic, changed it to *Don't write back* as its own line. She inserted a "just" to soften it. *Just don't write back*. She crossed out *back*. She wrote *please*. She crossed out *please*. The process made the lighting in the diner feel harsh in a way that it hadn't a moment before, fluorescents suddenly fluorescent. Her stomach tightened, trembled. She met up with the waitress at the register, where there was a rack of postcards. California, California.

"Do you have anything that already has something written on it?"

"California," said the waitress.

"Okay, never mind. Here's your pen."

"Good girl." The waitress took the pen that was behind her ear out from behind her ear, put it in the cup by the register with a bunch of pens that were similarly cheapo pens, and stuck the pen from Em behind her ear in its place.

Then, as she was leaving, Em thought, here's your pen *back* would have been better to say, concluded that she was just not that much of a writer, and thought of Frank, the way he wrenched his body around in the car backing out of her driveway, stones flying in the fierce effort of care. She remembered it with feeling, but the feeling was for the memory. When she thought of Frank as a person out there in the world, there wasn't a charge.

That was a lot of it—of not writing back. There wasn't a charge. But she'd also made that mistake people make thinking they can get it right. I don't think you can get it right. Not now, in these conditions. If ever. I think you get up near it. You have your shape next to it, and feel for its shape. You remember that you are insubstantial, that *matter* is the finest wordplay you ever held in your mouth. You bring a mouth to the idea of a mouth, you bring eyes to eyes, even imagined eyes. You bring your whole body up to the limits of your imagination. All you got.

There did come a knock on the house-sit door. Ad was in the hall with her cat in a zippered carrying case, a blue backpack, and a deck of tarot cards she knew how to use on Venice Beach. Em whispered, "You're here, you're here, come in, come in." So scared and happy. "I didn't know you could fly."

Ad said, "Ha," and Em did not ask questions.

The couch in the house-sit was a pullout futon thing that the cat immediately liked because she could sit on the back of it and look out the window. Long-haired American domestic *Felis catus*. Together, they put a sheet on the futon pullout thing—really the place just had two rooms plus bath, so the fridge was just over the kitchen counter from it. Em said, "I hope the fridge doesn't bug you, it's really loud."

"It's okay," Ad said. "I like humming."

They ate a supper of ramen and frozen peas at the coffee table and the cat kept trying to get her nose up high enough, making them laugh. Em knew from her father that Ad had trouble processing sensory experience into things like language and memory, so when Em asked, "Do you remember—" this was a real question, not a segue, and that made recollecting together intimate as it hadn't ever been before. Also because when you have had a lot of pain over what is real and what is a delusion, when you seem to have a baseline to work with, it feels delicate and special. Also, with the internet proliferation of video evidence of police actions, combined with the mainstream practice of reporting on TV and radio what was happening on the internet as news, the country was having a lot of fights about how you know what happened or didn't happen, or what, in video form, constitutes evidence of what. Now you could really understand someone's politics by just mapping which video recordings they responded to in what way.

"Do you remember telling me," Emilie asked her sister, "when you lived in that apartment on the top floor in that snowy town, that you'd open the window and the cat would take herself for long walks around the house on the gutter?"

Adeline had a new nervous gesture, she'd put two fingers to her lips and tap when emotions rose or she was struggling with her brain. She put her fingers to her lips and tapped. "Because she was afraid to hop onto the roof. She just went around and around," she said. "I left the window open for her even in winter. Not to mention—"

They both said, "Smoking!"

"It's funny because it kills you," said Em.

"Cute," said Adeline.

The cat batted around a plastic ramen wrapper that had not made it into the trash. "She was angry at me for a long time," said Adeline. "She used to sleep on my chest and then she stopped and she wouldn't come near me. She's just seen a lot, living with me. One time I was at my desk and she came over and smacked me in the face with her claws about half out. Nothing has hurt my feelings as much as that." She paused, and Em wondered if this was a pause for certain traumas that had occurred, that Ad remembered, or wasn't sure were real, or was sure were real but in a different way in her current state, or were any of those things combined, that she didn't want to say but was leaving a space so that Em would know they were there. She said, "But now look." She lay down on her back on the futon couch, patted her chest, and made a little friendly noise. The cat hopped up on her chest and settled there, then edged forward, up to Adeline's face, and peered at her. Little breaths came out of Adeline's nose because she was trying to keep from laughing. The cat shook her head for a second, and then resumed her peering. Their breath was tickling each other. "She's back," Ad said, turning to include Em in the quick light of her face.

Adeline, in this recovering and recovering state, was quiet, tentative, sincere. Em had once found a box of audiocassettes of Ad talking to herself and listened to one just long enough to recognize what they were. They were tapes of trying to understand what had happened and was going to keep happening to her. The quality of her sister's voice on the recording had been unadorned. The tapes were long lost, but she'd heard just enough of her sister's voice like that to have pined for it.

This sweet time was like that voice. But do not mistake sweetness for a pure state. What is sweetness, what is sincerity? A pause.

You're not supposed to be able to walk around Los Angeles, but it is possible to approximate a walkable city if you know the bus system and don't have time constraints. When Em went out, she tried to let the place sink in, as she'd been letting it sink in through the house-sit computer. Outside, colorful and dramatically shaped plants, roofs with clay tiles. At some point she'd meet someone who'd point at a street corner and say, "That's where this happened," and point at a sign and say, "Used to be, that was a place where we'd—" and that would add a layer.

Some days, Ad took her cards to Venice Beach, where she'd once been followed by a private detective.

Em said, "Use your magic for good, okay?"

What would it mean to return to a place in this new state? To sit with strangers and *read* them *to* them? She did not ask. She did not want to upset a balance. Also something about privacy when it came to the present. Also fear, when *reading* has a supernatural aspect. When your sister has a supernatural aspect you are afraid to remember or to forget.

Also Ad often returned to say that she didn't know how to talk to people. She said she didn't even hear what she wanted to say in her head. She said she could hardly think of anything, let alone whether she wanted to say it. "I used to be so good at language," she'd say.

So maybe she just took the cards with her and held them, as a possibility.

She said she was grateful and wanted to contribute.

Em was making a little money remotely, grading standardized tests online for a place called Measurement Incorporated. Maybe money is money. She still had some cash in a pile about a knuckle thick in a binder clip in a napkin holder on the kitchen counter quietly tempting fate. Meds that arrived in the mail from their father had Ad sleeping really late, and Em would often go out and kind of wander around looking for a job as if you could just spot one on the corner and take it. This was not counting the actual jobs you can spot that get posted on storefronts. She was not going to take a job like that anyhow. She was past that, she told herself, though she'd once told herself she'd never rent again and now look. There was a life path she'd heard of where house-sitting was perpetual, but she would likely end up with rent and she knew it, some dumb way of knowing yourself.

"How's Mom?" Em asked Adeline.

"When I left, she said I was leaving her in a hole and I'd end up in a hole."

What is it about getting to know a place? Em had not bothered with it in her last town or the town before that. Do you want to make it *yours*, do you want to be *from* it? Feeling yourself in relation with it may be the thing. Humming a standard, what is that song, *Getting to know you, getting to know all about you.*

Going to meet someone for a coffee, to run an errand, it was no longer jarring to see people talking all day long on tangly headphones, and they were no longer mistaken for madmen piecing, piecing, piecing their stories together for a listener who existed at an indecipherable frequency. Some of the people on headphones were wireless businesspeople, but some of them—"it's not like I was in love—I had a certain fascination with the man *forty years* ago—you know you can just fuck yourself—you don't even try to understand"—were just inside out.

Em, out getting in relation with the place, came around a corner and encountered a messy line of shabby people. Some of them were visibly crazy, some of them were passing a crack pipe, and some of them were, seemingly, not crazy or doing drugs right that minute, just injured or blowing their nose, and some seemed pretty healthy, for example, a kid with one leg of her orange shorts bunched up into her crotch, neither clearly accompanied nor unaccompanied, and one of the people that the messy line was aiming toward was, Em discovered as she made her way along the outskirts, Adeline, who'd apparently made ins with some people who were illegally distributing sandwiches.

How amazing, Em thought. Will you look at that? She thought, it's spectacular.

She marveled until she was afraid for no reason at all that she was outstaying a welcome.

Sometimes Em met up with Lu. There was a type of friendship Em had disparaged in the past because it was just one person absolving the other, back and forth, *oh my god that is not your fault, don't even put that on yourself,* stereotypically women. There was another type of relationship where the dynamic was egg each other on, put each other down, and understand it as *challenging*—a virtue— stereotypically men. Both types, Lu pointed out when they were discussing this over coffee, were invented by the patriarchy. Without knowing if they had the same reasons, they both thought that was *really* funny.

Em asked, "Did you have a Russian friend? A woman? Last time you lived in LA? She was very protective? Possessive? Like she wanted to sleep with you? A very sexually intense person like that? Was she sleeping with you?" She could tell, by this time, what Ad looked like when she was being shown something of her life that had been erased. It was terrible, piercing to witness. "It's okay," Em said. "It doesn't matter. I could have the accent wrong. I suck at voices."

When Em came back from being out there, walking around, in relation, and her sister was just waking up, taking a handful of pills with her bedside glass of water, making little noises back and forth with the cat—

When Ad returned wearing a LACMA sticker—
"It was free day," she said.
"You're so good at this," Em said, meaning, they both knew, being here and being alive.

When they walked together to Venice Beach—
"Just show me around," said Em.
"It's different," said Ad, as they walked around looking for a place to sit and watch.

Together with Ad, every moment comprised forgetting or remembering what had happened, as if it was all or nothing. If only you could hold everything that had happened in your consciousness, you could behave with regard for it. But so much of Adeline was present that it was possible for Em to stop looking for what was missing or changed, to slide right over it.

On the boardwalk they saw a kid with a hula hoop showing off for another kid. What's so great about hula hooping is it's a human in service to an object that makes nothing but motion. You move your hips infinity. The difference between a kid who can hula hoop and a kid who can't is which one can, how people say, *let go*.

A sign in the window of a karate studio: "Special Focus Inner Peace."

When instances occurred in quiet progression without prompting. When what people said fell into place. When Em was accessing the lay of the land—

Em remembered she could get tickets from that guy for the aquarium that had just been built last time Ad lived there but she'd never been. So they went. They watched the giant octopus crouch in a corner and read about all the amazing containers it could get in and out of. There were pictures of an octopus filling a jar exactly, and then filling a different-sized jar exactly. They watched the sharks swim at one slow speed and read about finning.

Even then, people liked to fantasize about what if California was its own country, with its own states. Walking around, being in relation, Em had an idea where the earth was occupied by regions where rich people lived in luxury climate-controlled skyscrapers (spoiled?) and went on vacation where it was verdant (unspoiled?) and everyone's job was to present authenticity. *Serve*, as drag queens say.

Lu took Em to a dinner party thrown by a colleague who had a house in Laurel Canyon. Em was seated at a corner with a view between guests of the sliding patio doors. Between entrée and dessert, people were getting up and coming back from the bathroom and getting new drinks. From her seat, Em saw a mountain lion looking in at them, layered with reflections of parts of the night and parts of the party.

When she saw the mountain lion, she knew it was not a vision, but she didn't tell anyone. She didn't want anyone, not even her new old friend Lu, to tell the story of the dinner party as the story of everyone looking at a mountain lion and what was it doing, acting out what they pictured it thinking of them. And even before that—she didn't want any of the possible outcomes of alerting people to the animal outside—people screaming or laughing. Even silent reverence—she didn't even want that no matter how good it might have felt at the time. She made an invisible internal adjustment that brought out an aspect of symmetry. She kept it to herself. She let the lion be.

Em, in relation with the place, came around a corner and encountered a Pan-Asian protest. *Pan-Asian* was new to her as a term and she learned it from the signs. She looked around to see if she could spot Lu among them. Such a dumb reflex. She bought a cup for water at a Burger King and snuck a little fake lemonade in with it, then walked alongside the protesters for a while, feeling out the periphery. When she got back to the house-sit she had an idea for utopia, which was that everyone as a birthright gets access to a view of the sky from wherever they spend their days. It seemed like everything would follow from that.

When Ad was out and came back and said, *I was doing this, I was doing that, you know I saw the funniest thing, you know I picked this up for us what do you think?* Time accounted for without effort, let me offer you an account—

When Ad came back or Em came back—

They walked right by a hotel like it was nothing, it was so *concrete*. Would Ad start making art again and if so what would it mean and what if the art was good or bad—

In the news, a guy shot to death a lot of people, the latest in a sequence of similar events. For a while, in the bloody aftermath, what people evidently wanted to talk about, according to the internet, was mental illness and its relation to "senseless violence." But maybe Em just wasn't that good at navigation.

On the house-sit computer, Em looked up "lather rinse repeat" to find out when they stopped saying "repeat" on shampoo labels, not to mention if it was a ploy to get you to waste shampoo. There was an answer. She looked at it in black and white. Also a pop song, which she did not click. This felt satisfying for almost seven seconds, perhaps the shortest high ever. If she'd been a social media type, she might have found a way to get a second hit.

In fact, it made her want a drink. There had been no alcohol in the house-sit when she arrived, and she'd decided to keep it that way. So she just sat there not clicking on the pop song until she felt something else.

When Em came back and Ad was on the futon thing, looking up—*Hi, Hi, how's it going?*—the gift is the answers are the questions.

When Ad came back and said, "Hey now what the *fuck* has been happening in Egypt?"
    Is this what she'd been like? Before something? In some past?

Walking around, Em kept encountering public demonstrations and observed that people were doing things without any apparent expectation of meaning anything, like you give someone something because you have it and they want it and it doesn't matter what kind of person you think they are. Entities kept saying to protesters, *name your demands*, and the protesters kept saying (in catchy and/or stupid rhymes) *this is wrong* and the entities came back with *name your demands* and Em realized they were having different conversations, and that seemed profound.

At coffee shops or walking along noticing and eavesdropping, Em surmised that people wanted to participate in history.

Do *I want* to participate in history? Em asked herself.

But how much does it matter what you want, right?

When Em woke in the night she believed the shape in the living room to be the shape of her live sleeping sister. Took it on faith, kept taking it on faith.

When Em woke and saw on the countertop a piece of paper that had a mark on it. Was she drawing? Did she start something? She went up to the paper and it was a smudge. Still—

When she went out in the afternoon to meet Lu at a rally—dogs on leashes, kids in strollers—and came back and Ad wasn't around—cat looking up, cat blinking in dust motes—that fear—and then in the night, the shadows, the body shape.

At the rally, Lu said, "I guess the revolution is going to be adorable," which they both thought was incredibly funny. "My boss let me off for this," she said, and they both thought that was funny, too.

When Em walked down the street with Adeline, and say they were passing an alley, Ad would just sort of swerve toward it, and inevitably there would be a group of people standing in a clump and the people would be street people, and it would be like they had a draw on her.

Em said, "Come on, Ad, let's go."

Ad said, "But my magic—"

Em came around a corner and a man in a turban was kneeling—bowing—right there on the street, and she had no idea if he was crazy or protesting or an actor playing someone or somehow simply truly devout. She worried about tarot, how literal it might be to Ad after spending so many hours in states where everything had been equally real. Ad was making friends and Em thought, she has to make friends, but she was afraid the friends wouldn't understand and would like

354 The Swank Hotel

all the wrong things about Ad and bring them back out of her. "I made a friend, she practices scent," Ad said, following with a joke about her nose always having been her dominant feature. Em worried about this *practice of scent*, so ephemeral.

As everyone knows, not far down the road in the country's history, there was going to be a rainy inauguration of a president who then said that during the ceremony it had stopped raining, which it had not. He said the sun came out just as he began to speak. It might not seem that hard to look up on your special occasion, identify the qualities of the atmosphere, and repeat them in words for the benefit of others. It was as if what he was, not to mention what he represented, was an inability to register the difference between an experience and the memory of a feeling. And imagine, a person reaching that pinnacle of his own estimation as it coincided with the apparent standards of his culture, and what it would do to a person like that, in such a situation, to have the atmosphere just go along with no regard for any of it.

When Em woke in the night and wasn't sure, she thought maybe it was just some blankets in the moonlit streetlight but she was afraid to look closer, but next day there she was—sister, sister—look I made a little something for us, we can put it in the pot.

   Still, that knowing feeling of your sister accumulating secrets, of *what do you have interred inside you—*

Em stayed up late, watching video footage of riots from around the country and other countries and back into history. On a video zeroing in on a chanting crowd, Em saw a female protester that the video seemed not to be about. She looked stunned, as if she'd recently been hit in the head and didn't yet realize it, not saying anything among all the people with their voices aligned.

   In the news, people feeling innocent were saying that we all have our own opinions but no one can blame anyone for just wanting to get to work. People feeling innocent were saying that violence tears us apart. In Em's favorite video, a guy was interviewing a man on the street with a flaming car in the background, and a looter skipped by swinging a jug of laundry detergent in each hand.

When Em showed a video of unrest to Adeline it was against a part of her judgment. But she thought, this is where we live, this is our country, this is what it's about, this is who we are now, this is what we're like. It's my sister, she thought. I want to be with her in the world. Into the night, together, they followed a pattern of videos, approaching gathering after gathering at all angles.

She woke Ad in the night and sat on the edge of the futon.
    "I'm afraid you're going to go, that you want to go."
    Ad said, "Sometimes. I mean, I might." Em dropped her head onto her sister's shoulder. You're not supposed to add emotional pressure.

Em picked up another kind of work to do remotely, which she sometimes did in coffee shops for the scenery, and to test herself on ways for Adeline to be out of sight.
    When Em woke in the night and wasn't sure, she thought maybe it was just some blankets, so placid in the moonlight mixed with streetlight, and this time she approached the blankets, the shape was blankets, and her sister wasn't in the apartment anymore after that.

When she watched the crowds in videos and approached them on the street, she tried to imagine being one, being part of a crowd, and being a crowd, how people say *spirit* of the congregation, how people say *will* of the mob, how people, dancing in a mass, *rave*. She stepped from near the edge into the edge, and kept up for a block, even though it hurt, before she let herself float back out. She tried to listen for what a crowd might fathom.

Em up all night online with the cat on her lap, watching *actions* in so many cities and towns in colorful festive daylights, in agitated dusks, in concerted nighttime, in nighttime bursting with fatigue and rage from when you reach a certain level of pain. There—she thought she saw it—a piece of her sister in a video of that crowd protesting what that politician did—that corporation—that higher court—and there—a piece of her sister in a video of that crowd protesting police—

When she did, as if finally, encounter a crowd in the street with emotions that covered her own and slipped into it, for a while she felt encompassed by people as colors, shapes, and sizes of bodies and outfits and backpacks and giant-sized words written by hand. She moved along with them without knowing if she was present other than being a body, or if being a body was actually fine. She let some physics do some work, and as the light shifted because of interruptions by the built and breathing environment, her body found a rhythm in exertion.

Then she was on a cusp with them, with people ready to go off. People were the toxic detritus of their own horrid history and also clear water droplets on the tips of the grasses of meadows in advance of fires. Em vibrated on the verge of dissipation in the moment between culminating and having happened, because there was Adeline in the crowd, glinting among everyone.

Acknowledgments

Support in the form of time, space, and money from these institutions allowed me to write this book: the American Academy of Arts and Letters and the American Academy in Rome, the Corporation of Yaddo, the Hambidge Center, the National Endowment for the Arts, the University of California at Davis.

The following editors published early versions of portions of this book: Jedediah Berry at *Hunger Mountain*, Mónica de la Torre at *BOMB*, Stewart O'Nan at *Ploughshares*.

The following people and groups gave me significant intellectual and emotional support for which I am immensely grateful: Lisa Hanks Baxter; Teresa Carmody; Andrea Cohen (every day); Rikki Ducornet; the Duke University English Department Working Group on the Paranormal; Rima Fand; Howard Hochman; Michael Lee; Ali Leibegott; Anni Liu; Melissa Malouf; PJ Mark; Megan McShea; Andriana Mendoza; Katie Peterson; Beth Pickens; Dominique Reill; my beloved 2012 Rome Prize fellows cohort as well as Louise Glück and Joy Williams who got me there; Sara Seinberg; Anna Joy Springer;

Susan Steinberg; K.T. Thompson; Deb Olin Unferth; Alexandria Wright. Many others also helped, and I hope I have thanked them all properly along the way.

This existence of this book is inextricably bound to the life and mind of Emily Hochman.

It is also bound to Ethan Nosowsky, who was here with me in its writing, in one form after another, the whole way.

I drafted much of this novel by gathering scraps from the world onto my desk. Those scraps came from many books, magazines, newspapers, websites, movies, and TV shows, as well as from many people. What follows are some of the sources I know how to acknowledge:

Pages 58 and 62–63
Phrases from "Near-Empty Tower Still Holds Hope," by Nicolai Ouroussoff, *New York Times*, June 29, 2010, appear here.

Page 70
I'm indebted to T. M. Luhrmann's *Of Two Minds: An Anthropologist Looks at American Psychiatry* (Vintage Books, 2001), and a phrase from that book is used here.

Page 78
David Bowie's live version of "My Death," by Jacques Brel, is referred to here, and I've appropriated and reordered some of the lyrics. https://www.youtube.com/watch?v=nKmBg-jOYUQ.

Page 80
The poem referenced is John Ashbery's "Saying It to Keep It from Happening," which appears in his book *Houseboat Days* (Viking, 1977).

Page 111
Lines from Tolstoy's *The Death of Ivan Ilyich* (1886) are paraphrased here.

Pages 121–22 and 130–33
Here I rely on Michael Shaw, Melanie Turner, and Kathy Robertson,
"Lyon Moves Fast to Stem Scandal," *Sacramento Business Journal*,
September 5, 2010.

Pages 139, 177, and 320
The poetry quoted is from *The Metamorphoses of Ovid: A New
Verse Translation*, trans. Allen Mandelbaum (Houghton Mifflin
Harcourt, 2017).

Page 149
A line from Andrew Marvell's poem "Upon Appleton House" ap-
pears here, as do phrases from Peter Bergen's *Manhunt: The Ten-
Year Search for Bin Laden from 9/11 to Abbottabad* (Crown, 2012).

Pages 168–75
The film Josie summarizes here is Chris Ward and J. D. Slater's
2000 film *Bound, Beaten, and Banged*.

Page 177
"Symbolic of the power of seeing and understanding that which
is unknown and unknowable" and "the four points representing
the elemental processes of earth, fire, air, and water" are lines that
appear in various similar forms in an array of articles found in
a Google search.

Pages 179–80
Lines here are paraphrases of an article by T. M. Luhrmann in
which she quotes Michael Taussig's *Shamanism, Colonialism, and*

the Wild Man (University of Chicago Press, 1986). Luhrmann's paper is "Hallucinations and Sensory Overrides," *Annual Review of Anthropology* 40, no. 1 (2011). That same passage also includes a sentence from Hélène Cixous, *"Coming to Writing" and Other Essays* (Harvard University Press, 1991).

Page 186
Image of the Snaptun Stone used with the permission of the National Museum of Denmark. Photo by Lennart Larsen.

Pages 187–91
Frank's letter draws in part on scenes from Knut Hamsun's *Hunger*, trans. Sverre Lyngstad (Penguin Books, 1998).

Page 197
This image is used with permission of the artist, Emily Hochman.

Pages 205 and 215
The lines about Bobby Fischer were informed by the following sources: Brian M. Carney, "Victim of His Own Success: The Tragedy of Bobby Fischer," *Wall Street Journal*, January 23, 2008; *Bobby Fischer Against the World*, directed by Liz Garbus, HBO, 2011; Nicholas Bethell, "A Poisoned Russian King," *Harper's Magazine*, December 1973.

Page 209
I closely paraphrase lines from Ronald D. Laing's *The Politics of Experience* (Penguin Books, 1967).

Page 210
The image comes from Cartoliste: https://cartoliste.ficedl.info /article2397.html?lang=fr.

Pages 211–14
I am hugely indebted to www.deadbabyjokes.com (now defunct).

Pages 339–40
This NASA video is the source for the transcribed dialogue: https://
earthobservatory.nasa.gov/images/82693/earthrise-revisited.

Pages 340–41
I closely paraphrased or took text directly from three articles:
"The Blue Marble," Wikipedia, https://en.wikipedia.org/wiki
/The_Blue_Marble; "Earthrise," Wikipedia, https://en.wiki
pedia.org/wiki/Earthrise; and "Blue Marble—Image of the
Earth from Apollo 17," NASA, https://www.nasa.gov/content
/blue-marble-image-of-the-earth-from-apollo-17.

LUCY CORIN is the author of the story collections *One Hundred Apocalypses and Other Apocalypses* and *The Entire Predicament*, as well as the novel *Everyday Psychokillers: A History for Girls*. Her work has appeared in *American Short Fiction*, *Conjunctions*, *Harper's Magazine*, *Ploughshares*, *BOMB*, *Tin House*, and the *New American Stories* anthology from Vintage Contemporaries. She is the recipient of an American Academy of Arts and Letters Rome Prize and a literature fellowship from the National Endowment for the Arts. She teaches at the University of California at Davis and lives in Berkeley.

The text of *The Swank Hotel* is set in Adobe Garamond Pro.
Book design by Rachel Holscher.
Composition by Bookmobile Design and Digital
Publisher Services, Minneapolis, Minnesota.
Manufactured by McNaughton & Gunn on acid-free,
100 percent postconsumer wastepaper.